Praise for *A Gentle Tyranny*

"Themes of justice, equality, . . . and abuse of power are
developed in this well-written novel. . . . A series opener with
an intriguing premise."

KIRKUS REVIEWS

"Corban's characters are charming and memorable, and the lush,
verdant Central American jungle setting offers a fully fleshed-
out paradise that is as tempting as it is freeing and readers will
likely be captivated enough to read through this mysterious,
imaginative plot in one long, thrilling sitting."

BOOKLIST

"Jess Corban has created a firecracker of a new world. . . .
A Gentle Tyranny is a fierce novel that forces readers to consider
what the right thing really is."

READER VIEWS

What Readers are Saying

"I decided to give this book a chance and I am so glad I did. . . .
I was sucked in immediately."

LIBRARIAN, NetGalley

"It's the kind of feminist fic that flips the script. . . . Corban's
narrative style is wonderful."

ALEX, Goodreads review

"*A Gentle Tyranny* passes the Bechdel test with flying colors . . .
[and] appeals to the adventurer in all of us. . . . I recommend
A Gentle Tyranny to female readers of any age."

EMWEIM, Barnes & Noble review

"Fascinating plot line; . . . thought-provoking social and cultural constructs; engaging characters and relationships. Highly recommend!"

EMILY, Books-a-Million review

"If you found yourself gripped by the pages of *The Hunger Games* or *Divergent*, don't miss this book."

CLAIRE Z.

"A masterpiece of fiction. . . . Jess Corban has breathed new life into a well-worn genre. . . . I'll make the prediction that this will be one of my favorite novels of the year."

JOSH, Goodreads review

"This is a fantastic book, authored by a fantastic author. The ability to craft a world that is the end-all for some and a nightmare for others and explain why the grass isn't always greener on the other side via narrative is an art form not many have mastered."

NICKIE, Goodreads review

"I read the first book in 3 days—I simply couldn't put it down. Intriguing, action-packed, and adventurous on every page, *A Gentle Tyranny* is well worth the read!"

GENEVIEVE Z.

"This book is a compelling example of how a perfect civilization is impossible, that corruption is not specific to any one gender, and how, ultimately, the person we are is who we choose to be. It's a unique coming-of-age story and I'm very much looking forward to how the series will continue!"

JESSICA, Barnes & Noble review

A BRUTAL JUSTICE

wander™
An imprint of
Tyndale House
Publishers

A
BRUTAL
JUSTICE

NEDÉ RISING SERIES

JESS CORBAN

Visit Tyndale online at tyndale.com.

Visit the author online at jesscorban.com.

Tyndale and Tyndale's quill logo are registered trademarks of Tyndale House Ministries.
Wander and the Wander logo are trademarks of Tyndale House Ministries. Wander is an
imprint of Tyndale House Publishers, Carol Stream, Illinois.

A Brutal Justice

Designed by Eva M. Winters

Published in association with the literary agency of Wolgemuth & Associates, Inc.

A Brutal Justice is a work of fiction. Where real people, events, establishments, organizations,
or locales appear, they are used fictitiously. All other elements of the novel are drawn from
the author's imagination.

For information about special discounts for bulk purchases, please contact Tyndale House
Publishers at csresponse@tyndale.com, or call 1-855-277-9400.

Library of Congress Cataloging-in-Publication Data

A catalog record for this book is available from the Library of Congress.

ISBN 978-1-4964-4838-5 HC
ISBN 978-1-4964-4839-2 SC

Printed in the United States of America

27   26   25   24   23   22   21
7   6   5   4   3   2   1

To the Brute who completes a part of me no one else can. Life is richer because of your love.

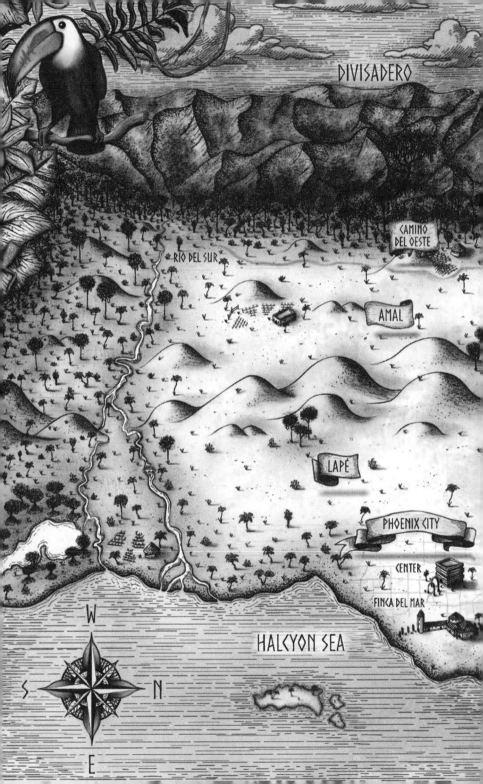

Part One

CHAPTER ONE

MY FINGERS REFUSE TO FORGET what they've done. A frantic pulse thrums in my ears as my fore- and middle fingers tremble against the corner of my mouth. The bowstring shivers with an echo of my unsteady grip on the riser. I blink hard, trying to focus, begging my mind to erase the memory of his face. But his eyes remain vivid with unexpected tenacity, boring into mine, pleading with me: *Do it. Do it, Reina!*

The Matriarch stands behind Tre's kneeling form, encircled by the Arena's towering bleachers, her sheer, multicolored robe lifting with a slight breeze. Her face twists in a jeering snarl. "What are you waiting for, Candidate?" Her mouth forms the words, condescension dripping from her lips like the blood I am about to shed, but the voice drifting across the Arena now is too grounding to be hers.

I know that voice. It's brave and beautiful and tinged with gold. *Trinidad.*

The scene mercifully melts into reality, a wooden target replacing Treowe's face, my mentor and newly appointed instructor analyzing my form, not Teera. Dozens of Alexia train around me. As I fight to find my bearings, Trin grows impatient, and she's not a woman one wants to irritate. "Let's go, Reina!"

Come on! I shout at myself, pushing down the haunting memories. Hesitation will bring questions I can't afford to answer. Still, I haven't shot a bow since—*Don't think about that now. Focus.* I've only been Alexia for ten minutes. Adoni might rescind her offer if I can't pull it together. I force my mind to clear, channeling every regret, every fear, every question I've battled since killing my best friend here three days ago, into a single shot.

If all the energy on the crowded Arena floor—the force of every thrust, kick, jump, jab—coalesced at this exact moment, it still wouldn't match the force of my arrow when I finally let it fly.

Crack! The tip burrows so deep it passes through the jute target, burying itself in the wood backing.

In a rush of anger, I unsheathe my sword and fling it for good measure. It spirals like a maniacal windmill before meeting its mark, centimeters from my arrow.

"Eager much?" Trin frowns. "Do me a favor and stick to the drills. You haven't been Alexia long enough to make your own rules."

When she turns, I quickly swipe what might be a tear with the back of my dusty palm. "Sorry. I'm just . . . excited." I infuse the word with a little too much pep, garnering a raised eyebrow from my instructor.

It's not that Trin doesn't know I murdered a Gentle in this

Arena. She was there, standing by with an expressionless face when I had hoped she'd offer some hint at a way out. She just doesn't know that Gentle was my best friend. That he was the only one who really knew me—understood me. The one who'd leave bloodred hibiscus flowers where he was sure I'd find them, the friend who would tease me by the bank of the Jabiru River, under the shade of our favorite fig tree, while we shared savory pastries stolen from the Bella Terra kitchen or ripe fruit from Mother's fields. She doesn't know the loss of him is threatening to undo me.

And I don't plan to tell her.

After the first shot, thankfully others come easier. Minutes turn into hours under a sweltering Nedéan sun. We train with bow and blade before practicing hand-to-hand combat techniques. A few familiar faces catch my eye throughout the morning, including Fallon and Valya, who were in my patrol group during Succession training. Fallon nods a greeting; younger Valya waves. Many of the drills are familiar too, transporting me to that time when my only concern was making Grandmother proud so I could become her Apprentice. The time before my familiar, safe world was upended. Before an unexpected plunge into the Jungle wilds proved so much of what I knew to be a lie.

By midday, the humid heat threatens to melt me faster than butter in a fry pan. I don't even try to hide my relief when our ranks file out for the noon meal. Returning my bow, I fall behind Trin and we weave through dozens of Alexia, racking their weapons and talking of strangely ordinary matters—hopes for lunch and troubles with neighbors—before slipping through the stone archway of the north gate toward the barracks and culina, where the Alexia take their meals.

Just outside the Arena walls, Adoni stands with her back to us, one foot resting on a raised planter. Even from behind, the leader of the Alexia is unmistakable, a rope of braid descending from the unshaved half of her head over a shoulder covered with a massive dragon tattoo. "Report back to the Arena in an hour," she says to someone obscured by her broad back.

I chance a look as we pass by, curiosity getting the better of me. A curtain of blonde bangs frames the visitor's angular cheekbones and thin nose. When she sees me, a familiar smirk spreads across her pale face. I nearly slip on the gravel underfoot as I halt midstride.

Brishalynn?

Adoni strides back toward the Arena, but I just stand there gaping at my former fellow Candidate, eyes probably bugging out of my face.

"What's wrong, Rei? You look like a hooked fish."

"What are you doing here?"

"What else would I be doing here? I'm joining the Alexia."

"But . . . you were a Politikós. In Amal."

"Why the change?" Trin cuts in.

I'd wager the Alexia second-in-command saw enough of Bri during Candidate training to be a little wary.

Bri flashes her signature bravado at us—90 percent show, 10 percent scared little girl. "Let's just say the Matriarchy isn't filling me with warm fuzzies of loyalty lately. With Apprentice Evil in line for power, I like the prospect of having a weapon in hand."

She turns the short sword in her palm casually, sun glinting off the polished metal. *Lovely.* The last time Bri had a weapon around me, it ended up centimeters from my chest while I slept. My turn to lose the warm feelings.

Trin raises an eyebrow in suspicion. "And Adoni let you in?"

Bri nods. "And since I know you're hoping, I'll spoil the surprise: I'm training with you." She accentuates her wide grin with a wink.

Since the first day of training, Bri's attitude has been a pain in my rear. As Amal Province's rightful Candidate, she let everyone know she wasn't happy about Teera selecting me to compete. Saving her life during hand-to-hand combat with Jamara did change our relationship some, I suppose. I wouldn't say we became *friends*—she did come very close to killing me—but we're not exactly enemies either.

Despite my lingering reservations, I can't help but snort at her audacity. "Lucky us."

By the time we break for the day, the western sun hangs as heavy as my own spent limbs. My forefingers throb in time to my footsteps, not yet used to shooting so many arrows. Not as bad as the first day of Candidate training, but as I rack my bow, I know I'll feel it in the morning. Taking a cue from the other Alexia, who look like they actually know what they're doing, I leave my short sword sheathed on my thick belt.

Fatigue notwithstanding, I held my own out there. Trin was proud, though she tried not to show it.

Bri racks her bow next to mine. Always full of surprises, she didn't do half-bad either. She worked hard and curbed her cheek, *mostly*. Just like our last time in the Arena, she picked up the techniques quickly. Before the Succession, Bri spent three years as a Politikós, enrolled at one of the prestigious Amal schools specializing in the destiny. Most attend to have a better chance at being elected as a Senator instead of being relegated to clerks, recorders, or tax collectors. They also learn about each of Nedé's nine core destinies—including Alexia—in case the ruling Matriarch initiates a Succession. Bri was professionally educated to have an edge over the competition. Unfortunately for her, Matriarch Teera added me to the mix. Who knows whether I actually ruined her chances, but

I'm still surprised she'd walk away from all that Politikós training and experience to start over. Destiny changes are rare in Nedé and usually require extenuating circumstances—like limb loss for an Agricolátio, or a Materno who has complications birthing children or something. I don't know what to think of Bri's defection.

"See you at the barracks," I say, peeling away to find my horse.

Bri wrinkles her nose. "You need a shower."

I shake my head.

Alexia stream from the Arena, black vests and riding pants powdered with fine dust. Those who trained with horses today hand them to waiting Gentles, then they're off to find showers and clean clothes before late afternoon turns to evening. Me? Doubting the stablehands will touch my "mutt," I decide to tend to Callisto myself. This morning Adoni reiterated that her offer to have Trinidad train me didn't extend to my horse. The Alexia ride only sleek Lexanders in shades of coal and dark umber. Their equines are as much a part of their uniform as their signature black vests and unconventional hairstyles. So tomorrow I'll have to figure out a way to get Callisto back home to Bella Terra, my mother's finca.

I flip the leather reins over her head to use as a lead rope. Not that she needs it. She has a habit of tailing me like a one-tonne puppy. I'm still not used to the saddle and tack of the Alexia. I prefer to ride bareback, a simple neck rope all I need for my spirited pinto. She watches me with glossy brown eyes, and I brush loose hairs from the white patch on her neck as we walk.

"You're a good girl, Callisto. It's not your fault you're prettier than the rest of them. They're just jealous of you—that's why they won't let me keep you." What started as jest catches in my throat. Even joking about not having her with me cuts too deep. I can't imagine doing this without her.

The Arena stables and adjacent fields house hundreds of horses, not to mention the rural fincas in other provinces that keep hundreds more at the ready. Here, dozens of paddocks flank a massive open-beam stable, where a parade of horses wait to be brushed and bedded for the night. Everywhere horses of chocolate, coal, and toasted allspice whinny, twitch, and graze. I inhale sharply, reveling in the smell of cut grass and sweaty steeds, letting the truth of where I am smack me sideways. I'm one of them now. I did it. I belong here.

After aspiring to—and failing to secure—the Apprenticeship, it seems silly now to think how long I spent worrying over the dilemma of my destiny. How many years did I practice at my secret teak forest arena, worried Mother would hate me for becoming Alexia? And for what? After all her warnings about Teera's need for control, she's probably *relieved* I've ended up here in the end.

I lead Callisto to the barn, bypassing a long line of horses awaiting the Gentles' attention. Inside, dozens of stablehands untack fine steeds as quickly as their gentled bodies allow, brushing sweat from their coats and leading them into stalls. Midas, Trinidad's horse, sniffs at a fresh bag of feed in her box while shooing a fly with her gold-tipped tail.

A crosstie opens up, and I seize the opportunity to steer Callisto into it, then quickly slide the leather saddle from her sweaty back. Adoni's jet-black Nyx stamps restlessly nearby, eyeing everyone around her with an air of superiority. Her handler—a stout Gentle with sandstone hair and a pockmarked face—balances precariously atop a short ladder, trying to slide the heavy saddle from Nyx's back. Someone drops a bucket; the metal clang startles the brawny horse. With a flick of her head she rears, knocking the Gentle off balance. He teeters a moment, then flails backward and falls a meter and a half to the ground. At the last second he thrusts an arm back to break his fall. The limb hits the dirt with a sickening crack.

A miserable scream reverberates through the breezeway. Two

other Gentles rush to his aid, trying to coax him to a sitting position. His right arm protrudes from his side at an unnatural angle, wrist bending awkwardly inward, a sharp point of bone protruding just below his elbow.

My stomach lurches. *Brittle bones.* Unlike a woman's, it doesn't take much to shatter a Gentle's skeleton. Just another unfortunate, natural weakness of Nedé's servants. Or so we've been taught.

Now, knowing the truth, I can't watch the stablehand shudder in agony without guilt pricking me deep. We've made them this way. To keep ourselves safe. Is their gentleness worth robbing them of health, of passion, of life?

For the hundredth time this week, Rohan's question bubbles in the thick stew of my uncertainty: *Which is better?*

When I encountered my sister Ciela at the Center weeks ago, she suspected Brutes were to blame for the raid on Jonalyn's finca. She was right—about the raid and about their danger. They're dangerous because we can't control them. But who gives us the right to decide their fate?

Protect the weak. Safety for all. Power without virtue is tyranny.

When the foremothers founded Nedé, women were the weak who needed protection. Women needed safety. They vowed to wield power better than the Brutes—with kindness and virtue. Have we?

The injured stablehand goes limp, passing out from the pain, and it takes four other Gentles to drag him to a cart. They argue over who will transport him to the Center, the only medical facility in Phoenix City. But a Gentle's heart handles trauma little better than his bones; I wonder if this one's will keep beating until they arrive.

What have we done? These are the weak among us, and rather than protect them, we treat them as servants at best, annoyances and liabilities more often. Worse, now I know *we're* the cause of their weakness.

The force of this Gentle's pain, the weight of our treachery, snaps something inside me, too, and I push my way into the commotion.

"Give him to me," I command, not waiting for a response as I snatch the harness from the nearest Gentle. It fits snugly around Callisto's midsection. I adjust the straps, then slide the cart's poles through the rigging.

I'll take him to the Center, and then I'll find Ciela—she must know something that will help me help them. If the vaccine makes Gentles like this, I have to find a way to stop it. Maybe there's even some way to reverse the damage we've done. Rash? Maybe. But I have to do *something*.

CHAPTER TWO

WHEN THE GENTLE REGAINS CONSCIOUSNESS, he moans with each bump over the cobblestones, making the thirty-minute journey to the Center drag twice as long. He cradles his mangled arm against his side, a circle of blood blooming through the right sleeve of his tunic. Should I speed Callisto to get the poor invalid there faster? Or slow her down for a smoother ride? Mercifully, another few blocks and the dilemma finally becomes irrelevant.

The massive square Center for Health Services rises above every other building in sight, nine stories of gleaming glass and smooth cement walls, skirted with neatly trimmed landscaping. Twelve arches create a tunnel toward the entrance, each laden with fiery-orange flame vine blossoms.

As I wrap Callisto's reins around a hitching post, Dom Russo's crooning lecture voice echoes in my memory, a relic of our

Succession training here: *to prevent a recurrence of the blight on human history—both of sickness and of Brutes—we place the utmost importance on maintaining the physical hardiness of our population. At the Center, we create life, then maintain vibrant lives.*

Right. Tell the Gentle curled up in this rickety cart, shaking from shock and pain after a simple fall, that he's leading a "vibrant life."

I loop my arm under his good side and force him upright. With a miserable groan, he stumbles forward, nearly tripping over his own feet. I half carry him under the archway to the front entrance. I almost expect Dr. Novak to greet us at the front desk, like the last visit, but instead, a receptionist inquires, "Can I help you?"

I hoist my charge a little higher. "This Gentle fell at the Alexia stables. He's hurt pretty bad."

"I'll call for assistance." She hands me a towel and smiles sweetly, but her tone remains matter-of-fact. "Keep the blood contained, will you?"

I wrap his arm with the cloth, trying not to jostle the piercing fracture. He winces and grunts, and I'm afraid if we stand here long, he'll pass out again.

I remember the basic layout of the floors from my tour a few weeks ago. "Don't trouble yourself. I know where to take him."

She seems mildly surprised, but maybe the Alexia uniform works in my favor, because she doesn't fuss when I head down the east hall without waiting for permission.

I pull the half-limp Gentle across shiny, smooth tiles, his shabby leather shoes sliding as he struggles to place one foot in front of the other. He shakes from the effort required to cross a mere thirty meters, but we finally reach the double doors marked "Gentle Care."

Before swinging open the door, I brace myself for what waits on the other side.

A downright putrid wave of sweat, old wounds, and unwashed bodies pours from the room. Yep, it's as foul and depressing as I remember. We weave between sick Gentles to the front desk, and I try not to wonder how many of the ailing will end their lives with the stinger before nightfall.

Can I blame them? I'd like to think I'd keep fighting, but if a clumsy fall snapped *my* arm like a twig, if I fell ill every other Tuesday, if I knew I wouldn't live past forty anyway, then quietus—a respite from life itself—would likely tempt me, too. I can't judge their resignation. I can only try to eliminate their need for it.

I intentionally meet the eyes of each suffering, swollen, tearstained face I pass, as if by acknowledging their presence I can validate their existence or soothe their pain. It's stupid, I know, but their bleak end—whether stinger today or phase-out tomorrow—threatens to crush me. I want them to know that. With each pair of weary eyes I meet, my resolve grows.

I have to put an end to this.

"You're going to be okay," I tell the Gentle I've brought, lowering him into a chair. He stares back with hollow eyes, either still in shock or offended by my blatant lie.

I feel bad leaving him, but there's nothing I can do to help in this room. My fight begins on the ninth floor.

After alerting a disinterested woman behind a tall desk to the newest Gentle in the room, I slip out the doors and practically sprint up eight flights of stairs. Halfway up, I pass a handful of Alexia headed in the opposite direction. Their shift must be ending. Good. It'll look like I'm part of the next crew, arriving for the night.

The lab hasn't changed much since the last time I was here, save an increase in Alexia. I keep to the edges of the room like the other black-clad peacekeepers. *I'm supposed to be here*, I tell them with my straight back and eye contact, begging my nerves to play the part. *Just another one of you.*

I scan the rows of desks, cluttered with beakers and microscopes. It's getting late; only a handful of workers remain. What if Ciela went home for the night?

A petite lab technician with a thick chestnut bun leaves her station, thumbing through a notebook as she moves toward an adjoining hall. I recognize those slender shoulders, that thin nose. I step lightly toward the hallway, turn the corner, then pick up my pace to catch my sister as she ducks into an office.

"Ciela," I whisper as I duck into the room behind her.

A jolt of surprise sends her notebook flying from her hands.

"*Bats*, Reina!"

I retrieve the notebook, smoothing the bent pages. "I didn't mean to scare you," I snap back. "I'm just—not exactly supposed to be here."

"You think?"

I'm used to Ciela's tart bite—bitter as a green mango. I'm not always honey sweet either, and I own my part in our frayed sibling bond. Maybe there's still a chance to fix it. The last time I saw her, our normal bickering subsided some.

"What *are* you doing here?" She recovers her composure, softening a bit, flipping through her notebook to find her place.

"I . . ." Where to start? I'll have to word my questions carefully. I can't reveal that I already know about the link to the vaccines, or my involvement with the Brutes. "Look, Ciela, I think you could be right about the raids being linked to Brutes. Have you discovered anything else? Like, how they might exist?"

She chews the inside of her cheek, then closes and locks the door. So she *has* found something.

"Why do you want to know, Rei?"

Think fast . . . "Same reason as you. If there are Brutes out there, we have to make sure they don't attack anyone else. For Jonalyn's sake."

This seems to appease her. "Alright. I did find something. But you can't tell a soul, okay? I could get fired or put in the stocks for tampering with specimens."

That would be an ill fate indeed. I know Ciela has had her eye on a director position since she was young. A director like the mother she adores. I'd never want her to lose that chance for my sake.

"Promise," I assure her.

"I've been analyzing Gentles' and newborn babies' blood samples. Something changes between birth and the time they enter the Hives. I traced the anomaly to the vaccine, and have been studying it ever since. At first, I was convinced some rare defect in the inoculation must be reverting the Gentles to brutish behaviors."

"That would make sense."

She lowers her voice even further. "But there were no defects—not one. In all the samples of Gentle blood I examined—hundreds of them—the only abnormality appeared in a handful of infants who were reported dead within hours of birth. Those babies wouldn't have received the vaccine—they died too soon."

Now we're getting somewhere. "What do you make of it?" I coax.

"I still can't connect the dots. But those infant samples, they contained large amounts of a substance not found in the older Gentles."

"A substance? Like what?"

"I don't know."

I bet I do. Tristan Pierce called it testosterone, and it makes a Brute what he is. If the vaccine blocks it during infancy, he becomes a Gentle. I'm going to have to lead her to that conclusion if I'm going to secure her help.

"Could it mean newborn babies are *born Brutes*, but the vaccine makes them Gentle?"

She purses her lips. "I'm still not positive, but . . . yes."

I'm proud of my sister. Her sharp mind has brought her to the truth, even without a dead Matriarch's tattered confessions. Good for her. And now I can ask what I really want to know.

"But that still doesn't explain how there could be Brutes out there." I gesture to the broader world with a flip of my hand. "You said the infants who had the anomaly died shortly after birth."

She looks thoughtful. "That's what I can't figure out. But I'm certain there's a link somehow. Once a Gentle receives the vaccine, he can't become a Brute. It's just not possible."

"Are you sure? There's no way to reverse the vaccine?" Now it's getting personal, and I feel my pulse quickening. I think of Treowe, and Neechi, and the broken stablehand on the first floor. "If a shot of liquid chemicals can turn a baby into a Gentle, couldn't there be a way to turn a Gentle back into a Brute?"

Her nose wrinkles, brows drawing together. "Why would anyone want to do that?"

"Just *theoretically*, could someone?" The words come out too hopeful. I try to add distance to my tone, falling into genuine confusion. "I mean, there must be some explanation why the Brutes are out there." Even though I know the vaccine gentles Brutes, I still don't have a clue how the Brutes in the Jungle came to exist. Every baby at the Center—at least those who don't die near birth—gets the vaccine.

"It's funny," Ciela muses. "Grandmother asked me the same question."

"*Grandmother?*" Gooseflesh prickles the skin over my arms and neck.

"Yes, Grandmother. You know, the moody Matriarch who made us dab our mouths with our napkins? She came by last week and asked me to look into it. Weird, right? I hadn't spoken to her since the last Initus, but she said it was a matter of Nedéan security, and she'd really appreciate if I'd put my 'sharp mind' to it. She all but promised me a director position if I could give her a definitive answer, and if I . . ." She cuts herself off, then starts again. "I've been working around the clock to figure it out."

"Wow, Ciela." I try, unsuccessfully, to force down the dread creeping its way up my windpipe. I barely manage a chuckle. "She's like a different Grandmother. That's amazing. And have you found anything for her?"

She shakes her head. "As far as I can tell, the effects of the vaccine are irreversible."

Irreversible. The word carries too much finality for the Gentles I've come to know.

"And you're sure?"

"I'm not saying it could never happen, but I've tried every combination of materials we currently have at our disposal, and none of them have made any measurable increase in a Gentle's levels of the mystery substance in live trials. So yeah, I'm pretty sure."

I go silent, shuddering at the implication of "live trials" on Gentles, and still trying to fathom how the Brutes exist. They must have avoided getting the vaccine, but how?

Ciela scans my uniform. "So you decided to join them after all." It's a statement, not a question.

"You're not surprised?"

"Let's just say you'd never make it as an actress in Ad Artium. Have you told Mother?"

I cringe at the thought of facing her, still afraid I'll disappoint her with my decision.

"No, but I have to take my horse to Bella Terra soon. I'll tell her then."

"She probably won't mind too much. There are so many Alexia

around the Center these days, it'll practically be like you chose the destiny she wanted for you anyway." She smiles slyly, and I genuinely laugh.

"Why *are* there so many Alexia around here?"

She takes up the question without concern. "They doubled the guard about the time Grandmother came by. Maybe there have been more raids. The Center is the heart of Nedé. I wouldn't blame her for being cautious."

Maybe, but something doesn't add up. If Teera has Dáin in custody, the attacks should have stopped. Could other Brute defectors be going after fincas?

Ciela cuts through my internal muddling. "I'd better get back to work."

"Right. Good luck with your research. I hope you find whatever Grandmother needs. You'd make a great director." I squeeze her shoulder. We're making progress toward sibling civility, but I don't think either of us is ready for a hug.

"Thanks. And good luck with *that*," she says, motioning to my uniform. Her gaze lingers on the short sword at my hip. Is it my imagination, or is she slightly impressed? "You'll make a great Alexia."

She goes back to her notebook as I slip out the door. Halfway down the hall, I realize I should have asked whether she has seen Jonalyn since the baby was born. I retrace my steps to the office door, but as I reach for the handle, a small glass pane reveals my sister's back, telephone pressed to her ear. Phones are rare in Nedé, reserved for important matters. I'd better not interrupt. Anyway, I'll find out soon enough.

I follow a different path to the stairwell to avoid encountering any fellow Alexia in the main lab. I should get back to the Arena. But as I descend the flight to the seventh floor, something Ciela said snags against a rough board of reason. The infants who showed the abnormal—or rather, *normal*—blood died before they could be given the vaccine. Why?

I remember passing a records room when we toured the Center, near the nursery. I wonder if they have documentation of anything useful, like what caused those Brute babies to die.

It wouldn't hurt to take a quick look around before I head back to the Arena.

CHAPTER THREE

AFTER TWO WRONG TURNS ON the eighth floor, I find a plain, windowless door between delivery and the nursery marked "Records." The air smells of sterile metal and clean linens, and the moans of a woman in labor echo through the hallway. I give a terse nod to a passing nurse. She notices me, though her gaze sticks to the floor. This Alexia gig is really paying off.

I tug the door open, hoping to find the records room empty. Instead a woman in a white lab coat leans over a broad ledger book, pencil scribbling quickly. Her graying dark hair is pulled back in a loose bun, and when she lifts her head to me, light hazel eyes stop me midstride.

"*Mother?*"

"Rei?" I'm not sure who is more shocked to see whom.

"I thought you were home, with Jonalyn." I quickly take in the rest of the room, relieved to find it empty. Two walls are lined with similar pale green and peach ledger books, the center of the room a maze of waist-high filing cabinets.

Instead of answering, she wraps me in a fierce embrace, kissing my hair and muttering, "Oh, my Reina." For the first time since I was old enough to resent my mother, I really hug her, and I make up for lost time. I feel her warmth and the slight give of her soft body in my arms. I breathe her in, and I *love* her. Really, really love her.

She releases her grip and holds me at arm's length. "I'm so sorry I wasn't there, Reina. She's a fool not to choose you . . . but I can't say I'm sorry she didn't."

"I know." The statement runs deeper than an answer to her condolences. My mother's distrust of Teera always confused me before, but now I know why she was so cautious. I've experienced Teera's power-hungry madness for myself. "I'm okay. Really."

For the first time she notices my uniform. She takes it in with a placid expression, and I brace for inevitable displeasure. But when her eyes find mine again, she looks peacefully resigned.

"It suits you," she says. "Serve them well."

"You're not angry?"

She sighs a little. "Oh, you know it would not have been my first choice, mostly because . . . well, it doesn't matter now. What matters is that you are my daughter, and I will always love you, no matter what. Besides, in my opinion, Alexia is still safer than *Apprentice*." Her quiet laugh disarms me completely.

"I guessed as much." I initiate another hug, the only gift at my disposal to thank her for understanding. "How is Jo?" I ask, remembering the reason Mother wasn't at the two-hundredth-anniversary celebration yesterday. "Shouldn't you be with her?"

Mother's demeanor instantly changes, her warm joy silenced by cool collection. "She's recovering. But because of all the trauma she's endured, the baby . . ." She pauses, seemingly searching for the right words. "The baby didn't make it. I'm here documenting the proper records."

"I'm so sorry," I whisper. "Was it a daughter?"

I instantly cringe at my own ingrained insensitivity, the prejudices that would make me assume losing a baby girl would be worse than losing a Gentle. It proves that my assumptions, hammered home through eighteen years of being Nedéan, run deep.

"No," Mother assures me. "Not a daughter."

But my comment stirs up the ocean of questions about Gentles and Brutes—the storm inside that I can barely seem to hold at bay. I need answers, and all the questions I've been waiting to ask threaten to spill out at once.

"Mother?"

"Yes?" She rubs my bare arms with smooth hands, taking advantage of the softening of my stone-cold demeanor toward her. I take a deep breath, lock her eyes with mine.

"I've been to the Jungle."

The words hang in the air as her hands drop to her sides like heavy stones. Understanding spreads across her face like shadows at dusk.

"And what did you find there?" she asks cautiously. Her deflection irritates me. Is she still trying to protect me? Or is she protecting herself? Why won't she just tell me what she has been hiding instead of making me go fishing for answers?

"I think you know what I found there, Mother." I don't mean to sound irritable, but nonetheless, old Reina makes an appearance. "I found Brutes. And one of them had your eyes. His name is Jase, and I don't know how you're connected, but there's something there, and I need you to tell me what it is." She takes so much time to answer that I throw in, "And the leader knows who you are. *Why does he know who you are?*"

"Keep your voice down," she warns, not angrily. Serene, unflappable Mother ages twenty years. She presses soft fingertips to her temples, then takes a deep breath before attempting a response.

"First, you need to know I've kept this from you and your sisters for your own protection. What I tell you now will be for the same reason. If anything ever happened to you three because of what I've done . . . I could never forgive myself." She smooths a strand of my hair made wild by a day of Arena training.

"I understand." Of course I can't, not really, but it sounds right to say if I'm to convince her to go on.

"Jason—Jase, as they call him—is my child, yes. Many years ago—when I was about your age, actually—I discovered what makes a Brute a Brute and a Gentle a Gentle. When I birthed Jase, I couldn't stand the thought of him being subjected to a life of pain and servitude. So I kept him from becoming one. Then I took him to Torvus and asked him to raise Jason."

"But how? . . . Why Torvus? How did you even know there was a Brute living in the Jungle? And why on earth would he take your baby?"

She closes her eyes, barely whispering the answer. "Because Jason was his child too."

My mind spins with the absurdity of it—with unanswered questions and fear and awe and . . . and . . . satisfaction. I *knew* it. I knew Jase resembled both Torvus *and* Mother. But . . .

"You had a child . . . *by a Brute*? Like in the old world?" I ask incredulously. I'm not sure what shocks me more, that Mother and Torvus had a child, or that my virtuous mother disregarded the Articles to do so. She nods once in answer, placing a hand on the table beside us, as if the weight of all this might topple her. "Even though he and I parted ways, I knew Torvus wouldn't refuse the child, because he loved me. And I loved him, Reina. Not in the way a mother loves a child or with the affection of a sister or a cousin. His heart and mine became intertwined with a oneness that defies explanation. I can only assume that's how it used to be, when Brutes and women coexisted—before we gentled them."

I don't think she meant to say that last part. *Before we gentled them.* She watches me closely, almost shyly, waiting to see if I caught her meaning.

"Domus gave me the journal. I know what the foremothers did—what we continue to do."

Is that a spark of pride lighting her eyes? "I'm glad he saw reason to show it to you, Rei of Sunshine."

"It's not right that they're changed without their knowledge. But I don't know how to help them."

"I know exactly how you feel," she says, and I can tell she does. "We have no right to play God, deciding what they should or shouldn't be—whatever the danger. Brutes are meant to be Brutes. And I've done what little I can to make sure at least some will get that chance."

What? What has she done? *So some will get that chance . . .* The Brutes at Tree Camp, all different ages. Dead infants with abnormal blood. I still can't connect the pieces until I remember exactly where we're standing.

"Jonalyn's baby—he's not dead, is he?"

Mother's lips part, but before she can confirm or deny my accusation, a distant commotion silences her. Our heads snap in unison toward the sound. Neither of us, I now realize, are supposed to be here.

"We have to go." Mother slips the ledger into its place and steps quickly to the door. Pushing it outward, she peers cautiously into the hallway to be sure we are alone. "Come with me."

Bright electric bulbs reflect off the hallway's tiled floor as Mother leads us toward the delivery rooms.

"I know a pla—" Her words are cut short by a trio of women rounding the corner toward us, not twenty-five meters ahead.

Two Alexia, armed with swords but no bows, guard a sharp-looking woman with cropped silver hair and a flowing multicolored robe. Her mouth tilts with satisfaction.

My heart free-falls into my stomach. Thankfully Mother speaks, voicing the words too afraid to leave my own mouth.

"Mother—what are you doing here?"

Matriarch Teera lifts her chin to better look down her thin nose at her eldest daughter. "I could ask you the same, Leda. With Reina?" Her nostrils flare as she says my name, a sure sign we're in trouble. "How *interesting*. Though finding you together is quite convenient. I have some questions I'd like to ask you both." Her head dips slightly toward the guard on her left. "Take them to the cells for questioning."

The Alexia advance with determined steps. As panic quickens my pulse, I know one thing for sure: we can't let them take us in. There's no telling what "questioning" Grandmother has in mind—even for her own kin. I grip Mother's arm, swinging her around.

"*Run.*"

We sprint toward the glass-walled nursery at the end of the hall. We have to get around the corner and find a place to hide before the Alexia close the distance. My limited training won't do us much good if this comes to hand-to-hand combat. I'm fast, maybe fast enough to outrun them, but Mother is already breathing hard.

Two sets of boots pound the tiles behind us, echoing like thunder through the corridor. Over their clatter, Teera yells, "Dead or alive!"

I hear the frightening slide of daggers escaping their sheaths. Just before we round the corner, the nursery's viewing wall explodes with the impact of a weapon, raining down a shower of glass.

Another step and Mother gasps, stumbles, nearly falls. She releases my hand, and I glance back, ready to yell at her to keep running. Her face twists in agony.

"Mother!" I slip my arm under hers, lifting and pulling her around the corner with every ounce of strength I possess. A bloom of red seeps through her white lab coat. The handle of a dagger protrudes from the right side of her back. *No, no, no.* I instinctively want to tear it from her body, use it to protect her, but that would worsen the bleeding.

Mother gives a valiant effort at stumbling on, but the Alexia will round that corner any second. This is it—we'll die here.

Two meters ahead, a door swings open. Before I know what's happening, Dr. Karina Novak pulls us inside.

"Come with me!" she commands, quickly closing and locking the heavy metal door behind us.

Mother drops to her knees, then collapses across the floor. The doctor rushes to kneel beside her, steady fingers moving quickly to tear the fabric away and examine the wound.

"Oh, Leda," she mutters. "This better not be about . . ."

Mother winces weakly.

The doctor turns to me, her large eyes urgent behind thin-rimmed glasses. "We don't have much time. Did they see us come in?"

"I don't know." I hope Mother's lab coat absorbed the blood. A trail would lead them right to us.

Not a second later, the doorknob rattles. I hold my breath. *Please, please, please keep walking.*

A distant call . . . The shadow under the door vanishes . . . Fading footsteps . . . I nearly collapse with relief.

Dr. Novak grabs a stack of cloth diapers from a cupboard and presses several around the dagger. "I need supplies. Press these here, just so, until I return."

The doctor sprints to the other side of the large room, then exits through a small door painted to blend into the surrounding wall. It creaks on its hinges, as if neglected for ages, grating so loudly in the dead silence I fear it will alert every Alexia in the entire Center. I hold stock-still for minutes that feel like days, hands frozen against the cloths, straining to hear any other footsteps approaching the door.

"Reina," Mother mumbles in the quiet. "I'm sorry—so sorry."

"Shhh," I soothe, wishing I didn't have to press the wound so I could hold her in my arms, cradle her the way she rocked me as a child, before tucking me tight in my four-poster bed. "You're going to be okay. We'll get you out of here."

Blood seeps through the cloths on her back, oozing between my fingers. Too much blood.

This can't be happening. Not Mother. Not my *mother.*

My tears fall freely onto the tiles. I have to keep her alive. She can't die—not here, not like this.

Her breaths become shallow, then stop. I shake her in a panic. "Mother! *Please*—don't give up. She'll be back soon. Stay with me!"

She sucks another breath, and relief pours from my eyes. With tremendous effort, she forces her eyes open a little.

"Rei," she rasps. "The baby . . ." Another labored breath. "Take him . . . Torvus."

Jonalyn's baby. I was right—he *is* still alive. Torvus can give him the life he'd be robbed of in Nedé. But I was drugged on the way into the Jungle and blindfolded on the way out. I'd never find Tree Camp on my own.

"I can't," I say through tears. "I don't know the way."

Her face twists with a fresh wave of agonizing pain, splitting my soul in two. I lean down close, kissing her forehead.

With trembling, bloody fingers, she yanks her necklace free, breaking the jute cord in a final burst of strength, and forces the pendant into my palm.

"Take this . . . him."

"I don't know the way," I insist again, frantic not to disappoint her, terrified to lose her.

"The song," she forces out. "Follow . . . song."

What is she talking about? What song? She must be losing too much blood.

"Promise," she begs, her eyes closing with frightening resignation.

"Okay, I promise." I'd promise her anything in this moment, no matter how impossible. I'd give her my very life if it meant she would . . .

Another creak of the narrow door and Dr. Novak is running toward us, then emptying her bulging coat pockets onto the floor next to Mother. All manner of needles, pads, scissors, string, and vials spill across the tile. I slip the pendant into my vest pocket and help her regather them.

She takes one look at Mother, and I don't miss the fear that passes over her face. But just as quickly she barks at me, "You have to get out of here."

"I won't leave her."

"You have no choice, Dom Pierce," she snaps. "I can hide a Center worker much easier than an Alexia. You'll endanger us all." She cuts away the lab coat and sops up the gush of blood. Seeing I haven't moved, she drills me with a forceful glare. "Leda is like a daughter to me. I promise I'll take care of her. There's nothing you can do here."

She leaves little room for argument.

"That door leads to an emergency corridor. Follow it right to the staircase. It will lead you outside, bypassing the lobby."

I want to ask if Mother will make it, but Dr. Novak's frantic movements—injecting the wound with a needle, jerking the dagger free—imply my questions will only get in the way. My lower lip trembles like a child's. Leaving her goes against my heart, but I'm sensible enough to understand Dr. Novak is right.

I kiss Mother's forehead goodbye—for now or forever. She doesn't stir. As I slip through the creaky door, I force myself to face reality: I will never see her again.

I stumble out of the room in a daze, through the corridor and down the abandoned narrow stairs, per Dr. Novak's instructions.

Dr. Novak. I suspected there was something different about her during the Candidates' tour. It wasn't just because Mother's codirector recognized me as Leda's daughter. What did she say? *This better not be about . . .*

About what? What secrets do they share?

The stairs descend in darkness, each passing floor marked only by a nondescript door centered in another corridor. I race down, down, down, listening for trailing footsteps, and counting the levels as they pass. *Seven . . . six . . . four . . .* and finally, *one.* The bottom level looks just like the rest, and for a moment I question whether I could have counted wrong. The last thing I need is to walk into the middle of a hospital floor. But the staircase ends here—this must be the bottom. I grip the cool metal handle and twist.

It doesn't turn.

It's supposed to turn. I try again. Nothing. I wrench the handle over and over, finally coaxing the rusted metal to budge slightly. Progress. I slam my body's weight into the door—once, twice—then try the handle again. Slam . . . twist . . . slam. The rust-swollen hinges finally concede, and the door shimmies open.

Night air floods the doorway and fills my lungs, heavy and too warm, but living. Such a stark contrast to the sterile hallways, beakers, and records I just left behind. Fresh grief bubbles in my chest as I recall other lifeless things—precious things I've been forced to abandon.

Not Mother, too. First Treowe, now Mother?

I bite my thumb to hold back a choked sob. *No*—I can't let myself descend into that abyss. Not here, not now. Grief will have to wait. I need to get somewhere safe.

The exit has deposited me into a screenlike alcove of tall shrubs, part of the manicured landscaping that rings the Center. With some effort, I close the door, then try to get my bearings. I'll have to escape this green tangle before I can figure out which side of the building I've come out on.

I duck and squeeze through tightly woven branches, twigs scratching my arms and leaves rustling in my ears, before emerging ten meters from one of the giant archways near the front entrance. That's unfortunate. I was hoping I'd be on the east side of the Center, nearer Callisto. I'll have to cross the front of the building somehow.

Straightening, I brush sticky pieces of shrub from my uniform. But my hand stalls midswipe.

I'm not alone.

A contingent of Alexia stride under the arches toward the entrance, and they've spotted me. *She* has spotted me.

Trinidad's golden eyes grow wide as a cat's, then narrow to slits, the briefest glimmer of confusion and betrayal eliminated by the cold steel of her training.

Granted, I can see why this wouldn't look real great.

"Trin," I say, stepping cautiously toward her, smart enough to know running won't work this time. "It's not what you think."

The dozen or so Alexia around her—some of whom I trained with just this afternoon—raise their bows and unsheathe their swords in unison, halting my approach.

"Oh, really?" Trin mocks. "'Cause I thought you decided to be an Alexia, Candidate, not a traitor."

INTERLUDE

LEDA PIERCE, the eldest daughter of Teera Pierce, was never meant to be a Matriarch's daughter. At least that's how she consoled herself when her mother forced her and her sister, Julissa, into itchy tunics to be paraded before Senators. Leda would much rather have been running barefoot along the Halcyon beachfront than forced to sit through Council meetings in the great room at Finca del Mar.

Leda's distaste for privilege ran deeper than a child's longing for freedom. From a very young age, she knew she and her sister were only the fulfillment of the Matriarch's duty to have at least two offspring, as an example to Nedéans.

But appreciation for duty does little to console a young heart that longs to be loved.

The summer of her tenth year, Leda and Julissa were sent to

visit Teera's cousin, Senator Salita Pierce, in Amal Province. Salita offered to keep the girls for the summer at her large finca in the countryside. She promised Teera she would introduce the girls to advantageous senatorial connections, and with their tutor along, their studies needn't even suffer. Leda later learned that Salita felt sorry for the sisters—ignored while Teera was home, cooped up at the finca while she was away—and hoped a few months at Bella Terra would provide a respite from that life. Leda prickled at the thought of others' pity, but not enough to refuse the chance of escape.

Among the fields and orchards of Bella Terra, Leda's young soul came alive. She loved to splash along the banks of the Jabiru and taught Julissa to catch frogs in the large pond by the sheep field. "Aunt" Salita, as the girls came to call her, was sometimes away on Senator business, but she allowed the girls as much freedom while she was gone.

Not surprisingly, Leda and Julissa begged to return to Bella Terra every summer thereafter. Matriarch Teera often agreed, clearly glad to be rid of the responsibility of children, free to oversee construction of the Arena or other matters. But had she known what these visits would birth in her eldest daughter, Leda knew she never would have acquiesced.

———————

Leda was thirteen years old the summer she lay on a blanket along Bella's riverbank, reading a delightful book under the shade of a massive fig tree. Absorbed in stories of the foremothers' accomplishments, she startled when a strange racket rose above the swirling hush of the water, interrupting her reverie.

Whack, whack, whack.

She traced the sound across the river and a little upstream, where a curly-haired Gentle about her age stood in water up to his bare stomach. With a long pole, he beat at a branch above him until a fat, scaly iguana—long as an arm—lost its grip, slipped from the limb, and plummeted into the water with a great splash. With catlike speed, the Gentle grabbed the thrashing animal, firmly clamping its mouth and tail. Then he plunged it underwater and held it there, his thin muscles tensed. Eventually the creature went still, and the Gentle tossed it into his boat. It landed with a thud next to three other dead lizards. Then he climbed into the boat and rowed toward her shore.

She watched the dripping Gentle lumber up the bank toward her, four scaly, limp iguanas bundled in his arms. She was curious—more so about this peculiar Gentle than the lizards. She knew her mother would never, ever approve of her talking to a Gentle for any reason other than giving orders, but she was particularly tired of her mother's control that summer, and the freedom of Aunt Salita's finca had incited in her a growing independence. What could it hurt to see the lizards? She asked to view his catch.

———

Leda often conversed with the Gentle that summer, and eventually without guilt. He was fourteen, recently assigned to the finca after the last Initus ceremony. To Leda he seemed different from other Gentles his age, though she couldn't put her finger on what set him apart. He looked like them, but the lizard-catching Gentle was more sure of himself, quicker with his words, and when he happened to be working nearby—more often than seemed coincidental—he made eye contact and went out of his way to help her.

The other Gentles called him Torvus.

When she returned the following summer, Leda caught herself scanning the fields for him, relieved to see him carting water nearby. And when he chanced upon her later that day, while she picked plumeria blossoms in a hedge far from the main villa, she realized she was hoping he'd find her.

Summers came and went, and Leda's interactions with her unlikely friend became more frequent. He taught her to hunt iguanas. She taught him to read, using as primers a *Holy Bible* and a few other volumes from Aunt Salita's collection of rare books. Her aunt would never notice their brief absences from the display in the back hall. Nedéans had no interest in reading books by long-dead Brutes; they only boasted about their "antique relics." But as Torvus learned to make sense of the letters on the page, he hung on the stories about a great quest and an enchanted ring, Dumas's tale of injustice and revenge, and a strange story about the senseless slaughter of songbirds.

Torvus was animated, attentive, asked questions, and made her little gifts. She trusted him with the secrets of privileged life, and he commiserated with her sorrows. She found relief in venting about her controlling, unpleasant mother, and his resulting dislike for the Matriarch justified hers.

As time passed, Torvus became different in other ways. He grew taller than the other Gentles. His face widened, his shoulders broadened. Confused and embarrassed by the changes, he wore baggy tunics to cover growing muscles, and kept to the outlying fields to escape the notice of female eyes.

Except Leda. He trusted Leda. He *loved* Leda.

By the summer of her seventeenth year, she could no longer deny his *otherness*. His voice had grown deeper, chin stronger, eyes more intense. That was the summer she suspected Torvus wasn't a Gentle at all, and worried what would happen when someone else noticed. That was the summer she realized she loved him in return. The summer she broke every Article, denied every virtue. The summer he told her he was leaving.

"Come with me," he whispered in the darkness, under a tangle of plumeria trees, their secret bower. "I can't leave without you."

"Where would we go?"

"The Jungle. I'll make a home for you there. I'll take care of you. I'll make you happy, I promise."

Her lips found his, their bodies entwined, and they sealed the promises made. He would venture beyond Nedé first, to build a home for them. She would return to Finca del Mar until he sent word.

If Torvus had known what Leda would discover when she returned home—what would tear them apart—he would have stolen her away that very night.

———

A few weeks after returning home, while her mother was away for a Senate hearing in Fik'iri Province, Leda browsed the Matriarch's personal collection of rare books for a volume her tutor had mentioned. She knew better than to be in the Matriarch's office without permission, but she assuaged her guilt by telling herself she *would* have asked if her mother ever had time for her. As she worked her way along the gleaming shelves searching for *Intelligent Virtue*, she stumbled upon an unmarked leather journal, the contents of which would turn her world upside down.

Through Tristan Pierce's words, Leda discovered the truth about the vaccines. The confirmation of what Torvus was—however

39

improbable—collided with all Leda had known of the Gentles. In contrast to their weakness and apathy, Torvus's strength, resilience, and passion—his belief that things could change—rang true. He was what they were meant to be.

She loved Torvus deeply, but as she continued reading the Scripture book she had taken from Bella Terra, she felt a deep responsibility to help other babies have the chance to be what God intended. So while she waited, she dedicated herself to combing through every book at Finca del Mar, and leveraged her status to spend hours at the Center, researching what could be done for the babies changed against their knowledge.

Then, one day, her painstaking research became unimaginably personal. Unable to deny the signs any longer, she was forced to accept the unlikely, terrifying truth: she was carrying a child of her own. And she couldn't tell a soul.

Months passed, and now Leda was the one forced to hide her changing body. The Matriarch's daughter loosened sashes and wore oversized tunics to hide her swelling abdomen, but time was shrinking as the baby within her grew. Fear threatened to suffocate her. Had Torvus forgotten? Even if he sent word, could she go? Could she deny the growing conviction that she needed to do something to help the innocent?

Finally, one night after returning home from the Center, Leda found a single plumeria blossom scenting her bed pillow, and beside it, a necklace strung with a small mahogany pendant, carved in the shape of a tree. She remembered her promise, and knew she couldn't keep it.

She met Torvus under the plumeria trees one last time. One last time, to tell him she couldn't go with him.

Her rejection shattered Torvus's heart into angry fragments. He wanted her to choose *him*; she wanted to give others a choice.

His pleading ripped at her heart, his touch nearly convinced her, but she knew she had to think of more than herself now.

Despite Torvus's deep grief, as she walked away, he told her how to find him, hoping she would change her mind. She touched the pendant strung around her neck, hoping someday she could.

―――――――

As her eighteenth birthday approached, Leda accepted another truth: fate had chosen her destiny for her. Only one future would enable her to deliver a baby secretly. Only one would ensure that her child—should it be a boy—would remain like his father.

When Leda chose Materno, she obliterated the last of Teera's faith in her. The eighth Matriarch of Nedé had hoped Leda would succeed her and was incensed at her "weakness." Yet she couldn't publicly disgrace a daughter who chose Materno—the "highest destiny" of Nedé. To preserve her own pride, she forced Dr. Karina Novak to share the Center leadership position with her daughter. Teera also begrudgingly granted her daughter the finca she requested: Bella Terra. Leda ensured Aunt Salita was relocated to a grander finca farther south, and consequently the benevolent Senator felt no ill will.

The day Leda arrived at the Center, Karina's contempt was evident. It wasn't hard to imagine why. Leda had heard whisperings. And she knew herself what it was to be manipulated by the Matriarch's whims.

"I know this isn't fair," Leda conceded, once they were alone.

"I've heard you worked for decades to secure the directorship. Why should an eighteen-year-old's connection to a meddling Matriarch sidestep years of study?"

The hard line of Dr. Novak's mouth gave a little. "Well, we'll see." Then a little more. "I've also heard you're not much like your mother."

Leda took to Dr. Novak as only a teenager starved for motherly affection could. She aimed to please and devoted herself to learning every process and procedure. As the weeks passed, she sensed the older woman soften toward her, take pleasure in her inquisitiveness, admire her willingness to work long hours, and applaud her patience under pressure. Perhaps that's why Leda trusted her with a secret she hadn't shared with anyone else, and asked something of her that could cost the Center codirector her job . . . or much, much more.

———

When Karina learned that Leda had encountered the Brute Torvus at Bella Terra, she doubted it could be a coincidence. Still, she couldn't bring herself to tell Leda about her own secret. Leda confided that Torvus was leaving Nedé, which meant Karina could avoid facing what she had ignored decades before. Still, suspecting her mistake was the reason for Leda's predicament, she purposed to help, whatever the personal cost.

Karina agreed to deliver the baby in secret. She supplied Leda with formula and diapers, blankets and the customary health vaccine, and urged her to hide the child at Bella Terra until he was old enough to transfer to a Hive. He could enter the Gentle system easily enough, and they could put the ordeal behind them.

Leda had other plans. With no record of her child's birth, nothing stopped her from declining to administer the vaccine. But with no vaccine, Leda knew she couldn't hide her boy in Nedé forever.

It took her a week to locate the place Torvus had spoken of, following his landmarks through the wild Jungle to the foot of an enormous mahogany tree. There she found the house he had built for her, a simple wood dwelling radiating safety and warmth, a plumeria blossom carved into the door like a seal of promise. Their reunion threatened her resolve to leave—and nearly dissolved his will to love—but in the end, Leda convinced Torvus to care for their child as he had promised to care for her.

She named their son Jason, hoping his presence would heal her absence.

CHAPTER FOUR

I DON'T BLAME TRIN FOR APPREHENDING ME, or for handing me over to Adoni. Any well-trained Alexia would have done the same. At least she was decent enough to have someone grab my horse before taking me to the cells.

Adoni didn't blindfold me on our way down the narrow stairs to this hole. I appreciate knowing exactly where I am: beneath the Arena via a vine-covered door near the northern entrance. Unfortunately, her indifference hints she has no intention of letting me out anytime soon.

"It's too bad," she said, clanking my cell door shut. "You'd have made a half-decent Alexia." Shaking her head, she left without giving any hint at what comes next—how long I'll be here, whether they'll feed me, if I'll get a chance to defend myself, what tortures Teera will employ to get what she wants.

The stone wall at the rear of my cell cools my bare arms and sweat-soaked vest. It might be dark, musty, and unsettling in here, but at least it offers a break from Phoenix City's incessant dry-season heat. I release a shaky breath, the aftermath of adrenaline leaving my chest hollow, my limbs weak.

A small prick of light from an electric bulb down the corridor to my left barely reveals my immediate surroundings. The opposite end remains a dark mystery. My cell runs about a meter and a half by three, with a slim cot taking up half that space and a bucket in the back corner. A single corridor runs the length of the underground prison, flanked on either side by enough identical metal-barred cells to surprise me. How many chambers does Grandmother need to subdue threats to Nedé? And . . . who has she actually banished here? Were they all Gentles? Or did she torture other women who stood in her way? I wouldn't put it past her to defy Nedé's protections against barbaric punishments and lock away anyone she deemed threatening.

In that case, I take my present occupancy as a compliment.

As the quiet minutes tick on, with no distraction from the enormity of the past hour, I'm forced to let it slam into me. Threads of grief and fear tease their way through my veins until I'm shaking. I can't escape the image of my mother spread across the floor, color drained from her face, can't erase the feel of her blood seeping through my fingers. There's no way she could have survived that wound. I pound my fist on the ground, sharp pebbles piercing my skin, and try unsuccessfully to stifle a sob. *Not Mother, too!* The tears come, and come, and come. One for every regret.

I didn't always treat Mother like an annoyance. I didn't always resent her nagging or prickle at her affection. When I was young, I welcomed her love as any child does: with both arms. But as I grew older, our differences emerged and instead of appreciating them, I resented her for who I thought she was. I assumed she was weak to choose Materno, a coward for leaving the privilege of Finca del Mar for rural Bella Terra. And I resented her for caring so much about my safety and having an opinion about my future.

Regret intensifies the pain of losing her. I didn't even know her—not really. I spent years dreaming of being a hero, and all along I was living with one.

But it's too late to tell her now. And I'll have to live the rest of my life realizing what a gift she was, too late to enjoy her.

You don't know that, Reina. Maybe Dr. Novak was able to . . . I twist away from my weakness, my neediness. Hope will only hurt worse in the end. I have to face reality. Mother is gone. And she asked me to take Jonalyn's baby to the Jungle. So I can't stay here. I have no clue how I'm going to get out, but there's no other option.

I squint toward the light at the end of the corridor and see what might be a door beyond it. If I could just talk to Trin. After the way she looked at me outside the Center, with such surprise, betrayal, and anger, I'd rather take an arrow to the arm than talk to her—but she's the closest thing I have to an ally. I doubt she's within earshot—there isn't even a guard posted in this secret prison—but I let my voice probe the darkness anyway.

"Trin?" The word cracks from my parched throat and echoes strangely through the row of interconnected cages, bouncing off stone walls. "Trinidad?" Then stronger, "Hello?"

Silence. I pound my fist again, sigh, and slump back against the wall.

From the unlit void, a rough, brutish laugh creeps along the damp earthen floor. The distinctly wicked, eerily familiar chuckle freezes me solid.

"Well, well," he says. "Isn't this a treat?"

Amid the shadows three or four cells to my right, a dark shape moves slightly, a hunched figure turning toward me. The weak light barely illuminates a mussed shock of red hair.

I scramble to the corner of my cell, slamming back against the bars with enough force to make the cage shudder. It takes a full minute for fear to recede enough to realize Dáin is also locked up. He can't hurt me, and I can't kill him.

"The only 'treat' is knowing you're going to die," I spit back at him.

He laughs outright, but a childish quality in it catches me off guard. It calls to mind the small Brutes at Tree Camp, chasing lizards and scampering up trees. Even Dáin was small once.

"Wouldn't you like that," he jeers, leaning back against his own wall.

"You deserve it—after what you've done."

"To you? I didn't hurt you, you sniveling, whining girl."

"To my sister," I bark back, "when you raided her finca."

"Your sister is lucky to be alive, after what she did to me."

His meaning eludes me until I remember the large scab across his face the night he attacked me. *Attagirl, Jonalyn.*

He sniffs loudly, then adds, "They weren't supposed to be there, anyway. My source told me the place would be empty."

"Oh, so it's okay to steal other people's stuff as long as they aren't around?"

"The sage has spoken!" he mocks, with a dramatic flick of his wrist. "You tell me, *is it* okay to steal something from someone, if they don't know it has been taken from them?"

His meaning is clear, and it shuts me up. He doesn't need to know I have my own doubts about Nedé's practice of gentling Brutes. His existence is the strongest case for continuing the practice.

"I thought so," he says, then spits toward the corner of his cell. After a moment of silence he speaks again, this time with less anger and more reason. "Sometimes people have to get hurt so the right thing can happen."

"It doesn't work that way," I mutter. "What if you hurt someone for a 'greater good,' but the good never comes? Then you're a devil, not a hero."

How puzzling that you can go through life thinking you're a pretty decent human being, then suddenly, in a single instant, you realize you're on par with pond scum. I killed Tre for the greater good. Dáin raided fincas. He had no business hurting those women, or killing anybody, but I can see how hope for a greater good could push someone to do the unthinkable. We're not so very different. How disgusting.

"I'd rather be a devil than a Gentle," he says, kicking the bars of his cell.

The metallic clang makes me jump, but I have nothing to say in retort. Deep, dark silence envelops us again—for minutes or hours, it's hard to tell. Without sun or stars, clock or food, one moment bleeds into the next like gray watercolor seeping across parchment.

Eventually I stretch out on the dirt floor and hope sleep can overpower despair.

I'm jarred from a fitful nightmare by the scrape of a door. As firm, confident footfalls echo down the corridor, I scramble to a sitting position, forcing stiff joints to bend. When the dark figure crosses under the single bulb, the backlit flash of gold on her biceps gives her away. She heads straight for my cell.

"Trin, I can explain," I rush. "It's not what you think."

She paces in front of the bars, avoiding my eyes. "Now you're an expert on what I think? Adoni's right—I shouldn't have been so free with you. I shouldn't have trusted you."

"But I—"

"It doesn't take an Innovatus to figure out what's going on, Candi—Dom Pierce," she says hotly.

The switch to formality stings, even though I'm not technically a Candidate anymore anyway. But more concerning is what she thinks is "going on." Could she know why I was at the Center?

"What are you talking about?" I probe.

"Teera told Adoni about your plan. Honestly, I thought you were better than that. It's low, Reina, even after what happened in the Arena."

"I don't have any plan, Trin."

"You come back here," she continues, ignoring my plea of innocence, "and say you want to be one of us, to give yourself an alibi so you can take out the winner." I stare at her, disbelieving, as she continues, "None of us wanted Jamara to win, but bats, Reina, what were you thinking?"

"*Take her out?* I have good reason to hate Jamara, but I wouldn't kill anyone—"

Trin raises an eyebrow at me, and I instantly regret the words.

"That was different," I defend. "I had to do what I did to—to the Gentle."

She stops pacing to stare straight into my soul. "What you do is your business. I'm just saying it surprised me. Made me wonder what else you're capable of that I wouldn't have guessed."

I want to scream. She can accuse me of wanting to assassinate Jamara, fine. It's not like the thought never crossed my mind. But not Tre. His death is sacred to me, and I can't have her thinking I shot him for my own benefit. Can I trust her? Can I tell her without breaking my word to Torvus?

My face burns with heat. I hope I'm not making a mistake.

"He was my friend, Trin. Okay?" A lump threatens to choke me. "She chose him to test me. To see if she could control me.

And I wish to Siyah I had failed the test. Yes, I shot him, but only because I wanted to help others like him."

"Help them? What do you mean?" Her eyes narrow.

I bite the inside of my cheek. I don't know if telling her more will help or hinder my case when I ask her to break me out of this place, but something in me needs her to understand why I'm in here, and why I have to get out.

"I believed that if I became Matriarch, I could make life better for the Gentles. Treat them better than my grandmother has. Maybe give them a chance at a better life."

"A better—?" She curses under her breath. "So you shot the Gentle to convince Teera you hate them as much as she does, so you can help them?"

"Well, when you put it that way . . ."

"And then you went to the Center to—*what*, save the world by taking out the competition?"

"No! Why would I go to the Center if I wanted to kill Jamara? Even if she were there, what would I do? Poison her with herb tinctures? Bandage her to death? I don't need any more weapons. Besides, only an idiot would think killing an Apprentice would land her the Matriarch's seat. It makes no sense."

She seems to consider my point, though her next words barely slip through her tight jaw. "So why *were* you there?"

"A Gentle got hurt at the Arena stable, pretty bad. I took him so he didn't bleed to death."

"And because you were doing a good deed you had to sneak back out?"

"No, Grand—*Teera*—ambushed us."

"Us?"

"I found my mother working that night. She's a Center leader." I force composure into my voice. "Teera ordered an attack and . . . my mother was hit with a dagger. One of the doctors hid us. She told me how to get out, and that's where you found me. I swear, Trin, I'm telling you the truth."

"Why would Teera want you dead? And Dom Pierce—her own daughter?"

I roll my eyes at her. "You said it yourself. She'd kiss a fer-de-lance to keep her power. My mother and I have . . . discovered things. The bottom line is she doesn't trust us."

"Should she?"

"I'm not trying to kill her or her Apprentice. You have to believe me. You have no idea what my grandmother is capable of."

She tilts her head, but her steely eyes don't give away what conclusions she might be drawing. Desperation presses my voice to a near whisper.

"She's going to kill me. You know that's why I'm down here." I let the words drift and settle, uninterrupted. I lock onto her golden eyes, begging her to trust me. "I need you to get me out of here."

She is literally my only hope of escape, and I'd have better luck reading the stars at noon.

Eventually Trin reaches into a pouch attached to her belt and tosses me a banana. "Thought you might be hungry."

"Thanks."

She still seems deep in thought, as if trying to decide: Am I lying? Or have I been framed? Maybe if I can press just a little further . . .

"You didn't have to come down here, Trin. You're here because something didn't add up. What they told you doesn't match who you know me to be. *Please*," I beg, "I'm asking you to trust me."

After another agonizingly long silence, she says, "I'm not promising anything." Then she retraces the corridor and closes the door behind her.

"Well, that went well," Dáin jeers.

"Shut up." My cheeks grow hot when I realize he just heard the entire conversation.

"No, really. I'm impressed. Maybe you're not as useless as I thought."

I refuse to grace him with a response. Instead I eat the banana slowly, meticulously exhaling, hoping the smell tortures him. But when I get to the last bite, nonsensical pity takes over my rational brain.

Without a word, I toss the final piece between the bars into his cell. It hits the dirt, but I doubt he'll be picky about it.

Then I curl up on the floor and beg my mind to sleep.

CHAPTER FIVE

IN THE GREAT EXPANSE OF SILENCE—HOURS? DAYS?—that follows, I have plenty of time to play what-if games with fate. What if Trin returns? What if she doesn't? What if I go mad before anyone comes to check on us?

The latter scenarios offer little substance to toy with, so I concentrate on the first one. If by some chance I've convinced Trin to help me escape, I need to have a plan.

A plan. Right.

First order of business, I need to get to Bella Terra to make good on my promise to Mother. That means I need Callisto. Get the baby, find the Brutes. How, I don't know, but I'll have to cross that bridge later. Once I find the Brutes, then what?

The gentling has to stop. I honestly still don't know which is better—safe Gentle or unaltered Brute—but it seems they should have that choice for themselves. The foremothers "played God," as Mother put it, and there were—are—other consequences.

I rub my temples to push back the headache forming from dehydration and probably—oh, I don't know—maybe a little stress. I try to focus through the pain. I have to believe I'll get out of here somehow. In the meantime, I could have weeks to figure out a plan, or scarcely minutes. So . . . *What are you going to do when you find the Brutes, Reina?*

For no reason I can name, Rohan hijacks my concentration, standing at the top of the mahogany tree, awash in evening charm, holding my eyes with his questions.

He can't have my allegiance.

And yet . . .

I want to see him. So much so that if there were no baby to take, I might still find myself searching the Jungle wilds for Tree Camp. Why in Nedé does he make me so illogical?

A plan, Rei—you need a plan. *And "see Rohan" isn't one.*

Hunger gnaws at my insides, thirst dries out my tongue and lips. I ignore the discomfort the best I can, trying instead to flip through my other options as the hours pass.

What about Jase? Could he help? Even here, alone in the dark, the thought of his easy-come belly laugh and familiar hazel eyes, so much like Mother's, puts me at ease. I imagine those eyes lighting up when I tell him I've heard the story that wasn't his to tell. He will help me if he can. I think. If Torvus even allows me back into camp.

The hulking Brute leader didn't technically forbid me from returning. Sure, he made me swear not to tell anyone what I'd seen, but that's not *exactly* the same thing, by my count. I'd never expect a warm welcome, but he'd have to take Jonalyn's baby, wouldn't he? To honor whatever arrangement he had with Mother? And maybe I can convince him to help me . . . do . . . something.

I go over my plan progress: get out, get baby, find Brutes, give baby, convince them to help me "do something." I cringe at the flimsiness of my plan just as a loud snore rattles the darkness.

With satisfaction, I add to the list: *let that beast rot in his cell.*

Teera will kill him once she has what she wants, and I'll never have to fear him again.

Once she has what she wants . . .

Bats.

Teera thinks Dáin—the "asset" she spoke of—is the leader. She's wrong about that, but she's right that there are others out there. What if she tortures him for information? *My dear,* she once told me, *anyone can be persuaded if the right tactics are employed.* Could she break him with those tactics? Tear from him the location of Tree Camp?

Would it even take much persuading? I remember the growl of Torvus's voice as he yelled at Dáin across the circle of fire, disavowing him. Being banished from camp might leave little motivation to protect his kin. It might not take much coercion for Dáin to snap, to give Teera whatever information she wants. *And once she knows where they are . . .* She made it clear that once the two hundredth celebration was out of the way, she planned to devote "every resource" to dealing with the Brutes. Time is not on my side.

The thought of Teera's forces flooding the Jungle fills me with surprising panic. The Brutes are strong, and I'm sure they are brave, but there can't be more than seventy-five of them, and many are too young to fight. What the Brutes possess in strength, the Alexia surpass in number. If Teera unleashes the full might of the Alexia into the Jungle, the Brutes won't stand a chance.

I have to warn them as soon as possible—Jase, Rohan, the little cubs who can't possibly have committed any great crime in their short lives.

I wish I could say for certain that the Brutes I've come to care for wouldn't ever hurt us. I have no such promise. Still, the thought of Teera suppressing them—killing them—for fear of what they *could* do? Tyranny never wore such obvious colors.

I can't let Teera get to Tree Camp, which means I can't let her get to Dáin. And to keep her from him . . .

A red-hot shudder creeps up my spine. *I'll have to face my greatest fear of all.*

CHAPTER SIX

BRUTES AS BIG AS HORSES CIRCLE AROUND the fire ring, trapping me inside. They sneer down, watching flames lick up my legs. Heart pounding, I beg them for water in vain. I scan the onlookers for a flicker of familiarity, desperate for a trace of kindness or humanity. For anything good. Anything safe. Any indication that one will help. But their faces are hollow, devoid of features. Behind them, withered, baby-faced Gentles look on with resigned sympathy, holding out flasks but unable to reach past the sneering Brutes.

Somewhere in the tree huts above, a door opens, and the sudden scrape of metal on wood scatters them all. I jolt awake, hitting my head against a metal rod.

In the foggy land between sleeping and waking, I struggle to get my bearings, but the bar that just collided with my head leaves little question where I am. I recognize the space; it's the same depressing view that has taunted me after too many fitful bouts of sleep. But I'm still here—haven't died from starvation or thirst, so my occupancy can't have been as long as it feels.

Against the familiar canvas of bars, stone, and gloom, something stands out of place. A person—just on the other side of my cell door. A rush of panic drives away the last remnants of sleep, until the *who* registers.

"Trin." The dry, groggy croak sounds so foreign I clear my throat and try again. "Hi."

She stares at me for a long moment before speaking, sadness—maybe dreaded pity—softening her features. I must look terrible.

"They'll bring food and water tomorrow—enough to keep you alive." She pauses, looks at her hands and what they hold, as if deciding. "But I thought you could use this tonight." She crouches down, slipping a dark, roundish object as big as her hand and what looks like a blanket roll through the bars, setting them on the floor. "I wouldn't wait to eat it. Won't keep well."

She turns to leave, seeming suddenly as eager as I am to get out of this hole.

"Wait, Trin . . ." I try not to beg, knowing how pathetic it must sound, but I can't help it. Not when I know my only chance of escape is striding out the exit. "Please, you have to believe me," I call after her, hoping my innocence will trail her, haunt her until she finally stares it in the face. Trinidad doesn't respond. She doesn't look back. And as the door scrapes shut, sealing my fate, something like a defeated moan ruptures from me, echoing through the darkness.

I wait for a jeering taunt from my fellow captive, expecting Dáin to rub failure in my face like a cow pie.

Silence.

Perhaps near starvation has tempered his tongue. Good. I wonder for a split second if he could have died while I slept and steal a glance his way. In the dark shadows layering his cell, he slumps against the bars, but his eyes are open and alert, watching me.

When I was ten, I visited the Rylo Animal Preserve in Kekuatan Province with my mother and sisters. A relic from before the fore-mothers, the original enclosures are hundreds of years old. A group of Agricolátios repaired them, and they maintain the preserve in an effort to help Nedéans appreciate our animal neighbors. Most of the residents are injured local creatures that workers have nursed back to health but can't release into the wild: a tailless kinkajou, a limping margay, a stork with a broken wing. But near the back of the preserve, adjacent to a pair of crocodiles, we saw a one-eyed puma pacing its cage—a ferocious cat that would have torn the flesh from our bones had those bars been removed. However, there *were* bars, and with the carnivore secure in its cage, we could consider the beauty of an animal we might otherwise have run from.

From the safety of my cage, I have a rare view of a Brute brought so low I can look in his eyes without terror. Without his harpy-headed club, without his rage, transformed by hunger and the same defeat that dogs me, I see . . . a human. A new connection freezes me solid: *Mother took him there.* She took them all to Torvus, rescued them from the fate of Gentles. She risked her own safety to give him that gift. He's a Brute because of her. I picture my mother carrying a redheaded baby into the Jungle, risking her life to give Dáin a better one. Should that make me angry at her, or cause me to hate him less?

The connection both fascinates and disgusts me, but mostly it makes me feel the loss of her, and I have to turn away. My gaze lands on the items Trin left for me, and I lift my creaky body and crawl across the floor to them.

The round object is brown-green with scale-shaped mark-ings, leathery and a little sticky around a puncture. The skin gives easily to the pressure of my suddenly greedy fingers. I tear open the custard apple with the ravenous haste of a starving prisoner, sinking my teeth into the creamy white flesh. I don't bother spitting out the large, smooth seeds. I've inhaled half of the fruit and started in on the other when my teeth scrape something small and metallic. I probe the white mush with a finger, retrieving a hard, sticky treasure too beautiful for words.

I nearly spew a mouthful of fruit. I laugh and sigh and squeal and whisper, "Thank you, thank you, thank you, Trin."

Euphoria blooms in my chest, making me jittery, in part from the hope of getting free from here, but more so because she believed me. I told her the truth and she trusted me. I can't explain why that's so important, but it is.

Slipping the key into my vest pocket, I turn to the bedroll next, untying the jute with sticky fingers. It's a thin blanket. Which would make perfect sense if I were staying another night. Or if it weren't the infernal dry season. I shake the cloth open anyway and am startled as a straight white stick thuds to the floor.

No, not a stick.

Anything would have made more sense than this—more food, a sack of coins, a change of clothes. Yet, strangely, there's nothing I would be happier to find lying at my feet.

The stark white bone of the knife is unmistakable, even in the dim light. The deep grooves of the basket-weave handle are so intricate, I can't help running a finger over them. The blade is nearly as long as my forearm, and it calls to mind the strangely thick arms of the Brute who carved it. I can almost see the concern in his dark eyes as he gave it to me just before I left the Jungle.

How Trin happened to possess Rohan's knife I can only guess. The last I knew, Teera had it. But I don't have time to wonder now. With no way of knowing how long I've been down here, I'd better be cautious. Trin said someone would be by tomorrow with food—that what she brought "won't keep." I'd better move quickly.

The jolt of sugar from the custard apple mingles with adrenaline, and I'm ready to take on the world, one lock at a time.

Once I figure out the right angle, the key slides easily into the hole and turns with minimal effort. I'm on the other side in three seconds, staring down the corridor toward freedom. Behind me, my cellmate croaks dryly, "Look at that. The girl got herself an accomplice."

"Shut up," I snap, already second-guessing what I'm about to do, even as I make my way to his slotted door. "Listen carefully, you pitiful excuse for a human. I despise you with every fiber of my being, and I trust you less than a snake with a mouse. But we have a common enemy, and I'm banking on the hunch that you hate her more than you hate me. Am I right?"

"Go on," he rasps, getting to his feet.

"I don't trust you to keep your big mouth shut if Teera gets to you. And I know you have supplies."

Because this animal took them from innocent finca owners like your sister, my better sense tries to remind me, but I snuff her like a stubborn candle and continue.

"And I know you want to . . . *change things.*"

He raises an eyebrow. "If by 'change things' you mean pay the Matriarchy back for everything it has taken from us, then yeah."

"Listen carefully, Brute." We're standing nose to chin now, and I'm surprised how little fear I feel in the face of him. "Your sloppy little band of revolutionaries is no match for the full force of the Alexia. You might have 'testosterone'—whatever that even is—but you are outnumbered and *way* out of your league. You need me, and I—" the words taste all kinds of sour sliding out—"I need your help. Time is running out, and you can get back to Tree Camp faster than I can. If I let you go, you have to warn Torvus that Teera knows about them and could come at any time. Tell them I'm coming and that I'll follow as soon as possible so we can figure out a plan."

Dáin's dense freckles bunch around his nose and eyes, features pinched in consideration. I wish he wouldn't take so much time. Every second of silence that passes is another opportunity to question the monumental risk I'm taking.

"Will you do it?" I ask, commandingly.

"I don't have much choice, do I?"

"Neither of us do."

So it's decided. My fingers shake, the key knocking against the hole as I try to ease it into the lock. But it won't fit.

"*Bats*," I mutter, trying again. It would be just my luck for each cell to have a different key. On the third failed attempt, I growl at the blasted lock and throw the key to the floor, grabbing the bone knife from my belt instead. The curved tip slides easily into the hole, and I finesse it this way and that, prying gently and willing it to work. I'm just about to crumple in defeat when a final twist clicks something free. I grab the door and tug. It swings out like a blessed miracle.

The elation of victory is slapped down by my sudden vulnerability. The protection removed, we glare at each other for a tense moment, and I consider slamming the door shut and making a run for it. I grit my teeth instead, trying to look more sure of my decision than I feel.

"Once we're outside, you're on your own," I tell him.

"Don't you worry about me, pretty thing. Shadows were made for the night." He grins devilishly, stepping toward me, sending a rush of panic through me. Then he reaches out and grabs the dark blanket tucked under my arm. "May I?" he asks, after the fact.

My temper gets the better of me, and I press the tip of the knife into his chest. "Just so we're clear, you won't take anything from me without asking."

"Simmer down, girl," he says, ignoring the blade. "I admit I have a habit of taking things I like, but I won't lay a hand on you." His crooked smile does little to reassure me, but I lower my weapon out of necessity. We have to move.

"Have you considered," he goes on, "that Torvus might not be willing to see me? In case you missed it, we aren't exactly on good terms." If I didn't know better, I'd swear hurt flashes in his crazed eyes. "I don't know what kind of deal you two have going on, but he might have a hard time believing I'm running with the enemy I offered to dispose of in front of the clan."

Of course I'm not sure. I barely know Torvus, and from what little I've seen, he's as moody as a pregnant llama. If only I had something I could give him, some token . . .

My hand tightens around the knife handle, protesting what my mind is considering. It's my only weapon, and . . . *Don't be stupid. It's just a knife, and it might work.*

"Take this," I say, flipping it to offer him the handle. "It's Rohan's. He'll know it's from me."

"*You* managed to steal *this* from Rohan?"

"No—he gave it to me."

Dáin whistles low. "Well, isn't that sweet?" Then he snatches the knife, twirls it once, and shoves it into an empty sheath at his hip. Waving his hand with unnecessary flourish, he motions me to lead the way.

We move through the corridor between cells and slip through the door Trin used. A short, narrow staircase leads to what I remember as the entrance.

It's locked.

"You've got to be kidding me," I moan.

Dáin grunts, then runs back toward the cells. Thirty seconds later, he's pushing me aside, producing the key I dropped outside his cell. The lock releases, and he cautiously opens the heavy wooden door into a curtain of tangled vines.

We're met with the fresh scent of field and the watery sound of a nearby fountain. After quietly closing and locking the door, we scurry through the moonlit darkness to a deeply recessed alcove in the Arena's outer wall.

"This is it," I say. "You're on your own from here. There are horses in the pastures if you know how to ride, but Jase said it was faster and safer for him on foot." Dáin looks surprised, and I wonder if he knows Jase has been in Nedé. "It doesn't matter. Just don't get caught, okay? I'll follow soon."

A niggling worry resurfaces—I still don't know how to find my way back, and someone who lived there is standing right in front of me.

"Hey," I whisper reluctantly, hating to ask him anything. "How can I find Tree Camp?"

Amusement sparks in his shadowy eyes. "What, you want a map or something? Street signs? If you don't know how to find it, you don't belong there."

"You ungrateful—" *Ugh*, I hate this wretched Brute. He probably doesn't even care if I get back to the Jungle, and why would he?

He raises his fiery red eyebrows like the real reason he won't help is obvious. When I still don't see it, he says condescendingly, "Look, if I had an hour, maybe I could give you some general pointers, but camp is meant to stay hidden to anyone who doesn't already know where it is."

A sound from the direction of the barracks startles us both. We scan the open courtyard nervously.

He growls, "This ain't exactly the place to chitchat."

"Fine," I say, like it's no big deal. "I'll figure it out." I want to kick him, but I have more urgent concerns. Namely, how am

I going to snatch Callisto and weapons from under the noses of my Alexia compatriots and get to Bella Terra without being seen?

Dáin wraps the blanket around his hunched shoulders, and before he's ten meters away I can't tell which way he went. *Like a shadow.* He wasn't lying. Let's hope he was as truthful about the rest.

I scan my surroundings to get my bearings. We came out just west of the Arena's north entrance, a safe distance from the barracks and apartments clustered to the east. Unfortunately, the weapon caches are located in the Arena itself. And to get to the outer paddocks, the logical place for Callisto, I'll have to sneak clear to the southern edge of the property.

The grounds are deserted enough to assume it must be the middle of the night. Still, there will be guards. At least I'm dressed as an Alexia. If I can keep my face hidden, I shouldn't raise suspicion. Besides, how many Alexia would know I was being kept in the *secret* cells? By definition, their existence shouldn't be common knowledge. So instead of slinking like Dáin, I hold my head high, hoping confidence works in my favor again.

I follow the gentle curve of the stone wall toward the west entrance, shuffling my feet through the dewy grass so as not to step directly on any of the croaking toads. Their bumpy backs shine a slimy moonlight silver as they jump away lazily, irritated at the disruption. Some of them meet my boots midjump.

A hundred meters and a few airborne toads later, I slip under the massive stone entrance and make my way across the tile courtyard onto the Arena floor. I'm in luck. Just under the awning, the weapons are unattended.

Make that *almost* unattended.

A medium-height figure in uniform and full weaponry slouches against the rack of bows, staring up at the night sky. Sensing my presence, she snaps to attention, whipping around to face the sound of my footfalls. When we lock eyes, she grins like a child who just got away with stealing a coin.

"I knew it," she nearly giggles.

Is it possible I have the bad luck of twenty people? Of all the Alexia to be guarding the weapons . . .

"What are you doing here, Bri?"

"You know, you really need to diversify your arsenal of inquisitions."

I sputter something unintelligible, making me feel small and stupid.

"Call it a hunch," she offers, "but your beloved Trinidad has been acting real strange the past few days. She had some lame excuse for you going missing, then didn't even flinch when I said old Teera probably did you in. So when I saw her sneaking out of her apartment tonight with some mysterious items, I offered to take Fallon's shift guarding the weapons." She caresses the shaft of a bow. "What escapee wouldn't need a few accessories?"

Once again, I don't know whether to be impressed or annoyed by Brishalynn Victoriana Pierce.

"Why do you care?"

"I was just so hurt by the thought you'd leave without saying goodbye." Her thin lips make a paltry pout, but just as fast, she drops the act. "I'm going with you."

"You're *what*?"

"Going . . . with . . . you," she says again, spacing the words like she's explaining them to a four-year-old Gentle.

"No. There's no way in bats I'm taking you with me, Bri."

She hands me a bow and quiver. "Then I'll be forced to let Adoni know some weapons went missing in the night."

"You're blackmailing me?"

"I could kill you instead."

"Of all the stupid, selfish—" *Ugh!* "You don't even know where

I'm going!" If she did, I doubt she'd want to come, but I can't tell her without breaking my promise to Torvus.

"Don't care."

I run a hand down my face. The nerve! "If you desert the Alexia and come with me, you'll never be able to return."

"Being a respectable citizen of Nedé is overrated."

Knowing Bri, she's more drawn to the rebellion of life on the run than anything else. Still, when she speaks again, I hear echoes of the vulnerability she showed when we snuck out of the after-party at Finca del Mar.

"Why do you think I joined the Alexia?"

"Because you don't trust Teera or Jamara, and you feel better about your chances armed."

"And?"

"And what?"

"And you, stupid. I feel better about my chances with you."

The weight of her words, the sincerity, stuns me into silence.

"You should've been the Apprentice," she continues. "And I know, I was jealous and almost killed you and whatever. But there's something in you I could follow. So I'm going to. And you can't stop me."

"Bri, this is so much bigger than the Succession. You have no idea."

"Then you can tell me on the way. Right now, we better get out of here before my replacement comes."

If there's another choice, I can't see it. My mind is too muddled with urgency, and incredulity, and . . . honor. I'm touched by Bri's words, even if she'll just as likely kill me by morning as follow me into the Jungle once she knows what I'm planning to do—once she knows about *them*. In fact, she'll probably bolt once I do tell her, so why not placate her now to get away from the Arena safely?

"Alright." I grab a short sword and a few extra arrows for my quiver, hoping I don't have to use them on my new tagalong, then make for the exit.

———————

Callisto is easy to find, her white patches and half of her mane glowing like electric light in the dark field farthest from the Arena. Her ears flick as I approach; she comes without hesitation, nuzzling my shoulder as I shower her neck with kisses and breathe in sweetgrass and safety.

"There's my girl." I rub her neck to ease her agitation before swinging onto the familiar curve of her back.

"Everything's going to be okay, I promise." The reassurance might be more for me than my steady companion.

Bri clucks in the background, trying to woo one of the dark equines nearby with an imaginary treat. When it trots away, she mutters, "Get over here, you miserable horse."

I didn't think it would be wise to chance raiding the stables, so Bri will have to ride bareback till we get to Bella Terra. *If* she can catch a horse.

"Hurry up," I hiss quietly.

She shoots me a sour look, but fresh determination to prove herself works in our favor. After two more awkward attempts, she lands a seat on an exquisite, Alexia-worthy mare.

Now . . . all we have to do is jump the fence at the far end of the paddock, weave through the streets of Phoenix City, and travel four more hours down a deserted Highway Volcán without being spotted. No problem.

"We should make it to my mother's finca before morning."

"That's your great plan? To go home?"

"I didn't ask you to come."

That shuts her up.

"I need to get a few things in order." I don't want to tell her any more than I have to, not yet convinced she'll be sticking around. Or that I can trust her. "Then I'll tell you where I'm going, and you can decide if it was a mistake to follow."

But I'm suddenly unsure whether confessing I'm headed to the Jungle without a plan—even telling her about the Brutes—will be enough to lose headstrong Brishalynn.

CHAPTER SEVEN

THE FIRST RAYS OF DAWN SPILL OVER the eastern horizon between familiar twin rain trees. Bromeliads grow in the crooks of the thick, mossy branches, and a flock of tanagers roost in the sparse limbs. The trees, gatekeepers of Bella Terra, beckon two tired travelers and their horses to turn down the lane.

Rolling green hills, zigzagged with neat crop rows, bend low to meet the hard-packed, red road. We wind the final half kilometer up, around, and down to the familiar villa tucked into fields and bordered by the Jabiru River on two sides. I breathe in the familiar, heavy orange scent, listen to the birds' chatter and Diablo's incessant crowing. *How long will that rooster live?*

I expect joy to follow—maybe relief—but the familiarity only reveals a deep, aching hole inside. Of the few anchors in my life, two have been severed since the last time I rode this path home, both ripped from my life by the Mother of Nedé.

Callisto's ears twist sideways and forward, recognizing, remembering, enjoying; her steps quicken as we near the large open-beam stable. For a moment I unconsciously expect to find a certain someone there. Almost as quickly, the flicker of hope snuffs out like a smoldering wick between wet fingers.

He won't be here.

Never again will I finish a long ride to the greeting of a flaxen-haired Gentle with kind eyes. No more chance meetings under the fig tree by the river. No hibiscus tucked under my horse's brow-band to let me know I'm seen.

My throat tightens. Through the watery blur of tears, my eyes play tricks on me. I can almost see Tre in the early morning light, raking out a stall as we approach. The rhythmic motions slow but steady. Pausing to catch his breath. Swatting at a fly.

No, not Tre. But someone is there, where my best friend should be.

The short figure straightens and turns at our approach, revealing a Gentle with earth-brown skin, a round face, and a shy disposition.

"Neechi!" I dismount Callisto and nearly run into the breeze-way. "You made it. You came!" Before I can think better of it, I've flung my arms around him, squeezing much too tightly.

"Yes, I came." His quiet, lilting voice makes mine sound too loud, too fierce. But our smiles match.

"How long have you been here?" I ask.

"Four days. I did what you said. Solomon let me stay in the Gentles' quarters with the others." His voice lowers to a near whisper of sadness. "There was an extra bed."

I bite my lower lip to still its tremble. "He would have wanted you to have it. He would want you to be safe."

"I didn't know him well, Dom Reina, but I would figure as much."

I catch a glimpse of Bri in my periphery, walking her horse toward us. What must she think? A Nedéan, talking with a Gentle like an equal? To her credit, apart from wide eyes and a stern mouth, she says nothing about it. If she's going to stick around, she'll have to get used to my unconventional views.

"Neechi, this is Bri. Bri, Neechi. He was a stablehand at Finca del Mar. After helping me, I knew he couldn't stay there." Then, to him, "But you'll be safe here. My moth—" The word catches in my throat, reality slicing me like a physical wound. If Mother is dead, she can't protect him. What will become of Bella Terra? Marsa and Dom Bakshi could find other employment within their destinies, but what about Little Boo and the other Gentles? And after I begged Neechi to come . . . Who will care for them?

"You're safe," I repeat, hoping I can make it true. I smile and lead Callisto forward. She stamps and steps back twice. "Easy, girl," I soothe. "These horses have had a long night, and we're going to need them to be ready to ride in an hour or so. It's not ideal. Just do what you can for them."

"Yes, Dom Reina," he says, tipping his weathered hat before turning to the steeds.

Bri follows me through the pasture toward the white-walled villa I know as home. Before we reach the entrance, I notice Marsa stoking a fire in the outdoor adobe oven; the delicious smell of rising dough warrants a detour. Marsa notices us coming. She wipes her floury hands on a towel as she jogs the distance between us, and in three seconds she has wrapped me in a hug so tight and fierce I fear my ribs might snap like chicken bones.

She pushes me to arm's length, scolding, "Wap kon Jorge! Bringing company without warning? And you bein' so scrawny, petit! They feed you nothin' in the city?"

I grin so wide my dry lips crack. "It's just that no one can make *arroz con pollo* like you, Marsa. How can you expect me to enjoy that excuse for food they serve at Finca del Mar?"

She clucks at me for fibbing, but as she turns toward her breadboard—piled with smooth rounds of sourdough sprinkled with goat cheese and allspice—I can tell she's standing a smidge taller.

"We can only stay an hour or two," I say, getting down to business. "But we're going to need supplies. Food that can keep awhile. Enough for three." I don't need to look at Bri to know she's already wondering if I'm really hungry or if I'm going to explain myself. I don't feel a particular need to keep her informed. In fact, I'm rather enjoying holding all the cards. Perhaps we should just make that arrangement permanent.

"If you say so, petit." Before I can turn toward the house, Marsa adds, "Dom Leda's in the city, but maybe she'll be home before you run off again."

I know I should, but I can't tell her. I can't say the words. Not yet. So I try to smile at the thought of Mother returning, as if I have any hope that she will.

———

I show Bri to Ciela's room so she can freshen up and rest for a few minutes. My middle sister spends most of her time in Phoenix City, only coming "home" on the weekends she can get away from her work at the Center. The rest of the time she holes up in an apartment I've never seen.

"I'll come get you when it's time to eat," I promise, then make a beeline for Jonalyn's room three doors down the hall.

I find my eldest sister in a rocking chair near a large, open window across from her bed, cradling a tiny bundle of cloth and pink skin. A scruff of fine, baby-soft hair the color of toasted wheat peeks from the light blanket, his impossibly small lips curled in a pout. Jonalyn shifts my direction when I walk in, a smile spreading across her lovely face.

"I thought I heard your voice," she half whispers, delight warring with her desire to let the baby sleep.

I bypass an unruly lock of her dark hair, which has fallen from the pile pinned on top of her head, to kiss her cheek. Remnant bruising from the attack has all but disappeared, leaving only a slight yellow tinge along the edge of a cheekbone. Despite the unusual paleness of the rest of her, she looks worlds better than during my visit three weeks ago. Marsa's cooking, and a healthy baby, seem to have done wonders.

"How are you?" I ask, taking a seat on a cushion near her feet.

"Getting stronger every day. I should be able to return to La Fortuna soon."

"But not the little one." I give her a meaningful look. The last time I was here, sitting on the end of Jonalyn's bed, she was honest about what Mother had told her. About the Brutes, about Mother's involvement. I know Mother shared the rest with her since then, so there's no point sidestepping the truth now.

"No, not the little one." She looks down at the baby with a mixture of awe and sadness.

"Jonalyn—" My voice nearly cracks, and I try with everything in me to be stronger. For my sister. "Mother asked me to take him to the Jungle."

Relief and confusion meld in her response. "I'm so glad you know, Rei. When I heard you outside, I wasn't sure I could keep it from you. But why you? Mother said she'd be back in a couple of days."

Tears pool against my lower lids, on the miserable edge between containment and release. *Hold it together, Reina.*

"Teera discovered us at the Center, and her Alexia . . ." I try again. "Mother—" It's no use. I lose the battle against composure. Jonalyn blanches.

"*What* about Mother? What happened?"

I try to tell her, the facts coming out in fits and starts. Somehow I communicate that I don't think she made it, and then we sit, in silence, for the time it takes to travel through an expanse of darkness, searching for light.

———————

Gentle kitchen hands deposit plates of creamy yogurt, citrus salad, and herbed pastries on Bella's oversized dining table for the breakfast meal. Bri, Jonalyn, Marsa, and I barely make a dent in the benches' capacity, designed to fit our family and staff, plus a fluctuating number of young Gentles who live at the finca until their seventh birthdays.

"Is the baby asleep?" I ask my sister.

She nods. "I just fed him."

"And when is it our turn to eat?" Bri whispers sideways at me.

As if on cue, Dom Bakshi strides through the doorway with seven Gentles trailing like a line of ducklings. My old tutor breezes into the room in a colorful sari, back straight, not a hair misplaced from the peppered bouffant topping her head. But when she sees me, she jumps, covering her mouth in surprise. "Oh, Reina!"

We embrace in the kitchen like old friends, such a change from the tutor-student relationship that used to mark our interactions.

A pint-sized Gentle with a mischievous grin breaks ranks and wraps himself around my leg.

"Dom Reina, Dom Reina!" he cheers.

Dom Bakshi pushes him toward his place at the table, but before she succeeds I kneel down beside him.

"Little Boo?" I say, tilting his chin this way and that, inspecting him like a parcel. "Is that you?"

He grins wide, revealing a new gap. "It's me!"

"Are you sure? I don't remember you being this tall. And I could have sworn Little Boo had all his teeth."

This garners a giggle from all seven Gentles, who scamper up the benches, where Dom Bakshi has arranged their places in order of height.

When they've regained decorum, she takes her own seat across from them, but not before noticing my Alexia uniform. "Leda told me about the Succession before she left. The old vulture's a fool not to choose you."

I can't help but laugh at her fiery pronouncement, so unlike the proper Ad Artium I know.

Bri chimes in, "You have no idea."

"Domina Bakshi, Brishalynn Pierce." The two exchange greetings. "She was a Candidate with me."

"I see. Well, if the present company will excuse me, I thought you would have made an excellent choice of Apprentice, Reina. I can't, however, say I'm much surprised by your choice of destiny." Her smile calls to mind many a conversation in the Bella Terra schoolroom—me voicing doubt and indecision, she gently setting me straight. A teacher who understood the influence and responsibility she held. "I have every confidence you will serve Nedé well."

Marsa says the blessing in Mother's absence, and the mouthwatering dishes begin their circuit around the table.

"Eat up," I whisper to Bri. "We're going to need it."

Dom Bakshi addresses Jonalyn hopefully. "We should expect your mother home soon, I'd think."

A loud clank rattles the lunch party. Jonalyn moves quickly to gather her fork and the mango and citrus chunks scattered across the table and in her lap. She gives me a pleading look.

I glance at Little Boo. I have to be strong. Straightforward. Assured. I can't let them know I'm crumbling inside.

"Mother isn't coming home." Ten sets of eyes snap toward me, and I can't handle the panic behind them. "For a while," I quickly add, hedging for the Gentles' sakes. *Come on, Reina. Don't give them hope that will never walk through that door.* But I can't help it. I can't bring myself to strip them of their beloved Dom Leda, the one person in Nedé who values them as they should be valued.

No, not the only person. Not anymore.

I lean forward so I can look the little ones in the eyes. "I'm not sure when she'll be back, but she wants you to know that everything will be okay." At least, I'm sure that's what she would want, if she could tell them. "Dom Bakshi and Marsa will take good care of you. I have to go on a trip, but I'll be back soon to check on you too. And . . ." I turn to the adults at the table. "If she hasn't returned by then, we'll figure out what to do."

Dom Bakshi inhales deeply and sets down her fork. Marsa looks toward Jonalyn, who stares at her plate. I can tell Leda's faithful chef—second mother to the children of Bella—senses something is very wrong, but she rallies like the strong woman I know her to be. When one of the older Gentles asks why Dom Leda must stay away so long, she says, "That's nothin' to you. Dom Leda'll come when she's ready, you hear?"

And that's the end of it. But when the dishes are cleared and the Gentles have been sent to morning chores, Marsa, Dom Bakshi, Jonalyn, Bri, and I sit around the table once more.

"Now, what happened, petit?" Marsa crosses her arms and leans back, expecting a full explanation.

I give her most of one, telling about the Matriarch's attack, Dr. Novak, prison, but purposefully omitting the minor detail that my own mother has been rescuing Brute babies and shuttling them to the Jungle.

Tears stream down Marsa's round cheeks before I'm through. Dom Bakshi stares stoically into her coffee. Bri drums her fingers against the table. This is news to her, too.

I ramble to a conclusion. "As far as I can tell, Teera doesn't know Mother—" I can't say the word. "I want to keep it that way. Alexia may show up here this afternoon. Tell them you haven't heard from Leda. If anyone else asks, she's still at the Center." That may be true, anyway. I don't know what Dr. Novak would do with her body. "I promised I would do something for her, and when I come back, we can figure out what to do here at Bella."

The two older women nod in resigned agreement. I give Bri a questioning glance.

"If that look means you want to know if I've changed my mind, I haven't," she says.

"Alright. Bri's going with me."

"I'm going too." Jonalyn's voice is quiet but strong.

"Jo? No. You're not . . . You don't have to—"

She cuts me off, suddenly forceful. "I'm *going*."

"What about the baby?" Dom Bakshi presses.

"I'll take him along. It's about time I return to my finca; I'll go with Reina on my way home."

She makes it sound as simple as planning to stop by the farrier on the way to market. Granted, her accompaniment will eliminate the question of why I'd leave Bella with Jonalyn's child, but still, I wonder if she's thought this through.

Dom Bakshi concedes, not having any reason, or authority, to counter her wishes. And there's nothing I can say in present company to make a case against her plan either.

I sigh. "Make that food for five, Marsa."

"Five, petit?"

"Five." There are only three mouths to feed, but I have no idea how long it will take me to find Tree Camp, and I don't want to run out of supplies in the likely event I lead us in circles. Besides, at the rate people are joining this merry parade into the forbidden wilds, I might as well pack safe.

With the basics settled, Jonalyn, Bri, and I take our leave. My old bed is calling my name, but there's no time for sleep. Adoni will likely discover my empty cell soon, if she hasn't already. When Teera gets wind of my escape, she'd be a fool not to search Bella Terra.

I find Neechi in the stable breezeway, rifling through a pile of saddle blankets.

"Hi, Neechi."

"Dom Reina."

"I need you to prepare a horse for one more rider, as soon as possible."

He gives a polite nod of assent, all Finca manners.

The dark Lexander Bri stole from the Arena occupies Estrella's vacant stall. With a pang of guilt, I wonder where my mother's horse is now. A freshly oiled bridle and reins hang on a hook next to her door. I expect Neechi went through four sets to find the perfect fit for the shiny, smoky-black mare.

"Where's Callisto?"

"Grazing. I'll turn this one out as soon as I figure the right saddle."

I notice another set of tack, freshly dressed and hanging outside the next empty stall.

"Callisto doesn't need tack. You know that."

"Yes, I know."

I stare at him, waiting for more explanation, but he seems suddenly very enamored with a thick woven blanket.

"And . . . ?" I prod.

He doesn't look at me, and his words sound as much like an apology as a statement when he says, "They're for me."

I roll my eyes and laugh out loud. "Who's next—Diablo?" At this rate, I wouldn't be half surprised if Ciela's rooster did strut in here and demand to join us too. "Neechi, you don't even know where I'm going."

Wait . . . It certainly wouldn't be the first time a Gentle knew more about my life than I did.

"Do you?" I ask suspiciously.

He shakes his head. "I just know it'd be important, if you're leaving the Alexia, leaving your home. And I've been thinking a lot since your friend died." He glances at me sideways, tentatively, probably trying to read my expression at his mention of Tre. "He wanted his life to count for something. I never knew a Gentle could care that much. We never had hope enough to care. But . . . if he could make his life matter, maybe I can too. That's why I want to go—wherever you're going."

Unbelievable. He has no idea what he's asking. Yet I probably have no idea the courage he mustered to ask it. Or how deep he had to dig to find such conviction. Who am I to deny him the chance to make his life count? How could I dishonor Tre's memory like that?

My first day at Finca del Mar, I asked Neechi what his name meant. *Friend*, he had said. I didn't know how much I'd need one. Maybe I still don't. With Tre gone, Mother gone, the Brutes to find, and a snarky Bri tagging along to boot, perhaps I need his friendship more than I realize. Or maybe this is for him. At my request, he walked away from everything he knew to come to a finca now devoid of its benevolent caretaker. I have no idea what waits for me in the Jungle, but leaving him here won't guarantee his safety either. Finding Finca del Mar's stablehand here would raise questions, at best. At worst, who knows what Teera would do to him to find me.

"Alright, you can come. If you're *sure* you're willing to go anywhere—even if it's dangerous."

"Anywhere, Dom Reina."

"Then pack a bag for the Jungle, friend."

Part Two

CHAPTER EIGHT

WHILE NEECHI PREPARES THE HORSES and Marsa oversees our provisions, I head to my room to change. As I slip out of my vest, something rattles to the wood-planked floor.

Mother's tree pendant.

I quickly snatch it up, mortified at forgetting about it. My negligence feels like betrayal—as though I've somehow forgotten about *her*.

My thumb rubs absently around the edge. For the first time, I notice the intricacy of the carving, the deep red-brown of the wood, the miniature branches reaching outward like a sunburst.

Mother said to take this to Torvus, with the baby. Why would she want him to have the charm? Is it connected to him? Some sort of message?

I consider the design again. The wood grain and color give away the material: mahogany wood.

From a mahogany tree.

Seemingly random bits of information fuse in a rare moment of clarity. Suddenly I know what song Mother meant would lead me to the Brutes. The only song I've ever heard that mentions a mahogany tree. The song I've strangely only ever heard my mother sing.

I hum the tune double time, silently running through the verses, scanning them for clues:

> You take one, and I'll take three,
> And I'll meet you there, at the mahogany tree,
> Where the fire don't burn, and the dark water's deep,
> We'll save them there, at the mahogany tree.
> You follow the mare, and I'll follow a stream,
> And we'll leave them there, at the mahogany tree . . .

I can't connect every reference, but the words have to be hints. The tree is obvious enough, the rest muddy. Am I supposed to ride a horse? That would certainly make things easier. And I guess I'll need to find a stream. There was a river near enough the camp— Jase and Rohan forced me to raft down it, through a dark, terrifying cave. The memory coaxes a smile: Jase's goofy laugh when Rohan pushed me from the bank on what I suspected might be a floating coffin . . . watching the two Brutes jump from the cliffs into the swift green water . . . feeling Rohan's body pressed against my back, protecting me from a flurry of bats.

Focus, Reina.

The song. What's the rest of the song?

> If there comes a day when you can't find me,
> Lay my flowers there, by the mahogany tree,

I'll be buried there, by the mahogany tree.
I lost my love, at the mahogany tree.

At the thought of not being able to find my mother, I lose my will to decipher the remaining lines and go back to the first half of the song. Why did she say *we*? Poetic license, or are there others taking babies? Or maybe she intended to enlist others someday. She sang the song often around my sisters and me. Did she hope to eventually tell us the truth? Did she somehow know we'd join her quest?

I press my thumb and forefinger against my temples. If I return to where I followed the raiders into the Jungle, I might be able to find some sort of trail. But I don't know what route Rohan and Jase took from the clearing where Dáin attacked me. They drugged me, and I woke up in a tree hut. Not promising. The only other option is to go to where Jase brought me out of the Jungle, near the intersection of Highway Volcán and Camino del Oeste. It would make sense for Jase to take the most direct route to Nedé when escorting me home, wouldn't it?

Well, it's a start. And with three—make that three and a half— people counting on me, at least we'll have direction for today.

I shake the dust from my filthy Alexia uniform out the window and fold it into an old rucksack, just in case. Looking official has come in handy before. But for today's journey, I slip into an old set of riding pants and a loose shirt, less conspicuous for the open road, though I opt to stick with my custom boots from Dom Tourmaline. They're supremely comfortable.

I search my room for other items that might come in handy, adding two scarves, a length of cord, a small knife, and an extra change of clothes to the bag. A poorly carved monkey stares at me from a shelf, looking very forlorn at being left behind. I roll my eyes at myself even as I stuff his lopsided grin under the flap.

After grabbing clothes for Bri from Ciela's room—hoping they're closer in size—I slip downstairs and out the kitchen door toward the stables.

Here goes nothing.

————————

So many people cram into Bella's stables, you'd think we were throwing a party. Neechi tightens the cinch under Bri's horse. Marsa drops neatly tied parcels, fresh fruit, and waterskins into our saddlebags. Jonalyn adjusts the fabric sling that ties the baby to her chest. Ironically, even Diablo has shown up, strutting his pearlescent green-black tail feathers outside the breezeway. Still, despite all the chaos, Dom Bakshi has no trouble keeping seven Gentles in a straight line.

She's lucky they're not Brute cubs.

I toss the clothes to Bri. "Better change into these for now. I hope they fit."

She curls a lip in disgust but doesn't protest. Maybe she's too tired to muster snark.

Finished with the saddle, Neechi makes his way to me. "Dom Reina," he says, concern deepening the creases in his forehead, "Callisto doesn't seem herself."

Panic seizes my chest. "What do you mean?"

"Can't quite figure it. She didn't eat much, and I found her lying on her side. Took three tries to get her up."

No. She's fine. I won't let myself entertain any other possibility. I glance over at Callisto's stall. She seems alert and healthy to me.

I smile convincingly, refusing to worry. "She's probably just tired from our ride last night."

He nods, though I can tell he's not convinced.

"Maybe take an extra horse, just in case?"

I consider his suggestion all of one second before making up my mind. Neechi knows horses, but I know my Callisto. "She'll be fine," I assure him, stepping between a cart and a post to get to her stall.

"Hey, girl." I pat her neck, noticing a small trickle of drool hanging from her lips. "You must be tired, ol' girl," I laugh. "Pull it together. We've got a long ride today."

She stands calmly as I lay my rucksack on her bare back. If she did get "the crazies," as Jase called it, from that bat bite in the Jungle, I'm sure she'd be acting more . . . *crazy*. Besides, Jase said she'd be fine. He was sure of it.

Dom Bakshi sidles up, and I'm glad for the interruption. "Do you need anything else, Reina?"

In one of those strange moments that transcend time, much is spoken between us without a word. She is proud of me. I am thankful for her. She is going to miss me. I hope I'll see her again.

But one thing must be said out loud, just in case. "If I don't come back," I whisper, turning my back to the others, "keep the Gentles here as long as you can. She would want it that way."

Dom Bakshi's face tightens in resolve. "Of course. For Leda."

Marsa turns me by the shoulder for a tight embrace. "Careful, petit. Wherever you're goin', there's enough food in your bags for a spell, at least. Gonna put some meat on you yet."

I smile. Good ol' Marsa, always thinking food is the answer to everything.

I wish I could promise her I'll be back soon; instead, I lead our pack of travelers through the breezeway and into the adjacent field.

Little Boo chases after me, running to keep up with the horses' long strides. "Will you come back? When will Dom Leda return?"

I don't have an answer to give him, and I turn away so he won't see my tears.

Jonalyn answers for me, the perfect Materno. "Everything will be fine. Run on back now, and mind Dom Bakshi!"

He reluctantly halts, and the distance between us stretches until we reach the lane that will take us to Highway Volcán.

Callisto and I lead the procession: my sister and her Brute baby, a Gentle fleeing Finca del Mar, and a fellow Alexia defector.

Quite the crew. And if I don't get us lost or killed, it will be a small miracle.

———————

The first hour passes in relative quiet. We take the road two by two, Neechi beside me and Callisto, Bri and Jonalyn just behind us. A scattering of puffy, stark-white clouds moves across the azure sky, creating drifting patches of blessed shade.

The wide dirt highway cuts through increasingly lush countryside, dotted with rural fincas, as we travel west. Crops of coffee, banana, citrus, sugarcane, and hardwoods crisscross the hills and valleys. Hundred-acre pastures corral long-eared cows, bleating goats, or, occasionally, horses grazing on Mombasa grass.

When we reach the top of a steep knoll, we're rewarded with a glimpse of the land beyond Nedé. Where the cleared, cultivated land ends, just west of our border, Jungle-thick foothills rise. The hilly knobs stack up and back like a great, green stone wall, protecting higher peaks at the farthest edge of the horizon. Nearly straight ahead, but maybe a half day's journey beyond the border, the formidable El Fuego volcano rises above the surrounding hills like a Brute warrior, warning intruders to stay away from the wilds. At least that's what I see now—now that I know who lives in that Jungle.

And I'm willingly returning. Going back to treetop huts and fire circles, uncertainty and danger. *If* I can find Tree Camp, I'll be returning to them. Returning to him. A nervous shiver races up my spine. Why does the thought of him do that? Why react any differently to Rohan than to Neechi?

I steal a sideways glance at the traveler beside me. I'm still shocked he insisted on coming. These Gentles keep surprising me.

We're making good time. If we keep this pace, we should be able to cross the border by early afternoon.

Not ten minutes later, a fussing, squeaking sound comes from under Jonalyn's wrap, followed by a full-blown baby cry. She tries to soothe him another half kilometer, to no avail.

"We'll need to stop so I can change and feed him," she says.

Bri snorts in irritation. I admit, I haven't given much thought to how an infant might affect our travel plans. But what can be done? I trust Jo knows what she's doing. If she says we have to stop, we'll stop.

I scan the thick underbrush lining both sides of the road for a suitable resting place, grateful our journey didn't take us east. The road toward Phoenix City cuts through coastal savannah, predominantly tall grasses and precious few trees. But this half of Nedé grows increasingly lush as the road nears the Divisaderos. We don't have to hunt long for a fig tree capable of shading us and our animals. As a bonus, a small, shallow stream runs behind the tree, perfect for the horses.

My rear finds a stump while Jonalyn unwraps her cargo. He's so little—no bigger than a cowhide fútbol. I'm not exactly a stranger to babies. But those that have come to Mother's finca from the Center were several months old at least. At scarcely a week old, Jonalyn's baby seems impossibly miniature.

But the sound that comes from him resembles a full-grown Diablo. His cheeks are as red as a rooster's comb too, his fists clenched in rage. How can his tiny lungs create that much sound? The racket could wake the dead.

Jonalyn removes his soiled diaper and rinses it downstream from the horses, lays it over a sunny rock to dry, then fastens on a fresh cloth.

Still he wails.

For the love of Siyah, I moan inwardly. I've never been more grateful I didn't choose Materno as my destiny. I wouldn't have made it a single day. Not *one*.

Jonalyn settles back to nurse the child, and instantly the incessant crying is replaced by contented suckling.

My muscles ease, until Bri plops down beside me.

"Are you going to tell us where we're going now?"

I wouldn't tell her, but I'm actually quite proud she has ridden blind this long. And I'm relieved she didn't ask this question before I found Mother's charm last night. At least I have something to offer today.

Neechi fiddles with his waterskin, trying not to appear interested in what I'll say.

"You have a right to hear too," I tell him. Taking a deep breath, I force myself to voice this ridiculous plan. "We're taking the baby to the Jungle."

"Why?" Bri asks, drawing out the word into an entire sentence.

"Because I promised my mother I would. There's . . . someone there who is going to take care of him."

"In the Jungle."

"Yes."

"And the Center's okay with that?"

When I don't answer, she narrows her eyes suspiciously. "Wait a minute. Does this have anything to do with that book you found at Finca del Mar?"

I stall, wondering how to respond without giving too much away. Bri made it clear how she feels about Brutes. When I told her about Tristan's journal at the afterparty—when I revealed that Gentles were born Brutes, then altered with a vaccine—she defended the foremothers, saying the Brutes must have been monsters or the women wouldn't have had to do what they did. But she didn't know about *these* Brutes. And I still can't tell her without breaking my promise to Torvus.

Why did I let her come? She is going to flip out when she discovers what waits in the Jungle.

Or maybe before, if she puts two and two together and realizes the baby Jonalyn is rewrapping against her body isn't a Gentle at all.

I decide to avoid a direct answer. "You're the one who wanted to come. Felt better about your chances with me—remember?"

"Yeah, but I thought you were going to, I don't know, get revenge or something."

"Trust me, Bri, this is better than revenge. You'll see." And I hope she will. I hope that if I can get her to Tree Camp, she'll discover what I have: that the foremothers' actions aren't as black-and-white as we've been taught.

She wraps a shoulder-length strand of blonde hair around her finger aggressively, but my promise seems to have appeased her—for now. Neechi listens attentively but has nothing to say.

Jonalyn has finished situating the baby in his sling, so I take the opportunity to avoid further interrogation. "We'd better get going. The earlier we cross the border, the better."

———

Roughly six hours and exactly five more stops later, we pass a familiar finca near the intersection of Highway Volcán and Camino del Oeste. But where inviting buildings once stood—candlelit windows and a neatly trimmed garden—charred walls and tumbled bricks lie scattered in scorched piles. I glance back at Bri, whose somber expression tells me she remembers precisely where we are. The raid feels like a lifetime ago, not a mere two weeks.

My stomach twists. I just freed the Brute responsible for the attack.

I *really* hope I did the right thing.

I still despise Dáin for what he did to Jonalyn, to this finca and others, for what he might have done to me. I don't trust him. I'm only banking on the hunch that his hatred for the Matriarchy will channel his recklessness toward a better cause. But if I'm wrong, I just let loose the very evil that could end us all.

We take a final rest at a campsite tucked into a bend in the Jabiru, where our Alexia contingent slept our first night of patrol. The spot where Bri nearly took my life. Can't say I have great memories around here.

While Jonalyn tends to the baby *again*, Neechi and I peruse the parcels of food in the saddlebags, deciding this would be a good time for a late lunch. Strips of dried lamb, rounds of sourdough, preserved mango, crisp-fried plantains, a wheel of hard cheese, a cured sausage, three bananas, a sack of taro flour, two rods of sugarcane . . . the food just keeps coming.

"Looks like Marsa was intent on fattening us *all* up," I laugh. "But let's eat light for now. Just in case."

"In case what, exactly?" Bri prods.

"In case it takes me longer than expected to find . . . the house. I've only been there once."

"Someone *lives* in there? She must be crazy."

I nod, avoiding her eyes. "It takes a special kind of fearlessness to call the Jungle home."

"So, where to from here?" Jonalyn asks, taking a chunk of bread from Neechi with one hand, cradling the nursing baby in the other.

I consider the foothills before us, which have grown into a wall between us and the world beyond. Highway Volcán ends a hundred yards ahead, abutting the perpendicular Camino del Oeste.

Beyond that, the only visible landmark is the top third of El Fuego, which towers over the closest foothills like a giant peeking over the wall. I'm not sure which hills or valleys Jase brought me through. Even if I hadn't been blindfolded, they all look eerily similar—solid green masses of leaves, vines, ferns, and the occasional tail-feather-like fronds of a cohune palm.

"Well . . ." I stall. *Now what?*

I run through the first clue in the song again: *Where the fire don't burn, and the dark water's deep.* Fire don't burn. When would fire not burn? The finca is a charred heap, but that just happened recently. Maybe it's referring to a sugarcane field, burned after harvest? No, that doesn't make sense. Why would there be sugarcane fields beyond the border?

El Fuego steals my attention, the intimidating beauty positively arresting. A silver line of waterfall cascades to its base. A ring of clouds at the peak gives the impression the old volcano is smoking again.

El Fuego. There's been nothing but a little smoke since Nedé began. The fire inside no longer burns.

I turn to my companions with a grin of triumph, pointing up at the mountain. "Now, we go there."

CHAPTER NINE

We canvass the intersection of Highway Volcán and Camino del Oeste for a trail, a marker, anything that might indicate a path through the impossible tangle marking the border of Nedé. The trees seem twice as tall, the space between them half as wide. *How are we going to get through this?*

After probing unsuccessfully for an easy entry point, eventually we're forced to dive headlong. I lead Callisto first, anxious and jittery. Not like her, but then, the dried vine obstacle in my teak forest arena couldn't have prepared her for this. With no visibility and unsure footing, this is a horse's nightmare. Maybe we should have tried to enter at the place I followed Dáin across the border. No, El Fuego has to be the clue. It makes perfect sense now.

If we can get there.

The others follow, reluctantly. The horses pick their way

nervously over downed logs, around prickly bushes, and through hanging vines. They give a noble effort, but before long we're forced to dismount and walk—no, *beg*—them along.

Hours pass. Sweat drips from our skin and mats the horses' coats, even in the near-constant shade of the canopy. My arms blister with itchy red bumps. Every mosquito in the Jungle apparently wants its fill of our blood.

I try to mark a course toward the volcano—no easy feat when it only graces us with a glimpse of its head every millennium. Shadows will have to orient us in the interim.

When those shadows grow long and the dwindling light warms to amber, it's clear we won't reach ol' Fuego by nightfall. Besides, Callisto seems exceptionally tired, even without a rider. And she's drooling again.

Don't worry about her, Reina. She's fine. She has to be fine.

"Let's find a place to camp for the night." My words break a silence that has stretched since our last baby stop. For some reason, no one has felt like talking. Maybe because when you open your mouth, you chance drowning in humidity?

Finding a suitable camp proves difficult. Eventually we settle for a *slightly* less suffocating section of Jungle at the top of a knoll. There's even a small window between two trees where we can see our next destination: El Fuego, appearing, graciously, a little closer. If we had a road or trail, I bet we could reach it in a couple hours. But judging by our pace today, we'll be lucky to arrive by nightfall tomorrow.

I tie Callisto to a nearby tree—plenty to choose from—using the rope circle around her neck and the length of cord in my rucksack. Neechi unsaddles the other horses, then stakes the reins. With the animals secured and happily nibbling nearby branches, we turn our attention toward our own camp.

"Reina, can you hold the baby while I help get dinner ready?"

Jo takes my surprised sputtering as a yes, thrusting a squirming bundle into my arms. I want to protest—aren't there other, more pressing things I should be doing? Clearing Jungle floor? Charting a course? Unrolling bed mats? Scratching my billion mosquito bites?

I glance down at the tiny human.

Ugh. At least he's not screaming.

Surely my sister realizes there's a very real chance I could break this small creature. He feels like a newborn lamb in my arms—featherlight and fragile. I try to mimic the way I've seen Maternos hold these things, laying him down in the crook of one arm, but that doesn't feel secure enough. In fact, I should probably sit. *There.* With him resting on my thighs and a hand on each side so he can't fall off, I stare at his features. Dark eyes open and close slowly, enamored by the dappled light in the canopy above us, and his hands twist and curl into each other. Those teeny, moist lips pucker and smack, and I can't help but smile. He *is* kind of cute.

"Hi there, little one," I say, instantly annoyed that my voice has taken on the cooing quality Maternos always get with babies.

I place a finger over his searching palm. His fingers curl around it, surprisingly tight. "You're a strong one, aren't you?"

How strange that this miniature, vulnerable creature will become a full-sized Brute someday. Like Jase, like Rohan . . . like Dáin. Within this child exists the potential for strength and for danger, goodness or wrongdoing. He will have the ability to choose, as Rohan put it. That's the gift my mother has given him. That *I'm* giving him, I realize.

Fear overtakes pride. What if Mother was wrong? What if *I'm* wrong? Are we unleashing a power we won't be able to stop?

I'm not unleashing anything, I console myself. *I'm only making good on my promise to take the baby to Torvus.*

And then? I don't know.

The baby's features sour, his mouth turning down in a tremble. "Don't cry. Please don't cry."

I quickly stand, shifting him to my shoulder, but that feels awkward too. So I bounce him, walking in a circle.

This is *so* much harder than shooting arrows.

"Jo?" I plead.

"You're doing fine, Rei. I'm almost done."

Right. I roll my eyes at her and keep bouncing and walking, bouncing and walking. Another circle around camp and his non-stop wiggling stills. His lips part in relaxed sleep. *I put him to sleep.* "I put him to sleep!" I yell excitedly. He jolts awake, then lets me know what he thinks of my rude interruption.

Jonalyn sets the last of the dinner portions on a large banana leaf and relieves me of my duty.

"Thanks," we say in unison.

She laughs. "You know, you aren't as much of a novice as you think. You looked pretty natural to me," she says with a wink.

I don't believe a word of it, but still, there was something surprisingly satisfying in holding him. Or did the golden hour of evening trick me into affinity once again? Love a thing at noon, and your amor is real.

Or at midnight, when he's crying his face off, I muse.

We eat bread and cheese, dried meat and banana in gratified silence. Neechi and I work to start a fire, despite the intolerable heat—for protection, as Fallon advised while on border patrol. After our meal, we gather piles of fronds and brush to create makeshift beds. Jonalyn, who has never slept a night away from a mattress, tosses and turns, trying to find a comfortable position next to the baby. Neechi settles easily enough, used to sleeping on straw mats. He's snoring in five minutes.

As the only present company able to fight, Bri and I agree to take turns standing watch over the others and the horses. But even while Bri takes the first shift, I keep my weapons close. Strange sounds awaken with the moon—croaking and chattering, howling and grating. Strange but not altogether unfamiliar. They remind me of sleeping in the tree hut. The pervasive hum of Jungle night grows louder, deafening but strangely soothing, and exhaustion eventually overcomes apprehension, sweeping me into the realm of dreams.

———————

Our second day in the Jungle goes by largely as the first. With each passing hour, the monotonous surroundings tighten their hold. The farther we trek, the more I sense the circle of untamable danger around us widening, weighing heavier—feel the pulse of it in my limbs. How many thousands—millions—of trees surround us? How many menacing fer-de-lance or deadly pumas lurk out of sight?

And for Siyah's sake, how many times does that baby need to be fed and changed?

Aside from an occasional interesting animal—a bright parrot, a particularly large iguana, a cat resembling a miniature jaguar— we rely on our only other form of entertainment: singing. Like good Nedéans, we three women rehearse every song we can remember, from the Nedéan anthem to the spirituals predating the foremothers. I sing to pass the time. I sing to distract myself from worrying about Callisto.

I found her dead-asleep on her side this morning. For a sick-ening moment, I feared the worst. But after three smacks to her rump, she lumbered to her feet. She seems okay now, so I sing and force my mind away from any other possibility.

By midday, a watery rushing tempts us slightly north. We aren't disappointed. Encountering a swiftly moving river, nearly half the width of the Jabiru, we fill our water flasks and let the horses drink their fill. After lunch, Neechi submerges his hat in the blue-green water, filling it like a basin and dumping it over his head. Water gushes down his face and neck, soaking his clothes. We all laugh. Then we realize he's onto something.

I'm first to shed my boots and run into the river, splashing up to my neck in the cool water. It pulls me gently off my feet, and I let myself float, bare toes poking above the current, taking in the cobalt sky above. Bri jumps in soon after. Even Jonalyn follows, wading waist-deep, letting the coolness tickle the baby's feet. The simple pleasure of moving water against skin, the distinct scent of soggy wood and river fish, sets all our nerves at ease, and we giggle like children. It feels good to laugh. To forget for a moment that our fate depends on my figuring out another clue, and soon.

While we dry out on a downed log, I contemplate the river. "I wonder if it's the same water as the falls on El Fuego."

"And that matters because . . . ?"

A pity our little dip didn't permanently dampen Bri's mounting testiness. Oh well. "If it is, we could follow it, that's all."

She stuffs a hunk of sausage into her mouth. "Trekking through hell along a river sounds slightly preferable to trekking through hell. Might as well."

I can always count on Bri's bluntness to boil a decision down to sense. "Along the river, then."

———

"Along the river" proves more difficult in practice than in theory. Fueled by a permanent water source, the tree trunks widen and the brush thickens. Thankfully, we also encounter lengthy sections where wet-season flooding swept the banks clear, leaving behind near-level terrain we can traverse on horseback. In other places the river widens, stretching itself so thin we can ride along the shallow edges.

And so we press on, climbing up and down, along and through. The heat, humidity, bugs, and obstacles become an ever-present suffering, acknowledged with every breath, every footfall. How can a place feel so expansive and suffocating at once?

I wipe a soiled sleeve across my brow for the millionth time, trying to mop my salty sweat before it stings my half-closed eyes. Across the river, a slight movement jolts me into high alert. I stare intently at the cluster of trees but can't make out anything unusual. Must have been an animal.

Or maybe you're growing delirious.

It's not out of the question. I can see how one might go crazy in this eternal thicket.

Crazy.

I run a hand along Callisto's matted, sweaty neck. She doesn't acknowledge my touch. Her mind appears distant; her steps drag like she's just run clear from the Halcyon Sea. "We're all tired, girl. You can do this. I *need you* to do this."

———

It's impossible to know how far we've walked through this Jungle, what with the curves of the river, the painfully slow going, and the lack of any visible landmarks. One kilometer? Three? Five?

As the light dims, the temperature cooling ever so slightly, I begin to fear following the river was a mistake. What if it *isn't* flowing from El Fuego? What if it's leading us away from the volcano?

The gentle incline we've been following turns suddenly steep. We're forced to parallel the river at a distance to bypass the slick, rocky banks. But even though our current path is relatively dry, the combination of rocks, loose dirt, and elevation gain makes summiting nearly impossible.

As we climb, Neechi stumbles twice; each time I have flashbacks of the Arena stablehand's arm snapping like a twig.

"Be careful," I warn him, like that will make a difference. But I can't help but worry. What would we do if he broke a bone or had a heart attack out here? There would be no way to save him.

Jonalyn's fatigue is obvious too, but her strength astounds me more. She had barely recovered from the attack, then had a baby, and now marches through the Jungle a week later, with an extra four kilos bundled to her chest. Her body's toughness isn't all I find remarkable, though; her fierce determination inspires me. She could have let me bring the baby to Torvus myself. She had every reason to return to her finca—to rest, oversee the rebuilding, regather the Gentles who were temporarily moved after the raid. She chose this instead.

I marvel as she climbs, takes one exhausted step after another, balancing a baby and leading a reluctant mare. The brio of that woman—my sister, a *Materno*—rivals that of any Alexia. Certainly mine.

How have I never seen it?

"We're almost to the top," I encourage.

She nods, understandably breathless. Then she steadies herself, placing a hand against the baby's back, and takes another calculated step, tugging at the mare to do likewise. The transfer of her weight causes a boulder to give way, sending dislodged rocks and debris tumbling down the hillside. She slips backward and lands hard, twisting instinctively to protect her child from the impact. Five meters below, Bri jumps over the largest rock before it takes out her legs, but lands on loose dirt and slides several meters down a steep incline into a tangle of ferns. In the chaos, her horse spooks and rears, hind legs prancing dangerously close to a crumbling ledge.

I scramble toward my sister. "Jo! Are you okay?"

Neechi starts toward Bri, but she barks, "I'm fine. Get the stupid horse!"

Unfazed by her stiffness, he takes unbalanced steps toward the spooked Lexander, speaking softly.

"Neechi, be careful!" I yell, trying not to imagine him getting knocked over the edge while I check Jonalyn for injuries. She winces from a scrape down her arm, but once she's sure the baby is okay, shoos me toward the others.

Bri's horse rears again and paws for footing. The seasoned stablehand eases closer, calming her with his voice, eventually his touch. By the time I reach them, he has snatched the reins and is tugging her away from the ledge.

Breathing heavy, he hands Bri the reins, then slumps to a sitting position on the ground, shaking with exhaustion.

I crouch down beside him and hand him a water flask. "You saved that horse, Neechi. Well done."

Bri wipes sweat from her forehead as she appraises him. "We need to rest. We better set up camp soon."

I nod, reluctantly. I really thought we'd make it to the volcano today. "Let's get to the top of this, then we'll look for a spot." This seems to bolster everyone's resolve, including mine. Just a little farther . . .

I lead Callisto over the last difficult push—sending her up first, then scrambling with my own hands and feet. When I reach the top, I prepare to collapse with exhaustion and relief, but the view keeps me on my feet.

A dark emerald pool the width of a large paddock shimmers beneath what must be El Fuego, though we can only see a fraction of the wide, shaley base of the mountain. To my right, the pool empties into the river we've followed all day. From a lush outcropping far above us, the same river drops through thin air, crashing into the pool below with a roar. A gust of vagrant mist blows cool and damp against my face, and I breathe in the fresh scent of falling water.

We made it.

"We made it!" I yell down to the others. Giddiness reenergizes my muscles as I help them to the top.

"That's more like it," Bri says, taking in the view.

She follows a staggering Neechi to the water's edge and splashes her face clean while he fills a flask. She throws a cupped handful of water at his hovering face. He sputters in surprise.

"Thanks for your help back there," she says. His bewilderment melts into a tentative smile.

"Thank you, Dom—" He seems unsure whether to use her surname.

"Bri's fine."

"Thank you, Dom Bri."

There's just a hint of pride in Neechi's tone, kindness in hers. Then the moment of humanity vanishes like the waterfall spray, and she walks away. I wonder if she has ever before thanked a Gentle.

Jonalyn sits next to me, unwrapping the littlest traveler. "That water must be deep in the center; look how dark it is."

She's right. The dancing blue-green edges of the pool slope to near blackness in the middle and under the waterfall.

Deep water . . . *water's deep.* That's it! *Where the fire don't burn, and the dark water's deep.* Both clues point to the moist ground underfoot.

"We found it."

"Found the Brutes?" Jonalyn asks, lowering her voice.

"No—not yet. But we're on the right track." Now that I know for sure, I explain the song to her.

"I always wondered why no one else had heard of it," she laughs. Then, as if catching herself, she grows somber.

I take her hand and squeeze it gently. But with daylight quickly slipping, grief is an indulgence we can't afford.

We waste no time finding a place to secure the horses and set up camp, far enough from the waterfall to keep the spray from dousing a fire, close enough to the pool to take advantage of the relative treelessness of its rim.

Two days of travel, and we're more than halfway through our food supply. When I discussed provisions with Marsa, I didn't account for walking all day doubling our hunger. Tonight Jonalyn mixes river water with taro flour over the fire, which we scoop with dried plantain chips. The combination would taste downright disgusting if we weren't so famished. But we are, so we eat it with grateful stomachs. At least the tacky sweetness and mealy texture keep us from overeating our dwindling supplies.

When Bri and I return from collecting cohune fronds for bedding, Callisto is lying down near the other horses. Neechi kneels next to her, his hand resting on her side. Her head hangs so low her nose touches the ground, legs tucked under, ears turned out and down.

I toss the fronds at Bri, rushing to the mare's side. "What happened?"

He shakes his head, confused. "She was twitchin' all over. She dropped down, then a minute later it stopped. I've never seen anything like it."

I push Neechi aside to crouch alongside her. Her ears turn toward me, and she raises her head in greeting.

"But she seems alright now?"

"I don't know, Dom Reina. Maybe she's tired, but something isn't right. I've never known a horse to twitch like that."

"It was hot today. I've pushed her too hard. Maybe exhaustion caused it." Even as I say the words, I cringe at my own stubbornness. I know she isn't okay; I just can't bring myself to face reality.

"You have to beat this," I whisper near her ear. "I need you."

Besides, there's no way I could ever—

I can't even finish the thought.

Then again, Jase didn't say I'd have to kill her—Rohan did. Maybe Jase was hesitant because he wasn't positive. Maybe animals can recover from the crazies.

"Move the other horses," I instruct Neechi. "I'll stay with her."

"Yes, Dom Reina."

Whatever happens, there's no way I'm leaving her alone tonight.

I bed down on a pile of fronds, two more covering me like a papery blanket. With my head propped against Callisto, I stare out at the waterfall, faintly glowing in a nearly pitch-dark world. Its roar drowns out the nighttime Jungle songs. In the treeless void over the pool, a different sort of canopy gradually appears—single stars at first, then patches and swirls of light, more stars than should be possible. Unimaginable beauty. But I can hardly enjoy it.

"You can't leave me, girl," I whisper. "I don't know how to be brave without you."

I remember the day Old Solomon said I could have the pinto filly. She was feisty, had little regard for training, and was a mutt besides. I knew we'd be perfect for each other. The first time I rode her bareback, directing her with only a neck rope, she sprinted headlong down the hillside, and I tumbled into a coffee bush. Earning her trust took time, but we had lots of that. The reward was a priceless bond. Not to mention . . .

"Just think of all the money you saved Mother in saddles and bridles," I tease, glancing back at her.

Callisto's chin rests in front of her, ears alert, dark eye aglow with the nearby fire, where the others already sleep soundly. In its reflective dome, I see a stranger.

A girl who killed her best friend. Who couldn't save her mother. Who released a dangerous Brute. Who, perhaps worst of all, is fiercely afraid.

Maybe I've needed my horse for courage because I can't face who I am. Who I've become.

I rest against her side, feel her rhythmic breathing under my head. Above, I search for familiar, grounding constellations. Siyah—named for our first Alexia leader—barely visible over the treetops ringing the eastern edge of the pool, bow aimed at the earth, sword at her side. The rooster crows at her heels. Saving the best for last, I trace the starry signposts westward.

"There she is, the Great Mare," I tell Callisto, craning my neck for a better view of the otherworldly horse. Tonight she gallops upside down across the sky, southward, deeper into the Jungle, like a brave Alexia steed. A meteor passes over her tail, trailing stardust. Callisto twitches. "I know, she's my favorite too."

With a hint of familiarity overhead, and the comfort of Callisto beneath, my eyes begin to droop. But I can't sleep yet. When morning comes, where to? I found El Fuego. Deep water. Now what?

You follow the mare, and I'll follow a stream . . .

I laugh out loud at the simplicity, the beauty, the rightness of it.

The Great Mare seems to stretch her muzzle another light-year southward, tail flying behind, confirming Mother's riddle. I don't know about the stream, but at least I have a general direction for tomorrow's slog through the Jungle. And that's enough to sleep on tonight.

I rest my cheek against Callisto's soft hair, feel her ribs rise and fall, and wish she were immortal like the celestial equine overhead.

CHAPTER TEN

I KNOW THE TRUTH EVEN BEFORE I open my eyes to a rose-glazed sky or feel her cold stiffness under me.

Somehow, as I slept, I knew she wouldn't wake. In my dreams, I screamed when I lost her. I caved in on myself, screamed some more. My tears filled the pool and poured down the river. My body nearly disintegrated with grief.

But here, now, in the actual discovery of loss, a hollowness begins in my chest and creeps outward to each limb, gutting me of emotion. I don't even move.

Maybe I have nothing left in me to release.

Or perhaps the girl I've become simply can't handle another loss—can't face the reality of another being I love falling victim to my poor choices.

If you hadn't taken her to the Jungle . . .

I roll away suddenly, bristling at the internal accusation. "I'm so sorry, Callisto. I'm so, so sorry."

You shouldn't have pushed her so hard.

I have no rebuttal, no excuse. "Please, not you, too."

She's already gone, and it's your own stupid fault.

"No," I whimper, a tear finally forming from the tiny fragments of feeling lodged impossibly deep inside. "No, no, no."

Neechi pushes through a nearby bush. "Dom Reina?" Seeing Callisto's still body, his face clouds over.

"Help me, Neechi. I can't leave her like this."

Without a word, he bends down and begins covering her with palm fronds, concealing her chestnut and white tobiano coat with a lattice of green. I wander along the edge of the pool, westward, searching for fitting burial clothes for my loyal friend. Sixty meters from camp, a small waterway stops me cold. The crystal-clear water cuts through the moist Jungle floor, swishing around mossy rocks and pooling in miniature eddies, its breadth just wider than could be jumped across.

A stream.

And it's heading roughly south, maybe a little west. Nearly the same direction the Mare was running last night.

If I had any emotions left in me, I might smile—maybe even whoop in victory. But as it is, I turn back to camp silently, arms full of leafy branches, vines, and sprays of delicate flowers.

Neechi has gone. I kneel beside Callisto, cut lengths of brown and white hair from her tail, and braid them into a circlet for my wrist. To keep a piece of her close to me. Then I use the foliage I gathered to arrange a meticulous shroud. A vine here, a giant monstera leaf there, bird-of-paradise and fuchsia, all blanketing her with life—vibrant life, to cover her absence of it. I brush the paper-thin, bloodred petals of a hibiscus against my lips before setting the flower on the center of the mound.

I don't know if horses and people go to the same place when they die, but just in case they do, I whisper, "Take care of them for me."

———————

Bri and Neechi keep a respectful distance as we pack up camp. Jonalyn offers a sympathetic hug, briefly sandwiching—but careful not to smash—the baby between us. "I'm sorry, Rei. I know she meant a lot to you."

I kiss her cheek in thanks, then gather my rucksack.

"We're heading south today," I say. "This morning I found the stream that should lead us in the right direction."

"You can ride with me," Bri offers, avoiding my eyes.

Used to the feel of bareback, riding pillion suits me fine, but Neechi insists I use his bedroll for padding anyway. The smoky black mare has no trouble carrying us both. She's strong and obedient, and as sleek as an Alexia steed should be. Bri has taken to calling her "Horse," which seems an appalling offense to such a fine animal, but I don't have the will to fight her on it just now.

As we mount the horses, that nagging feeling of being watched returns. I glance around but find nothing out of place, and the waterfall makes it difficult to hear much of anything. I'm probably just paranoid.

The shallow, largely sand-lined streambed creates a level path through the tangle of brush, making progress much easier than the previous days. Other than the occasional low branch or jutting boulder, we're able to move at a decent pace.

The enclosed Jungle world would almost be enchanting if I could contemplate beauty without it tearing at my raw insides. But grief makes loveliness painful, so I don't think about the delicate rays of light filtering through the canopy, or the unique texture of a strange succulent vine winding hundreds of miniature green pads around a rough limb. Nor do I let myself dwell on the too-generous slice of cheese Neechi passes me at lunch, or the tender kisses Jonalyn places on her baby's head while he nurses. Instead I let every fine detail pass in a thoughtless blur, unable to cope with beauty, kindness, or love for the aching void in my heart.

Before night falls, we discover a cave large enough to sleep in. We're not the first travelers to use the natural shelter; a charred fire pit marks its opening. I wonder if Mother slept here, a Brute infant lying on a pile of leaves next to her, the way Jonalyn tucks her baby to her side now.

Bri and I finalize our shift assignments, then try to get some rest. Even when I'm not guarding the cave entrance and horses, I barely sleep. Every snap, every rustling in the treetops, could be anything—a snake, a jaguar, or maybe Dáin, come to prove I made a mistake by releasing him.

On the third morning since crossing the border, we eat the last of Marsa's carefully packed provisions: one stale sourdough loaf, two strips of dried meat, and a cupful of taro-root mush portioned between the four of us. In the silence, I hear their collective fears: *What now?*

I splash my quarter of dry bread with a little water to soften it up. "There will be food when we arrive."

Bri shoots me an *And when will that be?* glare, but is either too exhausted to parry, or doesn't want to hear the answer.

I'm not sure I can handle the answer myself. I have no clue how to find food in the Jungle. If we don't reach Tree Camp soon . . .

Jonalyn stands and sways with the infant, keeping him soothed while slowly chewing her share of the meat. I hand her my bread.

"You eat it. For the baby."

Bri throws a sideways glance at the bundle in my sister's arms before handing over her share too.

I know Jo would never take our food for herself, but for his sake she doesn't refuse. I touch his tiny palm. His fingers curl around mine with slow, jerking movements, like a sensitive plant. His eyebrows arc, and his mouth works, grimacing, then widening in a big yawn. Something shifts in my chest, loosening the vise grip of grief. For the briefest moment, I can smile at this little life, so full of wonder and potential. In the span of seventy-two hours, he has made me dislike babies a little less. In fact, I feel a strange attachment to the child.

I don't want him to grow up in a Hive or get brittle bones. I don't want him to ever have to choose between the stinger or a phase-out facility. In bringing him to the Jungle, he'll become a Brute, but at least he'll have a chance at a long, healthy life. *He'll* be safe.

I just hope his safety doesn't come at the expense of ours.

Midmorning, the stream turns markedly west. About noon—observed not by lunch, but by our grumbling stomachs—it disappears into a crack under a massive rock face, half-covered in moss, vines, and tenacious plants growing on thin ledges. Our only guide, gone.

Bri gives me a pointed look. "Now what?"

"I . . ." The truth is, I don't know. Defeat threatens to completely undo me. Have I been following the wrong stream the whole time? Is there another clue? I quickly hum through the tune yet again, considering the words:

> *Where the fire don't burn, and the dark water's deep,*
> *We'll save them there, at the mahogany tree.*
> *You follow the mare, and I'll follow a stream,*
> *And we'll leave them there, at the mahogany tree.*

If there comes a day when you can't find me,
Lay my flowers there, by the mahogany tree,
I'll be buried there, by the mahogany tree.
I lost my love, at the mahogany tree.

I figured out the fire that doesn't burn, the deep water, the mare, and I *thought* we were following the stream. The only other landmark is the blasted tree! But instead of our destination, I'm staring at an impassable mountain of rock.

Collapsing on a log, I silently run through the song again. *Nothing.*

What am I going to do now? I'm responsible for bringing them here. We're out of food and probably surrounded by predators just waiting for nightfall. We might make it back to Bella Terra, but without food herself, Jonalyn won't be able to feed the baby. How long would it take for an infant to starve?

"Um, Reina?" Bri kicks my boot, interrupting my spiral. "Hellooo?"

"I don't know where to go from here," I admit. Defeat sounds even more miserable out loud.

"Great." Bri finds a rock to sit on.

Jonalyn moves closer. "There has to be a way. She said to follow the song."

"The stream is the last clue, and now that has been swallowed by the earth."

"I really don't like the sound of that," Bri grumbles.

Neechi dismounts and crouches low, looking at the base of the rock. "Could we go through?"

Bri snaps, "There is no way on earth I'm belly-crawling into that. You're crazy."

But I consider his question, stare at the slim gap between the water and the veritable mountain above. Could she have meant to follow the stream into *that*? Would we even fit? Besides, I wonder out loud, "What would we do with the horses?"

"We could leave them," Jonalyn offers.

"That's not an option," I say firmly. "They'd be helpless out here."

"I could stay with them," Neechi offers.

A beat of silence follows, his proposal catching us all by surprise.

"While I admire your courage, *you'd* be helpless out here," I counter. "You have no weapons and no food."

He doesn't press further, embarrassment coloring his dirt-smeared face. *Still a Gentle, but a Gentle who wants to be brave.* Like there's something in him that was made for more.

Bri brings it back to the point. "Then what now?"

I remove my boots and wade closer to the opening, peering into the darkness. I can't see more than a meter inside. The water echoes against the stone ceiling, which barely clears the stream's surface.

"Who knows how far back this goes."

Jonalyn shivers. "Or whether it drops off completely."

"No," I reason, thinking it through. "We've been following the water upstream since El Fuego. The water is flowing out of this rock, so it couldn't drop off inside, right? Or it wouldn't come out here at ground level."

Bri catches on. "So this has to be, like, a tube."

I nod. "Maybe a really long tube. We just have to find where the water enters."

With no other options, it's an easy sell, even though—without our watery trail—we're forced to walk the horses through dense Jungle again. We keep the stream to our right—at least, we hope it's buried under the bulging mass of rock and overgrowth rising fifteen meters alongside us.

An hour later, the incline we've been climbing softens, and the rock mass shrinks to ten meters high, then five. When it levels entirely, we round the end and nearly step into our stream, bubbling into the yawning mouth of a cave.

"Ha! We found it!" I wrap Jonalyn in a hug.

Neechi scoops water into his mouth with two hands, then fills our flasks.

Even Bri seems pleased. "Good job not getting us lost . . . yet."

I smirk back, this small victory momentarily overshadowing the heaviness that has sapped the life from me since the pool. Since I lost—

Wait . . .

A peculiar, cord-like thread sweeps between two high tree limbs in the distance, nearly obscured by the busy, intersecting green growth between it and us.

I drop my bow and scramble to the top of the cave opening, but I need higher ground. A secondary ledge allows me to clear enough of the canopy that I can just make it out. Rising above every other tree in sight, the strong branches of a giant mahogany stretch toward the welcoming blue sky. Tree huts dot the limbs like perching sparrows, connected with zigs and zags of rope, thin as spider's silk from this distance. A troop of howlers bark rudely from a safe distance, dispersing a flock of colorful birds.

I actually did it. *I found my way back.*

But relief quickly gives way to panic. The otherworldliness of their camp fills me with strange apprehension. These Brutes aren't tame. I'm not even sure they're good. And I haven't just come back, I've brought company. What will Torvus say? Standing within a hundred meters of our destination, I contemplate turning around and retreating right back to Bella.

What was I thinking, coming back?

I force myself to run through my reasons, beginning with the baby Jonalyn carries and ending with my vow to avenge Tre's death by helping the Gentles. For their sake, I have to try.

The stream leads us to within fifty meters of camp—I can just make out a row of the orchard's many fruit trees in the distance. We leave the streambed, which curves sharply west at a deep pool with a sandy shore, to keep a straight course. Away from the water, traversing through a clearing of sorts, I realize the Jungle has become eerily quiet.

Would it be better to announce our arrival or tread quietly?

"Stay close," I whisper to the others.

Bri brings Horse up beside me. "I don't know where you're taking us, Sunshine, but I have a really bad feeling about—"

Whooosh!

A broad, heavy net drops from the trees, covering us like trapped animals. The horses neigh and skitter, unable to rear for the weight of the ropes. Someone screams like a stuck pig—maybe Neechi. As if in response, a collective yell erupts from the Jungle around us, followed by charging bodies, barely clothed and dusty. Our captors encircle us, pointing spears and betraying no affinity. Bri draws her bow.

"Put that down," I yell at her through clenched teeth.

She looks at me like I've lost my mind but reluctantly does what she's told. Jonalyn wraps her arms protectively around her baby. Neechi trembles.

I muster every shred of courage I can dig out of my hollow chest and address the mob. "I'm here to see Torvus."

INTERLUDE

IN THE EARLY MONTHS OF Leda's unlikely destiny, she gradually learned to enjoy the dual role of Materno and Center codirector. She came to savor the smell of newborns, was soothed by the suckling of infants on bottles, admired the unmistakable love other Maternos had for their daughters.

Because of her position, Leda had greater freedom than most Maternos. Even as she became pregnant a second time—to fulfill her destiny—she absorbed herself in her work, splitting her time between Bella Terra and the Center, where she attempted to research antidotes for the vaccine. However, progress was slow; each lead seemed to end in impossibilities.

As months turned into nearly two years, she wondered about her son, saw his face in every toddler she tended to. She thought of Torvus, with his fearless dreams and passionate love. Would Jason someday resemble his strength? Share his features? The Gentles she worked with daily gave vivid glimpses of what her son's future would have been if she hadn't kept him from that fate. If she hadn't known the truth.

What if she could offer other babies a chance at an unaltered life?

A daring mission began taking shape. It was not terribly uncommon for Gentles to die in infancy. Could she fake other deaths? If she was careful, her codirector needn't suspect anything. The plan was risky, but knowing what she knew, how could she not act?

The first lie—"The Gentle didn't survive"—twisted her insides. But what was worse? Deceiving Maternos, who, she knew, had no attachment to their male babies before they were sent off to fincas, or allowing those innocent children to suffer the fate of Gentles?

The second time Leda followed Torvus's clues to the base of the mahogany tree, she traveled with two such "dead" infants—one with impossibly big, brown eyes, and another with wispy, baby-fine hair the color of red amber. Two babies, destined to be Brutes because of her deception.

Crossing kilometers of Jungle with the infants, a milking goat, and a mule carrying supplies was no small task. But the peril of the Jungle held no terror compared with the apprehension that pounded in her heart when she knocked on the plumeria-carved door. The door of the home Torvus had made for her.

When Torvus found Leda on his doorstep, he gathered her in his arms, breathed in the scent of her, kissed her hair, her cheeks, her lips.

"You came back to me," he said, lifting her from the ground and spinning her in a dizzying circle.

She let herself believe it for a moment, and, more cruelly, let him believe it too.

"I brought you something." She rifled through the mule's pack for the books she had bought from Aunt Salita the month before, in a bargain that revealed the Senator's lingering affection for Leda.

As he took the ancient, tattered books from her, a smile stretched his lips. She watched him remember their reading lessons on the banks of the Jabiru, where she patiently taught him to read using those very pages.

"And who are they?" Torvus asked, seeming to notice the babies for the first time.

"Torvus—"

When Leda explained who she planned to leave behind, she couldn't hide the real reason she had come. Torvus stepped back, his eyes brooding storm clouds.

"Leave me—and take them with you. I'm no Materno!"

"Please, Torvus," she begged. "They deserve a chance to be who they were created to be, just as you have had."

It took no small amount of pleading, but he finally conceded.

"They can stay." Leda's heart flooded with admiration, relief, until he turned his back on her and yelled, "But I don't ever want to see you again."

His pronouncement shattered Leda's heart into a million pieces. Didn't he understand that she *wanted* to be with him? That if it weren't for the duty of saving others, she would gladly unite herself with him forever? But the shock of his sudden coldness silenced any argument, and Leda resolved to honor his demand: he would never see her face again.

———

Once Leda departed and his anger cooled, Torvus was left with two babies and a mountain of regret. Though a twisted piece of him relished his ability to hurt her the way she had hurt him, he wished his final words back. He wished *her* back.

But wounded pride has no equal in its ability to blind love.

During his years serving Nedé, injustice had incited Torvus's disdain for the Matriarchy. Solitude had fed it. When Leda asked him to take the babies, he convinced himself her betrayal proved she was no different from other Nedéans: selfish, proud, only using males for their own gain. Her request offered hope. If he had other Brutes like him, perhaps someday he could end the tyranny.

If Leda knew the real reason he had taken them in, he doubted she would continue to supply his future army. Then again, when it came down to it, would he be able to attack, knowing it would put her in danger?

Torvus's crew of little Brutes multiplied, coming one, sometimes two or three, at a time. At first, he could barely resist the urge to speak with her—fought the desire to intercept her when she snuck onto his porch in the middle of the night, leaving the infants in a specially designed cradle. She came to the Jungle dozens of times to bring babies and supplies: bottles, powdered formula, scraps of metal, fruit tree seedlings, medicines—anything she thought they might be able to use and that she could transport easily.

He got his wish—he never saw her face. At first, he decided it was easier that way; as time twisted memory, he convinced himself it was what she wanted. How could she forgive him for what he had said all those years ago? He refused to mend the bridge he had broken, and time widened the river between them like a swelling wet-season rain. As the years passed, he saw no way to cross.

CHAPTER ELEVEN

OUR CAPTORS MARCH US TOWARD the tree, bound at the wrists, spears pressed to our backs. I scan the crowd for a familiar face, finding none. Three younger Brutes lead our animals. One reaches curiously toward Horse, but jumps away when she tosses her head.

"Was this part of your plan?" Bri hisses, as we near the center of camp.

"If they haven't already killed us, I doubt they're planning on it. Not without Torvus's permission, anyway."

"Very comforting. And who is this Torvus?"

"I think you're about to find out."

The imposing leader emerges from his dilapidated, wood-planked house and stomps down the steps, straight at us, as if he was expecting visitors. He's dressed in skins from the waist down, and his wild hair doesn't look to have seen a comb in the two weeks since my last visit. A fierce fire in his stride melts my courage. When he stops directly in front of me, I'm swallowed up by his shadow. Muscles bulge across his bare chest and down his arms, his skin tight and rough with hair. *This is the Brute Mother confessed to loving?*

"I told you not to come back." His deep voice reverberates with an otherworldly timbre. "And what are *they* doing here? Have you no sense, girl?"

I won't let him see fear. I set my jaw and stand straighter, rising to meet his volume. "*They* will be the least of your worries soon. Did you get my message?"

"Oh yes, that traitor came here, with more of his subversiveness. Asking for supplies and men. The same stupidity he's been jawing about for years."

I ignore Bri's gaping mouth for now. I don't even glance at Neechi or Jonalyn. First I have to convince Torvus to let us stay, then I can explain.

"It's not the same," I argue. "Things have changed in Nedé. Teera put the pieces together about the raids; she was planning on using Dáin to locate the rest of you. She won't stop until she finds what she's looking for. You need to make a plan."

Torvus's jaw tightens, twitches. "You sent word with the traitor. Why come yourself?" He motions toward the other prisoners. "Why bring more danger to us?"

A familiar face weaves slowly through the onlookers, making his way toward Torvus. His light hazel eyes find mine, and I'm overcome with the depth and familiarity of them—warm and trusting, like Mother's. In my relief to see Jase, I stumble over my words.

"Moth—Leda sent me. With a baby."

He notices Jonalyn's cargo for the first time. A flicker of confusion wrinkles his brow, quickly replaced by anger. "Oh, she did,

did she? Was she tired of sneaking in at night? Decided you could do the job just as well?"

How dare he speak of Mother that way?

"No! She—" I can't answer, my throat tightening from confusion over his response, anger at being treated so unfairly, grief over the real reason Mother couldn't bring the baby herself. I can't stop the tear that slides down my cheek, and I watch it erode his fierceness enough to absorb the meaning beneath my silence. His gaze flickers between me and the baby, then something in him snaps. Like an enraged, caged predator, he paces and shouts orders.

"Ori, take the baby. Jase, deal with the others." He storms away from camp, snapping a branch and smashing it against a trunk as he goes. Just before he's out of earshot, he growls, "Prepare a fire meeting tonight!"

Once the Brute leader has disappeared into the Jungle, Jase approaches. Before I can resist, he squeezes me in a tight embrace, lifting me off the ground.

"You came back!" He grins, setting me down but not releasing his grip on my shoulders.

At least someone is glad I'm here.

"Well, somebody promised to let me kill myself jumping from a cliff the next time I was in town."

He slaps my back with a laugh. "I'll hold you to it. And who are they?"

"Jase, this is my eldest sister, Jonalyn." I don't miss the way he processes the connection. Not sure of what she knows, he refrains from wrapping her in the hug I bet he'd like to give her, too.

I motion to the only Gentle present. "Neechi was Matriarch Teera's lead stablehand, until he helped me. Now he's on the run." The younger Brutes stare, even more curious about him than they were about the horses. I wonder, have they never seen a Gentle? "He wants to help," I add. With what, I'm not sure yet.

"And this is Bri." I nod in her direction. "She was a Candidate with me in the Succession, but now . . ." I consider explaining her unexpected loyalty, wonder if it would help him trust her, but decide it just sounds weird. So instead I say, "Now we've both joined the Alexia."

Bri fixes Jase with a signature steely glare while addressing me. "They're Brutes. They're *Brutes*, Rei? *They're* what we nearly died trying to find? They're supposed to take care of the baby?"

"It's a long story."

Jase looks puzzled. "She didn't know about us?"

"I kept my word to Torvus. I didn't tell anyone about you or the camp—not even Neechi or Bri. They came anyway. Mother told Jonalyn so they could bring her baby here. Before Mother—"

Again I can't seem to put words to what I know I should explain. Jase steps back, helplessness dragging at his features, but not angry as Torvus had been. He says simply, "Not here. We'll talk later."

Meanwhile, Ori approaches Jo, who has unwrapped the baby and cradles him in her arms. She hesitates before giving him over. I know my sister well enough to perceive a silent war raging underneath her calm exterior. And how could it not rage? As a Materno, she's trained not to attach herself to Gentle sons, but this week's events have shaken all we've known.

I recognize Ori. The day Rohan wrapped my arm in a sling in the kitchen hut, he led an adventurous troop of cubs through the brush, a baby strapped to his back. Now he takes this child with practiced ease, cradling its tiny head in his large palm. He seems younger than Jase by a few years.

"How will you feed him?" Jonalyn asks, tucking a stray end of blanket around the baby.

I'm amazed by her fortitude. As far as I know, this is her first time seeing Brutes, but she hardly seems shaken. Any other emotion is eclipsed by concern for that baby.

The Brute has honey-blond hair that curls just past his shoulders, and his skin is fairer brown than most of the Brutes around us. He stands almost a head above my sister and is nearly twice as broad, yet he seems more intimidated by this wisp of a woman than she is of the ancient evil standing close enough to touch her. His gaze hovers between the ground and her waist. "Goat milk. And some powder the Rescuer leaves. We mix it with coconut water."

"Will you give him a name?" she asks.

Ori looks to Jase, who answers for the bashful Brute. "Torvus names the babies—uses some old books the Rescuer left us."

She nods, looking for a moment as if she might ask something else, decides better, takes a deep breath, and turns away.

"Not to be rude," Bri interjects as rudely as possible, "but is someone going to explain what a fire meeting is? Because if it involves being tied up *and* flames, I'm not interested in attending."

"She's a live one," Jase says, slipping a knife from its sheath on his thigh. Bri tenses.

"You have no idea," I assure him. "Don't worry, Bri, they don't roast their guests the first night."

Jase takes the knife to the rope at my wrists.

"I'm glad you're all buddy-buddy," she hisses, "but last I heard there was a reason the foremothers ended the Brutes."

Jase hitches mid-saw. An uncomfortable silence stretches, and I feel the eyes of every Brute on us.

"Maybe you shouldn't untie that one," Ori half-whispers to Jase.

Jase meets my gaze. "Do you trust her?"

Bri's snark has always rubbed me raw, but she's here, isn't she? She knew I was questioning whether *all* the Brutes of old were evil, yet she followed me to Bella Terra, and now to the Jungle. Still, when it comes to how she would react in this situation, I can't say whether I trust her completely, or whether they should.

"I'm hoping you'll change her mind," I say, "like you did mine. Whether you want her hands free in the meantime is up to you."

Bri huffs, then slings a few choice words in my direction.

"And the Gentle?" Jase asks.

I glance at Neechi, realizing I haven't heard a word from him since we were captured. The quiet Gentle's hands visibly shake, and his wide eyes fixate on the strange shapes around us—bare chests, biceps corded with muscle, prickly jaws, thick thighs. What must he think of them?

"He's safe." I don't add, *All Gentles are.* What could Neechi possibly do to these Brutes, even if he meant them harm? Seen side by side, the contrast is glaring—Neechi's timid expressions, small frame, thin arms, and round face, next to Jase's sculpted bulk and confident movements. One appears harmless, the other . . . Remembering the way Torvus's rage squeezed my chest, I can think of only one way to describe these strange beings: *volatile.*

At my vote of confidence, Jase breaks Neechi and Jonalyn's bonds. Hopefully Bri will behave so they can cut her loose soon too.

Jase leads us toward the enormous mahogany tree. "You hungry?"

"Famished."

He changes course, calling on two other Brutes to follow. He dismisses the rest to their "regular duties," whatever those are.

On our way to the kitchen hut, I finally get the nerve to ask about the void I noticed as soon as we arrived.

"I haven't seen Rohan."

Not that I care, I want to add, but that might sound forced, and I'm suspicious enough of what made me ask for both of us.

"He's out hunting near the hollow. He should be back tomorrow. Ever since Dáin returned with the knife, claiming you sent him to warn us, Rohan's been busy building our food supplies." He chuckles. "It's his way of getting ready."

Disappointment mingles with relief. I've tried to picture Rohan's piercing dark eyes for the past two weeks, but now that I'm back—now that they could appear at any moment—I'm not so sure I'm ready to see them.

Speaking of what I'd rather not see . . . "Where's Dáin now?"

"It's complicated."

I wait for him to elaborate.

He sighs. "Torvus doesn't want him back in camp and refuses to listen to reason. But Rohan and Dáin have been meeting, talking about our options."

It probably shouldn't, but hearing their names together sends a shiver through me. I know I sent Dáin back here to rally support, yet the thought of Rohan working with that vile devil makes me want to scream at both of them.

"Rohan trusts Dáin?"

Jase scratches the short amber stubble along his jawline. "Not exactly. Dáin's a hothead. His temper makes him dumb as a peccary. But despite the stupid things he's done behind Torvus's back, if what he told us—what you told him to tell us—is true, we'll have to work together."

He says it so naturally, like working with Dáin is no more terrifying than rummaging through the underground storage pits for food.

He hands us each a bit of meat and fruit, which we stuff into our mouths with eager gratitude.

"And you're okay 'working together' with Dáin?" I probe further, swallowing a smoky-sweet bite of dried meat. "He did attack me, remember?" *And then Rohan beat him up for it*, I remind myself. When Dáin showed up to the fire meeting, Jase tucked me behind him. He didn't seem the least bit afraid of Dáin either.

"Like I said, dumb as a peccary," he says casually; then, noticing my unease, he adds, "But he'll be good to have around. He's fearless, and a good hunter. Always has been."

"A good *hunter*?" I'm having trouble connecting why this is a preferable trait in a potential partner.

"Yeah, he can track an animal better than most. He's sneaky, like a snake."

Finally, a metaphor that fits him. "Like a snake. And I should feel good about that?"

He laughs.

I stare back, dead serious.

His nonchalance about the Brute who haunts my dreams makes me testy. "I mean it, Jase. I only released him to protect you. He wanted me *dead*, remember?"

My change of tone catches his attention, deepening his sincerity.

"I'd never let that happen. Neither would Rohan. We'll knock his teeth out if he threatens you again, okay?" He gives my hand a quick squeeze.

He says it so easily, like he's promising to smash a little scorpion if it gets too close.

I suppose his lack of concern over Dáin should comfort me. If they're not afraid of him, and I'm with them, maybe I don't have to be terrified either.

"Okay."

"Okay," he echoes. "Now, let's figure out where we're going to put you all."

CHAPTER TWELVE

AFTER CONSIDERABLE DELIBERATION over where the four of us will sleep, eventually it's settled: the very top of the mahogany tree. Jase and Rohan's hut.

"It'll be tight, but you'll have the best view," Jase persuades. *Plus*, he doesn't say but I presume, *five dozen other treetop residents will be able to keep an eye on you.*

We cross through camp quietly, speechless in part from exhaustion, part awe. While I've seen Tree Camp before, my companions watch in silent absorption, considering the thatched huts, raised gardens, treetop bridges, and neatly ordered orchards. Two blackened animal carcasses smolder in the fire circle, filling the forest with blue-gray smoke.

Brutes attend to various tasks, carrying water in clay jugs, whittling the ends of sticks into sharper points, herding the smallest cubs into a netted pen strewn with simple wooden toys. Some stare at us outright as we pass. Though none seem as shocked as the first time I arrived at camp, our group is as unusual a sight to them as they are to us. Neechi seems especially bashful from the attention. He keeps his gaze low as onlookers pass by, whispering among themselves.

When we reach the centerpiece of camp—the enormous mahogany tree, stretching at least sixty meters into the cloudy blue—Jase says to me, "We'll have to go up in two groups. I'll take you and the Alexia first."

He reaches for Bri's upper arm to help her onto the meter-high platform, since her hands are still tied. Not surprisingly, she wrenches away, opting instead to flop across the waist-high wood slats and wiggle her way from stomach to a standing position.

Amused, Jase teases, "Stubborn, too."

Bri says nothing, just fixes him with a death glare.

I grab the railing and hop on behind her. "He was just trying to help."

"He can keep his help to himself," she says, loud enough to make sure he hears.

After securing a small gate, closing us in, Jase takes to the thick rope. Hand over hand he draws it downward; meter by meter we rise into the leafy limbs.

We're soon enveloped in a blanket of emerald leaves, each nearly as long as my arm, densely packed one minute; the next, sparse enough to reveal glimpses of the world beyond. Along the way, eclectic huts hug the trunk or sit sandwiched between stout limbs, compact but impressively designed. Since the terror I felt my first visit has mellowed to a manageable apprehension, I'm free to notice the finer details of their craftsmanship: smooth planks, curved awnings, netted windows. Dozens of rustic, but ingenious, dwellings.

From one of the porches, a slender Brute with upturned eyes and long, stick-straight black hair wraps his hands in two leather straps attached to a curved bar that arcs over a long rope. Then he takes two running steps and jumps from the platform. I gasp, expecting to watch his body writhe through the air, falling thirty meters to the unforgiving ground. Instead, the bar whizzes and zips along the rope, the Brute flying gracefully beneath, angling toward the ground at the far end of camp. Only now do I notice a dozen other ropes connecting huts up and down the tree to various parts of camp. My jaw drops.

"What's *that*?"

Jase looks confused. "Parrots?" he asks, considering a flock of green birds perched among the foliage, talking and squawking in their singsong way.

"No, *that*," I repeat, pointing at the figure bracing for impact.

"Looks like Jem. He's a quiet sort, but nimble as a monkey."

"Not the Bru—oh, never mind."

"Ah, you mean the speed lines?" He chuckles, and I realize he was teasing me the whole time. I bump him with my shoulder.

"Are they safe?" I ask.

He responds with a quizzical expression, and I remember we have very different definitions of the word.

Far below now, my sister, Neechi, and the Brutes guarding them have shrunk to doll size. As we crest the surrounding canopy, we're met with a view stretching clear to Nedé. Bri can't hide her awe any more than I could the first time I saw the Jungle hills roll away like a carpet, revealing the patchwork grid of Amal Province melting into Lapé, and farther still, the doorstep of the Halcyon Sea, obscured today by clouds. Threads of rivers curl and cut through the foreground, disappearing into the hazy distance.

The platform halts in front of Jase's hut, built so seamlessly into an L-shaped crook of the main trunk and a supporting limb, it could almost pass for an appendage of the tree itself.

Jase opens the front door. "We can rearrange the cots—the Gentle will have to take the floor—but you should be able to sleep comfortably."

"Are you sure you and Rohan don't mind? I feel bad taking over your place."

"Naw, we're happy to get kicked out. I mean, not that you're kicking us out. I just . . . I'm glad you're here." He smiles sheepishly, his growing awkwardness endearing. "Make yourselves at home. I'll be right back with the others."

When Jase disappears, Bri wastes no time getting right down to it.

"Are you going to tell me what's going on?"

"Uh, surprise? Brutes exist."

"Don't get smart with me, Reina Pierce! This is . . . Do you know how—?" She paces the small room as she fumes, glancing nervously out the netted top half of the walls—which reveal only foliage—and knocking into the three hardwood cots as she sputters in frustration. "How could you drag me all the way into the Jungle without telling me we'd be captured by monsters?"

"First of all, I didn't *drag* you—you insisted on coming. I'm sorry—I really did want to tell you. I promised Torvus I wouldn't reveal anything about them. But now that you're here . . . Bri, they're not like we've been told. You saw Jase. He's . . ." I run through a list of adjectives I've come to associate with him: thoughtful, pleasant, eager to please, a little goofy, but definitely, "*kind*."

"Maybe they were all *kind*, right before they murdered women in their sleep! Geez, Reina, where's your head? The foremothers wouldn't have subdued them if they could be trusted."

"I know," I say miserably. "I mean, I thought so too. But now that I know them . . ." Even as I say the words, I recognize what a thin argument it is. *Know them?* Hardly. I've spent less than forty-eight hours with these Brutes, and nearly half of that was spent drugged by one of *their* darts.

I move to a safer, more compelling line of reasoning, building on the conversation we'd had following the Succession afterparty at Finca del Mar. "What about the Gentles? They don't get a choice whether to take the vaccine. We force it on them. And once we do, they become completely docile and fragile. Who says we have the right to do that to them?"

"It's for their own good, to say nothing of ours. If they knew what they would become, they'd give themselves the shot."

Would they? "Then why didn't the Brutes of old give it to themselves?" I ask the question as much to myself as to Bri. Why *didn't* the Brutes of the past do something about their brutishness? If they were anything like these Brutes, they must have known what they were doing was wrong, but Tristan Pierce made it clear they continued to hurt women. She felt there was no other choice but to end their reign of terror.

"I don't know," Bri challenges, "but you better get your head on straight. I don't trust any of those beasts out there, no matter how 'kind.' And as soon as we get out of here, I'm telling Adoni."

Voices crest the threshold of the hut. I lower my voice to get in one last plea before the others join us. "Bri, you can't. Teera will kill them all."

She turns away just as Jase escorts Jonalyn and Neechi inside.

"Here," he says, arranging the cots to make a little floor space. Looking at Neechi, he says, "It'll have to do."

Neechi doesn't meet Jase's eyes as he says, "I'm plenty used to hard beds."

Jase stares at the slight Gentle, curiosity or pity—maybe both—weighing his mouth down at the corners. He looks like he wants to ask something, but decides against it. Instead, he fills a sack with the few clothes and personal items belonging to him and Rohan, then makes for the door.

"I'll be back by dark to take you to the fire meeting. Until then, you should rest." And with that, he lowers himself out of sight.

"He's out of his mind if he thinks I'm going to stay here," Bri says as soon as he's out of earshot. She waits about ten minutes for him to descend the tree, then makes a beeline for the door.

"And where do you plan on going?" I argue. "There will be Brutes all over camp."

She ignores me, throwing open the door and pulling at the rope with her bound hands to raise the platform back to the hut. The rope doesn't budge. She tugs harder. Still, it doesn't move more than a centimeter. Does the pulley have some sort of locking mechanism?

With an exasperated groan, Bri shoves the rope outward. "*Kind*, huh?" she directs at me.

I admit, being locked in a room at the tip-top of this enormous tree both surprises and unnerves me, resurrecting a familiar doubt about the trustworthiness of these Brutes.

"He'll be back," I try to assure myself.

Bri rolls her eyes. "That's not what I'm afraid of."

———————

A knock on the doorframe wakes us from a nap—all except Bri, who refused to shut her eyes. Pulling myself out of groggy sleep, I find Jase peering apologetically through the open doorway. Late-afternoon sun filters through the leaves beyond the netted walls.

"Reina," he says quietly. "Sorry to wake you, but Torvus wants to see you."

Adrenaline snaps me fully awake. "Torvus? Why?"

Jonalyn sits up. "Everything okay?"

"I'm sure it's fine," I say, picking my way over a prostrate Neechi to the door and joining Jase on the platform.

"We'll be back soon," Jase reassures her.

Bri gives me a look that basically conveys it's been nice knowing me, and dramatically mouths *goodbye*.

"I'll be back," I insist again.

As we make the descent from treetop to ground, jerking meter by meter, he says, "You and your sister look alike."

"I take that as a compliment." Being the younger sister, I've always admired Jonalyn's beauty. "I guess that happens when you're related. I mean—" I turn to face him—"that's why you have our mother's eyes, isn't it?"

His arm freezes mid-pull, but his eyebrows lift with relief as he sighs, "You know?"

I nod. "I knew you seemed familiar from that first night after the attack, but I couldn't figure out why. When I saw you and Torvus together, I knew there was some kind of connection there, too. I finally got to ask Mother, right before—"

I focus my attention on the passing leaves, not wanting to relive the moment, knowing I must.

He gently urges me on with a thoughtful sadness I can't refuse to answer. "What happened?"

I tell him about the guards' pursuit, and how helpless it felt to watch her drain of life, and Dr. Novak's insistence I leave them. I'm so caught up in my own grief that I don't notice the tears on his cheeks until he stops drawing the rope to smear them away with a forearm.

Brutes cry? The idea is so foreign—the sight so strangely moving—it momentarily overshadows my own feelings. To see this strong being express that kind of emotion undoes me. I have a strange urge to hug him, to comfort his loss, to ease his sadness.

Are you crazy? my better sense chastises. He's not a little girl—
he's a Brute. Still . . . she was his mother too.

"Did you know her well?" I ask.

He runs a rough hand down his face, inhales deeply, and just
like that, any evidence of the sorrow I saw just a moment before
all but disappears.

"No. I only saw her from afar. When I was thirteen seasons,
Torvus told me how the babies appear in the cradle on his porch.
He said one of the women in Nedé rescues them and brings
them to the Jungle to keep them from becoming *Gutless*, as he
calls them. I asked if she left me there too. He didn't want to
talk about it then, but eventually he explained that she was my
mother—that, unlike the others who came over the years, I was
his boy. I could tell he didn't like talking about her, so I let it
be. But about a year ago I made him tell me more. I found out
he met her at a place called Bella Terra, and that, last he knew,
she still lived there. Dáin had been staking out fincas, so I asked
him to help me find the place. I went a few times, just to see it.
I made sure to keep out of sight—I just wanted to be near her.
Wanted to see how she lived and what she was like. I was curious, I guess."

He dips his head, seeming embarrassed by the confession.

"That's why you were at Bella Terra the day you found me in
the teak forest—you wanted to see Mother."

We've reached the Jungle floor. He hops down and offers me
his hand in assistance, which I don't need but take anyway.

"I made Rohan go with me that time. We were supposed to be
out hunting, but I told him if he came, he could see the Rescuer
for himself. He didn't want to stay long, and we were just about
to leave when you got hurt. Of course, we couldn't just leave you
there."

I step around another dangling platform near the trail to

Torvus's house. "Oh, I think Rohan would have been just fine leaving me there," I laugh, remembering the big Brute's insistence that "girl or not," I wouldn't die from that blow to the head. He only helped me to pacify his friend.

Jase's grin admits my point. "But he wouldn't anymore. Not now that he knows you."

I raise an eyebrow, doubtfully.

"He wouldn't," Jase insists. "He gave you his *knife*. Do you know how long it took him to make that thing?"

I'm trying to work out the connection when an unexpected voice interrupts the conversation, deep and low, but laced with a hint of amusement. "If she did, she wouldn't have given it to that peccary."

I whip around to find Rohan closing the three meters between us with confident strides, his bronze chest smeared with crusty mud, dark hair mussed in impossible directions on its way past his ears. Stubbly hair darkens his jaw, and before he can reach us, the smell of unwashed Brute does. He's filthy . . . and still, strangely bewitching.

Jase jumps to clasp forearms with his friend. "You're back early."

Rohan grins. "Dantès suggested we try the hollow. Got four pacas in a day. No point killing more than we could carry." He glances back across the clearing at two equally dirty Brutes with a pole slung between them; it bows under the weight of several limp animals that could pass for enormous rats.

I have a bizarre urge to say something at the same time I clam up. I want him to look at me even as I beg the ground to swallow me whole. How can I simultaneously crave and despise the way he makes me feel?

When I finally muster the nerve to look at him, he's slipping the white knife from its sheath at his thigh. Fixing me with a steady gaze, he offers me the handle. "This belongs to you." The faintest smile plays on his deeply bowed lips. "Unless you really don't want it."

"I want it," I say a little too quickly, taking the handle, being careful not to touch his fingers. "I didn't know how else to prove to Torvus that I was sending Dáin."

"It was a good idea, though I don't think it had the effect you intended," he says. "Torvus doesn't trust women."

And I don't trust Torvus, so I'm not sure why this offends me, but it does all the same. "Why *wouldn't* he trust me? I kept my word—I didn't tell anyone about you."

Rohan shrugs, then crosses his arms. "Maybe it's not you. . . . Or maybe it's because you showed up uninvited."

"Only because *you* drugged me!" Heat creeps up my neck. "It's not my fault you knocked me out and dragged me here."

I realize a moment too late he was joking. He lifts his hands in mock surrender. "You asked."

The fact he finds humor in my defensiveness makes me even madder. I scowl and look to Jase for help.

But instead of backing me up, Jase says, "You did lie to Torvus's face."

"What? When?"

"When you tried to cover for me, remember? You claimed running around Tree Camp was your idea." He laughs at the memory with that unrestrained, free way of his that always extinguishes my anger.

I do remember, and smile in spite of myself. "He didn't buy it for a second."

"Nope." He turns suddenly serious. "But that's not what Rohan's talking about. You can't blame Torvus for being a little wary of women in general."

"Don't soften it, Jase," Rohan interjects, his playfulness gone. "Their kind took what wasn't theirs and reduced the Gutless to shriveled shells of what they were meant to be. Torvus isn't the only one with trust issues."

His fire makes me edgy. Does he mean other Brutes have trouble trusting women, or that "my kind" have our own trust issues?

Before I can puzzle it out, Jase says, "She brought some others with her. I gave them our hut."

Rohan pushes a mass of unwashed hair from his face. "Of course you did."

"We need to test out our new hammocks anyway." Jase grins.

Rohan sighs, but not in anger. More like he's used to dealing with his friend's inconvenient ideas and is resigned to going along with them.

I should thank Rohan for giving up his hut for us, but I'm too preoccupied with what he said. *Torvus isn't the only one with trust issues.* I barely hear him ask, "Where to now?"

"Torvus," Jase says. "Oh, and there's a fire meeting tonight. You better get those animals skinned quick."

"Alright." Rohan nods at Jase, clearly avoiding my eyes as he turns toward his hunting partners and strides away. Maybe he's mad about the hut after all.

"Come on," Jase says.

I want to ask him what Rohan meant, but there isn't time. Before I'm ready, we're climbing the rickety stairs to the Brute leader's porch. The state of this house stands in stark contrast to the rest of Tree Camp. You'd be hard-pressed to find a frayed rope or broken board anywhere else. But this building leans with neglect. Bushes crowd the porch, and the thatching is brittle as tinder. For some reason, Torvus appears to have stopped caring enough to maintain it years ago.

We step past a slatted crate against the wall and Jase knocks on the door, just above the carved edge of a plumeria petal.

The Brute who opens the door isn't the same Torvus who thundered at us earlier today. The fire behind his gray eyes has been extinguished, the whites tinged red, the rims swollen. He turns his back without inviting us in.

Jase closes the door, then swipes a billow of dust from a wooden chair before offering it to me. I decline, feeling immediately claustrophobic in the dimly lit space. The last time I was here, I was too terrified to notice the strange emptiness of the house. No piles of clothing wait to be washed, no paintings add color to the empty wood frames. Several tattered books occupy a single shelf, covered in so much dust I'm tempted to sneeze on their behalf.

Jase retucks the chair under a round-top dining table, hand-carved, just the right size for two. A washbasin stands in the corner, empty of water, and no blankets cover the barren bamboo-slat bed. The only evidence anyone actually lives here is the hulking Brute standing with his back to us.

The longer the silence stretches, the more nervous I become. Does he mean to punish me for bringing others to his camp? Banish me from returning? Or worse?

Jase must be used to waiting on Torvus's moods, because he stands straight and evenly balanced, unbothered by the stretching quiet. I, however, can't take it anymore. Maybe Torvus is waiting for *me* to say something. To confess my error.

"I'm sorry I brought the others," I blurt.

My words drift, unanswered, lifting and swirling with the dust particles illuminated in the ray of late-afternoon sun angling through the only unshuttered window.

Why did he bring me here if he has nothing to say? Is that a Brute thing? I try to settle into the uncomfortable silence, but it just doesn't work for me. Remembering the pendant, I try again.

"My mother wanted you to have this." I slip the charm from my vest pocket, holding it out in my upturned palm.

The bait works. The great Brute slowly looks over his shoulder and, seeing what I offer, steps toward it, seeming entranced by the object. With shaking fingers, he lifts the gift to his lips. His thick fingers curl around the tiny tree, as if afraid he might lose it.

"She came looking for you," he says. The unnatural depth of his tone softens in a way I didn't know was possible—the crack in his voice as unexpected as the words. Maybe he did care for her, as Mother said he did.

Wait—

"*Mother was here?*" For the briefest of moments I allow myself to hope that I was wrong, that she somehow survived—that she has been here recently. "When?"

"Just after you left."

"Oh." My momentary hope deflates like a ball kicked into a sharp stick. That would have been before our run-in at the Center. But still, why would she have come to Torvus? "She came looking for me *here*?"

"She heard you went missing near the Jungle. Asked me to send a search party."

That doesn't make sense. Then why was Mother surprised when I told her I had been to the Jungle?

"Didn't you tell her I had been here?"

"No."

"*No?* Why not?"

"Because she's a headstrong woman!" His familiar temper ignites, then extinguishes almost the same instant. He mumbles, "And I'm a fool of a man."

I want to ask more—to learn what ties this foreign Brute to my familiar mother. The way she spoke of him proves there was more between them than anger and secrecy, but something warns me the topic lies out of bounds. Jase once said his relationship with Mother wasn't his story to tell. Maybe that's true of Torvus as well.

Torvus's jaw tightens, twitches. "I knew what a snake her mother was. I shouldn't have let this go on so long."

Jase speaks, for the first time since we arrived. "It's not your fault. We weren't ready—we still aren't."

Torvus huffs in rebuttal. "The day Leda brought Rohan and Dáin, I knew I'd be raising the answer to Nedé's tyranny. They were ready last year, but I wanted a few more of age—needed a little more time to train them. It was my job to put an end to it, but . . ." His voice catches, and it takes him a moment to regain his composure. ". . . I knew if our existence got linked to her, I couldn't protect her, not from this far away."

In another flash of anger, he slams his fist against the table. "I should have done something!"

I know a thing or two of regret. Of wishing you could go back and act before tragedy takes what you love.

"Now you can," I say, drawing from some reserve of strength I thought had completely drained through the cracks in my heart. "You can't change what happened, but you can change what will. Teera knows you're out here somewhere, and she's furious. She has sworn to dedicate every resource to finding you, which means you'll have Alexia crawling through the Jungle before long."

The grit in Torvus's voice returns, commanding. "*How* long?"

"I don't know exactly. Maybe weeks, maybe days."

Jase silently ticks off calculations on his fingers. "We've got twenty-two old enough to fight. Some of the younger boys could be useful too. We could shelter the cubs in one of the hunting camps farther in."

Torvus shakes his head. "Too remote. And we'd need weeks to make them suitable for the cubs."

"If we keep them here, it will require more men to guard them, leaving fewer to fight."

"We don't have a choice."

"What about Dáin?" I ask. As much as I despise him, one of the reasons I let him go was to utilize his resources. "He has men, doesn't he?"

Jase looks to Torvus.

The older Brute fixes him with a hard stare. "No."

Jase presses. "Maybe we should recon—"

"I said no!" He slashes an arm through the air, batting the offensive idea against the wall.

Jase doesn't press his luck. Knowing he won't change Torvus's mind on the matter, he turns to me. "The Alexia—what are their weaknesses?"

"The Alexia *aren't* weak. And depending how many Teera sends, they could outnumber you a hundred to one. But . . . as far as I know, they have little idea what lies beyond the border. If they knew your location, they would have reached you by now. The terrain might be your best ally. If you could keep them from getting close . . ."

Torvus interrupts, "Hiding isn't enough. We have to end this."

"What do you mean, *end*?" I ask skeptically.

"I mean *end*. The Matriarchy has stolen from us long enough."

A cloud passes over the sun, plunging us in momentary shadow, though I doubt that's why a shiver runs down my spine.

"End the Matriarchy?"

I have witnessed enough of a Gentle's pathetic life to want to change their circumstances. And I admit, these Brutes have surprised me enough to make me question what great deficit warranted their alteration. But to end the Matriarchy—to destroy the only system I've known, everything safe—sounds sudden and drastic. I stare at the moody leader's breadth and unpredictability with sudden panic. I will not be able to control them. What havoc will be unleashed if they leave this Jungle?

Or maybe such talk only sparks fear because of the volatile Brute making the plans. Would I feel the same if it were *my* idea?

The fire in Torvus's eyes intensifies, but his voice remains cooly even. "We'll kill Teera, and anyone else who thinks they have the right to tell us we can't be men."

My gaze darts from Torvus to Jase, who looks like a pebble stuck between two stones.

"Is that what you think too?" I ask him.

He fidgets with his thumb. "I doubt the Matriarch is gonna welcome us with open arms, Rei."

He's right about that—she'll kill them without remorse. I have no doubt.

"I know things have to change in Nedé. I came back here not just because I promised Mother to bring the baby, but because I want to make things better for the Gentles too. But kill Teera? Then what? You'll single-handedly murder her Apprentice and a thousand Alexia so you can take over? How convenient. You know what? Maybe I was wrong. Maybe you really are the monsters I was taught you are." I back toward the door, shocked by the brazen volume of my own tirade.

Jase tries to soothe, "Reina, please."

I have a sudden urge to run from this house and never return. But where would I go? What do I have left in Nedé? Treowe is gone. Callisto is gone. Mother is gone. Teera can't be trusted, Jamara wants to kill me, and after reading Tristan's journal, I don't know what to make of anything anymore. I'm here because I *know* something needs to change. I'm just not certain how to go about it.

"Don't baby her," Torvus scolds. "What do you propose, then? You want to 'make things better' for the Gutless? How? By post-poning Initus a year? Offering the stinger to toddlers? The only thing worth giving them is their right to be men!" His face is red with passion, the intensity overwhelming. Nonsensically, I feel the urge to cry. No, I won't let his anger make me fragile.

I fire back, "You said to take a life out of fear would make you no different from us, remember?"

Torvus is undeterred. "This isn't about fear—it's about justice. Enough is enough."

Jase tries to break the tension. "I wish there were another way too. But . . . sometimes people have to get hurt so the right thing can happen."

I hate those words, the mantra Dáin cited as his reason for the raids. But somehow they sound different coming from Jase.

Of all the Brutes in Tree Camp, I realize, he's the one I trust most. He's warm and kind, has proven he cares about me, and . . . is the most like Mother. I take a step toward her child and hold his familiar, blue-green eyes with my gaze. For a moment I see Treowe in them, and I remember: I killed him. I took his life to give life to others. If honoring his death costs one more, it's a price I'm willing to pay. It's nothing the Matriarch herself wouldn't do.

My voice comes out barely above a whisper. "Is it the *only* way?"

He squeezes my shoulder gently.

I swallow the bitter fear burning my throat and hope I'm not played for a fool.

Turning to Torvus, I say, "I'll help you find Teera, as long as you promise not to hurt innocent Nedéans."

The hulking leader considers my offer the way he appraises me: silently and suspiciously. Eventually he steps forward and grasps my forearm, sealing our agreement.

CHAPTER THIRTEEN

Timid tongues of red and orange flames lick across the center of the fire ring by the time we leave Torvus's house, the small beginnings of the blaze to come. A few Brutes prepare, carrying bundles of wood, filling jugs, securing skinned animals to spits. As twilight settles over camp, the smell of smoke and the promise of a good meal momentarily replace the anxious knot in my stomach with cautious anticipation.

Jase leads me to the wooden dais on one end of the ring. "Wait here while I get the others."

"Without you?"

He chuckles. "You just went toe-to-toe with Torvus, and you're afraid of them?" He thrusts a thumb toward the milling Brutes. "You'll be fine. I'll be back in ten minutes."

I watch him walk away. I've always had Jase or Rohan with me around camp. I suppose he's right—what would these younger Brutes be able to do to me? Still, as I lean against the edge of the platform, my fingers run absentmindedly over the bone handle of Rohan's knife. I don't know enough of these Brutes to feel at ease around them.

I take stock of my surroundings, noting their positions. Apart from a few glances my way, they keep to their tasks. Still, their presence makes me a bit edgy.

A few minutes later, a rustle in a nearby bush catches my attention. Three cubs, no taller than my waist, crouch in the dense branches, arguing with each other. I only catch bits.

". . . a she."

"Why . . . ?"

". . . here before."

". . . a spy!"

"I dare you, Pip," one challenges, loud enough for me to hear clearly.

Next thing I know, a tiny warrior emerges from the bush, sprinting as fast as he can, straight for me, arm raised, clenching a long, thin object.

Before he can strike, I grab his wrist and twist his arm behind his back. The object falls to the forest floor. He's strong for someone so small, but my size affords an obvious advantage. I immobilize his neck with my other arm. In no time, I've eliminated the threat. Adoni would be proud.

But when I get a good look at the object in the dirt, I see it's only a stick. Hardly dangerous.

I spin the one they called Pip to face me, holding his arms tight against his sides. "What were you trying to do?" I ask, stern as Marsa when she's fed up with me and Ciela. "Stop squirming and look at me."

Pip's eyes grow wide as he obeys, the whites shining bright even in the dimming light. The rest of him is one solid shade of clay, from his hair to his skinny legs. He looks scared as a curassow in the kitchen.

"He dared me."

"Dared you to what?"

"To touch you. Please don't tell Jase."

I drop his arms, embarrassment warming my cheeks. I just apprehended a child for playing a game. *Way to overreact, Rei.*

"I won't tell him if you don't," I say, trying to soften my glare. "But the next time you run at an Alexia, she might not be so forgiving."

As he races back to the bushes, I hope he takes the warning to heart.

"Tell me what?" Jase says, coming from behind with the remaining Nedéans in tow.

"Oh, nothing," I say loudly enough for the cubs in the bushes to hear, glancing their way. At least I hope Pip's friends respect his bravery. He deserves that reward after what I put him through.

We take seats on a log adjacent to the dais, Bri sandwiched between me and Jase, Neechi and Jonalyn to my right. As night firms her grip on the land beneath the trees, curious flames continue to spread outward, setting multiple bundles of wood ablaze, until the whole ring burns with a beautiful, dangerous glow. Brutes stream in from the surrounding forest and thatched-roof buildings. They find seats on boulders, logs, and low-slung tree branches, some jawing, most rather somber. I suppose our presence affects the mood.

I try not to watch for a particular Brute, but I notice Rohan's arrival all the same. His skin absorbs the warmth of the firelight, his hair hanging in wet, dark waves over his ears. That strange flutter returns. Perhaps it was better when he was filthy.

I force my attention toward the other figures joining the

clearing, watching them carefully as they approach—some tall and thick, others lean and wiry, all distinctly Brute. They're full of a peculiar energy, like fast-moving water or compressed coils, ready to spring.

I steal a glance at Neechi beside me. I've never noticed just how low a Gentle's shoulders naturally sag. The shadowy light deepens dark rings under his eyes, and he fidgets with a corner of his shirt. Still, he follows the Brutes' movements with marked curiosity.

"You okay?"

It takes him a moment to register I've spoken, another to process my question. Finally, he answers, "At the Finca, I heard stories. Some gossiped of creatures more like us than women. I didn't believe them."

I sympathize with his shock, though I don't know what to say.

"What *are* they, Dom Reina?"

I consider how to answer. I could lie, but for what purpose? To spare his feelings? If we go through with our plan, he'll find out eventually. Besides, he tested his body and risked his safety to follow me here. He deserves the truth, no matter how painful.

"They are what you should have been."

Our eyes meet. I know I have to tell him the *whole* truth.

As I explain the general facts of the vaccine, understanding spreads across his face, but not sadness. To be told you've spent your life as a sickly shell of what you might have been—well, I expected indignation, injury, even bitterness. Instead he just nods, slowly processing the information in his gentled brain.

"I'm sorry, Neechi. On behalf of all of Nedé, I'm sorry."

His gaze sweeps the circle of Brutes, his expression impossible to read. Finally he says, "No need to be sorry, Dom Reina. A dog can hardly imagine being a coyote."

He says it so plainly, so free from longing or deprivation, I have to fight back the emotions bubbling up on his behalf.

Suddenly Torvus is taking the platform and calling for silence. I shake away the longing to comfort Neechi, forced to give the Brute leader my undivided attention.

Balancing his weight equally over a wide stance, Torvus seems in no hurry to begin. Our Politikós could learn something of commanding an audience from his confident ease.

"As you see," he finally begins, standing in front of his chair on the platform, "the Nedéan has returned. She warns of coming danger."

In a strange déjà vu, I'm swept back to the last time Torvus talked about me at a fire meeting. Dáin interrupted with plans of his own. So as Torvus explains that they shouldn't be alarmed by our presence, I subconsciously scan the perimeter for a cruel, freckled face.

"What about the cubs?" someone asks. I recognize the speaker as Ori, the Brute who was caring for Jonalyn's baby earlier.

"We mean to deal with the Matriarch before she has a chance to find us. Nevertheless, the fourteen cubs and the youngest boys will remain guarded here. Six men travel with me: Jase, Rohan, Galion, Dantès, Théo, and Jem. The rest of you will be assigned to scout, man traps, stand watch, and continue the normal duties."

"What about the Nedéan?" another Brute asks.

"She has agreed to lead us to our target."

Bri's knee bounces agitatedly; she strains at her bonds, as if testing their strength.

"They promised not to hurt anyone else," I whisper, defending myself.

"Oh? Perfect," she seethes. "'Cause we have a long history together to ensure they'll keep a promise."

I don't realize until it's too late that she has managed to slip a hand free. Quick as a tail twitch, she jumps up, steals a blade slung across Jase's back, and sprints toward the woods.

Jase meets my gaze for only a millisecond before taking after her, drawing a weapon from his thigh as he runs. I scramble behind, sidestepping trees and dodging limbs.

Stupid Bri! What will Jase do when he catches her? What will the *others* do? She might be as good as dead.

Realizing she won't outrun her pursuer, the brazen Alexia soon turns on her heel and slashes. Jase meets the blow with his shorter blade. The clank of bone on bone rings hollow compared to the metal Alexia weapons we're used to, but the sharp edges will cut through skin just as surely.

"Bri, stop!" I scream. "Jase!" Neither of them slow.

Bri thrusts viciously, her panicked movements consistent with fear. The Brute meets each thrust, protecting his body from her blows. I'm not an expert in a Brute's abilities, but it seems to me he's holding back, choosing the defensive when he could attack. *Why?*

Bri's confidence grows, making her sloppy. When she over-extends, he shows his real strength, chopping at her weapon so hard he knocks it clean from her hand. Before she can reach for it, he pushes her hard into a broad tree trunk. He grips her arm with one hand; the other presses the flat of his blade to her throat. She freezes, no doubt expecting the death blow she would have certainly dealt him.

"Get it over with," she barks, fear and defeat mingling with her usual sharp tone, sweat beading on her forehead. Jase presses more firmly; he could take her life with a quick slice.

His chest heaves, and he holds her gaze with burning intensity. Without moving the blade, he asks, "Why are you so afraid of us?"

"Because . . . you're Brutes!" she sputters, like it's obvious.

"And what of it? What have we done to you?"

She doesn't think before hurling back, "You hurt women!"

"Oh, and you've never hurt us? What do you call that *Gutless* you brought with you?"

I've never heard Jase so forceful. Then again, Bri brings out the worst in most of us.

"What about the attacks?" she spits back. "I saw one myself."

Jase leans forward, their faces now centimeters apart. "What Dáin did is inexcusable, but a man can only take so much." He suddenly steps back and lowers the blade, control returning to his voice. "We're not asking for anything that isn't rightly ours."

She stares at his lowered weapon, relief and confusion warring with pride.

"And the Matriarch is yours to take?" Her tone remains hot, but some of the fire in it has withdrawn, mirroring his blade.

"Teera plans to kill them all," I interject. "Every last one. How is that fair—to punish some for the crimes of others? These Brutes didn't attack Nedé. Shouldn't they have a right to defend themselves?"

Bri doesn't take her eyes from Jase. "That depends." She moves toward him, so close their noses might touch if she were taller. "You haven't struck yet, but *would you*, Brute?"

He doesn't answer. His broad frame stands unmoving; his eyes hold hers, unblinking.

Without breaking his gaze, she stomps on his foot with the heel of her riding boot and grinds it back and forth for good measure. Her body tenses, ready for a fight.

His brow furrows, but he doesn't strike—doesn't even twitch. If I were in his shoes, I'd deck her. Twice. That's obviously what she's aiming for—and probably deserves. Instead he remains still as a stone carving.

Jase controls his body with impressive restraint. If she's looking for proof they're not all animals, that they possess self-control, surely she has it. I can't say I'm not grateful to see proof of it myself.

"Fine," she concedes reluctantly. "I'll stay for now. But if they murder us in our sleep, Rei, I'll track your butt down in the afterlife and kill you again."

She bumps into my shoulder on her way toward the fire ring.

The small crowd that followed the commotion turns back too, eager to get on with the meeting so we can get to the food.

All the Brutes except one.

Rohan smacks Jase's chest. "You wanted to, though," he says, a little too playfully, I think, for the tense situation we just escaped.

Jase shakes his head, a half smile relaxing the marked tension in his jaw. "Maybe."

They exchange a laugh.

I can't help but ask. "Why didn't you?"

"Because brawn without control makes you an animal."

"Power without virtue . . . ," I muse quietly.

Jase raises a quizzical brow.

"It's the Nedéan motto: 'Power without virtue is tyranny.'"

Rohan acknowledges me for the first time tonight. I don't know why I know it's the first time. I just do.

I meet his gaze in the near darkness, surprised to find it holds the same strange urgency as that evening in the treetops during my last visit.

"Seems we all have to choose," he says, then turns away, suddenly deep in thought.

We make our way back to our seats. Understandably, even though Bri's hands have been retied, Torvus watches her closely while he answers a few more questions.

"When do we start?"

"Do we have enough weapons?"

"Does the Rescuer know?"

Torvus doesn't attempt to answer the last question. Instead he seems to grow simultaneously tired and agitated, flopping into his chair.

"Eat," he says.

Immediately the Brutes descend on the roasting animals, hacking away the outer layer of charred flesh to the tender meat beneath. They skewer chunks on long, stripped sticks and pass them around the circle, followed by jugs of chicha.

Twice I catch Torvus staring at me, slumped in his high-backed chair on the platform. The second time our eyes meet, he rises and makes for the Jungle without a word. Jase said the leader never stayed long after eating—that he tired easily of their antics. But I suspect tonight his hasty exit has more to do with the other reason Jase gave: I remind Torvus "too much of someone." It must be Mother. And now that she's gone, how the reminder must sting.

What little inhibition remained around the circle disappears with their leader's departure. With food in their bellies and spirits lifted with drink, their unrestrained mirth rises with the curling smoke, ever higher into the deep black of night. Once the music begins—a single drum at first, evolving into a rhythmic orchestra of eclectic instruments—the Brutes all but forget four outsiders invaded their camp today.

This time it doesn't take much for Jase to coax me into the fray of dancing. Though, even with a functional shoulder, I have as much rhythm as a spinning scarecrow. No one seems to mind my lack of talent; in fact, they seem genuinely honored I'm trying.

Jonalyn is a harder sell, but eventually I convince her that we should humiliate ourselves together. I've always found her especially beautiful when she laughs; tonight she radiates pure loveliness. If only for the briefest of escapes, she appears to forget the danger and loss of the past few weeks. In this moment, she is the sister I remember. The sister I have terribly missed.

"Oh, Reina," she laughs above the din. "Who knew they'd be *fun*?"

"Ha!" I return. "Definitely more entertaining than a roomful of stuffy Senators."

As we stomp and sway, spin and twist, between bodies I catch a glimpse of Jase approaching Bri where she sits on the ground, back against the log, arms crossed. He crouches down to hand her a coconut shell and skewer of meat. A figure passes by, obscuring my view; when it moves, I see Jase has braved sitting down beside her.

Jonalyn takes my arm and swings me in circles. With each revolution I crane my neck to make sure Bri doesn't do something stupid. Amazingly, it doesn't seem she plans to run him through. In fact, she even smiles at something he says.

Another revolution and I smack dizzily into something solid.

"Ow—I'm sorry," I laugh.

Ori regains his balance, mumbling his own apology. As he walks away, Jonalyn disconnects from me to follow after him.

"The baby?" I overhear her ask.

"It's Jem's night for cub duties," he says, avoiding her eyes. He begins to walk on, then, turning back, adds, "He named him Finch."

Halting, she repeats, "Finch." A thoughtful crease folds her brow.

Ori slips back into the throng churning around the fire.

Jonalyn calls back to me, "I think I'd better rest." Then she returns to her seat by Neechi.

I'm about to follow after her when a deep voice behind me says, "I heard you apprehended an armed cub tonight."

I wheel around a little too quickly, knowing who I'll find.

A smile curls his thick lips. "The clan thanks you for your service." He dips his head in feigned gratitude.

I smack his arm.

"Ow," he groans, pretending to be hurt. "Why are you women so violent?"

"Did you come over here just to make fun of me?"

"No."

"Then why?"

"To tell you that what you did was brave."

"Disarming Pip?" I laugh.

He shakes his head and says something, but a passing drum drowns out his words.

I shout above the music, "What?"

He leans closer, angling toward my ear. He smells of smoke and damp earth. "Rescuing Dáin," he says, clearly now. "It was brave of you."

One of the dancers bumps my back, and I stumble into Rohan's unmoving body. Heat immediately burns my cheeks, and I back up as far as the pressing crowd will allow, though it's barely a step. Rohan doesn't seem bothered by my unintentional breach of personal space. He glances around, then presses a hand to my back and guides me toward the perimeter so we can avoid being trampled by the escalating fire dances.

Once we're clear of the carousing mass, I confess, "Rescue Dáin? I'd say it was more of a *release*, and I don't know how brave it was. Stupid, more likely."

I wish he wouldn't smile. Now I have to try not to stare, a battle I'm decidedly losing.

"But you sent him. To warn us." He studies my face.

"Yes."

"Why?"

Why does he make me so nervous? I can't keep two thoughts together around this Brute. "I . . . I don't know. For the Gentles, I guess."

If I didn't know better, I'd say a flash of hurt burns in his dark eyes. "The Gutless?"

Is it my imagination, or does the Jungle suddenly cool? "I want to help them."

"Help *them*?"

"It's not right that we gentle them without their knowledge."

"But *with* their knowledge—that would be alright?"

I snap back, "No, I—I don't know."

He studies me with equal parts curiosity, urgency, and . . . something I can't place.

"I need you to know," he nearly whispers.

His gaze burns through me, searching, fierce, magnetic. I could run from those eyes. Or I could step into them.

For all the unusual events of the evening—Pip's antics, Bri's escape attempt, the merriment and food—none of them keep sleep at bay like the encounter with Rohan. I retrace his words over and again, replay each glance, every chance touch. There are dozens of Brutes at Tree Camp. None of them draw my attention the way he does. None make me stumble over my words or chase sleep away. *Why?*

Neechi snores, sprawled comfortably on the floor. Bri, lying on Dáin's former hardwood cot opposite mine, stares up at the ceiling. Jonalyn's is situated perpendicular to ours, along the wall, her head resting near mine.

"You asleep?" she whispers.

I shift my head toward her in answer.

"They're nothing like I imagined," she confesses quietly. "Why didn't Mother tell us sooner?"

"She said it was for our protection."

The thrum of insect chatter pulsates in the small room, drifting in through the netted half of the walls. Silvery moonlight traces my sister's lovely features.

"I don't know how I'll leave him," she says.

"The baby?"

She nods. A tear slips from her eye, illuminated like liquid starlight.

"Are you afraid they won't care for him?"

"No, not exactly. I can't explain it, Rei. It's just different, knowing what he'll become. I've never felt this way about a baby— I mean, about a *Gentle* baby."

"A Brute baby."

She sighs. "Maternos know better than to get attached—you know from the start you'll be sending them away eventually, and you know it's for everyone's good." She reaches across to play with a strand of my hair. "But now I don't know what's for our good anymore—or for his. And if letting them be Brutes is best, how can I forgive myself for—" her voice trembles, then cracks, "for the first one? The one I sent to another finca?" A second tear chases the first. I brush it away.

"You didn't know," I soothe.

"And now that I do?"

"You'll do something about it."

"Like Mother."

I smile, imagining her trekking through the Jungle with tiny Brute babies. Like we just did.

"No," I say, "like *you*."

She seems pleased with my confidence in her, and we rest awhile, each absorbed in our own private thoughts, until her eyes shut and her breathing slows.

But I still can't sleep. Not without knowing what Rohan meant by his questions. Why does he care so much why I warned them, anyway?

Here, now, without his striking features muddling up my mind, I can think of seven better ways I could have explained why I released Dáin.

I don't trust the Matriarch either.

I didn't want Teera to destroy them.

I wanted to see him.

No, I would *never* tell him that. Still, was my answer so bad? Why *wouldn't* he want me to help the Gentles?

Bri shifts restlessly, flipping to her side.

"I'm glad you stayed," I whisper.

"Yeah, well, I figured my chances one-on-one with a Brute were slim."

"Naw, you could have taken him."

She smirks.

I press a little further. "Do you see now why I came back? Why I couldn't let Teera kill them?"

She shrugs.

I'll take that as progress.

"I still don't trust them," she mutters. "You've obviously been here before. Was it—?"

"The night of the raid," I finish for her. "Callisto and I fell behind you and the others. I saw some of them making for the Jungle, and I took after them. I almost had a shot, but they got the upper hand. Dáin might have killed me, but Rohan and Jase got to him first. They saved me, then . . ." There's really no way to soften this part. "Then drugged me and brought me here."

Her incredulous stare makes me cringe. "Let me get this straight. One attacked you, and some others saved you by drugging and kidnapping you?" she whispers fiercely.

"Dáin is the one who was attacking fincas, not the Brutes here. Torvus was against it."

"But he didn't stop this Dáin?"

I have nothing to say to this. She's right—Torvus knew about the attacks, Rohan and Jase knew about the attacks. They decried his actions as inexcusable. Torvus kicked him and his accomplices out of camp. But why *didn't* they put a stop to it? Why didn't they put an end to *him*?

"Look," she continues. "They aren't quite what I pictured Brutes to be, I'll give you that. I can even see what Jase means about wanting what is theirs. But I still say there was a reason the foremothers gave them whatever it was that gentled them—the vaccine or whatever. The attacks themselves are proof they aren't safe. At least not all of them."

"But what of us?" I argue back, trying to keep my volume from waking Jo and Neechi. "Are we 'safe'? What we've done to the Brutes by gentling them—you saw the clinic at the Center, Bri. They were begging to die. You watched the Matriarch murder the Gentle at the Hive yourself, for no reason and with no remorse. And she'll do worse. If these Brutes are monsters, how is *she* not one?"

She rolls onto her back, chewing her lip. "I still don't trust them."

Something Rohan said tonight simmers to the surface, and I repeat it as much to myself as to her.

"Seems we all have to choose."

She turns to face me again. "I did choose. I chose to follow you into this death trap, remember? I have no problem killing Teera, or Jamara either, if it paves the way for you to become Matriarch. But if you think these Brutes are going to dance around a fire while you take your rightful place, you're delusional. They're in it for power, just like Teera."

Power . . . tyranny . . . Is it possible to have one without the other? I answer my unvoiced question with a single word: *virtue*. If power without it leads to tyranny, then virtue is the only way to keep a leader or system free from tyranny. So the question is, which of us—women or Brutes—have more virtue?

That's a question I can't begin to answer.

CHAPTER FOURTEEN

As we descend the tree the next morning, a heavy aroma of cit-rus and jasmine envelops us even before I notice that the ground resembles the fabled snow of the old world. Jase opens the gate, and I'm already jumping down, entranced by the peculiar sight, itching to get a closer look.

No, not snow. The ground around the base of the mahogany is carpeted with thick-petaled, pinwheel-shaped blossoms. Someone has created a living, fragrant frosting of plumeria flowers in creamy whites, palest pinks, and barely yellows. They gather in mounds and slip between underlying palm fronds.

"Who did this?" I breathe.

"Torvus," Rohan says, coming alongside us.

"*Torvus?*" I glance past Rohan toward the Brute leader's house, partially visible through the curtain of Jungle. The single plumeria blossom carved on his door echoes the otherworldly display. "Why?"

Rohan shrugs, but Jase grows thoughtful. "I suspect to honor her." He gives me a meaningful look, and I instantly understand.

"If there comes a day," I sing softly, "when you can't find me . . ." My throat tightens, choking me into silence.

Jonalyn picks up the refrain. "Lay my flowers there, by the mahogany tree." She turns away, covering her face with her hands.

Skirting along the edge of the extravagant display, I lift a single blossom and spin it in my fingertips, inhaling the rich fragrance as if it could conjure a memory of her. Torvus must have stripped the flowers from every plumeria tree from here to Nedé. To honor a woman he'll never see again.

What kind of deep devotion does that?

"But . . . wasn't he angry with her?" I question Jase.

He comes closer to answer, affording us a little privacy. "He couldn't forgive her for leaving him."

"Leaving? But she lives—lived—in Nedé."

"I don't know the details. I just know he made that house for her, but 'lost her' to Nedé. That's all he told me."

"Lost her . . . ," I whisper, the final line of Mother's song pounding like a downpour in my ears.

I lost my love, at the mahogany tree.

She did love him, and he loved her with the devotion of ten thousand blooms.

What must it be like to love someone that way? Not with the affection of a family member or friend, but with a oneness that defies explanation, as Mother said. For a heart to entwine with another, like a strangler fig enveloping a ceiba in an inseparable, strangely symbiotic embrace. To completely disregard the Articles and give yourself wholly to another.

Involuntarily, my curiosity wanders to Rohan, whose eyes are fixed steadily on me. As always, he exudes an untamed energy, like the Jungle put on clothes today. All the draw of the wild, embodied in two broad shoulders, within the set of his jaw, in the curve of his lips. And the smallest flutter of understanding ignites inside me.

I force myself to look away . . . eventually. But not before he's walking my direction. Or am I pulling him toward me with some kind of invisible magic?

He stops a respectful distance away. "I'm sorry," he says, and it takes me a moment to realize he's talking to me, even though Jonalyn is busy examining the flowers, and Jase has gone, and I'm the only other person in sight.

"For what?"

"Your mother. You were close to her."

"Not as close as I should have been. She was an angel. Me—not so much."

His cheek twitches, revealing a dimple I've never noticed. "We all have our faults."

"Do we? And what are yours?" I ask him, not really meaning to. I guess my conversation with Bri has brought my doubts too close to the surface.

He considers my question. "I've made my mistakes," he says. He has the look of someone considering whether to say more, but Jase interrupts before he has a chance to decide.

Already five meters off the ground, en route to retrieve Neechi and Bri, he calls down, "Rohan, take them to the kitchen. I'll meet you there."

"Breakfast already?" I ask, perfectly content to change the subject.

"Preparations," he corrects. "We've got a lot to do before nightfall."

Jonalyn falls in beside me as we follow him toward the path

adjacent to the orchard. But I can't help glancing over my shoulder one more time. *She would have loved them.*

———————

The kitchen hut and surrounding vicinity already swarm with busy Brutes, three or four dozen, gathered in smaller groups. Each cluster attends to a specialized task, some twisting ropes and tying thick nets, others carving spears and assembling bolas—the strange weapon that took Callisto down the night of Dáin's attack. Younger Brutes fill clay vessels with water and food, strip carcasses of their meat, and lug fruit from the orchard, dumping green mangoes, thick plantains, and rough-skinned mamey fruit into leaf-lined underground lockers.

The more time I spend at the Brutes' camp, the less reliable I find the limited facts I was taught about them. My initial assumptions seem to constantly shift and re-form, being molded by the tutor of experience with each new interaction. As I scan the group now, working with diligent focus on their assigned tasks, I notice even more variation than I've perceived to this point. Oh, they're all Brutes—no doubt about that. As a class of human, they're as distinctive as Gentles or women. But within their kind, they also possess variations in color, size, hair texture, and personality. Some are shy, like Ori, while others—hello, *Jase*—are as friendly as young pups. Their skin tones span every shade I see at home in Nedé—from weathered thatch to oiled mahogany, bronzed further by the sun. Their voices possess a strangely deep timbre, but they don't all rumble like Torvus's. And their bodies . . . obviously, they change as they get older, just as ours do, but even among the Brutes who seem about my age or a few years older—like Rohan, Jase, and the others Torvus plans to take with us to Nedé—no two are alike. Hard labor has done its work on them all. Even so, some wear their might like an understated garment: surprising strength concealed in a sinewy physique. Others resemble stallions, their pronounced muscles chiseled with peculiar definition.

Rohan leads us to a table lined with eight large rucksacks, made from hides and fashioned with two straps for carrying on one's back.

"Our job is to fill these with the supplies we'll need for our journey. We have three days."

"*Three days?* I thought Torvus said we'd have a week to prepare."

"Yeah, well, you'll find once a man has an idea, he's antsy to get it done."

I count the empty bags again. One for Torvus, six for his men, one for me. "We'll need two more. Bri's coming, and I'm not leaving Neechi here."

"Make that *three* more," Jonalyn interjects, looping her arm through mine. My older sister barely reaches my chin, but in this moment she somehow projects the commanding presence of an Alexia.

Rohan looks between us. "Torvus won't like it."

I feign annoyance at her. "My friends don't know how to take no for an answer."

When he goes to find more sacks, I grow serious with my sister. "Are you sure, Jo? This will be dangerous."

"Like marching into the Jungle and consorting with Brutes? I know, Rei. But . . . what you said last night, about me doing something, like Mother . . . that's my purpose now."

"What about La Fortuna? Your children?"

"Now I have children here to worry about too. I'm going with you for all of them, because something needs to change, for all of us."

Jase ambles into the hut with Bri and Neechi on either side.

"Where's Rohan?" the affable Brute asks. It's barely midmorning and already he appears ready to conquer the world.

"He went to get more rucksacks." I notice something missing from Bri's wrists.

"You let her go free?"

Jase looks sideways at Bri, playfulness warring with caution. "She promised to be good."

"Like an angel," she says, closing her eyes reverentially for effect.

Jase shakes his head. To me he says, "When he gets back, tell him I'm going to work on weapons with these two."

With eyebrow raised, I pull Jase aside for a private word. "Are you sure that's a good idea?"

"Absolutely," he says, loud enough for Bri to hear. "Better to put a weapon in her hand where I can see it than wonder what would happen if she found one behind my back." He laughs out loud at his own joke. That deep, goofy joy of his gets me every time.

"Alright. But could Neechi tend to the horses before he joins you? They're worn out from our journey here, and there's no one better to care for them."

Neechi's cheeks turn ruddy and he twists his hands, probably with equal parts nerves and pride.

"Sure," Jase consents. He calls for a nearby Brute who is busy assembling a strange contraption resembling a giant spoon on a spring which they call a catapult. "Théo, take this . . . *man* to their animals, will you? Make sure he has whatever he needs to care for them."

I'm struck by how closely Théo resembles a Brute version of Trinidad—with chocolate-bronze skin, fair eyes, and dark, thick hair twisted into golden-tinged clumps that would hang past his shoulders if they weren't tied back. He eyes Neechi briefly before instructing him to follow. "Come on then."

When they're out of earshot, I turn to Jase.

"You called Neechi a man. Didn't you mean Gutless?"

Jase stares after Théo and Neechi for a long moment. "Robbing a man of his spirit doesn't make him less of a man."

"Do the others agree with you?"

"No, not all. Not even half. But having people agree with you isn't as important as knowing you're right. Look at you—I bet most Nedéans would consider you a traitor for being here now, helping us like this."

"Yes, they would," Bri answers for me.

Jase ignores her. "But you're here anyway. Even if none of the others agree with me, I don't fault the Gutless—the *Gentles*—for what's been done to them. That Neechi? He's doing the best he can with what he's got. He followed you clear into the Jungle, even with the cards dealt him. I'd say that makes him as much of a man as I am."

He gives me a tight smile before adding, "That doesn't mean I won't fight so others aren't disadvantaged the same way."

I think I understand what he means.

Jase leads Bri to a pair of stumps outside the hut, next to an enormous pile of coconuts, moving a bundle of long sticks between them. Handing her a short steel knife, he sits opposite her and shows her the correct places to slice away the tree pulp, then how to lash the tip with a sharp, shiny stone.

"She's harder to read than a stormy sky," Jonalyn says, watching them. "Do you think she'll help us, or betray us?"

I consider last night's conversation with Bri, and the fact that she's sitting nearly knee-to-knee with a Brute today.

"We're talking about Brishalynn. Who knows what she'll do." Still, something tells me she has tabled her plans to reach Adoni. "I don't think she'll try the same stunt twice. Stab us all in our sleep, maybe—" I play-grimace—"but not run."

Within a stone's throw, other groups of Brutes mend, assemble, or clean a plethora of weapons: fat blades on stout sticks, bolas, thin spears, and catapults. Another group lashes thick bamboo poles together, creating what appears to be a type of cage, large enough for a small Brute to stand in. A quantity of similar cages are already assembled, lined in neat rows behind a long hut.

Rohan returns with one more empty bag slung over his shoulder.

"Only found one. We have more at the cave, but we can fill these for now."

"What's 'the cave'?" I ask.

"One of our hunting camps."

"You have other camps?"

"Six."

"Do other Brutes live in them?"

"Not yet. In another year some of us plan to relocate to make room for new cubs, but for now we use them when we hunt, and to store supplies. Oh, and for scouting."

"Scouting?"

"I forgot how many questions you ask," he says, with a slight twinkle in his eye.

"I forgot how many secrets you keep."

He sighs. "How do you think we knew you were coming?"

I recall my suspicion that we were being watched, by the river and in the Jungle. "I knew it—I knew something was out there." Although slightly unnerving, the realization also offers the subtle satisfaction of being right. "So where is this cave?"

"You've been there—or nearly there. It's upstream from the chute." He fails to completely push down a mischievous grin.

Jonalyn gives me an inquisitive look.

"Oh, I remember the chute," I say dramatically, snatching a bag from Rohan's grip. "I'm glad you think my near death is funny."

"She was fine," he defends himself to Jo. "It was just a little raft ride."

"Into the belly of the earth, with Brutes who darted me the night before! How was I to know you weren't going to leave me for bat food?"

At the mention of bats, I suddenly recall the press of his body against my back, a human shield against the onslaught of crazed creatures. I wonder if he, too, remembers the moment, because he smiles a little, briefly catching my gaze.

"I'd never leave you," he says. Then, opening the sack, he adds, "Not for bat food anyway. Jaguar, maybe. They're nobler creatures."

Jonalyn finds this funny.

I wonder why it makes my insides flutter.

"Here," he says, divvying up the remaining sacks. "Each will need some dried meat and fruit, cohune nuts, a water flask, and a sleeping net. We'll divide the rest of the supplies among the eleven of us. If we make most of what we need ourselves, we can leave more supplies for those who remain."

We spend the next two and a half days assembling everything eleven people will require for a weeklong journey. We'll skirt the western and southern borders of Nedé, under the cover of the wilds, all the way to the Halcyon Sea. There, something they call a two-hull will take us to an island, allowing us to approach Phoenix City by sea, so we don't alert the Matriarch and Alexia to our approach. The "by sea" part sounds terrifying, but Jase assures me it's safe. Again, not exactly comforting.

At least the preparations keep my mind off the hollow ache that surfaces whenever I'm not busy. What time is there to grieve

Mother, to mourn Tre, to suffer the loss of Callisto, when we're working from sunup to sundown?

So I give myself wholly to the tasks assigned. We mend the sacks where the leather has worn through with thread made of hibiscus tree fibers and a bamboo needle. Sleeping nets are woven with three-ply sisal twine. We wrap servings of dried meat in banana leaves, roast the nuts, and make a paste from plants and cohune oil that Rohan swears keeps bugs from biting. As we forage for fresh herbs to replace the dried bundles we pack, Rohan patiently explains to Jo and me the properties of each leaf, bark, root, and flower we collect. We assemble hunting supplies, fashioning snares and fitting arrows with a strange, clawlike cage for a tip, which Rohan says captures birds with less waste. He seems to know everything there is to know about hunting and the uses of plants, weather patterns, and, gratefully, surviving in the Jungle.

His manner softens toward Jonalyn and me with each new interaction, eventually trusting us to work alone for periods of time while he attends to other matters. I secretly hope his disappearances aren't tied to Dáin, but if Jase was serious about us all needing to work together—and with Torvus refusing to yield—I can't, unfortunately, rule out the possibility.

Talking with Rohan becomes more natural, at least on matters of net sizes and plant genuses. I don't gape at his strangely shaped muscles, or flinch when he accidentally brushes my arm. As fear gives way to familiarity, I study him while we work. He always wipes his hands on his trousers before holding a weapon, as if he must remove any impurity before touching something so sacred. I notice his intense concentration when he's working, oblivious to conversation around him. Everything the Brute does reflects precision and purpose. No task is frivolous, no movement wasted.

I notice my own strange tendencies too—that I am painfully aware of his presence, or lack thereof, at any given moment. I catch, too, the slight tilt of my body toward him whenever we're within sight of each other, like a helianthus flower bending toward the passing sun.

Aside from the strange spell he puts on me, as the days pass, we ease into a comfortable partnership.

The other Brutes, too, grow accustomed to our presence, sitting with us at meals, acknowledging us as we pass, asking questions about Nedé, and telling us stories around the fire at night—tales of hunting misadventures, exceptionally large prey, and mischievous Brute antics.

By late Wednesday afternoon, Rohan, Jo, and I have nearly finished packing the sacks with the needed supplies. Bri, Jase, and Neechi have made enough weapons to outfit every Brute in the Jungle, let alone our small contingent of eleven. There hasn't been a single sighting of Dáin. Despite our tenuous circumstances and unclear future, in this moment I feel peace. As the midafternoon sun slides west, my shoulders relax a little. I actually take a moment to savor, rather than inhale, the unique flavors of the smoked meat, juicy mango, and fresh coconut milk of our meal.

Bri leans across the table to steal a strip of my meat.

I slap at her hand half-heartedly. "So, how's it going?"

"Fine, I guess, if one can ignore the endless drip of optimism from a certain Brute." She tips her head, not so subtly, toward Jase. "I have to hand it to them, though—Brutes like their blades even more than Alexia do." She concludes her hesitant compliment by swiping another strip of peccary from my banana-leaf plate.

"I can get you some more," Jase offers her.

"Where's the fun in that?" she asks, the fringe of her blonde bangs framing an exaggeratedly innocent face.

Of all of us, Jase finds her response most humorous, and I smile at his easy acceptance of my testy friend.

Friend. Two months ago, I never would have imagined using

that word to describe Bri. Not even two weeks ago. But I suppose that's what she is now. Of course, our touch-and-go, unpredictable friendship won't keep me from dishing out a little of what she so easily gives.

I lean toward Jase, only pretending to whisper, "I'm shocked she hasn't driven you crazy yet."

He grins. "I think she's holding back."

Bri feigns offense at Jase before downing the last of her coconut milk, but in the split second it takes her eyes to meet his and dart away, her act momentarily slips, revealing the smallest flicker of respect for the amiable Brute.

As we finish our meal and the others return to weaponry, Rohan speaks for the first time since we sat down. "Let's fill the flasks at the stream so we won't diminish the stores here."

Jonalyn and I stand to accompany him just as a slew of cubs rustle into the kitchen with Ori and one of Rohan's hunting partners—Dantès, was it? He's slightly shorter than Ori, with wild, sun-bleached brown hair, and smooth, deeply tanned skin. A cord strung with shells hangs around his neck. Jonalyn watches the troop with intense interest. I soon realize why: Ori has a tiny passenger on his back, baby Finch, riding snug in a sling.

"Might I help with the cubs instead?" she asks Rohan, a little too hopefully.

He seems unsure. For her sake, I push a little. "Jo's an amazing Materno. She'd be a big help, and she won't give anyone trouble."

While Rohan consults with Ori and Dantès, a familiar muddy cub comes running up with his friends, stopping just short of my legs. He stares up with big, round eyes.

"Seems you learned your lesson," I tell bold little Pip. "And so have I." I crouch down so we're eye to eye. "And I kept my promise," I whisper, winking at him. "I didn't tell Jase."

Pip's tiny, gapped teeth glow bright white against his clay-brown face. The smallest of his two companions slowly scoots closer, then places a curious, sticky hand on my cheek, as if testing whether I'm real. I cover it with my own.

When Rohan returns, the three boys scamper back to Ori and the other young ones.

"You'll take Dantès's shift," Rohan instructs my sister. "But these aren't Gutless cubs. Follow Ori's instructions."

She nods, then crosses to the other end of the kitchen to help Ori prepare food for the rambunctious lot.

"Thank you," I tell him, smiling at the way Jo so easily slips into the role of caretaker.

Rohan and I gather up the flasks and make our way to the stream, about half a kilometer from camp. When we passed this bend yesterday, I didn't notice the deepened bottom here, which looks to have been dug out to create a type of bathing hole. Two Brutes shake themselves dry on the bank, their sparse clothing dripping wet, having been washed right along with their bodies.

We trudge upstream another ten meters. The bubbling water creates a soothing backdrop to jabbering birds and monkey chatter, and the thick foliage along the streambed fills the visible world with vibrant shades of palm green, brilliant red, and cassia yellow. Violet hummingbirds hover and zip from scarlet-bush flower to flower, pausing to drink their fill from each tubular carafe before dashing off again.

When we reach a filling station, I crouch down next to Rohan on the wood platform. Here, a ring of large, mossy rocks surrounds a deeper well of clear water. Using one of the wooden ladles, I begin filling the flasks.

"Will this be enough water for the journey?" I ask.

"There are plenty of water sources on the way. But the first day, to the ruins, we won't pass a stream until afternoon."

"Ah."

We fall into silence, filling three more flasks. I want to talk, but I can't think of anything *not* obvious or idiotic to say. Besides, it seems half the time I open my mouth I offend him. So I opt instead to keep my lips shut, trying to enjoy the peaceful collision of water against rock and ignore the confusing drumming of my heart against my ribs.

Despite the endless curiosities of the plants and animals around me, I'm more aware of Rohan's movements—the bend of his elbow as he positions another flask over the stream, the flex of his thigh as he rocks back on his heels, the twitch of his cheek when I accidentally miss the flask's opening and water splashes off the rim into his face.

Twice I catch him staring at me, twice his gaze darts away, quick as the hummingbirds.

Though no words pass between us, I find myself pouring the water slower than a sloth, lengthening the moments I have here, with him, alone in a world of emerald ceiba and richly scented earth, singing kingfishers and an azure sky. And when I hear a branch snap nearby, why do I hope it's not another person—someone who might interrupt this quiet moment?

But when the last flask has been filled, I have no choice but to stand and prepare to return to the noise and interruptions of camp. As I sling a few flasks over my shoulder, the waterskins collide with a lump in my pants pocket.

"Oh, I have something for you," I say, trying to sound nonchalant.

Bemusement is far too endearing a feature on this Brute.

I reach into my pocket and, feeling the lumpy wooden gift, I have second thoughts. He's going to think me a fool.

"Actually, it's stupid. . . . Never mind."

"Come on," he coaxes, pulling my hand from my pocket. "Out with it."

My fingers reluctantly uncurl, revealing the small token. "I mean, it's nothing like what you gave me, but I *did* make it."

Rohan's lopsided grin nearly matches that of the roughly carved wooden monkey.

"Wow. It's amazing," he says.

Taking the angular token in his big hand, he turns it this way and that, examining my ten-year-old self's craftsmanship.

"I told you it was stupid," I laugh. "It's the first thing I ever carved."

"That makes sense."

I huff, snatching at it, but he keeps it just beyond my reach.

My cheeks warm with embarrassment. "I cut myself carving it and vowed we'd never part."

"I can see why. It's good. Really good," he exaggerates.

"Liar." I bump him with my shoulder playfully, and he instinctively grabs it with his free hand, holding me steady.

"Thank you, Reina," he says. It's a simple statement of gratitude, but hearing my name on his voice has a strange effect. Like the shade of a palm on a blistering day, winking starlight, or rich cream in morning coffee. I catch a breath and let it go all at once.

With one hand still on my shoulder, he positions the monkey next to my face. "I see a resemblance."

Even as I laugh, the word coaxes a flash, a question, from a teak leaf–littered forest.

"That day you found me at Bella," I start, "when I woke up, you were saying something about there being a 'resemblance.' What did you mean?"

"You were awake?"

I find a dangling vine suddenly bewitching. "While you carried me, yes. I was scared into shock, I think."

"I'm sorry I frightened you," he half-grins. "Jase had a hard time convincing me to go with him to the finca. Eventually he fessed up to his connection with the Rescuer, and with you. When I saw you, it was clear you and Jase were related."

"But," I tease, wanting to embarrass him just a little, "you said I was beautiful."

He doesn't stumble as I expect. Doesn't even blush. Instead he trails a surprisingly confident fingertip down my cheek, little pricks of electricity igniting in the wake of his touch. "You're the most beautiful creature I've ever seen."

Suddenly, it's as though the hanging lianas have wrapped themselves around us, tightening, drawing us inexplicably closer. He leans over me, and I feel the heat of him, find tiny flecks of amber in his dark eyes, notice the smallest cracks in his unsmiling lips.

I have the incomprehensible urge to know how those lips would feel against mine . . .

A sudden shout erupts from the bathing hole, snapping us out of the strange trance as quick as a blade severs cord. Other voices join the commotion, and Rohan springs into action, taking me by the arm as he runs toward the sound.

The two Brutes who were drying out near the bank are sprinting toward Tree Camp. In their place, a midsized, shirtless Brute is doubled over, sweat dripping down his smooth back and arms, panting like an overheated dog.

Rohan rushes toward him. "Galion—what is it?"

The Brute straightens as we approach, revealing dark, bushy eyebrows that angle toward his thin-bridged nose like a deep V. His face glistens with perspiration, except where a shadow of stubble covers his protruding chin and upper lip.

His voice is as thick as his wild, soot-colored hair. "They're coming."

"How many?" Rohan asks, calmer than I'd expect from someone who just discovered their enemies were approaching unannounced.

Galion takes a water flask I offer, gulping down its contents before answering. "A hundred by my count."

"That's all?" I ask, surprised.

Rohan scoffs. "*All?*"

"Knowing how mad Teera is, I expected her to send half the Alexia force."

"She'd be a fool to leave her land exposed, especially before knowing our location or numbers. It must be another scouting patrol."

Galion doesn't seem so convinced. "We've never seen a patrol that large. Besides, if they were scouting, they wouldn't have someone important with them."

"The Alexia with the dragon tattoo?" Rohan asks.

Galion shakes his head. "No. This leader isn't Alexia. But she's riding in like she and that bright tunic own the place."

"Jamara," I whisper.

Rohan straightens. "Who's she?"

I consider how to answer: The Matriarch's Apprentice? A Gentles Regimen worker so cruel I pity Kekuatan's entire labor force? The woman who tried to kill Bri and succeeded in beating me unconscious?

I settle on "No one you want to meet."

Rohan and Galion exchange a glance.

"I don't think we'll have a choice," Galion says. "They have a trail to follow." I don't miss his gaze darting my way. Neither does Rohan.

"It doesn't matter," the latter says, sensing my embarrassment. "They would have found us eventually."

Whether or not that's true, I can't say, but I feel awful knowing it's our tracks guiding the Alexia—led by none other than Jamara Makeda—straight toward Tree Camp.

"I'm so sorry."

Rohan rubs his jaw agitatedly, ignoring my apology. "How long do we have?"

"They passed El Fuego early this morning. I spotted the patrol from the lookout above the waterfall. I expect they'll arrive by nightfall—they're making good time."

I cringe anew at the reason why. And, without a baby requiring frequent stops or a Gentle's slower pace, they'd beat our time even if they didn't have a blasted map underfoot.

"Bats," I mutter. The surrounding Jungle has already taken on the softer quality of early evening. "We don't have much time."

"An hour, maybe two," Rohan agrees, seeming to make internal calculations. He smacks his fellow Brute between the shoulders. "Good work, Galion." Then he makes straight for Tree Camp.

I nearly jog to keep up with his long, purposeful strides, panic settling in. "I'm sorry, Rohan," I offer again, miserably. "I never considered someone might follow us." The reality of what I've done nearly suffocates me. It took all my courage to protect the Brutes by releasing Dáin—and for what? I led the danger right to their door like an idiotic child.

Rohan stops abruptly and turns me toward him, squeezing my arms a bit tighter than perhaps he means to. His expression isn't soothing or even forgiving, but neither does he reveal a shred of anger at my carelessness. His jaw might be tense, but his words are softer than I deserve. "Even if the entire Alexia force had followed you here, Reina, I'd still wish you back."

CHAPTER FIFTEEN

A LIGHT BREEZE RUSTLES THE BROAD LEAVES, crisscrossing around me like a botanical shield in the quickly fading light. As the sun sinks, the usual nighttime choruses rise. Buzzes, chatters, hums, and croaks fill the deep Jungle like an earthen vessel, drowning out any potential warning of the coming intruders. Bri crouches beside me on our perch a third of the way up the mahogany tree, bow in hand but not aimed, an ample supply of arrows stacked between us on the platform.

We didn't have time to test the Brute-crafted arrows on our Alexia bows before Torvus stationed us here, but it might not matter whether they fly true—we may not shoot them at all. When Torvus pierced me and Bri with a hard stare and asked whether we would fight *with* them, Bri said, "I won't shoot you, if that's what you're worried about. But I don't promise to shoot them, either."

She had voiced my own unease. I'd do anything to protect my sister or Neechi. I'd probably act rashly for Jase or Rohan. I might even go to *some* effort for Bri. But how could I attack my fellow Alexia, who are only obeying orders—innocent women, the brave defenders of Nedé? All they know of Brutes is what they've been told by the system ordering their approach. For the love of Siyah, part of me *still* wants to be among their ranks—standing for the Virtues—even as I perch in the enemy's camp.

When I met with him earlier, I reminded Torvus about our deal—that I would only help them find Teera if he didn't kill innocent Nedéans. I was admittedly a little fuzzy about where self-defense fell into that equation. In the end, I simply urged him to spare their lives if he could. Not surprisingly, he gave no indication he heard my request or planned to honor it. The Brute leader was impossible to read, per usual.

He did, however, strategically place us here in the tree, and made us swear we wouldn't shoot at all if we were conflicted. Should we find ourselves sympathetic to the Brute cause, he said, at least we'd be in a good position to use our archery skills. *And if we turned on the Brutes*, I surmised, *we'd be as far from him and his men as possible.*

Who could blame him for being cautious? One of us is the reason the Alexia know how to find Tree Camp, and the other tried to make an armed escape three days ago. Adding to our list of faults, we could count on two fingers the number of Nedéans Bri or I would shoot without hesitation, and according to Galion, only one of them is among those approaching. I guess you could say we're not exactly trustworthy allies. The fact that Torvus didn't tie us up and stuff us in his house for the duration of the night actually speaks to a measure of trust.

I'm glad to say I've earned it.

My sister, who, to my knowledge, has never held a weapon

in her life, valiantly offered to hide Finch and three other cubs in a cavernous tree trunk hollowed out by a strangler fig, so the assigned Brute could join another detail. I'd prefer to take my chances with the Alexia over the impossible task of keeping Brute cubs quiet. But she's a Materno, and as such, possesses something akin to magic with smallish humans.

When Jase asked Neechi whether he could fight, the Gentle looked as scared as a kitten dangled over the Jabiru, though devoid of frenzied clawing, which made him even more pitiable. As an alternative, Jase suggested that since they "don't have stumps big enough to hide the horses," Neechi should lead them half a kilometer south, and instructed him to stay hidden until he was sure it was safe to return. Then he gave Neechi two weapons and slipped one more into each of the three horses' saddlebags. Apparently, even a Gentle can't have too many knives. When Neechi disappeared into the darkening brush, I thanked Jase for taking care of my friend. If we're going to face an impossible foe, I feel better knowing Neechi and Jo are safe.

Funny—I guess I do understand something of Rohan's protectiveness.

Earlier, after he and I returned with news of intruders, he disappeared. I thought he must be readying the camp with Jase and the others, except just before I ascended the tree to join Bri at my post, he emerged unexpectedly from the outlying Jungle, heading *toward* camp. At the sight of me, he stepped double-time, making sure to intercept me before I reached the last hanging platform.

Rohan seemed especially rigid, but then, everyone had been jumpy in the hour since Galion brought news of the Alexia's approach. His brow furrowed as he appraised each of my weapons: the bow slung over my shoulder, a Brute-crafted blade strapped to my thigh, and his own bone dagger occupying the sheath at my hip.

Seeming satisfied with my arsenal, he asked, "Where will you be?"

"Up there," I said, pointing lamely toward the canopy, as if the meaning of "up" were ambiguous. Why does he make me so awkward? "With Bri."

Relief softened his stance some. "That's good."

"Why? You afraid I'll stab you in the back?" I teased.

"No."

"Worried I'll get myself killed?" When he didn't respond, my pride bristled just a little. "I can take care of myself."

"I'm sure you can," he conceded, but something else seemed lodged between his heart and his voice. With some effort, he finally put words to whatever led him to find me when there were a dozen other tasks probably calling for his skill. "I just . . . all hell might break loose tonight, and I don't know if I can protect you if it does."

"You don't have to protect me," I countered.

"Yes, I do."

He said it so urgently, as if begging me to understand. I think I did. He wanted to keep me safe, not because he thought me weak or incapable, but because he was afraid of what could happen. Because he cared . . . about *me*. Rohan protects those he cares about, like a Materno nurtures, like an Ad Artium creates, like an Alexia rides. It's just who he is.

"Whatever happens when they arrive," he said, "no matter *what*—promise me you'll stay up there?"

I considered his urgent sincerity, weighed it against my lingering pride that wanted to prove I didn't need safekeeping. Truthfully, I was still conflicted about the coming confrontation. Even if I found cause to fight, without Callisto to bolster my courage, it was running thin. And before me stood a Brute who seemed made of the stuff. If I sliced his skin, he'd probably bleed valor. In that moment I chose to trust his strength for the both of us.

"Okay," I promised.

He took my face in his hands, touched his forehead to mine. "Thank you," he said. "I'll find you when this is over."

I knew he would do anything to keep that promise.

Something told me he wanted to stay with me as much as I wished he would. But a moment later, he ran off to join the other Brutes scrambling to attend to the last details of Torvus's plan.

I watched him go, my skin tingling where his had touched mine, stunned by the strange longing welling up within me.

Was that what Mother had felt for Torvus?

I barely remember my ascent up the tree. I couldn't stop puzzling about the strange way Rohan made me feel—nervous but safe, exposed but . . . beautiful.

When I had reached Bri, I figured her sharp tongue would give me a respite from the swirling conflict inside. Instead, she stoked it.

"What was *that*?"

"What?"

She rolled her eyes. "You and Big Chest down there?"

Though she peered at me expectantly, I didn't answer. I didn't know *how* to answer.

Finally, she slumped back against the door of the tree hut. "Fine, keep your secrets. But you better be careful, Rei."

"You and I both need to be careful," I deflected. "The Alexia could be here any minute."

We took our positions and watched the outskirts of camp for movement.

We haven't budged since.

From our perch, we have a clear vantage point of the surrounding Jungle floor. Tree Camp itself seems hollow without the usual

Brute activity. No one carves or builds, prunes or yells. There's no gray smoke curling from smoldering coals in the fire ring, curing various strange kills on spits. Not a single hammock sags with the weight of a night guard catching up on sleep. With all of the cubs divvied up between hiding places, no small Brutes play tag among the mango trees in the orchard. Not a single laugh, grunt, or deep voice reverberates through the forest.

All is still and empty.

Within and beneath and above the seeming void, we wait, holding our collective breaths, hoping Torvus knows what he's doing. My fingers absently trace the weave of Callisto's horse-hair bracelet as we keep watch. Evening slips away, draining the surrounding Jungle of its vibrancy, replacing it with the color of uncertainty—the moments just before nightfall.

The Brute leader stands on the outer edge of Tree Camp like a living landmark, a proud statue, strong and unmoving, ready to intercept the Alexia when they make the final approach from the stream to camp.

And approach they do.

Their advance is heralded only by the quiet swish of bodies against brush, the snapping of a twig underfoot, the occasional snort of a horse.

"Well," Bri whispers, "I guess you don't have to worry *I'll* tell Adoni about the Brutes."

I'd laugh if I wasn't about to pitch my last meal.

There's at least a hundred Alexia—outnumbering the Brutes of fighting age more than four to one—advancing as close to orderly as the Jungle will allow, in five waves of twenty, more or less. Most ride, but some walk their slightly disheveled steeds. I notice immediately that a few Alexia don't have horses, and I wonder how many they lost on the approach—to injury, escape, or predators.

The Alexia close the distance to Torvus timidly, each with a bow or sword drawn, as if feeling intrinsically that something doesn't add up. They were expecting more.

Galion was right—this is no patrol. This is a contingent ready to carry out Matriarch Teera's greatest wish: the elimination of the Brute problem. And to do so, she sent her new protégée—no doubt to endear the people to Jamara when she eradicates the mysterious attackers.

Torvus draws himself up to his full height. "Who is your leader?"

Jamara maneuvers to the center of the front line, halting beside a familiar horse. I can just make out its gold-fringed dark mane, and though I can't quite see its rider from this angle, I know who the ranking officer is. There's only one Alexia fit to ride Midas— the second-in-command I long to see most, but want to see fight least.

Torvus, hopelessly outnumbered, doesn't flinch. His jaw remains set, his broad back and half his legs concealed by an array of weapons.

Jamara sits back on her horse like she's riding a throne, her features placid. Still, I notice she doesn't come within ten meters of the formidable Brute.

He bellows at her, "Why have you come?"

"To exact justice," Jamara seethes, gathering her nerve, "on those that dare attack Nedéan soil. And," she adds, "to retrieve any Nedéan traitors aiding our enemies."

"There are no such perpetrators here."

Jamara sneers with the calculated coldness birthed the moment she won the Succession. "Then we'll start with you."

She turns to Trinidad on her right, motioning for her to shoot.

The horses shift just enough that I'm able to see Trin's metal armbands as clearly as her concern. Her gaze quickly darts from a thick tree trunk to a shuttered hut, up to the network of bridges and buildings in the mahogany tree, then back to Jamara. She mutters something to the Apprentice, too quietly for us to hear. Jamara snarls back an impatient answer.

With a subtle resignation visible, perhaps, only to me, Trin obediently raises her bow, an arrow already nocked. My mentor's aim is unforgiving. If she shoots, not only will Torvus die, the might of the Brutes will be unleashed on her. That's the plan. I can't let that happen. I won't.

Before I can think about the merit of what I'm about to do, I scream, "Trin, don't!"

She hesitates at the sound of my voice, glancing toward my hidden perch in the great tree, peering carefully into the tangled limbs. The tip of her arrow sags at the same moment an impatient Jamara raises her own bow and shoots, poorly, at Torvus. Jamara's arrow misses by three meters—an embarrassing attempt at assassination, really. But Jamara's notoriously bad aim doesn't matter. Torvus instructed the Brutes that a direct attack was their signal to defend their home, their cubs, their lives.

When we were kids and feeling particularly adventurous, my sisters and I would canvass the brushy borders of Bella Terra, imagining we were wild animals, mystical fairies—whatever suited our age and mood. In these ventures, we'd occasionally spot a termite mound bulging from the brown earth or clinging to the bark of a palm. If my adventurous spirit turned mischievous—which, for some reason, only ever seemed to happen to me—I'd bat at the thing with a long stick. One strike was all it took for the inanimate structure to come alive, seething with tiny, angry mites that rushed around like a swirling cloud over the surface of the earth.

Jamara's intended strike stirs the camp like that now, drawing buzzing Brutes from hidden tree trunks and canopy huts like a frenzied wave, the air suddenly filled with yelling, whooping, and flying coconuts. So many coconuts.

Torvus is no fool. He knew the Alexia's bows and horses would give them the advantage in the open. Instead, the Brutes utilize their network of high perches and treetop bridges to handicap their enemy. For now, no Alexia can shoot; their hands are busy holding the reins of their bucking, prancing horses, or shielding their heads from the barrage of catapulted fruit.

Already some Alexia scatter, losing control of their panicked horses and galloping headlong into the darkening Jungle. Others fall into carefully concealed pits, horses and all, or get tangled in heavy nets dropped from the canopy.

Brutes zip from one end of camp to the other on the speed lines, creating the illusion that they can fly. The sky flyers carry axes but don't throw them. In fact, as I scan the frantic commotion, I realize the Brutes don't seem to be killing Nedéans at all. Arrows hit horses and a few women hold injured arms, but I don't see a single fatality. Not yet, anyway. Could Torvus actually have listened to me? Could they be trying to spare Alexia lives?

A dozen of the oldest Brutes join Torvus on the ground. Galion, Jem, and Théo immobilize horses with windmilling bolas, which bind the animals' legs and send their riders sprawling. As soon as a rider hits the ground, Jase, Rohan, or Torvus jumps into action, disarming and quickly binding her, wrists to ankles. They move through the ranks this way, impossibly fast, working their way outward from the tree.

It appears the Alexia force has already shrunk by half—bound, netted, trapped in pits, or knocked unconscious by coconuts. Jamara walks her horse backward toward the outskirts of the skirmish.

Bri sees her at the same moment I do and rocks forward onto her toes. "Oh no she doesn't," she protests, suddenly jumping to her feet.

"What are you doing?"

"There's no way she's getting out of here alive."

She slings her bow over her shoulder and practically jumps for the quickest route down: a speed line angling from our platform to a landing point fifty meters from the tree's base. Gripping the curved wooden bar, she flies down the rope like a hawk zeroing in on its prey, though landing with far less grace. Undeterred by her near-face-plant dismount, Bri picks herself up, draws an arrow from her hip quiver, and weaves in and out of horses, trees, and bodies toward our former fellow Candidate, dodging coconuts and ignoring everything and everyone else in her way. When she gets within ten meters, she takes shelter behind a trunk to steady herself, then leans into the open and takes aim.

Jamara turns her horse in a circle, trying to calm the steed amid the mayhem. She catches sight of Bri just as Bri's arrow strikes her horse's chest. The animal stumbles sideways, sending Jamara careening into the ground.

I hold my breath as Bri sprints toward the fallen Apprentice, swapping her bow for the Alexia short sword at her belt. Jamara struggles to rise, barely managing to get her own sword in a defensive position before Bri comes down with a hacking slice. Jamara blocks the attack, then pushes herself to her feet. For such a large woman, she moves with surprising speed. Bri and I have both been the unhappy recipients of that quickness, and we understand the strength of her fists. No one could beat her in hand-to-hand combat during training. Bri and I both had the bloodied faces to prove it—one of the few memorabilia we shared. If Bri loses her weapons, she'll be in trouble.

The duel is marked by adrenaline and fury on both sides, but Bri's thirst for revenge fuels her with uncanny precision and a skill I've never seen in the Amal girl.

A sudden, pained scream rattles the other side of the tree, one level above me, stealing my attention from the face-off. I watch in horror as a young Brute pitches forward and tumbles toward the ground, dropping his bow, smacking into branches and ripping through leaves as he falls.

Scanning the ground below, I can't see who shot the arrow, but one thing is clear: the steady stream of aerial projectiles from above has lessened to a trickle. The Brutes are running out of ammunition. As the supply dwindles, the Alexia have the good sense to reach for their bows.

I know I promised Rohan I'd stay in the tree, out of danger, but how can I let Bri go after Jamara alone while I sit here fiddling with fletching like a frightened child? No—even if I can't bring myself to shoot any Alexia, I can at least help Bri keep Teera's Apprentice from escaping.

I fumble for a handful of Brute arrows to supplement my quiver, stuffing the wooden shafts tip-down into the leather slots on my thigh.

Bri's hasty exit on the speed line leaves me only one option to get down from this tree. Scrambling onto the platform, I draw the rough rope hand over hand, lowering myself haltingly and not nearly fast enough, meter by agonizing meter. In a sparser section between branches, I'm helplessly exposed. An arrow whizzes past my ear and I shudder, quickening my pace. Apparently, my Alexia uniform doesn't offer me immunity. Jamara mentioned apprehending traitors. Are they watching for me?

Another arrow grazes the rope just above my head, confirming my suspicion. Several strands pop and fray. What remains of the rope creaks under the sudden strain.

My arms pull frantically, muscles burning with effort. "Hold, you stupid rope!" My only hope is to reach the bottom and find cover. Twenty meters to go . . . fifteen . . . Another arrow thunks into the platform railing, and the splayed rope looks ready to give way. If it snaps, I'm dead.

I scan the ground for the attacker just as the Alexia archer disappears under Théo's bulk as he slams into her. They tumble like Jungle cats, rolling into the brush. She struggles mightily, but the Brute pins her arms, then wrenches her weapon away, tossing it to the side.

The rope frays further, dropping the platform another few centimeters. I could try to reach above the tear in the rope and climb it back to the ledge, but I'd still be exposed. Panicked shouts and clanking metal fill my ears, muddling reason. My heart races with every tip and sway.

Sway. Sway! Maybe I can create enough momentum to reach a nearby branch. I start swinging side to side, carefully at first, then with more force, coaxing the platform into a rhythmic swing. *Closer, closer* . . . If I can just . . .

Suddenly, the last strand of rope gives way. The platform drops from beneath me, the momentum of my final swing carrying me just far enough to wrap my fingers around a thin limb. My feet grope for a foothold, finding nothing but air. The platform shatters against the Jungle floor, alerting every Alexia in the Jungle to my precarious position, including the last archer on earth I'd want to have sights on me: Trinidad.

She turns Midas away from the Brute she has just shot, spots me, and for a split second we lock eyes. Hers narrow into the same suspicious golden slits as the night she caught me outside the Center. She doesn't hesitate to take aim.

Trinidad—no! I scream. At least I mean to, but the sound gets blocked by the panic squeezing my windpipe. Weeks of secret training under her remarkable skill leave me no doubt what will happen when she shoots.

This is it. I'm going to die here. And not at the hand of just anyone, but the mentor I abandoned, the friend I asked to risk everything for me. Honestly, I suppose I deserve what's coming.

From the edges of my vision, Rohan careens into view, glancing from me to Trin, then racing to reach her before she can release her arrow.

Before he can get there, Trin tightens her grip on the riser, steadying herself for the long-distance shot. She squeezes her eyes shut, then focuses again. At the last second, the tip of her bow shifts left, almost imperceptibly. When she lets the arrow fly, it slices through the air as fast and straight as a shooting star, burying itself into the thick bark of the mahogany's trunk three meters from me.

Trinidad doesn't miss. She had a clear shot at an immobile target, yet I'm still dangling here, very much alive.

But Rohan doesn't know her like I do and is still in motion, rushing her horse. Midas swirls and snorts, but the massive Brute launches himself deftly from a boulder, tackling Trin from her mount. Her bow flies from her grasp as she hits the ground under him, knocking her head hard. Dazed, but coherent enough to keep fighting, she uses her momentum to roll him onto his back, then connects a direct blow to his nose before reaching into her boot for a familiar small blade. Blood surges down Rohan's chin as he flips her over, pinning her under him. He grabs her armed hand and wrenches the blade free. Then he reaches to her belt and draws her short sword—her last weapon. For a sickening moment, I fear he might run her through with it. But instead he glances above him, then jumps up and retreats several paces.

"Now!" he shouts to hidden fighters overhead.

As the Alexia scrambles to her feet, an enormous weighted net falls from the tree, knocking her back to the ground and pinning her in place. Lightning-fast, Rohan draws a cord that cinches the net like a coin purse right under Trin's legs, then fastens it tight.

Once she's secure, he searches the canopy for me. Finding me still dangling, his eyes betray uncharacteristic panic. "Hold on, Reina!" he yells, sprinting toward the tree.

My fingers barely keep their grip on the rough bark.

He shouldn't worry about me. He should be helping the others.

As my arms burn with the strain of holding on, a bizarre, alarming thought flashes like a storm cloud releasing its charge. *Would it be so bad if my hands gave out? Would an arrow to my chest be unwelcome?* I'd join Tre, and Mother, and Callisto on the other side—be free from the ache of missing them. I'd leave this frightening, cruel world behind . . . could forget about injustice and Teera, the Brutes and my terrible decision to murder my best friend. I'd be free.

Then, like a whisper, like a breeze in the leaves, my mother's voice brushes against my cheek.

Remember who you are, Rei of Sunshine.

I squeeze my eyes shut, as tightly as my hands grasp the fragile limb tethering me to this world.

Remember who I am.

And who am I?

I'm Reina Pierce, daughter of Leda Pierce. I might be flawed and afraid—a murderer, no better than Dáin—but I have fight left in me. I'll face what I've done, and I won't let Tre's death be for nothing. I will live to thank Trin and tell her the truth. I will live to repay Rohan for trying to save my life with no thought for his own.

I hear him shout my name a second time, and I know I have much yet to live for. So I reach deep down for the brio I must still possess somewhere inside, and wrench it free. It shakes loose with a guttural cry.

The thin branch arcs under my weight as I force one hand over the other, bobbing and floundering toward the trunk.

"The ledge!" I hear Rohan shout. I make the mistake of looking toward his voice. The void between us makes my head spin, and my pulse beats wildly. But I see the wide ledge fastened to the trunk, maybe two body lengths below my dangling toes.

Swinging my legs like a pendulum, I try to gain enough momentum for the jump. *Back. Forth. Back. Forth. Release!* For a terrifying moment I'm falling through the air—long enough to decide this is the stupidest idea I've ever had—then my feet collide with solid wood. My momentum slams me into bark, but I'm too elated to feel pain.

I made it! I didn't die. A juvenile laugh gurgles from my chest, and I fling my arms wide against the tree.

I scan the ground for Rohan, eager to share my momentary euphoria, but he has been drawn away by two Alexia—Fallon and Valya—parrying both their swords with his own weapons. Nearby, Torvus and the others, bloody and growing weary, struggle now to keep the Alexia from the heart of camp. Their circle of protection is shrinking. At least two dozen Alexia surround the eight remaining Brutes, and they're closing in.

Swords flash and arrows fly. Jase swings with practiced precision, but his wounds and evident weariness are taking a toll. Covered in sweat and blood, he calls out warnings and looks to defend the other Brutes even as he fields a barrage of attacks himself.

Jem jump-flips from a boulder over an attacker's head, but when he lands, another Alexia's arrow pierces the back of his thigh. He hobbles backward, trying to pull the tip free even as the first Alexia advances. Théo takes her out just in time, but not before his arm is sliced by an incoming blade.

I scan the chaos for Bri, finding her on the outskirts of camp, still locked in a vicious fight with Jamara. Bri's hair is matted across her cheeks and neck, and a line of blood trickles down her right arm. She holds her short sword in one hand, a Brute spear in the other, alternating between weapons as she tries to find a weakness in Jamara's defense. Bri appears to be slowing, the fiery passion that rent her from the tree fading into sheer exhaustion.

The Apprentice's tunic has been slashed through, leaving a gaping hole on one side of the multicolored robe. Her skin is smeared with mud, perspiration, and blood, but she's still fighting. Frighteningly, she looks to be gaining the upper hand.

I have to do something.

A speed line runs from this platform to the ground, maybe a hundred meters from Bri. Unfortunately, the curved bar used to glide down the rope is missing. It should be here, or attached to a guideline on the other end to draw to myself. I glance around but don't see anything else to use. I consider Rohan's bone knife, but holding a blade isn't going to work unless I want to slice my hands or the rope on my way down.

Arrows? One seems too flimsy, but four together might hold my weight. *It's risky,* I think, then laugh at the irony. More risky than breaking out of hidden cells, marching into the Jungle unannounced, dangling twenty meters above the ground? I suppose I can take my chances.

Holding the bundle of arrows over the rope, one hand on each side, I jump from the platform and fly over the battle below. As I soar through limbs and across camp, my stomach bumps into my tonsils in a strange, weightless rise. But it's not just the thrill of flying that forces my gut into unnatural places. The carnage on the ground twists my stomach too.

The second my boots touch soil, amidst the chaos and danger, I long for Callisto. For speed, for strength, for courage. A passing arrow rattles my resolve, but I force my feet to run. I can't let Jamara kill Bri. Their battle has taken them far from the center of camp, and I hunch to keep low, darting from one stump, one bush to the next, keeping my eyes on them all the while.

When Bri trips on a protruding root, Jamara knocks her sword from her grasp. Bri takes the spear in two hands and runs at Jamara, who shifts at the last moment. Bri lunges a step too far. Jamara drops her own weapon to wrench the spear from Bri's hands.

I run faster, jumping over logs and ducking under branches, but I'm still too far to save her.

Jamara lunges at her with the Brute spear. Bri sidesteps just in time. But with no weapon of her own, Bri's speed will only grant her luck so long. She's running out of tricks. Jamara has her cornered now, pressed against a boulder.

"You should have gone back to Amal," Jamara sneers victoriously, drawing her arm back, ready to deliver the final blow.

"*Nooo!*" I scream, still ten meters too far.

My voice grows and reverberates, echoing through camp like a mighty call to action. Alexia and Brutes alike pause at the guttural sound increasing in volume even though I've fallen silent.

A unified Brutish cry, followed by more than a dozen Brute bodies, bursts from the Jungle toward us. Some run with torches, all are smeared with mud, baring their teeth and brandishing weapons.

A Brute with a shock of red hair, illuminated in torchlight, leads the charge.

Dáin reaches Jamara within seconds. In a flash, he swings his harpy eagle club over her outstretched spear, cracking it in two. Then, without so much as flinching, he runs her through with the blade in his other hand. The Apprentice from Kekuatan drops to her knees, then falls face-first onto the Jungle floor.

Dáin glances at Bri and cocks his head to one side, as if trying to remember why he shouldn't kill her, too. Then, as if recalling that reason, he sprints off in search of another target.

For once, Bri is stunned into silence. We stare at Jamara's fallen body. Though the world is undoubtedly better without her malevolence, standing over the crumpled form of someone you ate dinner with a fortnight ago is sobering. The loss of any life, however justified, carries weight.

Dáin's men sweep through the clearing like a grass fire. They may be few, but they're fresh, eager, and have arrived not a moment too soon. They rush toward the center of camp, dividing the remaining Alexia with Torvus and the others. I run behind, drawing my bow, not sure whom I intend to use it on. It's just, with Dáin present, I'd rather be armed.

"It's about time!" I hear Rohan growl at Dáin.

"What?" the rebel leader pleads innocently, dodging a blow before using his club to take the legs out from under an advancing Alexia. He scowls toward Torvus. "I wanted him to realize he needed me."

Torvus returns Dáin's glare as he ties the Alexia he has bested, then climbs the dais adjacent to the fire ring. Like Bri just learned, losing a fight robs you of the luxury of choosing your savior.

As much as I hate to admit it, for once Dáin is right: these Brutes needed him and his defectors tonight. *We* needed him.

CHAPTER SIXTEEN

"SECURE THE SURVIVORS!" Torvus booms from the platform.

Every able-bodied Brute immediately sets to work carrying out his order, first hastily tying bandages to stem the worst of their bleeding. Some cover the dug-out pits, filled with trapped Alexia, with latticework lids made of long boards and netting, then secure the edges with stakes. Others transfer bound prisoners across camp to the bamboo cages. Dozens of cages. Those trapped under heavy nets, like Trinidad, remain as they are. I locate her bundled form again, ensuring she's still secure and relatively out of danger, about fifty meters from the base of the mahogany tree. She'll be safe there for now. So I turn my attention instead to the Brute leader, who's descending the dais.

"Torvus!" I call, running to intercept him.

He reluctantly halts.

Veins pulse in raised ridges up his neck and down his arms, and his hands and chest are mottled with dirt and blood. So much blood, mirroring the devastating loss all around us. Still, it could have been much worse. Torvus's tactics did succeed in limiting the death toll.

"Thank you," I say, "for sparing so many."

He grunts, wearily, and turns away.

"And I'm sorry," I blurt, the guilt I've been ignoring for the past hour resurfacing. "I should have been more careful. This is my fault."

He looks like he might tell me exactly what he thinks of my carelessness, but Jase jogs up, breathing heavily. Mottled bruising blooms across his body, beneath a patchwork of seeping lacerations.

"How many?" Torvus asks him.

"Six," he reports, straining to keep the word steady.

The Brute leader stills in reverence. "And them?"

"I count forty-two captured, twenty-seven slain. The rest escaped to the Jungle."

Torvus curses under his breath, then glares at me while addressing Jase. "We must assume our location will be reported. We'll have to evacuate."

I wither under his stern gaze.

"Take the bodies to the outskirts of camp," Torvus continues, "for the cubs' sake. We'll bury them tomorrow."

Jase nods and runs off again, nearly colliding with Rohan, who had been making his way toward us. Toward *me*. Rohan's waist is wrapped with a wide brown cloth, bandaging a wound that already bleeds through, and he limps slightly as he nears. But his chest heaves in relief at finding me alive. Before we can say a word, Jase grabs his arm and pulls him away, recruiting him and several other Brutes to help with Torvus's unpleasant errand.

They're all injured, yet each one keeps moving. Tonight has

revealed new depths of their strength, and not just their physical might.

I fight the urge to follow them—to assure Jase his sacrifices are not lost on me. To tell Rohan how his voice steadied me while I dangled between life and death.

Now is not the time. Instead, I let Torvus's mention of the cubs steer my purpose. As the Brute leader joins the efforts to secure the Alexia, I jog toward the hollowed-out tree near the kitchen where I assume Jonalyn is still hiding.

Halfway between the mahogany tree and the orchard, a group of younger Brutes, gangly and sweaty, descend from the canopy using a rope ladder. I barely glance their way until I notice that the last to climb down is going much slower. And he's oddly shaped compared with the others. Intense focus keeps his gaze glued to the rungs. He carefully reaches down with one foot, probing the air with his toes until he finds the next foothold, with the caution of a Gentle.

"*Neechi!*"

I immediately regret interrupting his concentration. As his head snaps up, the ladder sways, nearly pitching him backward. I run to steady the bottom and prepare to catch him if necessary.

"Never mind," I say. "Get down first; then you can tell me what you're doing here."

When he reaches the ground, his dark hair is matted with perspiration, and he looks as though he might faint. But he grins with the triumph of someone who has conquered a mighty challenge.

"Now, what *are* you doing here?" I gawk. "I thought you were with the horses."

He lowers his eyes bashfully. "I was, yes. But I didn't get far before I decided that was cowardly of me. If my life is going to count for something, it won't do to hide from danger. So I brought the horses back, and Jase said I could help up there." He grins real wide. "I threw lots of coconuts, Dom Reina," he says with a musical laugh that makes me grin from ear to ear.

The courage it must have taken for him to come back, to climb up *that*, to join the fight. "Neechi, I'm so proud of you." My cheeks warm. "You helped more than I did tonight."

"Reina!" My sister's voice rings through the clearing, welcome as a sea breeze. I sprint toward her, gathering Jo and, consequently, Finch in my arms. A wave of relief washes over me, and I embrace her like we've been apart for years. Right now it feels that way.

"You're okay?" she both asks and celebrates at once.

I nod, taking in the troop of little cubs around her, Pip among them. I ruffle his hair.

"Where are you going?" I ask Jo.

"Looking for Ori. I'm not sure where to take these little ones for the night, and they're getting sleepy."

I marvel for a moment at the odd normalcy of it. How strange that people have breathed their last while these children hid, protected, from the horror of it. Safe enough to "get sleepy." I peer down at their little faces and want them to always have routine. To always be safe.

"I'll get him for you," I say. "You should keep these sleepyheads away from the center of camp for now. Head to the kitchen. I'll send someone to you."

She nods, and we embrace again.

"Neechi—would you stay with Jo till then? If there's any trouble, I'd rest easier knowing she has a coconut-throwing warrior with her." I wink at him, then run to find Ori.

Someone has lit the fire ring, and the growing red-orange light illuminates everything within a twenty-meter circle of the stones. In the darkness beyond, torches bob and weave through the outskirts of camp, as a few Brutes canvass the surrounding area for any missed bodies or weapons, or stand guard around the pits.

I locate Ori in a group of less-injured Brutes distributing bundles of herbs, flasks of water, and shreds of cloth. After explaining Jonalyn's predicament, I take his share of the load so he can help her.

The area around the fire ring has turned into a makeshift Health Center. We give our supplies to Brutes who bandage each other, craft slings, and stitch deep wounds. A broken bone is set, and pained grunts mingle with the smoke.

Bri marches into the fireglow with an armful of salvaged Alexia weapons. When she catches sight of Dáin, recognition flickers across her face. She drops the weapons like hot coals and storms up to him.

"*I* wanted to kill her," she seethes.

Dáin's freckles bunch around his forehead and eyes as he tries to place her, or perhaps is startled by her vengeance.

"My apologies, mighty warrior," he says sarcastically, sizing her up.

She punches him in the face.

I gasp, then scramble for my bow, preparing to defend her from the retribution that will surely follow. But instead of returning Bri's attack, a faint smile stretches Dáin's lips, even as he rubs his sore jaw. Amusement, not anger, flashes in his eyes.

"Fiery," he says, sounding strangely pleased.

Jase has just returned from the search and quickly steps between them, holding his torch at an angle that tells Dáin he'd better back off.

"Easy, killer," Dáin says. "She's the one who clocked me." But when Jase holds his ground, Dáin shrugs and walks away.

"Are you hurt?" Jase asks Bri, scanning her limbs for injuries. He finds and assesses a deep puncture in her left arm, and a gash across her neck.

She shrugs. "You should have seen the other girl."

Driving his torch into the soft earth, Jase makes her sit down and gathers some chicha, herbs, cloth, water, a bamboo needle, and hibiscus-fiber thread for suturing her.

If Jase is back, maybe . . .

I scan the area for Rohan. He's leaning, unbandaged, against the edge of the dais, mashing leaves into a green paste with a mortar and pestle and smearing the mixture on his exposed injuries. For once I don't care if my concern is obvious. I weave through the wounded toward him. When he catches sight of me, he hands the bowl to another Brute. His dark eyes pull me to him, drawing me closer, even as he lessens the distance between us.

But while we're still five paces apart, Dáin steps between us.

"I knew you still had it in you," Dáin says, slapping Rohan's back while pretending not to see me.

Rohan grimaces. "Not now, Dáin."

I pull up short, repelled by Dáin's presence like a horse who spots a croc along a riverbank. Rohan's eyes hold mine, but he seems distracted now, nervous.

"It was just like old times tonight, eh?" Dáin smirks.

Rohan's jaw tenses. He looks like prey caught in a snare, exhibiting a strange nervousness I've never seen in him. A sickening dread heats my gut as I take another tentative step forward. "What does he mean?"

Half of Rohan's face dips in shadow as he turns to avoid my eyes.

Dáin finds this amusing. "You mean he didn't tell you?"

I take the bait. "Tell me what?"

He grins wickedly. "He's fought alongside me before."

Rohan shoves Dáin's chest. "Leave it be," he growls.

"I don't understand," I say, confusion and worry mingling. What opportunity could they have had to fight together that would give Dáin such mischievous delight? Nothing good, I fear.

Dáin recovers from the shove and raises his hands in surrender. "I just thought she would want to know that the one who gave her that pretty knife has tasted revenge on Nedé before. You remember, don't you? When we relieved a certain finca of its supplies? What was it—Fortunato? Fortune?"

No. Not—

"Rohan—" His name cracks in my throat. "What is he talking about?"

The moment I ask the question, I know I don't want to hear the answer. My feet back up of their own accord, slowly at first, then with broad steps, turning away just as Rohan's fist connects with Dáin's ribs.

"Reina, wait!" Rohan calls after me, but I'm already running—where, I don't know.

Rohan fought *with* Dáin? In an attack against Nedéans? And not at just any finca—La Fortuna? I recall Jonalyn's bruised face, her weakened body, and the tears fall freely. I want to believe Dáin was lying, but Rohan didn't deny it. On the contrary, he had the look of someone who had been caught.

Hurt fuels my anger like a log to a flame. I run, burning, into the darkness, defying the folly of facing the Jungle night alone. Let a predator find me. *I dare it.* I'll tear it to pieces and feed it to my fury.

The rising gibbous moon casts a blue glow over the Jungle, filtering through the canopy like gauzy fingers. I run through its grasp, refusing to slow, until my feet slosh through a silvery strand of creek, and I collapse on the bank.

I was beginning to trust that Rohan was different, that he was good. That he was *safe*.

My own sister's finca? *How could he?*

Perhaps the better question is, *How could he* not? He's a Brute. Isn't that what they do? Injure, hurt, endanger?

Teera's words surface in my memory, mocking my trust. *You have no idea the horrors they're capable of,* she had said. *It only takes one Brute to bring evil back into the world.*

Maybe Rohan simply can't be what I had hoped.

But he had said they had a choice. That night in the canopy, his eyes reflecting the rose gold of sunset, he had told me Brutes could choose good or evil—no one had taken that from them.

What's worse, then? A Brute who can't help but do harm, or one who willingly chooses to?

A sob racks my body. Somehow, inexplicably, my heart opened to him, which gave the dagger of betrayal easy access.

I splash water over my face and down my arms, washing away the filth, and regret, and my tears. Let it seal me back up, seal him back out.

No matter what he makes me feel, I can't let myself trust him. *He can't have your allegiance, Rei.*

How could I ever have thought otherwise?

CHAPTER SEVENTEEN

THE DAMP JUNGLE EARTH IS COOL BENEATH my bare toes as I reach down from the platform, trying to lower myself soundlessly. The moon has traveled most of its nightly circuit. Judging by its position, I'd say it's an hour or two from dawn.

Jase urged me to take Bri, Neechi, and Jonalyn to the treetop hut to get what rest we could, but I didn't sleep. I had no intention of it. Instead I spent hours staring at the woven zigzag pattern of the thatched roof, waiting for the noises below to still.

I tiptoe from the base of the tree, slowly melting into the shadows and away from the center of camp. Exhausted Brutes sleep by the fire ring, low flames flickering in time to the pulsating hum of nocturnal noises. Most lie on bedrolls, sleeping at awkward angles to accommodate their injuries. A few patrol through camp or guard clusters of cages, where my fellow Alexia await morning light. I wouldn't blame the women if they were terrified, even though the Brutes slipped bandages and water through the bamboo slats to their prisoners.

I knew from the moment Trin was captured what I'd have to do. After all she's done for me, there's no way I could leave her alone down there, with only her ill thoughts of me for company. It's my fault she's in this mess. If I hadn't led the Alexia to Tree Camp, she wouldn't have been captured. Fallon wouldn't be in a pit. Valya wouldn't be dead.

I try not to look for Rohan, but even in sleep his form is hard to miss. It reminds me of the first night I spent in the Jungle, on a cot in the treetop hut, watching the moonlight shift across his face, wondering why I found him so mesmerizing.

I shake the memory away. I should have known better, even then.

I slip past a grove of fig trees undetected, toward the spot Trinidad fell, then hide behind a curtain of vines hanging from a young ceiba.

The net lies still, cord as thick as my hand latticed over her body. *Too* still. My heart races. Could she have been more badly injured than I thought? Did some Brute recognize her as the Alexia second-in-command and exact justice for those she killed?

"Trinidad?" I whisper, the urgency of my voice betraying fear.

Her golden eyes snap open.

"Trin," I say again, relief buoying my resolve.

It takes her a moment to register who I am and where she is, but when she puts it together, a flame of anger ignites alongside understanding.

"You—" She seems to have difficulty deciding which insult fits best, so hurls several. "I can't believe I trusted you."

"I told you the truth," I defend. "Maybe not the *whole* truth— I couldn't tell you about these Brutes; I swore not to tell. But I wasn't lying about Teera wanting to kill me, or my desire to help the Gentles."

She ignores my plea, still fuming. "I risked everything to let you go—*everything*—and you repay me by releasing a known threat to Nedé! I'm lucky to be alive."

My mouth drops open. "I didn't mean to—" I stop mid-sentence, realizing I have nothing to say that can counter her accusation.

"What did you think would happen? Teera came the next morning to interrogate you. When Adoni escorted her to the cells, you *and* the Brute were gone. I got called in, of course, right after Bri didn't show up to conditioning. If you hadn't taken that obnoxious brat with you so I could pin the breach on her, I'd be dead. I hated lying to Adoni, but what was I supposed to do? If I told her I let you go free, Teera would have run me through right then and there." Her face falls in a rare moment of vulnerability. "How could you be so selfish?"

Her words couldn't have cut deeper if they were actual steel. "Trin, I'm so sorry—I didn't think about how it would affect you. I—I needed him to warn the others."

"Ohhh, of course," she sneers. "You needed to release an enemy of Nedé to warn his friends. Thanks for clearing that up."

I can't defend my actions, but I can, at least, defend the Brutes. "They aren't what we thought, Trin. I'm not saying I understand them completely, but they're not all responsible for the attacks . . ." A twinge of hurt resurfaces at the memory of Rohan's guilty face. Not all are responsible, perhaps, but one more than I thought. Still . . .

I explain how Rohan and Jase saved me the night I left my patrol to pursue Dáin near the border. "You can't deny they didn't act like monsters tonight. *You* marched on their home. Jamara shot first. And still, how many Alexia are alive because of their mercy?"

She glances toward the cages. She knows I'm right.

"Are Nedéans using their power any better than the Brutes of old did? Tell me the truth," I press. "What were Teera's orders? Hmm? No survivors?"

She locks eyes with me again.

"With one exception," she says. "Teera ordered Adoni to stay close to her, but she tasked me with bringing you back—dead or alive. Except for having to bring Jamara along, I took the orders gladly." She leans forward. "You were my responsibility. Bri was my responsibility. And I failed. I wasn't going to let that happen again."

"You had the shot," I accuse, remembering the fierce look in her eyes as I hung exposed in the treetops.

"I missed."

"You're lying."

She considers the canopy overhead, as if reliving the moment.

"Alright, fine. Something still didn't add up. I'm no fool. I could see they weren't fighting full force. I knew it was your voice warning me not to shoot. I had my orders, but still, I wavered."

"Why?" I press, trying to get her to admit what I hope is the real reason.

She grabs the net between us. "Because some foolish part of me still wanted to believe you were the woman I thought you were."

I place my hands over hers and lean in closer. "I don't know if I'll ever deserve your trust, Trin, but I'm going to do everything in my power to try."

I slip the bone knife from its sheath and set to work on the net.

She watches me saw at the cords. "How do you know I won't kill you when I'm free?"

"I don't," I say, concentrating on the fibers beginning to fray under the blade. The rope is as thick as my wrist—this is going to take a while.

While I work, she eyes the blade, stark white in the moonlight, and I remember how much it meant to me that she included it with the contraband she slipped me in the cell.

"Why did you return it?" I ask, not looking up.

She takes her time answering. "What you said about the Gentles—I could tell you really cared. You reminded me of Nana, I guess. The knife seemed important to you, so when I saw Adoni lock it in the armory for Teera, I thought you should have it back."

"Thank you," I say. "It *is* important to me." I don't, however, think it will be helpful to mention that it ultimately allowed the Brutes more time to prepare for her attack.

She smiles slyly—reminiscent of the confident, charismatic Alexia I first met. "You paid me back by leaving a nice, wide trail to follow your sorry butt."

I humph at her. "You're welcome." Since we still have some time till I'll get through these impressive ropes, I ask, "But how did you know where to begin your search?"

She grows serious again. "Teera sent us to Bella Terra first, but Adoni said if you weren't there we should begin at the last known raid site. That's the spot near Camino del Oeste where, well, you know where it is. Some Gentle field-workers reported a group of horses had passed that way—something about a crying baby—and we found your tracks near the border. From there, it wasn't hard."

"Well, with such an obvious map, you should be able to follow the trail back the way you came." Another segment of net pops open, and I'm breathing heavily from the strain. "About a hundred meters north, you'll find Bri's Lexander waiting for you. There's a little food and a weapon in the saddlebag."

"Will they come after me?"

I remember the Brute slipping bandages into the cages, Torvus's mention of relocating. "I don't think so. We have enough to do in repairs and preparations."

"*We?* You're staying, then—with them?"

I consider sidestepping the question, but the last time I kept back the whole truth from Trin, I almost got her killed. I won't deceive her again. I take a deep breath before confessing, "I'm leading them to Teera."

"*What?* Why?" she whisper-shouts.

"Because power without virtue is tyranny, that's why. We—Nedé, Teera, all of us—we're gentling Brute babies without their knowledge."

The confusion in her eyes is justifiable.

"Gentles aren't born Gentles. A vaccine we give them at birth makes them that way. Where's the virtue in forcing them to be what they're not—in harming them without their consent?" Another segment breaks loose. "We've been told they can't help but hurt women, but now you've seen for yourself—they have the capacity for goodness. Harm, too, yes. But don't we? Who gave us the right to take the choice away from them? You know we'd never give it up ourselves."

She scans the breadth of Tree Camp, the structures and impressive ingenuity visible in the moonlight, even after battle. "She has known for years, hasn't she?"

"Who?"

"Teera. I've always wondered why she focused so much on building the Alexia."

I remember the day Trin talked about her Nana with such fondness, explained that she was much of the reason Trin had joined the Alexia. She wanted to serve Nedé as her grandmother had. But her Nana had been able to keep peace with only a single small dagger, which she reportedly never had to use. Trin confessed that since her Nana's time, the Alexia had become "both more and less."

A fifth link of rope unravels, creating a hole just big enough for her to wiggle through. She crouches in the shadows beside me, listening and waiting to ensure no one has heard us, then gets to her feet.

"I know you don't agree with the direction Teera has taken the Alexia," I say. "I also know she'll stop at nothing until she has killed every single one of these Brutes. I don't expect you to trust them—not yet. But maybe you can understand why I can't let her destroy them. I believe gentling the Brutes has made *us* less too. You don't have to lie for me again. Tell Adoni this location if you need to—we won't be here by the time she can send you back with more."

Her gaze flits to the clusters of secure cages. "I'm responsible for them, too."

"There's no way we can break them all out tonight."

She chews her thumb. Trin won't leave if she thinks they need her here.

"Look," I reason, "if the Brutes wanted them dead, they wouldn't have gone through all the trouble of keeping them alive. I'll make sure they're treated fairly. I promise."

She grasps my forearm, and I return the gesture, then pull her into a tight hug.

"Be careful, Candidate," she whispers in my ear.

"You, too," I say, then give her the handle of her Nana's dagger—the one she had pulled on Rohan. It surfaced in a pile of weapons reaped from the Jungle floor after the fight. I knew immediately whose it was and that she deserved to have it back. More than I deserved Rohan's knife from her, anyway.

She rubs the turquoise and ivory stones with her thumb, cleaning mud away until they gleam under the moonlight.

"Just returning the favor," I say.

The corner of her mouth lifts as she slides the knife into her boot. Then she disappears into the night.

INTERLUDE

ONLY DR. NOVAK KNEW OF Leda's first pregnancy, and people would notice—ask questions—if the Matriarch's daughter avoided fulfilling her unexpected destiny. And so she birthed three more children, all girls. The first, Jonalyn, was born only a year after she left Jason with Torvus. Ciela came two years later, and, following an unexpected miscarriage, her Rei of Sunshine completed their family and taught her to hope again.

Her daughters filled her heart with light and joy. They brought a sense of permanence to her life, and her love for them helped fill the deficit left by her separation from Torvus and the ache of leaving Jason. Jonalyn, Ciela, and Reina reminded her that duty must come before pleasure, and that, strangely, pleasure can be found even in duty.

Her role as a Center codirector, combined with frequent treks into the Jungle, limited her capacity for more childbearing. But that didn't matter to Leda—she had no need of the stipends or pension offered Maternos for more births, and her hands were full with Center business and overseeing Bella Terra. As a finca-holding Materno, dozens of tiny Gentles were assigned to live with her over the years, the offspring of other Maternos. With the help of a capable tutor, Dom Bakshi, and her trusted chef and friend, Marsa, Leda cared for them as if each were her own Jason, giving them seven years of dignity before reluctantly releasing them to Hives.

Knowing what she knew, Leda treated the older Gentles who came to work at Bella with all the fairness and respect she could, without drawing too much attention. She even allowed her daughter Reina to become friends with an unusually sharp, kindhearted Gentle she had named Treowe.

Regardless of her full life, Leda never forgot Torvus. Sometimes, on hot, dry-season nights, she'd wander the plumeria hedges, allowing the scent to transport her to another time— a world when forever felt as sure as his embrace. But as the years passed, her resignation grew. She had to put duty over love, no matter the cost. Besides, Torvus continued to give her no other option.

No matter how many times she left babies on his porch, he never made contact with her. He could have, she knew. She always timed her journeys with the full moon, making night travel easier. If he wanted to see her, he could leave her a message in the crate—a note, a flower, anything. His silence placed exclamation point after exclamation point on the last words he had spoken to her. He didn't want to see her *ever* again.

The only thing stronger than Leda's fear of facing Torvus was her love for her daughters.

When an Alexia came to Bella Terra to inform her that Reina had gone missing after investigating an attack, Leda packed a rucksack and left that very afternoon. She crossed the kilometers of Jungle in half the time it usually took, marching up Torvus's steps in broad daylight.

When the aging Brute opened the door, her resolve nearly faltered. Seeing him face-to-face made her feel seventeen again. Despite decades of separation, her heart began to beat a forgotten rhythm.

She watched him watch her a long moment, dappled Jungle light softening his harsh edges. Did she imagine a flash of tenderness in his eyes? It almost seemed he wanted to embrace her.

"Why have you come?" he asked quietly.

She hoped, for the briefest of moments, that he had changed his mind—that he'd tell her to stop leaving the babies in the middle of the night—to come in daylight instead, to be *his* instead. But he had asked her a question, and she felt he deserved the truth.

"My daughter," she pleaded. "She went missing near the border."

At her answer, his gaze hardened.

"What's that to me?" he snapped.

No, nothing had changed. How could she have thought otherwise? "I was hoping you might have heard something."

He grunted, then turned and reentered the house.

She followed him inside, uninvited, her own conflicted anger growing with each step. Suspicions she had tried to bury suddenly seemed more feasible, given his response to her.

"I've tried not to assume, but there's talk in Nedé about attacks on fincas . . ."

Torvus's anger flashed then. He whirled on her, his hurt unmistakable. "And you think I'm responsible?"

Did she? The Brute before her barely resembled the Torvus she had known—the passionate, untamed soul who had stolen her heart under the plumeria trees. But now? Had he become what the foremothers claimed Brutes were—selfish, violent, untrustworthy menaces? No, she had to believe the real Torvus was still there somewhere, underneath his graying beard and sharp tongue. But perhaps when she left him all those years ago, she buried that man too deep in anger for her to ever reach again.

So she quickly sealed her heart back into the cocoon of duty and left the Jungle as empty as she had twenty-five years before. She had made her choice then—had chosen to give life to others rather than live it herself.

———————

Torvus followed Leda all the way to the border, remaining just out of sight, ensuring her safe passage—just as he had every night she had brought infants to Tree Camp.

Speaking with Leda after all these years was unexpected, the effect she still had on him more so. Thirty years had passed since a curious girl on the riverbank had asked him about his armful of iguanas, but she was still herself. The gray woven through her dark hair, the lines settled around her eyes, hadn't changed Leda Pierce—not really. She had only come to ask for his help once again, not to make amends. Why should he be the one to apologize? How dare she accuse him?

Even as pride strangled his affections, he couldn't deny what once was, or the timeless beauty of *her*.

He wanted to forget her.

He longed to hold her.

But pride won out as he watched her disappear into Nedé, just like the last time he had foolishly let her go.

Leda had kept her secrets close to protect her family. When Jonalyn gave birth to her first child, a boy, Leda couldn't risk telling her, not even to rescue him. When La Fortuna was attacked, it brought questions from her eldest daughter that had forced her hand. She had no choice but to tell Jonalyn the truth, and once she knew, no choice but to offer to take the baby.

But when Reina revealed she had been to the Jungle—in the Center records room, of all places—Leda suddenly worried that her daughter might fall for a Brute the way she had. In all her years of rescuing babies, she had focused on the injustice of gentling humans against their knowledge. She hadn't considered the repercussions her actions could have for her own daughters. Reina was strong, but hadn't Leda been strong once too?

In the fresh sting of rejection, having just returned from the Jungle four days earlier, she wanted to spare her daughter the heartache she had endured at the hand of someone she loved that deeply. Where had it gotten her? And she planned to warn Reina . . . until they were interrupted.

Facing eternity distills what matters most. That night, bleeding onto the tile floor, slipping in and out of consciousness, Leda finally realized what a fool she had been. With death clawing at her broken body, her mind hovering between the world and what comes after, she ached to be held by the strong arms of her true love—to be comforted by his voice, steadied by his strength. She wanted to tell him she finally understood that life without him was no life at all. That she loved him.

Like the swelling of a plumeria bud just before it unfurls, she felt her heart might burst with longing for what might have been.

But "might have been," Leda mourned, consciousness slipping away again, *can't save me now.*

CHAPTER EIGHTEEN

THE SUN IS HOT TODAY, even with the canopy to absorb some of the strongest rays.

Bri looks as wilted as I feel, sweat dripping down her temples despite her blonde hair being swept back into a ponytail.

"You want to get some water?" I ask.

She nods, setting the sack she was working on—a patchwork of netting and leather—on the wood bench.

"We'll be back," she tells the Brutes.

Jem's mouth twitches, wrinkling a thin line of hair above his lip, his eyes barely flitting to us before returning to his task.

Théo nods brusquely. He doesn't say anything either, but his dour expression communicates that we don't have to return. We could just as well go back to Nedé. I don't blame them for hating me. I'm the reason they have to leave their home. And they don't even know I released their highest-ranking prisoner.

Well, one of them does. A few hours after freeing Trinidad, once the sun climbed to claim a new day, I confessed my crime to Jase.

He didn't seem as concerned about my releasing the Alexia's second-in-command as I thought he would be. He only asked me why.

"Because she saved me first."

That's all I felt needed to be said. I didn't disclose that a few hours before releasing her, I had discovered a certain Brute I was growing to trust had secrets of his own, which had led me to question their kind as a whole. That may have had something to do with my actions. I didn't mention it, though, because standing beside Jase this morning—his mussed hair falling around earnest, hazel eyes—I couldn't remember why I doubted. I couldn't imagine *not* trusting Jase. His warmth, his openness, his easy laugh and desire to please make the strongest case—of all the Brutes I've encountered here in the Jungle—for trust. For partnership. For fighting for their right to be Brutes.

He put his hand on my shoulder, bent down so he could look right into my eyes, and said, "I trust you, Reina. If you needed to do it, you had your reasons."

As with Trinidad, his trust was a gift I hoped to prove I deserved, and so I asked, "Should I tell Torvus?"

He stuck his tongue in his cheek before answering with a slight smile. "I don't think he needs to know just yet."

I'd be lying if I said I wasn't relieved. Torvus had enough to be angry with me about, even before I released Trin without consulting him. Because of me, Tree Camp was compromised. I had cost six Brutes their lives, all of them their home.

Shortly after my talk with Jase, Torvus called everyone together to explain the necessity of abandoning camp, glaring pointedly at me more than once.

"The Alexia may return at any time," he said, "with more force than their first attack. Tomorrow we make for the ruins."

A murmur went up from the gathering, but it didn't last long. For one, who could argue with Torvus's reasoning? The Brutes barely prevailed last night—they might not be so lucky again. Second, there wasn't time to object. Twenty-four hours isn't long to salvage what you can from years of living in one place, especially while tending to the wounds of battle.

Consequently, instead of beginning our journey toward Phoenix City today, as was previously planned, every able-bodied Brute has been preparing for relocation. Tomorrow they'll travel a day's journey south through the Jungle, where they'll attempt to make the ruins home as Tree Camp has been. The eleven of us will accompany them to the ruins, make sure they're settled, then continue our mission.

Today, my companions and I have been helping where we can.

After gleaning the last of the mangos, bananas, and mamey from the orchard trees, Neechi rounded up eight Alexia horses lingering near the fringes of camp, who seemed more afraid of the big, scary Jungle than of these big, scary people. They were begging to be taken care of. Along with the two remaining horses we brought from Bella Terra, the ten animals will go a long way toward carrying needed supplies, even if the route to the ruins will make leading the animals tricky. Neechi has spent the afternoon tending to their wounds, repairing tack, and helping a few of the Brutes get acquainted with the horses so they can lead them without fear tomorrow.

Jonalyn invented a game for the cubs of transferring fruit from the underground lockers into woven baskets. Pip took the challenge quite seriously, mowing down three other boys in his effort to get the most mangos into the goal. Since the attack, she hasn't let Finch out of her sight, usually wrapping him to her body with a colorful scarf—the Materno style. She keeps him close, like she's afraid to let him go. Maybe she is. Once at the ruins, she'll have to leave Finch behind. Perhaps forever.

Bri and I have spent the day working alongside Théo and Jem, sewing simple rucksacks out of any available material—animal hides, netting torn from tree hut windows, woven floor mats. Anything that can hold blankets, weapons, food, rope, or the few practical items the Rescuer brought to camp over the years: baby bottles, clothing, or, as I recently learned, the curious dusty books on Torvus's shelf. Even without Théo and Jem's coolness to remind me, I'm painfully aware each sack we create will be filled with items that could have remained here if it weren't for me.

Hence the need for frequent water breaks.

As we pass by the fire ring on the way to the stream, Bri grumbles, "I liked them better when they had fewer reasons to hate us."

As I'm mumbling a half-hearted agreement, I catch sight of Rohan descending the mahogany tree. His bare back is mottled with deepened bruising today—not that I'm staring. I admit, it would be easier to be angry with him if he weren't so . . . so . . . *him*. He climbs down the ladder with one arm, the other holding a bundle of mats over his shoulder.

I walk faster, trying not to look his way, hoping he doesn't spot us before we reach the cover of the overgrown path. So far today, he has asked to speak with me three times. Three times I've ignored him. It's not that I want to be rude; I just don't trust myself to think rationally around him—to hold onto my anger. I know he can't be trusted, but one look into those deep, dark eyes, flecked with the tiniest specks of gold, and I just might forget that fact. Yes, distance is my best defense against irrational thought.

"What's the matter with you?" Bri asks, a little too loudly for my preference. "I thought you two were—I dunno, close or something."

I avoid answering till we're concealed by leafy banana palms. "It doesn't matter," I dodge. For some reason the subject of Rohan feels especially vulnerable. Plus, I'm not sure I want to stoke the fires of Bri's distrust by telling her he was part of an attack against Nedé.

Still, I have no one else to talk to, and as we make our way toward the stream, the feelings of betrayal swell like an abscess, begging to be lanced. Eventually I blurt, "I just . . . I heard something that made me realize he's not who I thought he was."

Bri actually laughs out loud. I brace myself for her epic *I told you so*. Prepare for her lecture on not being able to trust these Brutes as far as we can throw them.

Instead she says, "Were you even *there* last night? Nothing is what we thought it was. Not the Matriarchy. Not the Alexia. Not these Brutes. The whole world's flippin' like a flatbread and you're worried he's not *who you thought he was*? That's hilarious, Rei. Seriously funny."

She snaps a hanging liana that brushes against her face, then breaks off pieces as we close the distance to the stream, throwing the woody bits into the brush.

It's too hot to argue. If I told Bri exactly what Rohan did, she'd be as angry as I am. Then again, some annoying voice reminds me that *I* don't know his exact crimes. Sure, Dáin clearly enjoyed conveying the information—which doesn't exactly add credibility—but Rohan didn't deny his accusations either.

Even if there's more to the story, would it matter? He was somehow part of the attack on La Fortuna. How can I trust him again?

We crouch on the stream-side platform where Rohan and I filled the flasks—was that only yesterday afternoon?—and splash water over our heads before filling our containers.

"So are you telling me that *you* trust them now?" I ask Bri.

She splashes her face with another handful of water, then shrugs. "I wouldn't call it trust. More like 'calculated risk.' I wouldn't let that redheaded Brute so much as take out the trash behind my back, but he did eliminate one common enemy. Teera obviously has to go, and they're motivated to do the job."

I peer at her suspiciously. "That's not the only reason, is it? Admit it, Bri—they're growing on you, aren't they?"

She douses me with a ladleful of water. "Fine. Some of them . . . have proven they don't mean to murder us in our sleep."

I don't think I'm the only one disarmed by Jase. I haven't missed the way her chin lifts when he laughs at her excessive wry sarcasm, or the way she has softened, albeit slightly, to his instruction over the past four days. She even accepted some Brute clothing he gave us to alter into outfits better suited for our coming trek.

"Jase is my mother's child," I tell her softly.

Her head whips around so fast that her ponytail flings a wide arc of water against the surrounding leaves. "He's *what?*"

"Something about him was eerily familiar. I couldn't place it at first, but the last time I saw my mother, she confessed the truth. The craziest part—" and I don't know why I'm sharing this with Bri, other than that it feels good to get it off my chest—"is that Torvus is the other parent."

Her eyebrows shoot up, then furrow in confusion. "What in Siyah's name—?"

I shrug. "I didn't ask for details."

"Let me get this straight: Your mother, Leda Pierce, and that big Brute with anger issues had a child—like in the old world?"

That pretty much sums up what I know. "She brought Jase to the Jungle so he wouldn't grow up as a Gentle. Can you imagine— Jase, a Gentle?"

Imagining confident, capable, strong Jase reduced to a fragile, sickly, unmotivated Gentle is almost too much to bear. Bri must be entertaining a similar image, because she grows thoughtful too.

"She brought all of them here," I continue, "because she believed they deserved the chance to be what God intended."

She shakes her head slowly. "Even if her actions meant putting all of Nedé at risk?" Her expression changes as she answers her own question.

"Even if it meant risking her very life." I choke on the words.

Remembering my mother's sacrifice does more than rip open the wound of losing her. Remembering her convictions buoys my own.

I, too, have a cause. I was willing to sacrifice my best friend for it, and I can't let one Brute's secrets derail me from my mission. I can't let Tre's death be in vain. *Protect the weak.* I will ensure justice comes to the Gentles, even if it means leading Brutes straight into Nedé to remove its tyrannical ruler. *Safety for all.* I will help them take down the Matriarchy because I believe, as my mother did, that every person deserves the chance at their fullest life—even those who could hurt us.

We return to camp to find a strange commotion humming near the great tree. A scout guards a figure obscured by surrounding Brutes.

"She asks to see Torvus," the scout shouts, and one of the boys immediately sprints down the path to the leader's house.

Bri and I jog toward the disturbance. I scramble onto the dais for a better look, but only catch glimpses of the prisoner's back.

Even from this poor angle, I can tell the intruder is a woman— tall, with dark hair peppered with gray, piled loosely on top of her head in a disheveled mess, strands sticking to her neck and shoulders. She hunches forward slightly, appearing weary. I scramble down and run the perimeter of the encircling mob, peering between shoulders to catch a better glimpse of her.

The woman's face is paler than it should be, and uncharacteristically dirty, but I'd know those eyes anywhere.

"Mother!"

Her gaze flits toward my voice, and I begin shoving Brutes out of my way to reach her.

"*Mother!*" I yell again, pushing forward.

And then she's in my arms—breathing, solid, alive—and I can barely keep my feet on the ground for the giddy weightlessness that threatens to lift me right out of this world. My cheek presses against the soft familiarity of her gently aged face.

"I thought I lost you," I whisper, barely able to believe my senses.

"My Rei of Sunshine," she says, then sucks in a pained breath as her body sags under my eager embrace.

I set aside relief for worry. "Are you alright?"

She tries a weak smile. "Considering I was run through by the Alexia not two weeks ago, I'd say I'm better than 'alright.' Karina did an admirable job stitching me up."

"What are you doing here? I mean, I'm so relieved, but why—? How—?"

"I got word Teera was sending a hundred Alexia into the Jungle. I feared the worst. As soon as I was able to ride, I knew I had to come warn Torvus." A flash of sadness accompanies the next words. "No matter the cost."

I don't have time to wonder what cost she could mean. The leader of the Brutes has already caught sight of us and strides double-time toward the crowd. Bodies give way before him like a receding tide. Even I find myself stepping aside as he approaches, unnerved by a strange fire igniting his storm-gray eyes that I worry could burn us all.

Fear flashes in Mother's eyes, briefly, but as he blazes toward her, she defiantly lifts her chin, stands straighter, musters every shred of dignity she possesses.

"I know you don't want to see me," she blurts, "and I wouldn't have come except I heard—"

She's unable to finish. Torvus engulfs her in an earnest embrace, pressing his lips to hers. He holds her like he's at once afraid to break her and afraid to lose her. Then he caresses her cheek with a large, weathered hand.

"You're alive," he breathes, with more tenderness than I'd have thought possible from this hardened Brute. "I was a fool to ever let you go."

Mother melts into him like he's the safest place in the world, allowing his arms—arms that could snap a bow in half—to cradle her weary body.

Her lips tremble. "I never stopped loving you," she says, tears slipping down her dirt-smeared cheeks.

He presses her to his chest and kisses the top of her head. "Nor I you."

Not a foot shuffles, not a throat clears as we witness this vulnerable moment between two unlikely people. There's something sacred in their reunion, and none of us dares interrupt the transcendence of it.

Still, heat creeps up my neck and cheeks at the intimacy of their affection. It's as if they're the only two people in their own private world. Like the rest of us aren't even here.

For a moment, the memory of Rohan's touch tingles along my cheekbone, and I remember the way time stood still when he looked at me—when he *saw* me. When I trusted enough to open my heart to him.

Even as I warn myself that I can never be so careless with him again, I find myself scanning the area for a set of broad shoulders and dark, unruly hair.

Beside the weapons locker to the north of the fire ring, Rohan whispers something solemn to Jase, who's staring slack-jawed and unblinking at Mother and Torvus. The faintest smile lifts Jase's lips at whatever he's hearing, then he slaps Rohan's back and sets off with intent.

Rohan watches his friend make his way through the crowd toward its center, then catches me staring at him.

Without words, without my permission, his gaze penetrates my soul.

Look away, Reina.

How is it possible for someone to seize control of my own heart's beating?

Reina! Look away.

Confidence sets his jaw, quiet pleading furrows his brow. The juxtaposition of sufficiency and yearning—asking me, without words, to allow him to explain himself—almost breaks my resolve to avoid him. Why do I want to trust him so badly, even when he has proven I shouldn't?

For Siyah's sake, Rei!

My better sense finally breaks through, like a slap to the face, and I force my focus back to my mother. Jase has breached the circle of Brutes surrounding her and Torvus, waiting a respectful distance from the pair. When Torvus slips an arm around her back, turning her toward the path to his home, she catches sight of Jase.

The woman I have always known as calm, collected, soft but unflappable, freezes in recognition. When she breathes again, she slowly places a hand over her mouth as fresh tears well up in her eyes.

"Jason?"

She moves toward him, reaches trembling fingers to touch his cheeks. She smiles, and laughs, and cries, as if shocked that this tall, strong, kind-eyed Brute was once the infant she brought through the Jungle to Torvus.

Jase places a wide palm over her delicate hand, his lopsided grin mirroring her joy.

"You don't know how long I've wanted to meet you," he says, his voice even more throaty than usual.

His words seem to complete her joy. Her body convulses with a sob, and she winces at the still-healing wound. Torvus is at her side in an instant, bracing her with a steady arm.

"You need to rest," he says, some of his usual commanding tone returning.

She nods, though clearly reluctant to leave the child she has only just been reunited with. To Jase, she says, "We have much to talk about. We will, soon."

I can't say I've ever seen her this happy, and her joy spills into me. "Once you've rested, I'll come see you," I promise, kissing her cheek. "And I'll tell Jo you're here."

She slips an arm around Torvus as he leads her down the path to his home. She leans against him, head resting on his arm, as if they've never been apart. I know little of love between a woman and a Brute, but I can already tell her affection for Torvus is . . . different somehow. It's not quite like the love of a Materno for her children, though equally passionate.

It's a kind of love, I think, that could drive a person to make irrational decisions. To risk. To open oneself. Perhaps even to forgive.

Two hours later, the sun's setting signals an end to the day's preparations. Grumbling stomachs coax us away from our growing pile of patchwork sacks toward the kitchen. Only Jem insists on finishing a final bag, his fastidiousness trumping hunger. Surly Théo reminds him we still have tomorrow to finish, but the quiet, narrow-faced Brute ignores him.

"I'll meet you there," I tell Bri and Théo. "I want to check on my mother."

I peel away from the pair, making for Torvus's house. It's my third time following this hard-packed path, barely visible through the tangle of encroaching Jungle plants, but this is the first time, I realize, I haven't been nearly choked with apprehension on my way.

The shoddy structure yawns at the approaching night. Nothing has changed about the outside of the house—the loose board over the door hasn't been secured, nor the bushes trimmed—but the rise and fall of voices, an ember of candle glow through the window, creates the illusion that the home is different somehow. Warmer. More welcoming.

I strain in the low light to see the stairs as I climb, pausing to listen. Not to eavesdrop, exactly, but to consider the foreign combination of their voices together—like a horse whinny accompanying an oriole's song. Each endearing in its own way, but curious together.

". . . some of their horses," the Brute leader is saying. "I could take you myself tomorrow."

A weighted silence stretches between them before Mother's soft voice replies, "Is that what you want, Tor? For me to return home?"

Against my better manners, I find myself edging closer to the crate against the house so I can peer into the window without being seen.

The two sit across from each other at the wooden table, Torvus's back to me.

"I can't lose you again," he says, "not when you've only just returned."

She places her hand atop his in the center of the table. "Then what is it?"

"We are leaving Tree Camp. Moving south, to the ruins, deeper into the Jungle."

"Then I'll go with you. We can make a home there, together."

"They'll find that camp too, eventually. Now that your mother knows for sure . . ." A bit of grit roughens his words. "I have to put an end to this, Leda."

Her expression is unreadable. "You're planning something. What?"

He doesn't answer right away, instead rubbing her hand with his thumb, watching their entwined fingers intently.

When he speaks, his tone is softer. "A woman once taught me that true strength is shown in sacrificing for the greater good." He meets her gaze. "I understand now. I know why you couldn't come to me—couldn't live here with me. It's the same reason I can't stay with you now."

She closes her eyes slowly, sending a tear slipping down her cheek. But when her eyes open again, they reveal compassion, not anger.

"This has always been beyond us," she says, smiling softly. "But to have your forgiveness, and to know you understand how it tore me in two not to be together . . . I can return in peace."

He shifts from his chair to the floor, kneeling in front of her. "I don't know how this will end, but I know I have to stop her—for your protection, for those you brought me, for the future." He cups her chin in his hand. "But if I survive, I *will* find you. And I will never, *never* let you go again."

He kisses her, and I sink down below the sill, take a moment to breathe in the thick evening air, balmy and full of life. A monkey scuttles through a branch overhead, chasing another's tail. Nearby, a crimson tanager alights from its neatly wound nest.

All creatures long for companionship—find meaning in adding their lives to a greater whole. It's a fact I've been taught since childhood. It's why Nedéans value family, celebrations, our destinies. Why we esteem our very society, our common heritage. Why we need each other. Only in the past few weeks, since meeting these Brutes, have I found those familiar opportunities for connection—the places I've found wholeness in the past—to be lacking somehow. Meeting them . . . finding Rohan . . . has exposed a deeper part of me—an ingrained absence—that no mother, sister, friend, or destiny has filled.

It's the only way to explain why, despite all these years apart, Mother would choose Torvus over her life in Nedé.

Once I hear the scrape of a chair against the floorboards, movement around the room, Torvus asking what else she needs, I figure it's safe to interrupt. I knock tentatively on the door, noticing again the gently curving petals carved into the wood. The design has always struck me as odd, but as I remember Jase's words now—that Torvus built this house for Mother—it makes sense. Every board and thatch, stair and window, was meant for her.

The door swings open and Torvus fills the frame, his shoulders somehow even broader than before. Out of habit, I half expect him to grunt and turn away, but he remains, unmoved, weight evenly balanced over a wide stance. His leathery skin still bears the signs of age and battle, the thick stubble of his chin still tinged with gray. But there's fresh life in his eyes that wasn't there yesterday— a humming energy that radiates from him. He is, somehow, a man made new.

"I'm here to see my mother," I say, a little awkwardly, wondering if my cheeks bear any lingering pink from listening in on their private conversation.

"Reina?" Mother calls from somewhere within.

Torvus shows me to where she rests, then respectfully takes his leave, claiming he needs to check on the cubs. I suspect he aims to give us some privacy, and I'm grateful to him for it.

Torvus's transformation isn't the only change. The house seems different too, and not only because the washbasin sits full, the sparse furniture relieved of its layers of dust, the windows unshuttered, and the bed frame where Mother rests covered with a woven mat and thin blanket. No, the clearest difference is more of an ambience, a feeling. She hasn't been here three hours, and already love lives here.

"Sit," she invites, motioning to the narrow space beside her on the bed. I obey, sidling up to her in a way I haven't since I was probably, oh, seven years old—before I discovered I was vastly different from her and my sisters. Before I began bucking at her affection.

"Are you going with them?" she asks, getting right to the point. I nod.

"And do you know what Torvus means to do?" She angles to better read my expression.

I nod again.

"I learned long ago that I could not control Torvus, and I know better than to think I can dissuade you once you've set your mind to something. But I will tell you this, and I beg you to listen. To withhold forgiveness is like drinking poison and expecting the other to die. Yes, sometimes things must be done for the greater good, and perhaps this is one of those situations. I really don't know. But bitterness will destroy you. Seeking revenge never offers the closure one hopes it will."

She strokes my knee a moment, then adds softly, "I know what she asked of you, Reina."

My eyes fly to hers, instantly on the verge of tears. Somehow, realizing my own mother knows what I did to Treowe unearths a depth of shame I haven't felt since that day in the Arena.

"I don't blame you," she says quickly. "My mother can be very . . . *persuasive*. But I do worry what guilt might lead *you* to do."

I don't pretend not to know what she means. She worries I'll kill my own grandmother, ironically, to avenge the life I took at her command.

She might not be wrong.

But my distrust and distaste for Teera isn't my only motivation. "Torvus and Jase—they say it's the only way to fix this. To make things better for the Gentles."

"Perhaps they're right. Or perhaps there's another way they can't yet see because they're blinded by the injustices done to them." She sighs, leaning heavily against the polished wood headboard behind her. "Forgiveness often gets thwarted by pride. That's something I know all too well. But where forgiveness grows, new paths appear."

The quiet reflectiveness of her tone, the impossible goodness of her words, would have made me testy not so very long ago. They would have reinforced my belief that she was naive to the world—too much a Materno to understand me. But after witnessing the strength she displayed at the Center—and in light of what I now know she's risked for others—I purpose to sit with her words awhile. See if they have merit. She deserves that, at least. So as I reluctantly kiss her goodbye and walk toward the kitchen hut, I play her words over in my mind.

Forgiveness often gets thwarted by pride. Perhaps the pride that kept her and Torvus apart—at least, I think that's what she meant—could have been prevented by forgiveness.

That makes sense, even without knowing the details. Torvus is a new man in the span of a few hours, just by making things right with someone he loves. I watched the weight fall from him—from both of them. But I don't see how that applies to Nedé's eighth

Matriarch. What she has done—what she continues to do—to Gentles is beyond forgiveness. How can we change the future without removing her from power? I'm afraid Torvus is right: I don't see another way.

But that last part . . . *Where forgiveness grows, new paths appear.* Her words pulse in a puzzling rhythm, and instead of thinking about Teera, I find I'm remembering Rohan's pleading eyes this afternoon. The way he seemed so restless to talk. I can't fathom trusting him again—not completely. But, if Mother's right, perhaps I have it backward. Maybe forgiveness needs to come before the path will appear.

CHAPTER NINETEEN

THE NEXT MORNING, I find Rohan in the kitchen, packing a small satchel with food. He straightens slowly as I approach, shifting a rucksack hanging on his back. I can't help but notice the weapons strapped snugly to every limb—more than usual for around camp.

It appears he's leaving, which inexplicably saddens me. "Where are you going?" I ask, irritated at the disappointment in my voice.

"To the cave. We need some supplies kept there."

"Oh." I just stand there, still as a frightened gecko. He wasn't supposed to be busy. I was going to find him unoccupied and ask him to talk, but now . . .

"I was wondering—" I begin, at the same moment he says, "Reina, I—"

I chew the corner of my lip. He runs a hand through his thick hair.

After sufficient awkwardness to make me clam up, he asks tentatively, "Do you want to come with me?" As my eyes widen, he quickly adds, "I could use some help carrying everything back. Jase said he'd come, but I know he has a lot to do here."

I consider the question: a Brute who has drugged me and attacked a Nedéan finca just invited me into the Jungle with him. Alone. Any rational person would say no. *No, no, no.* In fact, a smart woman would run the other direction. Following him would take an enormous amount of . . . *trust.*

And there's the crux of it. I came here to let him tell his side of the story, hoping his answer would lead me toward a path of trust. But maybe—if what Mother said last night is true—forgiveness has to come first, before I *can* trust.

The bandages around his waist remind me that he went out of his way to make a sling for my arm my first time at Tree Camp. He was the one to save me from Dáin. When Fin spied me, and when Dáin returned, Rohan took a protective stance. He was frantic to help me the night the Alexia attacked. Someone who wished me harm wouldn't look at me, talk to me, the way he did at the stream, would they?

Can I forgive him for his involvement in the attack on my sister's finca—for other offenses I might not even know about? I honestly don't know. But I think he has proven I should try.

"Alright," I hear myself say.

He grins with all the enchantment of a sunburst through storm clouds.

———

When we pass a large patch of bird-of-paradise flowers, their spiky heads peeking up from oblong wing-shaped leaves, I recognize the trail. It's the same we took with Jase on the way to the chute. I forgot the other day Rohan mentioned the cave was just upstream from that landmark, the place I first learned Brutes have a playful streak.

When we pass low bushes of fernlike sensitive plant, I trail my finger along dozens of fronds just to watch them curl in on themselves, like Jase showed me.

It's warmer than a pig's armpit, per usual, and I'm grateful Bri and I had a chance to repurpose the clothing Jase gave us into something better suited for Jungle travel than Alexia uniforms: lightweight breeches, cropped just above the knee, and a simple sleeveless top. Dom Tourmaline would probably cringe at the rustic fabric, but I find it surprisingly soft and blessedly cool.

We weave along the narrow path, through encroaching plants of myriad greens, angular shapes, and striking peculiarities—trunks covered in spines, broad leaves punctured with irregular holes, stalks of flowers so vibrantly crimson or pink I can't help but touch their waxy petals. The Jungle is nothing if not fully alive. Dangerous, mysterious, but abounding in sights and sounds that ignite something wild in me, too.

Walking in time to Rohan's steps, I watch his calf muscles flex and relax, flex and relax, as they march out a soothing rhythm. I could almost be content with the chatter of animals and insects for conversation—avoid bringing up the subject he seems happy to ignore for now. Maybe in his mind, my coming with him has put the issue to rest. But just because I'm here doesn't mean we can forget what happened. I hate to ruin this peaceful moment, but I need to know. Deep down, I need to know.

"Rohan?" My voice does little to fill the vast Jungle around us. "Why were you at La Fortuna?"

The predictable beats of his stride stall. His head hangs forward a moment, as if he's gathering the courage to turn around. Searching for the strength to face me.

When he does turn, his resolve to tell me the truth is written all over his face. Right alongside regret.

I press further. "Was Dáin telling the truth? Were you part of the attack?"

"Yes."

"Why?"

"I don't expect you to understand," he begins, "but we've been waiting a long time. Waiting to *do* something about the injustice." He rubs the back of his neck. "It's not in our nature to stand by when things need to change. Dáin said they were getting some supplies from a finca that would help us when the time came to fight. But when we got there . . . it didn't seem pruning hooks and coin were worth . . ."

My throat tightens as I imagine Jonalyn at the mercy of a nightmare she hadn't even known to fear—the panic she must have felt.

"Did you hurt—?"

"No!" he interjects. "But I didn't do anything to stop it, either. It was before I really knew you—before I realized . . ." He trails off, hanging his head. "I didn't hear until later about your sister."

"Why didn't you tell me?"

"I would have . . . eventually. I—" He struggles to find the words. "At first I didn't see a reason for you to know. By the time I realized I should tell you, I was afraid if I did, you wouldn't—" His gaze falls to the packed dirt underfoot.

"Trust you?" I finish, wrapping my arms tightly around myself.

He takes a step closer. "I know I don't deserve your forgiveness."

I want to stay mad. I want to channel all the anger I feel toward Dáin into resentment of this Brute. He put so many innocent people at risk.

My own hypocrisy slams into me like a runaway mare.

My anger deflates as I whisper, "No less than I deserve yours."

His brow furrows.

"It's my fault the Alexia found Tree Camp," I continue. "I practically led them to your door. You might have had a hand in an attack against my people, but I'm responsible for the death of *six* of yours."

He doesn't deny it—doesn't minimize my guilt. In fact, he doesn't say anything. Just fixes me with an unreadable gaze—both welcoming and distant at once. I crumple under it.

He forgave me so easily when Galion returned with the news of the approaching Alexia, but that was before Brutes died because of my carelessness. I was so quick to judge Rohan's motives, even after he trusted mine. An entirely new kind of fear suddenly cripples me: What if he won't forgive me for what *I've* done?

Rationally, he has no reason to.

"Please, Rohan," I say, begging him to reconsider a rejection he hasn't yet spoken. "Please forgive me."

He sighs, not with resignation, but with conviction. "Sometimes people have to get hurt so the right thing can happen."

"Why do you all keep saying that?"

"Because it's true. It's the way life works. There will always be terrible things in this world, Reina. But there will also be good. It's our job to make sure there's more of the latter, even if it means sacrificing our very lives." His intensity rises. "It's part of being a man. Those who died in the Alexia's attack understood that. They died with honor."

They died with honor. I can see how choosing death to overcome tyranny carries inherent nobility—a unique type of strength. I've watched it firsthand. The corners of my eyes sting with threatening tears as I remember Treowe's insistence that he face me in the Arena, his eyes urging me to shoot.

"Brutes aren't the only people who would sacrifice themselves for the good of others," I say. "My best friend—a Gentle—he understood it. He died with honor too."

"A Gentle?" he asks, incredulously.

"Yes, a Gentle." My own insecurity over my unsanctioned friendship with Tre warms my cheeks with embarrassment. "It's forbidden to talk to them, let alone form a friendship, but he—"

"No," Rohan interrupts. "I mean, a *Gentle* sacrificed himself? For the good of others? I didn't think—Why would he—?"

"I killed him," I confess. If we're going to forgive and trust each other, telling Rohan the whole truth is probably important. Still, I look away, unwilling to watch his opinion of me sour.

I feel his eyes on me, hear concern in his question. "Why?"

"To prove to Teera I was Apprentice material. Tre knew it was coming, but he chose death anyway. He chose to take my arrow because he believed I was the Gentles' best chance of change. But I've regretted *my* choice every day since."

Rohan grows somber. Once again, I find myself wishing for a pat *It's okay,* or *Don't beat yourself up, Rei.*

Instead he says, "We'd better get going."

I follow silently, imagining what terrible things he must think of me.

Not five minutes later, he veers off the trail into seemingly unmarked territory. "There's something I want to show you," he says. "It's not far out of our way."

———

We climb an exposed hillside covered in ferns, drenched in sun, and punctuated with towering cohune palms. When we reach the summit, Rohan shimmies through a narrow crevice between two boulders taller than both of us combined.

"Through here," he says.

I don't particularly like being squeezed between slabs of stone, but when we reach the other side, I swear I'd crawl through far worse for the chance to see what awaits us.

We've emerged into a lush paradise so breathtaking I wouldn't have imagined it possible ten seconds before. Delicate ferns and spongy moss cling to dark rock walls on all sides, which enclose us like a living arena, the deep green peppered with vibrant strands of white, violet, and peach orchids. At our feet, a crystal-clear pool stretches ten meters across. From the ridge to our right, a waterfall cascades down an incline of rock, sliding along slippery moss and smooth stones before tumbling over a ledge into the rippling pool below. The rich scent carried on the mist can only be described as deliciously living—fresh and pure and even greener than the plants surrounding us. A single morpho butterfly—bluer than the azure sky above—pumps its papery wings, fluttering haltingly up the rock wall and down again, then around the perimeter, nearly brushing my cheek as it passes by.

Speechless, I slowly step straight into the pool, letting the cool water inch up my legs as I spin to take it all in. Beauty like this shouldn't be possible.

Anywhere my gaze lands, new details demand awe—from the tiny yellow-and-black frogs sunning on a rock to the riot of red leaves unfurling from a nearby bush. The place is stunning in its detail, marvelous in its combined effect. I spin another complete circle.

That's how I see him. Just looking at me.

He wears a grin as wide as that time he flipped me off our raft outside the chute. He dropped the subject of Tre so abruptly that I've been worried what he must think of me. But I don't see a trace of condescension or anger.

Stepping in beside me, he cools his limbs with handfuls of water. I try not to notice the way his wet skin glistens like the pearlescent multicolored pebbles under the dancing surface of the pool.

"It's amazing," I say, though the word seems a fiercely inadequate descriptor. "Thank you for showing it to me."

"I thought you'd like it."

We stand shoulder to shoulder, watching the hypnotizing water fall, fall, fall, breathing it in, in, in.

Then he splashes me before diving into the dark center of the pool.

"You Brute!" I laugh, as he quickly escapes toward the waterfall with effortless strokes.

"Come on," he calls back to me.

I'm easily convinced, and swim to join him on the other side. He treads water right under the flow, purposefully angling his head so the water splashes into my face. I dunk him, which takes considerable effort. He pulls me under, too easily. We both emerge laughing and spitting water, drinking in the uncommon euphoria only available on this side of sorrow and loss, confusion and pain. For this moment, I feel like a child—free and alive.

We drift on our backs, letting the falls push us slowly toward shore. When he can stand, he lifts me out of the water and drops me back in, then laughs at my irritation.

"You're worse than the cubs," I tease, recognizing a clear reflection of Pip's brashness in this full-grown Brute.

The thought of Pip reminds me of Tree Camp, and my sister Jo. Guilt sweeps in, overshadowing the bright joy I felt just moments ago. How can we be so selfishly occupied when others need us? My self-reproach must show because he says, "What is it?"

"It just seems unfair, that we're here, enjoying this, while everyone else is preparing to leave their home."

He shrugs, in a half-conceding sort of way. "Sometimes you have to live in the moment."

He steps closer, reaches out to remove a twig from my hair.

Just that touch, the slightest brush of his fingers in my hair, ignites an overwhelming wish to be *closer*.

"We should go," I say, though unable to look away from his gaze. "We still have to get the supplies."

My words have a strange effect. He looks like he wants to say something, or do something, but now isn't sure what's best. Still, he doesn't draw back when he says, "I asked you a question once—you didn't know the answer then." He pauses a moment, as if still trying to decide whether to bring it up. When he speaks again, I know he's taking a great risk. "Do you know now which is better?"

I know exactly what he's talking about. It's the question he asked me high in the mahogany tree, as the glow of sunset tempted me to find him endearing. *Between us and the Gentles*, he had asked then, *which is* better? I couldn't answer him that night because I honestly didn't know. Gentles were predictable, helpful . . . *safe*. I had only known for twenty-four hours that Brutes existed, and my experience with them was markedly *mixed*. Despite the near-instant affinity I felt for Jase and the strange electricity I experienced with Rohan that day, I couldn't definitively say whether their charming qualities outweighed their potential to harm us. My interaction with Dáin ensured that.

But since then, so much has changed.

I search his eyes, hungry for an answer. "I think you know."

"I need to hear you say it." His wet hair drips into his face and down his shoulders, and if I didn't know better, I might think he was holding his breath.

"*You* are better, Rohan."

He places a broad hand against my cheek, brushes my lip with his thumb. He leans toward me, and the world around us freezes. No cloud shifts, no bird ruffles its feathers, no shadow lengthens, no cell divides. The world shrinks in on itself, until it contains only his being and mine, drawn inexplicably together by a force as ancient as the universe itself.

My heart pounds through my chest.

I *want* him to be closer—want to feel his lips against mine. The desire feels as uncontrollable as the untamed Jungle around us.

I suck in a breath.

There's a reason Article V exists, Reina Pierce. And it probably has everything to do with this.

Desire must be mastered. Its dangers destroyed the world of the foremothers. It's the antithesis of self-control. These are truths I've been taught my whole life. So I intuitively know I shouldn't feel this strongly . . . especially for a Brute.

And yet I do.

Somehow, quickly, I muster every ounce of self-restraint I've ever possessed to turn away, to reject the arms I want around me, and slip through the boulders into the fern-carpeted glade beyond.

Part Three

CHAPTER TWENTY

JASE AND BRI WALK JUST AHEAD OF ME. "Not far now," he tells her.

I certainly hope not—we don't have much light left.

A line of ants intersects the path underfoot, each segmented insect hoisting a jagged section of leaf overhead like a stiff green sail five times its size. Undeterred by the danger around their ranks, they march on, tipping and jostling under their flat loads, determinedly crawling over sticks and through decaying debris.

I scan the long line of Brutes in front of and behind me, carrying large packs of supplies, stepping resolutely over logs and between branches, not unlike the insects underfoot. Some of the younger cubs rest between bundles on the horses' backs. Others ride in one of several wheelbarrow-like carts Galion constructed yesterday, salvaging wood from the huts destroyed in the battle and round pulleys from the speed lines. Even though the cubs are probably tough enough to make the journey on foot, we wouldn't stand a chance of reaching the ruins by nightfall. So the older Brutes take turns pushing the carts or guiding the horses, in addition to carrying their own packs.

Torvus leads our procession through the unmarked forest, from memory or by camouflaged signs, I can't tell. He's careful to take us through long stretches of creek or shallow river whenever possible, minimizing our tracks. He won't let history repeat itself.

Rohan positions himself last to ensure we don't lose any stragglers. We've barely had time to speak since returning from the cave yesterday afternoon. Maybe that's best. He has seemed distant since. I don't blame him, but neither can I make sense of the strange longing our encounter ignited in me. So how can I explain my fears to him? I need more time to process my weakness, figure out how to be stronger around him.

The rest of us are sandwiched between Rohan and Torvus— Bri, Neechi, and me, plus every Brute from Tree Camp, Dáin and the other defectors included. Torvus reluctantly allowed them to return to the clan under fierce and detailed threats of injury if they subvert his authority again.

We've been walking since dawn, forced to leave a good home because of my stupidity.

I told Mother how terrible I felt about my carelessness in the gray stillness just before dawn, as we reluctantly said our goodbyes on Torvus's porch. She assured me it wasn't my fault—not really. "Teera has been searching for years, Rei," she had said. "It was only a matter of time before she discovered their location. He knows you were trying to help."

He knows . . . The thought of her and Torvus talking about me behind closed doors made me feel like a child, but I tried to bottle my guilty conscience so I could focus on the mother I just got back instead of beating myself up.

"I wish you'd come with us," I told her again.

She sighed, tucking a strand of hair that had escaped my braids behind my ear. "It's for the best. Marsa and Dom Bakshi need to know I'm alive. And as long as my mother thinks I'm *not*, I might be able to do some good yet."

The mention of Teera seemed to make her more urgent. She cupped my face in her hands. "I know she is harsh, self-serving, and unpredictable—" valid points, all—"but remember, Reina, regardless of a person's motivations, all actions have consequences. I'd hate for yours to be dictated by hers."

She kissed my forehead, lingering close, as if trying to seal the memory of my scent.

I glanced toward my sister then, expecting her to give Mother a final embrace as well. Instead Jo stared back apologetically.

"As much as I want to be there for you, Rei, I can't let Mother journey home alone. She's too weak. Besides, Cassia needs me, and La Fortuna must be rebuilt. Then, depending on how things go in Phoenix City . . . with the *plan*, I want to help Mother rescue more babies."

I smiled. "I knew you'd do something to help—in your own way."

"You're not disappointed?"

"Having you with me has been amazing, but you're absolutely right." My arms wrapped her tightly. "You are so much braver than I ever knew. But this is my fight now. You're not abandoning me—you're staying alive for Cassia . . . and your other son, and Finch." I kiss her forehead. "They need you too."

At that, she squeezed me tighter. "I love you."

"You too, Jo."

She swayed Finch tenderly, kissing his hair, cheeks, and fingers before handing him to Ori, tears running unapologetically down her dusty cheeks.

Jase enveloped Mother next, tucking her into his arms with a tenderness I thought only daughters could feel for the women who gave them life.

"Be careful, Mother," he said softly.

"Oh, Jason. If only there were more time."

Mother and Torvus must have already said all that needed saying; they embraced silently, a single tear the only indication of Mother's reluctance to leave. But when Torvus restrung the tree pendant around her neck, I felt the loss for her. And when she began her journey back to Bella Terra, she carried pieces of our hearts with her.

The rest of us trekked south, leaving behind orchards and aqueducts, the fire pit and tree huts, supplies we couldn't carry and the beautiful, otherworldly mahogany tree. And forty-one bamboo cages, occupied by Alexia prisoners.

"Do you think they've figured it out yet?" I ask Jase, remembering the fierce women's wide eyes when, at Torvus's command, Brutes cracked open a hundred green coconuts littering the Jungle floor and slipped the husks through the bars of their cages—enough creamy, gelatinous meat to last them at least three days. Then Torvus gave one Alexia a small, sharp rock. "Be resourceful," he said, before stomping away from Tree Camp.

Jase purses his lips. "Maybe. Depends whether she realized the stone will carve through bamboo faster than it would saw through lashing."

I nod. Either way, once she gets free, she'll find something to pry open or smash the other cages. With a stroke of luck, they might even uncover the pit a hundred meters from camp where the Alexia weapons lie buried. Well, the weapons the Brutes didn't pilfer for themselves. They might have been magnanimous enough to free their enemies, but when it comes to blades, they have a greedy streak. The Alexia will have to walk back to Nedé—Torvus insisted we release the horses we weren't taking with us—but they'll make it home alright, despite their injuries. They're Alexia, after all.

Alexia like me.

Pride buoys me as we ascend another hillside, one of a seeming thousand we've trekked up and over today. My thighs burn and my shoulders are painfully raw where the sack's straps rub against them. My feet ache in my boots, and my shirt is soaked through with sweat. But if these Brutes can hike all day without complaining, so will I.

As we near the crest of the hill, a jolt of gold sprays across the canopy—the sun's last breath exhaled overhead. So much for making it to the ruins before nightfall.

But as the incline flattens, we're not met with another kilometer of crowded green Jungle as I expect. Instead, a vast lawn of overgrown grass stretches before us, hemmed in on three sides by enormous stone structures.

I'm not sure what I was expecting. A broken-down building, maybe. Some decayed boards or concrete rubble, like the sites in Nedé that predate the foremothers, where the Innovatus sometimes find materials to repurpose. But this—

Three pyramids rise from the Jungle, one each in the north, south, and west—layers and layers of stones stacked one upon another, reaching toward the sky. Steep stone steps lead to the upper levels, which are so tall they clear the very canopy. And they are eerily intact. If it weren't for dislodged rocks littering the grass, and dark lichen streaking the otherwise sand-colored stones, I might wonder whether these towers were built in my lifetime.

The sun melts into a bank of clouds behind the western pyramid, infusing the sky with orange-gold warmth. The rest of the sky fades to gray, lending its vibrancy to the spectacle in the west. I drop my pack, but my feet are drawn up and into the light like a moth to a candle's flame. The stairs lead me up, up, up until

I'm above the canopy too. The world rolls away, all shadows and gold, the enormous sky stretching from one horizon to the other. The vista presses my chest with the weight of all three pyramids combined. It's a sacred view.

Whoever created it must have known the power of such things. Could they have been—

A Brute voice interrupts my thoughts. "Incredible, isn't it?"

Rohan climbs the last step, joining me on the platform.

I wonder if he can tell I'm glad it's him. "Who did this?"

He shrugs. "Don't know. But they knew what they were doing. Look at the position of the sun." He leans closer, showing me the correct angle. "Each of the pyramids aligns with a particular star or constellation. Jem figured that out. And the carvings—I'll show you tomorrow—they seem to tell stories of rulers and battles and sacrifices."

"Sacrifices?"

He shakes his head with a laugh. "They weren't Gentles, I can tell you that much."

I hate when he talks about the Gentles like that—like they're less than. But the view inspires me to ignore the snub. "What do you mean?"

"It looks like if they won a battle, they'd kill the other leader to thank their gods. Or rip out his heart or something."

"They were Brutes then." I grimace before realizing how that might sound to present company. I guess we both have our ingrained assumptions.

He deflects the insult. "We all have to choose."

"So you keep reminding me."

"And I'll keep reminding you until you understand. I don't know if they were good men," he says, turning his back to take in the ruins, "but some of them cared, at least. They must have worked hard. Thousands of people would have lived here—men, women, children. They couldn't have survived if they were all what Nedéans suppose us to be."

I consider this while howler monkeys shout their final daily threats to neighboring troops.

Roofless structures dot the perimeter of the lawn between the pyramids—a maze of catacombs filled with grass, debris, and a few determined trees. Storage rooms, perhaps? Long-abandoned houses? I try to imagine the buildings in their former glory, thatched and whole—with people coming and going, cooking and creating. Children playing ball on the lawn. Women and Brutes, living together.

Dom Bakshi taught us there was a time before the foremothers when Brutes and women coexisted in the world. My general Nedéan experience—formal education supplemented with neighbors' gossip, Initus ceremonies, and Grandmother's patronizing lectures—combined with my imagination, led me to believe it was a terrifying existence for the women of old. Even before the Brutes were wiped out by the Great Sickness, they cared nothing for women. Women lived in fear for their safety. The foremothers escaped, and the Gentles they cured of inferior genetics now serve us. We are all the world has left, but we have all that we need. We're happy. Safe. It's a history I accepted as fact—I had no reason to question it, until reading Tristan Pierce's journal.

Hundreds of steps below, the Brutes unload horses, light fires, and prepare dinner in this mythical place, and I consider how these people have surprised me. They've challenged so much of what I considered fact. And these ruins—I never imagined something like this existed, so close to Nedé yet completely outside our knowledge. It makes me wonder what else I've been wrong about. What other realities might hide just beyond my sight.

A terrifying possibility suddenly seizes me, and I blurt, "Could there be other people out there?"

He presses a fist to his lips, studying me carefully. "Are you sure you would want to know if there were?"

What a dumb thing to ask. Of course I—

Actually, with everything else that's already upending my world, maybe I'm not entirely sure I want an answer. Still, he'll think me a chicken if I back down now, so I say, "Yes."

He snatches one of the many sticks littering the platform and begins peeling the end, seeming in no hurry to answer, or maybe deciding how much to share.

"I don't know," he finally says. "There might be. I haven't seen anything definite myself, but Dantès swears that one time when he was exploring the sea south of Nedé, he saw a sail in the distance. Maybe it was a trick of the light. Maybe not. When he told us, Torvus played it off. But I have my suspicions."

His suspicions aren't fact, at least. There's a chance he's wrong, and I cling to it. I have enough to worry about in the near future without adding "unknown threats" to the list.

Sun-fire has faded to dusk, and a host of Jungle insects coax the coming night with their serenade. The rolling canopy, spreading in every direction, sighs in the deepening shadow. With it, I try to rock back to sleep the impossible possibility this place has tried to awaken.

CHAPTER TWENTY-ONE

THE NEXT DAY, we do what we can to turn the ruins into a suitable home for the Brutes. Bri, Neechi, and I help clear the rubble from the stone chambers, dig new storage pits for the fruit, nuts, and dried meat we transported from Tree Camp, and gather some of the pyramids' dislodged rocks to create a new fire ring. Although Torvus and the seven oldest Brutes will continue southeast in the morning, plenty of able-bodied, hardworking younger Brutes will remain to hunt for meat, finish thatching roofs, and generally improve the place in our absence. They won't be left unprotected. The weapons cache—a mixture of Brute and Alexia blades, bows, bolas, and spears—fills a whole stone storeroom.

By the second morning, as we prepare to depart, the ruins already hum with busy routine. Traps are set, wood gathered, water from a nearby river hauled into stone vessels. Torvus gives last-minute instructions to the oldest Brutes staying behind.

"Will they be safe here?" I ask Jase.

"Safer than we'll be," Dáin answers for him. The moody Brute shoves final supplies into his pack. Last night Torvus announced the defector would be joining us—doesn't trust him out of his sight, I'd wager—bringing our cohort to eleven.

Bri snorts. Of course *she* would find his snark amusing.

Jase ignores them both but doesn't soften his answer for me. "Safe isn't the highest goal, not now." He squeezes my shoulder. "Unless the Alexia figure out this location, they'll be alright. They know how to take care of themselves."

I observe the clearing again: the progress on a roof, a growing pile of brush and sticks beside the fire ring; dozens of Brutes—none seeming older than eighteen—armed and busily making this place their new home.

As we say our final goodbyes and shoulder our packs, I certainly hope Jase is right.

———

For two days we trek through the unforgiving Jungle, south and slightly east, stopping only to eat provisions, sleep in our tree hammocks, clean still-healing wounds from the battle, and reapply the insect salve Rohan wisely portioned for each of us. I don't care that, in this stifling heat, the oil feels like tar against my already-tacky skin. Without some kind of shield, I suspect we'd all fall down dead—completely siphoned of blood by the swarming, whining mosquitoes barely held at bay by his magic ointment.

Hour upon hour we tromp through the undisturbed forest, at a pace only the Brutes could set: somewhere between a trot and a canter of death. Torvus nearly always leads, using a machete to hack a path through lianas and dense networks of fronds and vines. Sometimes Rohan, Jase, or Théo take turns at the lead, but Torvus seems to prefer the role. I think he likes thwacking things—brings him inner peace or something.

Neechi does his best to keep up, but more than once I wonder whether he'll survive the journey. Jase promises it will be easier for him once we get to the river, so I urge him on, reminding him he's stronger than he thinks. Galion, who avoids Neechi whenever possible—doesn't even glance at him unless he has to—surprises us all the second morning. Without a word, he fits the Gentle's pack across his chest, counterbalancing the supplies already on his back.

Bri holds her own, silently weathering the heat and pace like an Alexia. I often forget she was a Politikós before the Succession— that the Bri I know isn't the woman she trained to be. At the Exhibition of the Arts she conversed with Amal Senators like a respectable Dom, revealing she could tame her harsh bravado if she thought it was in her best interest. And here she is, keeping pace with Brutes she didn't even know existed much more than a week ago. Full of surprises, she is.

Rohan rarely ventures far from me, but neither does he linger within arm's reach. If we're climbing a bank, he sends me ahead of him, makes sure I can reach the rock ledge. If we're crossing a river, packs held high above our heads, I notice he positions himself downstream. Without the luxury of time, I make little progress toward sorting my feelings about him. I just know I like when he's around.

We consume water as though our bodies are sieves, every drop we drink sweated back out in seconds. Though we follow streams when we can, eventually our flasks run dry. About the time my mouth puckers like I've been chewing on banana skin, Jem silently fells a nondescript woody vine as thick as Torvus's forearm and taller than Théo. Laying it flat along the ground, he chops it into meter-long sections with his machete. Galion is the first to lift a piece overhead, angling it until water trickles from the bottom of the vine into his mouth.

"Water vine," Jase explains, noticing my slack jaw. He hands a section to Bri, then Neechi.

Wondering if there will be enough to go around, I scan the area and notice an identical branch nearby. I go to work hacking off a section for myself, feeling pretty smart. Rohan ambles casually beside me, then puts a hand on my arm.

"Not that one," he says, his mouth warring between concern and amusement. "That one'll kill you."

I stare at the rough wood in my hand, then back at Jem's vine. They look *indistinguishable* to me, except for a coating of black sap on one side of mine. Some of it has rubbed off on my hand, and a strange burning sensation spreads quickly across my palm.

"Ow!" I squirm, watching my skin redden. "Am I seriously going to die?"

"Not yet," Rohan says absently, scanning the surrounding area.

"Not *yet*?" I cry after him, but he either doesn't hear me or thinks my panic's funny.

He makes for a tree with flaky red bark and gathers a handful of its oval leaves. With no mortar or pestle, he twists the leaves with his bare hands, massages them with a bit of vine water, then presses the moist wad into my palm, curling my fingers around it.

"Hold this for a few hours," he instructs. Noticing my wide eyes and shaking hands, he concedes, "It won't really kill you—not unless you eat it."

I want to kick him in the shin for scaring me like that, but I'm too grateful for his remedy to strike. I guess we'll call it even.

On our way to rejoin the others, I ask, "How do you know so much about the Jungle?"

He shrugs. "We've all had to survive out here."

"I know, but how did you *learn* about it, without getting killed by water vine look-alikes?"

He grins. "I guess you start to see patterns, plant families. It's like a game—a puzzle—to figure out what each has to offer. I've been playing since I was a cub. The dangerous ones usually let you know in some way."

"And if they don't?"

"If they don't, there's usually an antidote growing nearby."

"Lucky for me."

"For us both." He grins again. "I knocked myself out half a dozen times trying to get the right concentration of sordy root for the darts."

"That explains a lot," I tease. Still, I'm a bit relieved to hear I wasn't the first test subject for that tranquilizer my first night in the Jungle.

Torvus is already twenty meters ahead, vigorously hacking a path as though he hasn't been swinging his arm for two days. Bri and I reluctantly pick up our packs to follow.

"The moral of this story," she says, after draining the last of her *real* water vine, "is to stay out of the Jungle." She tosses the empty wood into a pile of leaves.

"Awww—is the little Alexia tired?" Dáin taunts as he saunters past, making sure Jase isn't around, I notice.

Her eyes narrow. "Does the little Brute want to taste my fist again?"

Dáin barks out a laugh, seeming to enjoy their exchanges more and more.

Jase waits a dozen paces ahead for the rest of us to catch up.

I squeeze the ball of leaves tighter against the sharp pain prickling my skin. Small blisters already form along my thumb and forefinger. But Rohan was right: a few hours later, nearing dusk, my legs threaten to seize up and fall off from exhaustion, but my hand is nearly pain-free.

We reach a broad river just before nightfall, twice as wide as the Jabiru. If I'm not mistaken, it's the roily, gray-green water of Rio del Sur—the river that marks the southernmost boundary of Nedé, though we must be kilometers yet from reaching Nedé's western border.

Exhausted, Neechi slumps against the trunk of a gumbo-limbo tree. "Are we camping here?" he asks, taking his sack from Galion in anticipation of dinner and sleep.

"Not tonight," Jase apologizes.

Met with blank stares, he explains the plan: we'll run the river at night, divided between three canoes that lie hidden in brush along the riverbank. Nedé's southern border is sparsely inhabited, but we can't take the chance of being seen. If we paddle swiftly, we should reach the Halcyon in two nights, resting during the day on the south side of the river.

Dantès interrupts to brag that he and Jem have single-handedly dug out ten of these canoes from Santa Maria logs—felled themselves—with plans for ten more, in the event they needed to relocate camp quickly. Brutes certainly spend a great deal of time imagining eventualities.

So instead of sleeping in gently swinging hammocks, cocooned in breezy trees, we spend the night earnestly paddling down the swaying currents of Rio del Sur.

I understand now why Torvus was so determined to reach the river by dusk. Even a bright gibbous moon—like the one illuminating our watery highway tonight—hides us better than the sun would have. Despite the cover of night, we keep to the southern bank as much as possible, to blend in with the thick Jungle backdrop of the wilds.

The canoes are sturdy, if not as wide or sleek as the Nedéan rivercraft the Gentles use to transport produce and goods up and down the Jabiru, trading from each of the four provinces with Phoenix City. These keep out the water, though, which is all that matters tonight.

Torvus strategically arranged us to spread the weaker paddlers across the vessels, putting Neechi in the boat with him, Galion, and Dáin. Ten meters behind them, Jase, Bri, Dantès, and Jem paddle in impressive sync. And in our boat, Théo and Rohan's combined muscle makes up for the empty seat between me and Théo, who takes the front. Rohan claimed the bench behind me, and I can't say I mind, even with the strange tension between us. I like having him close, even though I know better than to speak above the slightest whisper. Even his silent presence makes me feel somehow safer.

If I weren't so tired, I might actually enjoy the unique enchant-ment of the river at night—the swish of our paddles through the black water, the wide swath of stars mirroring the break in the canopy, the occasional owl swooping from one bank to the other. As the hours pass, the moon arcs slowly overhead, in and out of wispy clouds, casting a soft light across the sleeping world, illumi-nating flittering bats and the glowing orbs of crocodile eyes. The nocturnal river reveals yet another side of the wild Jungle I didn't know existed.

Neechi paddled slowly but consistently through the night. Now his oar lies across his lap, his torso folded over on itself. By the time the moon disappears behind the foothills and the black of night morphs from coal to darkest gray, blisters bleed where the wooden paddle rubs against my still-tender palm and fingers. My eyes beg to close, my body sways like the water beneath, longing to slosh against the bottom of the boat to quench the agony of exhaustion.

Still the Brutes paddle. The consistent *slip-slosh-slip* of Rohan's sure strokes hasn't hitched all night, and neither of the other canoes have trailed more than fifteen meters apart.

When the predawn glow brightens enough to differentiate colors, we follow the lead boat into a brushy alcove in the bank. We hide our canoes, climb into the trees, and sleep the day away like moss-streaked sloths.

But as soon as darkness lends cover, we climb back into our respective canoes, recharged by rest and food, ready to paddle to the world's end if necessary.

The burst of energy lasts an hour or so before the monotony of paddling returns, the eerie shapes and sounds of the surrounding Jungle banks calling attention to how very little stands between my rear end and whatever hides in the pitch-black water beneath our boat.

On the upside, Dantès suggested wrapping the handle of my oar with a smooth banana leaf, and that—combined with another batch of Rohan's pulpy green mush—makes for slightly more comfortable paddling.

Our second night on the river seems to pass much slower than we paddle, even though Torvus paces us even faster than the night before. More than once I wonder why I decided to join this mission. In fact, I'm pondering what was so important that we needed to paddle to our deaths when Torvus suddenly veers toward a cut in the southern bank. We follow into a near-tunnel of black mangrove, rising like a wall on either side, strangling the moonlight and shrouding us in near-complete darkness. My eyes strain to see even my own paddle, and twice Théo alerts us to low branches by getting smacked with them himself.

Thirty minutes later, the mangrove walls open up into a bankless expanse beneath a dome of stars. We've entered a lagoon of sorts, I think. I strain to glimpse a tree line, but see only stars above, blackness beneath, and . . . I must be more exhausted than

I realize. I blink hard, rub my eyes. When I open them again, Jase's boat, just ahead of us, appears to be floating on blue starlight, its wake stringing behind like a phosphorescent motmot tail. I glance down at my paddle. Each time it dips into the water, a glowing blue shadow swirls around it.

I draw back with a gasp.

"What is this place?" I whisper, my pulse beginning to race.

Rohan chuckles softly at my fear. "Watch this," he says, then slices his oar backward into the water, spraying glowing blue droplets across the side of our boat, soaking us in warm lagoon water.

"Hey!" Théo barks, a little too loudly, then sends water ricocheting back toward Rohan.

I receive a face full of cross fire. It drips down my cheeks and nose, tastes salty on my lips. A shiver races up my spine, from chill and awe.

A school of fish swim alongside, like an underwater meteor shower—their every movement igniting ethereal squiggles. Pulsating circles—jellies, maybe—bob and weave alongside our canoe, then disappear underneath.

"Unbelievable," I whisper. I don't think we're in danger of being overheard here, but this place demands a reverence incompatible with noise. I try to concentrate on keeping pace with the others' strokes, but I'm completely captivated by the dreamworld around us.

Rohan leans closer with hushed words. "Dantès and Jem discovered it, when they were building the two-hull."

"Why does it do that?" I ask, trailing a finger through the water as we glide.

"Don't know. Something in the water gets agitated when it's disturbed—but you can only see it at night, only at certain times of the year, and it doesn't happen during a full moon."

"How strange."

"Kinda makes you wonder what else is out there, you know? What other strange, beautiful places exist beyond what we've seen."

I think of the ruins, and the people who once built them—about the possibility of "what else" might be discovered if we went looking. It's a new question to me, but not to Rohan. I rest my paddle across the canoe and turn to face him.

"Do *you* want to find out?" I ask quietly. The moon offers just enough light to recognize his features, not enough to read his eyes.

"A few of us have been thinking about it."

"Of leaving Nedé? I mean, the Jungle?"

He paddles three strokes before answering. "Once things are settled, yes."

I don't know why this makes my chest ache—why it dims the brilliance of the eerie light show around us. In the remaining hour it takes to paddle across the lagoon, the glowing blue shadows hold less appeal. Instead I fight against a sorrow directly opposed to my better sense.

I don't want him to go.

———

Night still twirls her dark skirts when we reach the shore, and we take the opportunity to sleep on a very narrow stretch of sandy bank, trying to rally a few hours of sleep before we attempt what Dantès brags is the most difficult crossing yet. Just like a Brute to relish the challenge.

When the sun nudges us from sleep, warming our backs and illuminating the world where we've landed, I'm glad we waited to enter the swampy marsh and tangled mangroves in daylight.

"We're going through *that*?" Bri gawks.

Jase seems genuinely sorry to put us through it. "It's not fun, but it's the fastest way to the sea. Just try to stay up on the roots.

You'll be fine." He offers a reassuring smile as he slips his bare arms through his pack.

In response, Bri slicks her hair back with cool lagoon water, resigned determination hardening her features. Neechi looks as though he might crumple as he lifts his pack, but before he can shoulder it, Galion swipes it up again.

I give the swarthy Brute a grateful smile as he tromps into the mangroves.

Rohan says, "I'm impressed with him."

"Me too. I got the impression he felt weird around Neechi when we first arrived."

"I meant your Gentle."

Ignoring the supposed compliment, I huff, "He's not *my* Gentle." What is it with this Brute and condescension? "And he has a name, you know."

His jaw stiffens, but he offers an apologetic tip of his head. "I didn't mean to be rude . . ."

"Well, it is rude," I interrupt, "to assume that just because someone is weaker than you, they don't deserve the decency of respect, the benefit of the doubt."

My ire rises with each word, reflected in my building volume.

His steady gaze forces me to take a deep breath.

Rohan isn't the only one who dismisses them—*bats*, all of Nedé does! So why does his ambivalence make me so mad?

Maybe I'm taking out my collective frustration on him, though I couldn't say why.

Maybe I care what Rohan thinks about the Gentles because I care about them.

That can't be the whole of it, though. I don't get this testy with fellow Nedéans when they're harsh or patronizing to Nedé's Gentles—not even people I know. That leaves only one other explanation, and it makes me rock back on my heels.

I care what Rohan thinks about the Gentles because I care about *him*. And that being the case, I want desperately for him to see them—to see the world—through my eyes.

Rohan lifts my pack to make it easier for me to slip it on. "You're right."

Wait—what?

In all my blustering, I wasn't expecting him to actually see my side so quickly. I turn to face him as the others start gingerly picking their way into the swamp.

"I am?"

He pierces me with a meaningful stare. "It would be foolish to make assumptions about people based on their level of strength." He leans in closer, and I think I stop breathing. "Wouldn't you agree?"

He holds my gaze, long enough for me to work out his meaning. Rohan is wrong to think less of Gentles for their weaknesses—just as Nedéans are wrong to assume everyone with a Brute's strength is dangerous. Just as *I* did.

"Yes," I finally whisper. "I do."

He smiles a little, then shoulders his own pack. "Besides, for what it's worth, *Neechi* can throw a mean coconut."

For roughly two kilometers, we slog through a tangled mangrove swamp. Jem demonstrates how to jump nimbly from root to root like a graceful monkey swinging between limbs, but more often than not, my attempts to hop from one oddly angled perch to the next land me knee-deep in thick red-brown mud. If Torvus hadn't pointed out a poisonous coral snake slithering menacingly through the muck, I'd contemplate stripping out of my boots—for Siyah's sake, maybe even out of my breeches—to make the going easier. But I suppose mud-filled boots are preferable to dying by snakebite in this miserable tomb.

Even the Brutes seem more irritable through this leg of the journey. All except Jase, who still offers encouraging words to me and Neechi and laughs heartily at Bri's increasingly sarcastic gibes. "Why bother taking over Nedé when you could live in *this* paradise?" she shoots, and "For all your nifty Bruteness, you'd think you could have made a *bridge*, or *canal*, or *something* useful."

Eventually the mud thins a bit, along with Bri's jawing, and brave coconut palms occasionally shoot up from among the mangroves, like feathery umbrellas. Soon bromeliads grow in the branches of broadleaf trees, and after another hour, a delicious salty breeze cuts through the stagnant swamp air like life itself. When, through the tangle, I catch my first glimpse of distant lapping water, I nearly whoop in jubilation.

We made it.

CHAPTER TWENTY-TWO

THE HALCYON SEA DANCES UNDER a brisk wind, lapping gently against piles of frilly, glistening green-brown kelp along the shore—mounds and mounds of it, fermenting in the sun. At Finca del Mar, Gentles rake the beaches before any debris can accumulate. This untouched, unruly shoreline underscores the very reason I've never been farther than I can swim from Nedé's coast.

Years ago, when I was nine or ten, Mother took my sisters and me to a particularly fine beach in Lapé Province for a holiday. While we canvassed the grainy sand for shells, I overheard some women talking about an incident that had occurred the week before. A group of three Gentles had been fishing for red snapper a hundred yards out. Somehow the long rope securing their boat to the dock untethered, and a strong afternoon current swept them away, never to be seen again.

The memory unnerves me.

The sea is unpredictable—everyone knows this. One false move and she could drag you from the safety of Nedé to who knows where, or swallow you whole if you're not careful. That's why only a few brave, nautically inclined women—and a small task force of courageous Alexia—venture out in little sailboats. And even then, they watch the wind and stick to the calmer waters near the shoreline—never beyond the reef.

It was easier to push down my apprehension about this leg of our journey when we were kilometers away. Now the place where sky meets sea, usually so bewitching, appears exponentially distant.

The Brutes scout the beach for safety before we wade into the dark blue-brown water. Mud and sweat melt from our skin like the sediment stirred by our steps. Most of the Brutes rinse quickly, though Rohan unwinds his bandages to soak the still-healing wounds with seawater before returning to shore.

I dip under the cool, salty water to keep from staring and to tame my unruly hair, braids tangled from days of travel and the stiff breeze. When I surface, Bri joins me, and we wade deep enough to rinse our trousers clean.

When we emerge, refreshed and blessedly free of mud, Torvus and Dantès have already cleared masses of concealing brush from a boat resting a few meters from the waterline. It takes four Brutes to slide the vessel into the water, and as they maneuver it, I can see why they dub this the "two-hull."

Twin canoes—each easily six meters long—run parallel, connected by a raised platform three meters wide and two-thirds as long as the hulls. A mast rises from the platform, straight and tall as a queen palm—about as thick too. An oily cloth drapes from the mast, dingy brown, fringed by a few slack ropes.

"Half on each side," Torvus orders. "Dantès and Jem, take the rear; Dáin, where I can see you."

"Our packs?" Jem asks.

"Lash them to the platform. We'll need them on the island."

The island. When Jase first explained the plan to approach Phoenix City by sea, he mentioned it. At the time, I received the information with as much concern as his voice held— *none*. But now, climbing into a boat that sways atop wind-swept rivulets, I barely restrain the panicked curses itching my tongue.

In theory, I know what an island is. The foremothers left record of several they passed when they arrived two hundred years ago, and the knowledge has been passed down in geography lessons ever since. But no living Nedéan, to my knowledge, has ever ventured beyond the reef to actually see one. Why would we? Why face the possibility of being lost to the sea just to step on a tiny dollop of land, when we have all we need within our borders? It wouldn't make sense.

Perhaps Bri is following my line of reasoning because she stalls midstride. "Just so we're clear, this 'island'—you've been there before?"

Dantès appraises her, then shrugs a shoulder. "Once."

"*Once?* I don't like the odds of *once*. How do you know you can get there again? Does this thing have reins?"

Half the Brutes seem to grunt, sigh, and roll their eyes in unison. But Jase calmly takes her pack. "Relax. Dantès was born for the sea. If he says he can find it, we're as good as there."

Bri glares at Jase—who winks at Dantès when she isn't looking—but she allows him to guide her into a seat in front of him. Neechi glances nervously at me, and I force a nod. What choice do we have now? To the island we go.

We draw short paddles stored along the bottom of each hull, beneath the single-wide seats. At Torvus's mark, we row in sync away from the shoreline.

"Draw! Draw! Draw!"

The wind picks up as the beach shrinks behind us. When I can barely distinguish one tree from the next, Dantès and Jem scramble deftly onto the platform. With sharp tugs, they raise the mainsail, tying complicated knots to ensure it stays put. The stiff fabric snaps to attention, and Dantès quickly makes adjustments to harness the oncoming northeast breeze. When Jem attaches a smaller sail in front of the mast, we really start to speed across the surface, rising and falling in a rhythmic, strangely soothing sway. We're traveling fast now—faster, maybe, than Callisto could run.

The thought of her guts me, and I close my eyes to hold back tears. I imagine I'm straddling her bare back now, fingers curled in her two-tone mane, gulping down salt air as she gallops across the Halcyon.

Théo taps my shoulder, startling me out of my private grief.

"Stow the oar," he grunts.

My cheeks redden as I realize I'm the only one still holding mine aloft, and slip it under my seat.

At least we won't have to paddle the whole way to the island. I mean, I knew the sea was vast, but surrounded by water on all sides, with just the smallest sliver of land in the west to guide us, only now do I comprehend the word.

Magnificent frigate birds circle suspended above, their bent wings angled like black kites against the cloud-strewn sky. Dantès and Jem stick close to the ropes, making occasional adjustments to zigzag along. As we sail, kilometer after kilometer, our watery highway transforms from blue-brown to brilliant cerulean. Dots on the horizon grow in mass until they resemble piles of floating kelp—no, not seaweed, heaps of land no longer than a Phoenix City block—covered in tangled mangroves from tip to very tip, the trees' spindly roots dangling into the sea like so many spiders' legs.

"If that's an island," I whisper to Neechi in front of me, "I don't know how we're going to land this thing." There's nowhere to come ashore, let alone stand or sleep.

When he faces me, his brown eyes are as big as saucers, smile lines creasing every corner of his awestruck face. "I don't care if we ever land, Dom Reina. I've never seen anything so beautiful in my life."

His wonder widens my own grin. Maybe Neechi's courage has been bolstered by these fearless Brutes too. I doubt *I'd* have ever ventured into the open sea by myself, trapped in a carved-out tree, at the mercy of the temperamental wind and a worn rag of a sail, and yet with them—I steal a sideways glance at Rohan, opposite me in the other hull—with them, this somehow resembles adventure.

So I join Neechi's shameless delight, staring out across the ever-moving water.

We soon cross the long, snaking reef that marks the end of Nedé's waters—indicated by a natural wave break I've only ever heard about in my studies. White-tipped waves froth along its edge, creating a literal line of demarcation between Nedé and . . . whatever dangers lie beyond.

Past the break, Dantès turns us northward. In another hour, cerulean water gives way to vast pockets of the truest turquoise I've ever seen, faceted like liquid, moving precious stones—more vibrant than I thought possible. I lean over the edge of the hull, entranced by the otherworldly hue and striking clarity, and wonder what creatures might live below.

Still we sail, free and fast, and though my shoulders, face, legs, chest—everything—begins to burn from the blazing sun ricocheting off the sea, I'm apt to second Neechi's sentiment: I could sail like this forever.

Suddenly Jem points and Dantès is shouting at Jase, "That's what I was trying to tell you about!"

The rest of us snap right, in the direction of Jem's still-outstretched finger. Three fins slice through the water a stone's throw away, keeping pace with our boat. I shield my eyes and squint to get a better look. *What in Siyah's name?*

Without warning, three nearly human-sized gray creatures with long snouts leap from the water in unison, curving in bascule before diving back into the water. Again and again they leap through the air, then splash down like playful children. I'm laughing in delight, breathless and wondering what they could be. I've never seen such a fish—never even heard of a creature like this. The Brutes, too, jaw and point at the curiosities.

I don't know how, but I'd swear the fish are grinning at us too. One opens its mouth as it jumps, as if to call out a greeting.

Rohan's words echo in my mind: *What other strange, beautiful places exist beyond what we've seen?*

What lands, what creatures—what *people*—might wait beyond the horizon that stretches endlessly away, no matter how far we sail?

I glance again at the big Brute. He's leaning over the side of his hull now, vigorously pulling at a line, drawing it in hand over hand. I sit up straighter to get a better look. With a quick jerk and a great heave, he hauls a narrow silver fish—longer than his arm—into the boat.

"Roast fish tonight!" Galion cheers, as Rohan pins the shiny, large-scaled fish atop the platform, avoiding its snapping jaws lined with sharp teeth.

When its fluttering gills finally still, he uses a knife to cut out a small chunk of its flesh, then wraps the rest in a wet cloth and slips it under his seat—the only shade we have. Attaching the hunk of white-pink meat to his hook, he drops the line overboard.

"Always hunting," I muse aloud.

Théo chuckles. "That's 'cause we're always eatin'."

By the time the sun begins the final third of its daytime circuit, Rohan has caught three more fish, one of which I recognize. Most Nedéans have an appetite for the bug-eyed, red-scaled snapper. I'm suddenly very anxious for dinner.

Occasional clouds and a steady wind keep our skin from sweating, but not from burning. So after nearly a whole day of sailing, we're all starting to wilt from the incessant glare of that gem-like water. Despite my earlier claim that I could sail forever, I'm not terribly disappointed when Dantès points confidently ahead and shouts, "There it is!"

I'm even less disappointed when we navigate close enough to take in our destination.

Vastly different from the tiny mangrove islands we passed earlier, this swath of land resembles a hunk of Nedéan coastline, plopped right into the sea. Though I can't make out its entire shape, as we skirt east around the southern tip, it appears long and narrow, and curves slightly, like a banana. It's also flat as parchment and encompasses more hectares than Finca del Mar. The turquoise sea brushes against sun-bleached sand, and tall palms line the perimeter, their fronds rustling restlessly in the never-ending wind. A flock of pelicans floats just offshore, riding the rise and fall of the sea.

Jem drops the smaller sail and Dantès tries to maneuver us right onto shore, but the unruly wind forces us to drop the mainsail and row the final thirty meters. Once the front of the two-hull touches sand, we jump into knee-deep water—warmer than I expect, and so clear I can see my toes beneath its surface—and push the boat up onto the beach.

I'm parched, burned, soaked to my waist, but unmistakably, deliciously alive. The island dances with peaceful energy. I curl my bare toes into the strange sand—bone white and soft as sugar. I've never seen anything like it. Like *any* of this.

Bri stomps into the crystal-clear surf, sloshing through the water in a wide circle. Her blonde hair blows every which way, but the thrashing strands can't mask her grin. I don't know if I've ever seen her this happy. Something about this place infuses us all with fresh life.

While Torvus and Dáin gather driftwood to roast our fish, the rest of the Brutes shed weapons and shirts and make a run for the water.

"Come on!" Jase calls to the three of us, then dives in headlong.

I question Neechi, "Can you swim?"

He shakes his head. "You go."

"Are you sure?"

"I'll help with dinner." As he makes his way to Torvus, the contrast of Gentle and Brute strikes me again. Yet they have more in common than I would ever have expected.

Bri has already removed her weapons belt, which we've been wearing over our Brute clothing. Nedéans do enough swimming to know soggy clothes aren't buoyant, so I'm not surprised when she slips out of her breeches. It's nothing we wouldn't do at the swimming holes back in Amal, but for some reason I feel a bit shy about shedding mine around the Brutes.

Any inhibitions, however, fade to the background as we tumble pell-mell into the waiting arms of the sea. Jase and Rohan circle back when they see us swimming toward them, then lead us out to the spot where the others are already diving down like fishing pelicans.

"It's going to sting your eyes a bit—" Jase grins, treading water—"but trust me—it's worth it to keep them open."

He slowly draws a lungful of air, then flips under the swaying surface.

Bri follows, diving after him not a second later. I glance at Rohan, suddenly a little nervous. I'm no stranger to swimming in the sea, but this is deeper, more tumultuous, and farther from shore than I'm used to.

He must sense my apprehension. "You can hold on to me if you want," he says, offering me his hand.

I grip it tightly.

He squeezes once. "Ready?"

I nod.

We each suck in a breath and dive down, down, beneath the surface.

My first thought is that someone has seared my eyeballs with hot coals. Sting *a bit*? Really, Jase?

But my second thought, quickly overshadowing the first, is that I've left my own world and been transported to a realm of sheer fantasy.

A school of flat silver fish with yellow fins shimmy past, circling around a large boulder. The rock itself is covered with all manner of oddly shaped plants—fanlike, tubular, spiky, ridged—in muted pinks, greens, and blues. Among these plants, brilliantly colored fish nibble and dart—stunning azure with lime-green tails, striking yellow with black patches, flat and round, narrow and long, some covered in spines, others with snouts like a pig's. An enormous gray dinner plate with wings hovers above the sandy floor, flapping its body like an underwater bird, whiplike tail trailing behind.

Everywhere is movement. Seagrass bends and straightens.

Shadows shift and dance. A giant turtle lumbers slowly past. Even a "stationary" group of fish, sheltering in a cavernous opening, sway left to right in unison.

Rohan pulls me closer to the rock, pointing to several protruding worm-like creatures with feathery burgundy tops. He snaps his fingers next to one, and they instantly retract, disappearing into themselves. I giggle, bubbles escaping like iridescent marbles. *Oops.* Within seconds, my lungs begin to burn.

I point up, and Rohan follows me back to air.

Breaking the surface I squeal, "This is *amazing*!"

He grins at my delight, rubbing his sore eyes. He appears different somehow, with his hair slicked back and cheeks burned brown-red. Younger? Untroubled? I can't place the change, but it's bewitching. If the underwater world weren't enough to marvel at, the little droplets of water suspended in his lashes, the sea's mottled reflection against his wet skin, could be enough to captivate me all afternoon.

"Again?" I beg.

"As many times as you want, Rei."

I don't think I need his hand anymore, but I take it anyway.

The sun nears the western horizon, bathing the island in a warm glow.

Eight Brutes, two women, and a Gentle laze around the fire atop palm fronds, stomachs full of fish, clothes stiff from drying in the breeze. Our bloodred eyes sting like they've been pickled in salt water, and my body still sways in time to the waves' echo. Empty coconut husks litter the shore, emptied of their tangy water. Aggressive gulls swarm around the discarded fish skin and bones we flung on nearby rocks. But us? We don't do anything for once. A day full of sailing and swimming—on the heels of five days trekking through the Jungle—has settled us all into quiet exhaustion.

I lie back on my frond mat, staring up at the clouds and papery palms, listening to the quiet lapping of water against sand. I'm thrilled Torvus decided we'll stay here through tomorrow evening before setting out for Phoenix City. Our mission—finding Teera, upending the Matriarchy, restoring justice—feels like a dream just now—this, a truer reality. Surely it can wait one more day.

Most of the Brutes, plus Neechi, sun-spent and satiated, sleep comfortably in the sun's final rays. Dáin whittles alone, Jase shows Bri how to remove the stubborn animal from a large conch shell they found while diving, and Neechi sorts other curious shells he collected in the shallows.

I'm just thinking that I haven't felt this happy in months—that I wish nothing would have to change and we could go on like this forever, for as long as the sea is wide—when Rohan's deep whisper tickles my ear.

"Walk with me?"

———————

He leads me west along the southern tip of the island, affording us a perfect view of the sun's descent through low-lying clouds; it sparks them to life like tangerine electric bulbs. I still don't understand how the sun can set in the very place Nedé should be. So many curiosities I've never had occasion to ponder.

For a long time, gulls' cries and the nonstop rustling of palms are the only sounds. I sense Rohan wants to talk about something, but, perhaps, doesn't know how to start.

I focus on dragging my big toe through the sand as we walk, trying to give him the space I've learned he needs to sort out words.

But his larger-than-life presence makes it terribly difficult to ignore him, so eventually I cave and try for idiotic small talk.

"I still can't believe how beautiful it is here."

"You're going to love the stars." He grins. "Without any trees or mountains to block the sky—it's unreal. More constellations than you could imagine."

"Wait—so you *have* been here before? Dantès said he had only been here once."

Rohan chuckles. "Think about who he was saying that *to*." *Bri*, I realize. "Who wouldn't want to get her goat?"

I have to give him that. She certainly doesn't shy away from giving them plenty of grief. "So you *have* been here."

"Twice. Dantès and Jem are most interested in the sea, but I've tagged along a few times to learn the basics. Mostly south."

South. Away from Nedé.

"Are you going to tell me why, or do I have to ask?"

He sighs. "I've taken a couple runs with Dantès to see how the two-hull holds up. As you saw today, it's impressive. The plan . . ." He stalls a bit, grows quieter. "The plan is to load it up with supplies and see how far it can take us."

He eyes me sideways, as if eager to catch my reaction to this piece of information.

"You said you were *thinking about* seeing what else is out there," I press, turning to face him. "You didn't mention you already have a plan in place."

"We weren't expecting things to come to a head so quickly, but now that we're making our move, things are speeding up."

"Why didn't you just tell me?" I don't know why I wish he would have. He doesn't owe me the courtesy of sharing the Brutes' inner-circle plans.

He ignores my inquiry, lobbing a question of his own. "Why does it matter to you if I go?"

I stiffen, irritated that he changed the subject and put this on me. "If your mind is set, why bother telling me about this 'plan' at all?"

The exchange is heating, and I expect him to fire back a defense or, more likely, call me on yet another layer of my seemingly eternal hypocrisy, as so many of our conversations go.

His jaw tenses, but his eyes flash less with anger than a strange, helpless earnestness.

"I don't know!" he says miserably. "It was easier before I met you. Jase and I knew what we had to do: cripple Nedé, explore the unknown. But since the first time I—I *saw* you . . . you changed all that . . ."

"Well, I'm sorry for interrupting your life."

His eyes snap to mine, and he runs a hand through his salt-tousled hair as he steps closer. "That's not what I mean."

Weakness, and indecision of any kind, are so foreign in this Brute that I can't help but soften a little. "Then tell me what you mean."

"I'm trying to say . . ." He leans even closer, searching my eyes, as if the words will appear there. When he speaks, his voice is as soft as the sand underfoot, deep as the sea beyond. "I'm trying to say . . . that ever since I met you, none of it holds purpose anymore. All I can think about is *you*, Reina—being near you, understanding you—" he traces a finger across my cheekbone—"taking care of you."

I melt under his touch, like the sun rapidly dissolving into a puddle of orange liquid on the horizon. I want to tell him that I know exactly what he means, that I feel it too—whatever this is—even though it scares the bats out of me. But no words come.

He hesitates at my silence, yet risks taking my hands in his anyway. He stares at them as he says, "I want you to come with me."

"*With* you?"

At my surprise, he adds, "You don't have to decide right now. But I wanted to ask—wanted you to know—before . . ."

"Before we die?"

He grins at my bluntness. *By Siyah*, his smile undoes me.

"I don't know what's going to happen when we reach Nedé." He grips both my shoulders as if already imagining how he'll protect me. "But when it's over, Rei, I don't ever want to leave your side again."

I stare into his eyes a long moment, considering his words. I think of Mother and Torvus—the long-standing connection they share. I think of the people who lived at the ruins ages ago, and the implication that there were good men, men who cared for women in times past. And I can't ignore the strange magnetism that has drawn me toward this Brute—the inexplicable, subconscious longing I've had for this very moment since my first sunset in the mahogany tree, when he asked me which was better: Gentle or Brute.

If Article V doesn't make allowance for this, for us, then perhaps our Virtues—those Nedé recognizes as absolute, yet even our own Matriarch abandons—maybe they aren't sufficient after all.

The desire welling in me now doesn't rage uncontrollably like the emotions that frightened me at the waterfall. This feels rational and right: I want to be with Rohan too. *Always.*

If he ventures from Nedé, I'm going with him. Wherever he goes, whatever wonders he discovers or distant lands he explores, I want to be by his side, facing what may come together.

In answer, I let myself lean into him, pressing my cheek against his chest. This time, a seeming decade of experiences later, my initial fear in the teak forest has been replaced by a deep, courageous trust in this Brute—this man.

He enfolds me in his strength, wrapping one arm around my waist, sliding the other hand into my disheveled hair, and draws me against him. I let myself savor the warmth of his breath in my hair, the scent of sea salt on his skin, the rise and fall of his sigh, the rhythmic, steady beat of his heart. This has to be the safest place in the entire world.

His fingers brush down my arm, leaving pinpricks of heat in their wake, then intertwine with my own. My heart swells like a rainy-season cloud, impossibly full, threatening to burst with . . . with *love*.

How could *this* be a violation of the virtues? No . . . I suspect it's the truest of them all.

CHAPTER TWENTY-THREE

His fingers remain woven in mine as we continue north up the western shore. Though we're virtually silent, this time I don't mind. To speak now would disturb the recollection of what came before. I prefer to let his confession linger.

On this island, even muted twilight seems magical somehow—an airy, softer side to the blazing sun, azure sky, and underwater rainbows of daytime. The gray-blue expanse overhead preludes the starry display I can't wait to witness.

Or perhaps the magic has everything to do with my present company.

Rohan squeezes my hand and says, "Tell me about the Gentle you—" he stops, kindly redirecting his phrasing—"the one who died with honor."

It hurts to think of Tre; it hurts doubly because I *haven't* thought about him much in the days since Tree Camp. Not as much as he deserves.

"My mother named him Treowe. He was kind, sharp for a Gentle—" I suddenly recall sparring bananas with Tre until we both held mushy lumps—"and he put up with my impulsiveness."

Rohan chuckles at that. "He must have been *exceptional*."

My elbow finds his ribs. "He was," I say, smiling. "He was a good friend."

He rubs my thumb with his. "You said you regretted your choice. Why?"

So he *was* listening on the trail to the cave. I suppose he just chose to move on in that moment—literally and figuratively. Perhaps the skill is something I should learn from him.

"Because I miss him. But mostly because it didn't work—Teera chose Jamara as Apprentice anyway. I don't see how his death means anything now."

Rohan stops abruptly, then turns me to face him.

"Honor itself means something." There's an urgency to his words, unmistakable conviction. "Even if the outcome doesn't go as planned."

A warm tear slides down my cheek. He finds it with his thumb. Though I nod, I'm having a hard time reconciling that possibility.

"You have to understand that, Reina. Especially with the odds we'll be facing."

He presses his lips to my forehead, takes my hand, and leads us on.

This side of the island has less sand and more vegetation; the pebbly ground grates on my feet, and we have to pick our way around stands of mangroves.

In the fading light, a dozen of night's first stars announce their existence. We haven't walked ten meters before I notice another light—a strange glow farther down the beach, red-orange and . . . *smoking*.

Rohan stops short, releasing my hand and gripping my forearm instead. With his other hand, he slides a blade from its sheath on his leg.

That's a fire—no mistaking it.

I follow him away from the sandy shore into the cover of dense palms, thankful the sand dampens the sound of our footfalls. We need to get a better look. Maybe another Gentle fishing boat got loose and washed up here. My eyes roll of their own accord. Of all the stupid theories. But why would anyone else be here? I thought Nedéans didn't sail this far.

The fire grows larger as we approach undercover, illuminating two wooden sailboats at the water's edge. Their polished sides shine in the firelight; the lax sails appear brand new. Around the fire, no fewer than a dozen Alexia lounge, bows leaning against a nearby tree.

We crouch behind a mangrove, strain to hear their conversation.

". . . Adoni would never agree," one says. "She won't take any chances, or we wouldn't have been sent out here to our deaths."

"You're so dramatic. Sailing wasn't as bad as I thought it'd be. It was kind of fun, actually."

"I didn't mean the boats, stupid."

Another voice says, "I wonder what they're like."

"Trinidad said they fought with the strength of two women apiece."

"I'll take my chances," a gruff voice cuts in. "I'm not afraid."

"Look, if they actually come this way—and we have no way of knowing whether they will—we'll do what we can to stop them. Whether or not we triumph, we won't fail to send up the signal. As long as Teera knows they're coming, we can say we did our job."

"I'm just saying," the gruff voice retorts, "if they show up here, they're not leaving alive."

A few assent, then settle into a quiet unease.

I want to tell them they don't have to be afraid, that they don't know what Brutes are actually like, but apart from Trin—who, I'm relieved to hear, made it back alright—I haven't had any experience trying to convince the Alexia of the truth. I don't know how understanding they'd be. And I don't like the odds presenting themselves tonight.

Rohan scurries to another vantage point, motioning for me to follow. From here, he points silently to a handful of arrows lying near the fire. Each has a narrow cylindrical rod lashed to it, with a threadlike tail protruding from the bottom. Those must be the "signal" they spoke of. They resemble the fireworks Innovatus sometimes supplies for the Initus celebrations.

Rohan's moving us again, this time deeper undercover.

When it's safe to whisper, he says, "No matter what direction we leave this island, they'll see us once we make for Nedé. If they send that signal, their leaders will know we're coming, and this is going to get a lot harder."

"Should we get the others? Attack first, while we have the element of surprise?"

He shakes his head. "We need to save our strength and numbers for the real fight."

"So we need to relieve them of the signals before we get the others and set sail."

His brow furrows, and I can tell he's thinking very hard about the best way to play this. Finally he says, "Not *we*. You have to warn Torvus to get moving. I'll meet you at the southern tip of the island."

"But I can help. Just give me a blade—"

"I only have one knife," he blurts.

"One—are you kidding me?" These Brutes are veritable walking weapons caches, and he's down to *one*? "Of all the times to pack light!"

I didn't mean to insult him, but I'm afraid I've hit a very Brute nerve. You'd think he was caught with his pants down the way he reddens.

"I didn't—I was afraid you wouldn't walk with me if I—" He blows a mouthful of air. "Look—it doesn't matter now. I have one weapon, and you have two legs. I'll wait twenty minutes. That should give you time to reach them. Tell Dantès to get that boat in the water and be ready for anything."

I don't move.

"*Go*," he urges, and the grit in his tone leaves no room for argument.

The thought of leaving him rips my heart to shreds, but I trust his judgment. At least, I'm trying to. So I press my forehead to his and whisper, "Be careful."

He cups my face with his broad hands. Then I run like I've never run before.

I weave through palms and jump over debris, straining my eyes because the only thing that could make this situation worse is if I slammed into a tree or face-planted into a rock. At least, that's what I tell myself. In actuality, there are probably quite a few scenarios that could be worse. I just can't think about those now.

Finally the shore widens out, and I sprint headlong across the sandy beach. My side aches from breathing all wrong.

I'm sure more than ten minutes have elapsed by the time I round the southern curve of the island to find those we left stringing hammocks between palms and lazily drinking coconuts by the fire.

They startle as I approach, several reaching for the blasted things Brutes *usually* have strapped all over their bodies. Gratefully, the only bows in our cohort belong to me and Bri, or I might've been skewered before they had a chance to see who approaches.

I stumble into camp, panting and doubling over. "Alexia . . . West side—"

Torvus crosses the beach in three strides.

"How many?" he demands, even but brisk.

"We counted twelve."

"Where's Rohan?"

As I explain Rohan's instructions, Torvus stiffens. Then he begins shouting orders to anything breathing—including me, though I can barely suck enough oxygen to qualify.

Within seconds, Théo and Dáin fill coconut husks with seawater to douse the fire. Jase, Bri, Jem, and Dantès get the boat floating, then we shove our supplies into our packs, stuff the packs in the twin hulls, and wade out to the boat. Left with only moonlight to guide us, we paddle quietly into open water, and wait.

Waiting is hardest of all. Even if we were close enough to see or hear any hint of what's happening at the Alexia camp, the curve of the island would prevent it. So I keep my eyes peeled toward the night sky, dreading I'll see a signal—not because I fear what will happen to us, but because I can't bear what that would imply has happened to him.

The complete, eerie silence, broken only by the *slip-slosh* of our paddles as we work to remain in one place, doesn't bode well for my nerves. My pulse won't stop racing until Rohan runs down this shore and swims safely to our boat.

A sudden *whizz-thunk* startles us all—none more so than Dantès, who stares down his nose at an arrow embedded in the mast, centimeters from his chin. He scrambles back as another *thunk* reverberates from the right hull, just below Jase's elbow.

Torvus booms, "Paddle! Raise the sail!" just as an Alexia ship materializes in the hazy moonlight.

"No!" I yell. "We can't leave Rohan!"

Torvus ignores me, sinking his paddle and drawing mightily. *How can he not care?*

Jase interprets from across the platform, paddling double-time. "First priority: make sure we're alive to help him." He ducks as another arrow flies past, then shouts, "He'll be alright." But he's not convincing enough to douse my panic.

An arrow narrowly misses Jem, who's trying to tie complicated knots in the darkness. The Alexia's sail versus our oars doesn't make for good odds. We need to give Dantès and Jem a reprieve so they can focus.

I scramble to retrieve my quiver and bow from under my seat. The rocking surf isn't going to make this easy, is it? I brace myself by wedging one foot in the hull and the other on the platform. *It's just like riding a horse*, I tell myself, trying to imagine I'm swaying in time to Callisto's four-beat gait. I disconnect my lower body from my upper, focusing on the mechanics. The Alexia's stark-white sail makes spotting their ship easy enough. Nocking the arrow quickly, I set my sights on one of the six dark shapes in the boat.

Steady, Rei.

But even as I adjust for wind and distance, something holds me back. I might not know her name, but she's Alexia. I have no desire to kill her, for the same reasons I couldn't fight those who attacked Tree Camp. I just want them to quit chasing us so we can go back to Rohan.

At the last moment I shift my aim, sending the arrow barreling toward the taut sail. The tip rips through the fabric, and the strong wind instantly takes up the mission, tearing the sail bit by bit with mighty gusts. The Alexia scramble to hold the fraying pieces together, but it's too late. Their boat already drags to a slow stop, the sail rent in two.

Whoops and cheers erupt from our boat. Théo slaps my back as I retake my seat in front of him. A second later, Dantès gets us into position and the two-hull lurches forward. I squint to see the island, only a jagged coal outline against the moonlit sky.

Dantès keeps a steady course northward, waiting for orders.

"That's half of them," I reason with Torvus. "And Bri and I can shoot from the front as we approach. There's still a chance. They haven't—"

But before I can finish, a shrill whistle pierces the silence, followed by a crackling *boom*. An enormous ball of light explodes overhead, sparking and swirling, showering orange and yellow fire dust into the sea. The signal's as bright as the sun—there's no way Phoenix City could miss it.

"No, no, no!" I scream. "We have to go back—we *have to go back*!"

Torvus's face goes slack. No one makes a sound.

"What are you waiting for?" I yell at them. "He needs us!"

I see the impossible decision all over his face: go back for his own and risk being overtaken by whatever that signal was meant to set in motion, or leave one behind to save us all.

Dáin says what I suspect they're all thinking—what I refuse to accept: "That thing wouldn't have gone off if he could stop it." His matter-of-fact grimace makes me want to tear off his face and feed it to the fish.

"It's an honorable death," Théo mutters.

"He's not dead. *He can't be dead.*"

I slump in my seat, numb.

Jase, reassuring to the end, offers, "You said there was a second boat."

I want to turn away before he can feed me his false hope, but I'm too weak to refuse it.

At Torvus's command, Dantès turns the boat west, toward Nedé and whatever we'll face in Phoenix City. As we sail into the blackness, I lift my gaze toward the night sky. It's as Rohan said it would be: a million stars twinkling overhead, a dome of celestial stardust cast from horizon to horizon, every constellation bigger and brighter than I thought possible. But he was wrong about one thing: I don't love it. Without him, the vastness doesn't inspire; it stretches enormous and aching, like the gaping hole in the universe of my heart.

Every tear that falls dries instantly in the night wind. Apparently I won't have the luxury of grief tonight. Not ten minutes into our sail west, Jase sounds the alarm.

"Boat!"

Another white sail glows faintly in the darkness, trailing us like a jaguar marking its prey. It's identical to the Alexia boat we lost—except this sail's intact, and it's gaining on us. Having set off the signal and finding our camp deserted, they must have abandoned their post to come after us.

Torvus climbs onto the platform with Dantès and Jem, assessing our options. The rest crouch low in the hulls, anticipating the volley of arrows that will come any moment.

"Turn us around," Torvus commands. "We won't run this time." He meets my gaze and nods once. "You know what to do."

He says it like I'm one of his men—with the confidence and trust he has in them. I scramble for my bow and quickly buckle the quiver to my thigh. Dantès has successfully tacked southeast, roughly toward the island. The other boat adjusts its sails accordingly, keeping us in its sights.

The wind blows hard against my body as I wedge my foot in the hull and lean against the platform. The distance between the vessels is still too great—I'd be lucky to reach the sail at all, let alone hit it with enough force to pierce the stiff material.

"Closer!" I yell. Jem and Dantès make adjustments. We're nearly running a straight course for their boat now, rising and falling on the surging water.

I breathe in and out slowly, trying to steady my nerves, hoping the Alexia don't get a clear shot at me before I can disable their boat. I lift my bow and nock an arrow.

Steady . . . steady . . .

A hundred meters separate us now. Seventy-five.

I draw the arrow back, fingers trembling against my damp cheek, eyes fixed on the white sail. Every second gives me more clarity as the distance between the boats shrinks. *Just a little closer . . .*

Fifty meters . . .

I release the arrow just as a swell tips me backward. I don't need to see where that one went to know it was a complete miss. *Bats!*

We're only twenty-five meters away now; there's no way I can miss the broad white sail this time. As I quickly nock a second arrow, I vaguely wonder why they aren't shooting. No matter—lucky for us. I draw my fingers to the corner of my mouth and take aim.

Two things become clear at once. First, the boat isn't full of Alexia. In fact, it appears empty except for one figure, manning the sail. Second, that figure is too large to be an Alexia, and it's waving one arm overhead, like it's trying to get our attention.

"Don't shoot!" Jase yells suddenly.

"I've got the shot—"

"Rei, no—look!"

Twenty meters . . .

I peer closer at the boat as we approach in the darkness; a muffled shout struggles to break through the wind. It's near enough now that moonlight illuminates a broad, bare chest, and dark hair blowing wildly in the wind.

"Rohan!" I yell, already dropping my bow into the hull. Without thinking, I dive overboard.

I swim as fast as I can through liquid night, longing to see, to touch him for myself—to make sure he's real.

He drops the sail as I approach, stalling the boat while I close the ten meters between us. When my hands finally touch wood, he grips my arms and hauls me in. I collapse into him, dripping wet and choking on seawater.

"You're alive! I thought I'd lost you."

He cups my face in his hands, smiling. "It'll take more than a few Alexia to keep me from you."

Then he presses his lips to mine—salty and sweet and warm, and I lose all sense of time and reason. I'm falling, falling into him, and the places where I end and he begins grow opaque, as if our edges are bleeding into each other.

In this moment, there's nothing in the whole universe besides us.

Except, of course, the boat drifting up alongside ours.

"Weird," I hear Bri say.

"What happened?" Jase asks eagerly. "When we saw the signal, we thought . . ."

Rohan draws back, grinning like a cub, and takes my hand. That's when I notice the trickle of blood running down his left arm, and the reopened gash on his side.

"You're hurt."

"I'll be alright," he says quietly. Then, answering Jase, he explains, "I decided that since I only had one knife, I had a better chance of outrunning them than fighting. So I snuck in, snagged the signals, and took off running like a scared peccary back into the trees." The Brutes guffaw heartily at this; my mouth is hanging open with horror, picturing Rohan rushing into a camp of twelve Alexia with a single blade. *He could have been killed.* He's going to get a piece of my mind later.

Seemingly oblivious to his mortality, he continues, "As soon as I disappeared, half of them got in a boat and sailed away, probably looking for my boat and anyone else with me. The rest took off after me. I lost them, but I must have dropped one of the signals along the way. When I heard it go off—" he shakes his head like he can't believe he was so careless—"I had to head back. I drew them into the trees after me. Once we were far enough away from their camp, I circled back and . . ." He sweeps his arms wide, presenting the prize of his trickery.

I lean against the side of the hull, deliberating whether to smack or hug him.

Torvus stands with arms crossed, but his eyes dance as he nods once. "Well done, Rohan."

Jase makes up for Torvus's stoicism, hollering, "The rest of us might as well go home—you can take down Nedé yourself!"

His exuberance is met with hearty cheers and congratulations, but the well-meaning sentiment rings strangely to me.

Take down Nedé. I still don't like the sound of it. It unsettles the part of me that still doesn't understand what these Brutes plan to do once we remove Teera from the equation.

I find Bri across the water. Her mouth is set in a thin line. When we lock eyes, she raises a brow as if to say, *What did I tell you, Rei? They're just going to take the power for themselves.*

Rohan puts an arm around my shoulder. "Want to help me sail

it the rest of the way? I can show you how." I nod, grateful for a reason to stay near him.

But as the boats travel northwest, nearer and nearer Nedé's shore and whatever awaits us there, I can't completely shake the unease.

I know Teera has to go. I'm committed to changing Nedé and putting an end to gentling. But what then? Who decides how we move forward? I agreed to come with these Brutes, to lead them to Teera, because I've come to trust them—their intentions and their virtues. But is my strength enough to keep theirs from becoming corrupted? To keep them from taking more than they should?

If, without virtue, power inevitably degrades into tyranny, then we need to know which of us—women or Brutes—are more virtuous. I'm still not sure, and I'm running out of time to figure it out.

I curl up next to Rohan in the single hull—his broad body makes an excellent windbreak—as he explains how we can be moving one way when the wind's blowing another.

How strange life is, I muse. I'm skin to skin with a Brute, and I'm not the least bit afraid. Instead, he has brought meaning to my life I never realized was lacking.

He shifts so he can put one arm on either side of mine, gently guiding my hands to the right ropes as we make adjustments to the sail's angle.

"Why do I *doubt* this was how Dantès showed you to sail?" I tease.

He laughs, and his hair tickles my ear. "You get special treatment."

"I accept."

The cocooning sense of safety I felt on the beach returns.

When did I decide that Rohan was safe? When did I allow myself to trust that *this* Brute wouldn't hurt me?

Maybe the shift occurred when I realized he *could* be safe, if he wanted to. *We all have to choose*, he had said, that first night in the great tree.

He has chosen me; I have chosen him. I don't completely understand what that means, but I do believe we'd do anything for each other—I know it in my bones.

Rohan has made mistakes. He's been rude, he's misunderstood me—he attacked my sister's finca, for Siyah's sake. But he has also been brave, and sacrificial, and shown me forgiveness I didn't deserve. And what of my faults? I killed my own best friend, I recklessly led the Alexia to Tree Camp, and I've held on to too many grudges. I hope I've also shown kindness, and had courage, and done the right thing when it counted.

Maybe we need each other. I need his strength; he needs my loyalty. He calls me on my hypocrisy, and I suspect I bring beauty to his world. Together we are more than the sum of our parts.

A single star breaks loose overhead and shoots across the black canvas of glittering pinpricks. I suddenly know something with absolute certainty, as sure as the stars blink overhead: neither of us—Rohan nor Reina—is inherently more or less virtuous than the other. But together? Together our virtues multiply. Together we may be able to stomp out the embers of tyranny.

CHAPTER TWENTY-FOUR

Rohan hands me a full water flask, and I take a long drag before handing it to Neechi. Nine of us crouch in a thick cluster of cattails between the sea and Finca del Mar's border, which, along with the darkness and enough frog croaking to muffle an explosion, provides perfect cover.

"They should be back by now," Théo whispers, to no one in particular. No one answers, but we're all thinking the same thing. It's been nearly thirty minutes since Galion and Jem set off to scout the finca.

We landed half a kilometer south of Phoenix City on a largely uninhabited stretch of coastline and had no trouble hiding the boat or making our way through the swampy sea marsh. We didn't spot a single Alexia until we reached the finca's boundary, which was easy to find, what with the zillion electric bulbs illuminating windows and garden paths. The whole place is lit up as bright as the signal that alerted them to our approach.

A rustle makes me jump at the same moment Galion and Jem's heads pierce through the reeds. *Bats*—I can see why Torvus chose them to scout.

"What did you see?" the Brute leader asks in a husky whisper.

Galion's scowl isn't promising. "The dragon woman is here . . . and four hundred Alexia, at least."

Jem adds, barely audible, "It's completely surrounded."

I admire the inner strength that allows these Brutes to meet the news with such stoicism, especially Torvus.

Bri certainly has no such poker face. "Well, that's just great. The big explosion in the sky sent every Alexia in Lapé a personal invitation to our execution."

Dáin meets her bravado with indignation. "If you don't want to be here, then why did you come?"

Jase shushes them both like a mother reprimanding bickering siblings. "Knock it off." He looks to Torvus, who meets his gaze. Some unspoken conversation passes between them. Then he says, "I'll be the woodsow."

I don't like the boldness in Jase's eyes—it looks too much like sacrifice. I rock up on my toes. "What's the woodsow?"

They both ignore me, Torvus considering. "It could work."

Rohan leans forward. "He's not going alone."

Jase grips his unbandaged shoulder with a grateful nod.

"Is someone going to tell me what the bats you're talking about?" I hiss.

Dáin says blandly, "*Woodsow.* Wooden curassow? Carved look-alikes, positioned to draw in your real prey."

I whip round to Jase so fast I smack Neechi in the face with my braid. "*No way.*"

"What choice do we have?" Jase asks.

"Plenty others. Maybe a million. Starting with the two of you *not* walking into the middle of four hundred Alexia ready to kill any Brute who steps foot in Nedé!"

Jase glances at Rohan, but neither appears the least deterred. "Sometimes people have to—"

"Shut up!" I seethe. "Just shut up. If I hear that phrase one more time . . . Sometimes people are reckless and the right thing *doesn't* happen." They have to listen. I can't lose either one of them. Not like this. "*Please*," I beg.

"I'm going to have to agree with Reina here," Bri interjects. "Seems like a pretty stupid idea to me." Her eyes flit quickly to Jase and then away again. The corner of his mouth twitches, and he discreetly places his hand on hers. She doesn't flinch or pull away. *Holy mother of Siyah . . .* I bounce my eyes away to keep from staring.

Torvus silences us all when he speaks, even his hushed tone commanding our attention. "We've run out of time."

"*Why?*" I challenge. "They saw the signal—they're expecting us tonight. What if we surprise them by *not* attacking straightaway?"

Torvus's jaw ticks, and I take his hesitance as an opportunity to press my point. "Eleven of us against hundreds of them? Even with Jase as a woodacow—or whatever—we won't make it past the first floor of the villa. You think Teera's just going to be sitting in her suite, all alone, waiting for us to kill her? I promised I'd lead you to the Matriarch, but what good is that if you're intent on dying before you reach her?"

"We knew the mission would be dangerous," Jase counters.

"Dangerous?" I gawk. "This is suicide!"

Rohan doesn't meet my eyes, but Torvus stares at me, silently, for a long moment. Finally he asks, "Do you have a better idea?"

All eyes are on me now, waiting for me to share my grand alternative. The one I don't have.

I chew the corner of my lip and squeeze my eyes tight.

"Let's just think about this rationally," I say, more confidently than I feel. *Breathe in. Breathe out. Think, Reina.* "If we can't get to the Mother of Nedé, where else could we strike? What else could we cripple?"

The question hangs in the air for a long moment, and I can practically see any sway I was gaining seeping into the marsh beneath us.

I don't miss the apologetic despair lacing Neechi's words when he weighs in. "Maybe the Brutes are right. What else is there, Dom Reina? She's the heart of Nedé."

Fantastic. Even my timid, gentled friend thinks we should fight. I try not to take his betrayal personally.

But his words worm their way into the spinning wheels of my desperation. *Nedé's heart . . . the heart of Nedé.* Where have I heard that before? *Ciela*, I recall suddenly. I squeeze my temples, mentally rehearsing our conversation. We were talking about the vaccines, and how Grandmother had sent . . .

"No," I gasp. "Teera's not the heart of Nedé. The Health Center is."

"Not to be difficult," Bri interjects, "but how are we supposed to cripple Nedé by striking a bunch of doctors and dying Gentles?"

She has a point. "There must be something valuable there," I reason, tapping my lip. "Ciela said Teera doubled the Alexia guard when trouble started."

Bri clears her throat. "The Center does more than care for sick patients," she says, intoning a perfect Dom Russo imitation. "It's a vital part of the Materno destiny, without which—"

"There would be no Nedé," I say with her.

"They create life using the life serum . . ." Pieces are falling into place, and my volume shows it. "It has to be tied to the bank Tristan Pierce wrote about in her log. She said it was all they needed to start over." But where would it be kept? The Materno area would be logical. I retrace the steps of our eighth floor tour: delivery, exam rooms, records, the nursery, the life serum clinic . . . I screech to a mental halt when I remember the glass-paneled room housing steel-topped tables, microscopes, and the strange large box sweating from "refrigeration." That *has* to be it.

"I think I know where the bank is," I blurt, "and if we destroy it, they won't be able to create any new life—no babies to gentle, no women to rule them. They'd *have* to listen to our demands for change."

I pause, waiting for each and every one of them to stand in applause—to express that they're as proud of me as I am.

A few frogs' croaks accentuate the silence.

Not the exuberant response I was hoping for, but a few slow nods are better than nothing. Rohan gives me a small, encouraging smile. I'm grateful for his support, at least.

"I still say we kill Teera," Dáin mutters.

But Torvus settles back on his haunches, sifting through this new information. He stares toward the bright blaze of the finca, then back again. "Alright. How do we get to the Center?"

The Center for Health Services towers above the cobbled streets like a watchful defender. The gray of early dawn still mutes the fiery orange flame vine covering a dozen arches at the entrance, but now that it's light enough to see our feet plainly, I'm anxious to get inside.

We keep low, moving quickly through the lush vegetation circling the building. The front entrance is all but deserted, guarded by only two Alexia who converse with a Center worker, likely coming in for the day. Even at this distance, I recognize the older woman's tall frame, wiry silver bun, and narrow-rimmed glasses perched on her thick nose: that's Dr. Novak. Under different circumstances, I'd rush to her side to thank her for saving my mother's life. Instead, I hope she keeps the guards occupied long enough for us to reach the hidden door leading to the passageway she showed me the last time I was here.

Getting the Brutes *gracefully* through the wall of shrubs between us and our entrance without snapping every second twig proves challenging. Almost as difficult as wiggling the door open without it screeching. At least it hasn't rusted shut since my shoulder's last frantic encounter with it.

We file into the narrow corridor and ease the door closed.

"Alright," I begin again. "This passageway should be clear. But once we enter the eighth floor, the clock will start ticking as soon as we're seen. There shouldn't be many Center workers at this hour, but we can count on plenty of Alexia. If *anyone* sees us, we have to assume Teera and Adoni will get wind of it as qui—" The rest of the words trickle out sour as star fruit. "As quick as a phone call." *A phone call.* I picture Ciela's back through the square pane of an office window, phone pressed to her ear. How long afterward did Teera intercept me and Mother?

I think I might be sick.

"You okay?" Bri asks.

Ciela? Could she have betrayed us? There was a time I wouldn't have put it past her, but . . . our last conversation—I thought we were finally putting our petty sibling quarrels behind us.

"Reina?" Rohan nudges my foot. "You alright?"

I shake the image away, hoping the suspicion will disappear with it. Right now, we have other priorities.

"It's nothing. Let's go."

I take in the group one more time, hoping we haven't forgotten anything. The Brutes' many blades glint in the light cast by a single electric bulb. I'm sure they carry just as many I can't see. Bri and I opted for our Alexia uniforms and weapons, to try to blend in with the guards. And Jase insisted Neechi—

"Wait—where's Neechi?" I ask, suddenly very aware of his absence.

Heads turn and shoulders shrug, but Neechi is absolutely, terrifyingly missing.

"Who saw him last?" Galion asks.

There's a lot of murmuring, mentally retracing our steps through Phoenix City's back alleys and shadowed streets in the hour before dawn. But the last time anyone actually remembers seeing him was the moment we left the reeds outside Finca del Mar.

My stomach twists in terror.

"You've got to be kidding me," Bri moans.

Théo's gold eyes grow somber. "Maybe he finally ran out of courage."

I glare at him in disbelief. I wouldn't blame Neechi if he was tired of risking his life, but I know him better than that. He wouldn't leave without telling me. Would he?

I plead with Torvus. "We have to go back. If he got caught . . ." *Then I'll lose him like I lost Tre*, I don't dare finish.

Rohan turns my shoulders to face him. "We'll find him, Rei," he says earnestly. "But we can't go back. We're not going to have any leverage until we do this, here. Think with your sense, not with your heart."

I know he means well, but I want to punch something. I'm angry with myself for losing Neechi, and . . . and because I know Rohan is right. If Neechi *has* been caught, storming Finca del Mar to rescue him would be as stupid as the Brutes' earlier plan.

So I set my jaw and say, "Then let's create some leverage."

The hidden door to the eighth-floor medical room cracks open with a groan. A sliver of hallway light spills under the office door on the far end. Even in the dark, the space makes me shudder. Mother might be alive, but the horror of holding her limp body comes rushing back.

I force my feet to cross the room, and turn the door's handle. A quick check reveals a hallway filled only with stark-white tiles. I squint in the sudden brightness.

"Okay," I whisper, "coast is clear."

Still, I have to take two more deep breaths before I muster the courage to leave our cover. For all I know, I could be leading them into a trap.

I run through my mental map of the eighth floor—what I remember of it—one more time. There may be a quicker way to get to the room in question, but I'll have to stick with familiar landmarks so we don't end up lost in the maze of exam and delivery rooms, offices, and seemingly endless hallways.

From this office we head for the nursery. I see they've already repaired the three-meter glass panes destroyed the last time Teera suspected treason.

From the nursery we take a right, but just as we pass records, we have to squeeze into an empty exam room to avoid two Alexia guards on the far side of delivery. In the moment we're waiting, Jem peers strangely at a doctor's instrument, and Jase canvasses a wall, touching charts and dials. How strange the Brutes look in this setting; how otherworldly this place must seem to them. Only Torvus doesn't appear curious—just impatient to get moving.

"Alright," I whisper, as soon as the hallway clears, "we're almost there."

After one wrong turn in delivery, we reach the life serum clinic, and at the end of the hall, just as I remembered, the glass-walled room that holds the key to our success.

Except it isn't empty.

———

Ciela stands with her back to us, carefully removing a thin vial from the open bank with gloved hands.

She startles when I open the door, and the vial drops to the ground, shattering. She whirls on us and, catching sight of her sister and eight Brutes, turns as pale as her creamy-beige lab coat.

"What are you doing here?" I hiss.

"I could ask you the same thing," she says, without taking her eyes from the Brutes crowding the space.

"Who is this?" Torvus demands.

"Torvus," I say, "meet my *other* sister, Ciela, who is just about to tell me why she betrayed me and Mother."

What little color was left in her cheeks drains completely.

"Rei, please. It's not what you think . . . I mean, I can explain."

I take a step closer, unsheathing my sword and pressing the tip to her chest.

"Did you call Teera?" I ask slowly, teeth clenched.

"Yes."

I almost run her through right then and there. "Mother could have *died*!"

"You think I don't know?" she says miserably, her chin trembling. "You have no *idea* what it did to me when Dr. Novak took me to her."

"Then why did you do it?"

"Grandmother said to call her if I saw you or Mother around the Center because she needed to talk to you. I didn't think . . . Rei, she said I was *this close* to getting the director position when

Mother retired, and—" She breaks off, choking on a sob. "I hate myself for not seeing through her. You have to believe me."

I reluctantly lower my sword, and she surprises me with a tight hug.

"Not to break up the family party," Dáin says, scanning the hallways outside the two adjoining glass walls, "but didn't we say time was of the essence here?"

Ciela glances nervously at my companions. "Are they—?"

"Brutes, yeah." I glance at Rohan and can't help but grin, recalling *my* first impressions.

She scans their faces, and her gaze hitches on their weapons. "Mother told me about them, but they're nothing like I imagined."

"She did?"

"After Dr. Novak staged her death, I hid her at Bella so she could recover. When she could talk, she told me everything—what Gentles really are, and that I should help you if you came back. I was mad at first. Do you know how much that information could have sped my research? I understand why she couldn't, but still, with her help I've already nearly isolated testosterone in my samples."

"I don't know if that matters now," I say, peering behind her at the box, then glancing at Torvus.

"Why not?" she asks incredulously.

"Because we're here to destroy the bank."

"The what?"

"The bank—you know, the thing behind you that helps them make the life serum." Recognizing how ignorant I sound, I get irritable. That's all I know, and I'm suddenly keenly aware how little it is.

She scrunches her nose, humoring me with one raised eyebrow.

I sigh, exasperated. It's just so like my sister to enjoy making me feel stupid because she knows so much more than I do or whatever.

"We're going to destroy the stuff that lets them make babies, okay? Clear enough for you?"

This gets her attention. "But . . . why would you want to do that?"

"I don't have time to explain. We're sitting curassows in this room. Mother told you to help me, right? You're going to have to trust me." *Or be forced to cooperate*, I think, but let's hope it doesn't come to that.

She seems to need more reassurance.

I press, "It's the only way we know to stop the gentling and keep Grandmother from killing the Brutes. From killing Jonalyn's own baby."

Ciela's face softens. Though perhaps she's not completely convinced, I think we have her cooperation.

"Can we smash it already?" Dáin asks, fingering his club. The other Brutes glance repeatedly out the windows, clearly uneasy with how exposed we are.

Ciela shields the box with her body. "Hold on." She draws another vial from the still-open box. "These contain prepared life serum, but only the auxiliary ingredients are stored in this room."

"In English, please?" I mutter.

She rolls her eyes. "If you want to completely eliminate the ability to create life serum, 'smashing' this box won't do it. You need to find the source of *this*," she says, removing a tiny glass vial, no longer than a bean.

"What do you mean, *the source*? There's more somewhere?"

She nods. "This isn't my department—I'm only here to get some serum to test against . . . that doesn't matter. It's my understanding they only store here what they need for, oh, a year's worth or so of serum."

"Okay," Jase says. "Where's the rest?"

"No idea. Only Center leaders have clearance to know the

location, but wherever it is, that could be the bank you're looking for."

I squeeze my eyes shut, begging my knees not to give out under me. The room suddenly feels very small and very exposed. I can practically hear a clock ticking in my head. I brought them all here, and now we're stuck inside a tiny room in a nine-story cube that will sound an alarm if we're spotted, and we're no closer to finding the bank than when we left Finca del Mar.

"Now what?" Bri asks.

Galion bounces, peering out the windows. "Time to go." A single Alexia comes into view, spots us, turns and sprints the other direction.

Every Brute springs into action, hands anxiously grabbing for weapons.

Torvus asks, "Back to the passageway?"

"We can't leave without destroying the serum," I insist. I turn back to Ciela. "You said Center leaders have access. Mother's a Center leader."

"Who is supposed to be *dead*. Even if I knew where she was right now, she wouldn't be able to set foot in the Center, let alone a sensitive area."

"Dr. Novak," I nearly shout. "She's here. And she helped Mother."

Ciela tilts her head, considering. "She's probably your best chance."

"Where would she be?"

"Her office, most likely. She works more hours than I do. Ninth floor."

Before I can think why, I squeeze Ciela in a tight hug. Then we hightail it out of the glass box like curassows fleeing the kitchen, hoping to live another day.

Ciela hides us in a clinic room a few doors down marked with a number eight. She assures us no one will be using it this early in the day, though as she closes the door behind us, she adds,

"If anyone *does* come . . . run?"

"Super helpful. Thanks."

Though none of us are real excited about being packed in a strange room with no windows while the guard alerts Adoni, Teera, and hundreds of Alexia to our presence, we don't have much choice. Waiting here gives us a better chance of an audience with Dr. Novak than forcing our way upstairs.

Bri and Jase lean against a wall behind a long exam table, shoulder to shoulder. Galion and Théo peer down at a counter covered with strange metal devices, probably figuring out how to turn them into weapons. Torvus paces, Dáin sulks, Rohan fidgets with the end of a knife, Dantès yawns, Jem twirls a blade between his fingers, and I don't know if I can take a single minute more in this room when we hear footsteps approach.

In the time it takes the door handle to turn, all eight Brutes have drawn at least one weapon. They resemble tense Jungle cats, ready to pounce. So when Dr. Novak slips through the doorway, wire-rimmed eyes round as oranges, I can't really blame her. In fact, I'm proud of her for not fainting, because the absolute shock registering on her face makes it clear Ciela didn't give her a clue why she dragged her down here.

My sister shuts the door.

"You didn't tell her?" I mouth.

"I didn't think she'd come if I did," she whispers.

Unbelievable. I've always questioned Ciela's judgment— I mean, who keeps a *rooster* as a pet?—but I'm starting to seriously doubt her ability to reason.

"Dr. Novak," I say quickly, weaving through the Brutes toward her before she can do something rash. "Thank you for coming."

"Don't thank me yet, Dom Pierce." Her slender body is as rigid as her voice, but I notice her eyes crinkle as she examines the Brutes—her gaze sweeping over their peculiar features, not just their myriad weapons. As a doctor, perhaps she's better equipped than most with curiosity.

"I haven't had a chance to thank you for helping my mother. And me."

"You're welcome. Though if Leda had told me *before* she was injured what she did with the child, and what she has continued to do since, I might not have been so generous."

I'm not entirely sure what Dr. Novak knows, or what she means by "the child," so I decide to keep my reasoning vague. "She didn't do any of it for herself. I think you know that—it's why you trusted her. And I need you to trust me now."

She's listening, and she hasn't screamed for the Alexia yet, so I press on.

"Mother has always cared about Gentles because she believes they are people, just like us. She understands that *we* are the reason they suffer. You may not have known the details of what she was doing, but when you showed us the Gentles clinic during Candidate training, I saw your own conflict."

I observe that battle on her face again as she scans the room full of Brutes. "Leda knows I've never completely agreed with our treatment of Gentles, but I didn't realize she was taking them—" She cuts herself short, flustered, and presses her thick lips together. "What do you intend to do?"

"We need to force Teera—*to help Nedé*—embrace a better way—" here goes nothing—"by destroying the bank."

She gasps. "Did Leda tell you—?"

"No." I shake my head for emphasis. "I don't know what it

is, not exactly, but I've read Tristan Pierce's private journal, and I gather it holds the key ingredient Nedé needs to create new lives. If we destroy it, the gentling will have to stop."

Her face puckers like she's been punched. "Yes, but only because there will be *no* new births. Destroying the bank would destroy life completely—set in motion the end of Nedé itself. There's no way I can allow it."

A ten-kilo weight slams into my chest. "But—"

"I'm sorry, Dom Pierce. I own up to my actions, and I understand why Leda did what she did. Changes need to take place, and I freely admit the road will be difficult. But eliminating *all* new life? Preposterous."

With a dead end looming in our faces, the Brutes instantly grow antsy.

Jase comes alongside me. "If she's not going to take us there, we need to get moving before more Alexia arrive. We'll find another way."

"There *is* no other way, Jase," I snap.

Dr. Novak freezes at my words, turning toward us. She peers curiously at Jase. "You're Leda's child."

"Yes," he stammers, as confused as I am.

My mind whirls. "Dr. Novak, how do you know about Jase?"

She fixes me with an affronted glare. "Because I delivered him."

"You *what*?"

She sighs. "Leda was to take you to a Materno finca in Kekuatan. Of course, I felt bad for her when, before she could take you, you died."

Her final word hangs in the air, and she smiles slightly.

"I *died*?" Jase asks. But I'm putting two and two together. Mother told me about faking infants' deaths that night in the records room.

Dr. Novak continues. "Only while fighting for her life did she apologize for deceiving me. She explained she had fabricated your death, and the deaths of others, before taking you to the Jungle to live as Brutes with—" She cuts off suddenly and stares at Torvus, as if seeing his presence fill the room for the first time.

In the ensuing silence, Bri suddenly interjects, "Am I the only one wondering why a Center leader would help some woman hide a baby?"

Dr. Novak doesn't shift her gaze from the formidable Brute. "I felt responsible."

"Responsible for what?" I ask tentatively, not sure I want to know the answer.

Dr. Novak takes one step toward him, then another. Galion and Théo edge out of her way as she closes the distance. When she speaks, her voice sounds remote.

"I knew there was a Gentle who exhibited unusual tendencies from birth—a baby who cried when the others were still, who challenged what I had learned in Materno training. For the three months he inhabited the nursery, I watched him closely, wondering if it was my imagination. But when he left the Center, my curiosity wouldn't let me rest. I tracked his movement through the Gentle system, from a Materno finca in Fik'iri to Hive IV. Gentle 35208's last record indicated he was sent to work at a Senator's finca in Amal: Bella Terra."

My breath catches in my chest. *Torvus worked at Bella Terra? As a* Gentle?

Torvus shifts his weight. "You knew . . . about me?" I don't know if he realizes his hand has tightened defensively around a knife hilt at his hip. "Then why didn't you alert the Matriarch?"

Dr. Novak sighs. "I was so young. I couldn't be completely certain whether what I observed in those three months was genuine abnormality or . . ." She seems to be reading him, as if trying to decide whether *he* wants her to continue.

"Or what?" he prompts.

"Or the inexperience of a first-time mother."

The room goes completely still.

Torvus draws back, the wall stopping him from moving far. But he shows surprisingly little emotion for someone who just heard the answer to a question he must have asked his whole life.

"Have you ever wondered why you were different from the other Gentles, Torvus?" she asks.

"Of course."

"Me too."

"Wait," I interrupt. "You mean *you* don't know?"

She reluctantly breaks eye contact with him to answer me. "I didn't, not until very recently. Even now I can't be certain."

Torvus's jaw tightens. "But what do you *think* happened?" he presses.

She smooths stray curls away from her lined face. "While I was caring for Leda following the attack, she explained the connection between the vaccine and the Gentles. She helped me revisit that time in my life when I birthed my first baby. They whisked you away into the nursery, just as they do now. But after an hour, I was so curious I made my way there, to see if they would let me study you for a little while. I hoped to work at the Center after birthing a few children—dreamed of a high position, and had ample ambition to pursue one. The nurses weren't there to ask, so I took you back to my room—just for a little while. I returned you no more than thirty minutes later. When I approached, I overheard two women in the nursery. One said something about another nurse always forgetting to record the fatalities properly. I waited until they exited, then returned you to the bassinet."

"He never received the vaccine," I say slowly.

She meets my hypothesis with the matter-of-fact expression of a doctor. "That's my best guess now. But I had no reason to suspect that then." Her features soften when she returns her gaze to Torvus. "I wasn't sure whether I had imagined the abnormalities. It wasn't until Leda came to me pregnant and told me about her . . . *relationship* with you, that I wondered whether I should have intervened and tried to help you somehow. By that time, Leda said you had gone off to the Jungle. I assumed Nedé would never hear from you again." She grows quiet. "I didn't know Leda knew how to find you, or I would have made contact." Her eyes glisten behind the glare of her glasses. "I wouldn't have abandoned you."

Torvus slides a hand down his reddening face and tilts his head toward the ceiling. His arms seem restless, like they're not sure whether they want to punch something or wrap the silver-haired woman in an embrace. But he says nothing.

"Leda did love you, that much was easy to see," Dr. Novak says quietly, then steps back, giving her words time and space to penetrate Torvus's rough exterior. To the rest she says, "And I'm sorry I can't help you all . . . at least, not the way she did. Not if it means ending new life in Nedé."

Despite her stubbornness, her affection for my mother is clear. She has a soft spot for Leda Pierce, the Rescuer who sacrificed everything to offer these Brutes a chance at life. I'm so proud to be connected with her. To have taken up her mission to do *something* about the injustice.

I lock eyes with Rohan. Like Mother and Torvus, we've opened ourselves to a mysterious, life-altering virtue, wondrous and wild. A virtue built on sacrifice and forgiveness, filled with promises and beauty, ignited by passion and embraces.

I glance at Jase.

A virtue that can birth life itself.

"But, Dr. Novak," I whisper urgently, "you and I both know the bank *isn't* the only way to create life."

She peers at me curiously, her lips pressed tight together. The silence stretches and my heart pounds wildly.

Once she has worked out some internal puzzle, she smiles slightly. "No. I suppose it isn't."

CHAPTER TWENTY-FIVE

As soon as we venture from the room, trouble begins. Guards patrol both ends of the hallway, checking offices and calling out to one another. They see us immediately and take chase, swords drawn.

Torvus and Jase shield Ciela and Dr. Novak, and the rest of us position strategically to protect them.

"Back to the corridor," I holler, as the distance closes between us and two sets of patrols.

"And which way is that?" Jase shouts back, just before his weapon collides with the first Alexia's sword.

I relay instructions above the clang of weapons as we fight our way down the narrow hallways, the tight quarters protecting us from too many Alexia at once. Surrounded by Brutes, unarmed Dr. Novak and Ciela are cocooned from the onslaught, yet every intersection produces more guards, drawn by the commotion. Fists fly and daggers plunge as we press quickly forward, shouts and moans echoing against the tiles.

Somehow we make it back to the nursery. Then, in a rush, Torvus beats back three Alexia to get us to the door. I swing it open, pulling Ciela and the doctor in with me. One by one, the Brutes back their way in, Torvus and Rohan holding the guards at bay until we're safely inside. Then they slip in themselves, and lock and barricade the door.

Dr. Novak turns on the light, and we do a quick assessment of injuries. Jem has a nasty gash across his neck and Dantès has a punctured leg. The doctor rummages quickly through supply drawers, gathering a few rolls of bandages and a bottle of antiseptic, then quickly patches them up.

"That needs stitches," she says to Jem, "but we haven't time now. They'll retrieve the keys before long. Now—" she glances at the door in the corner—"we can take the corridor to the first floor. It should deposit us in the Gentles' health supply closet." Her brow furrows. "Or is it the pharmacy?"

"You don't know where it leads?" I ask, a bit flustered.

"Really—I hardly spend my time skulking around ancient corridors, Dom Pierce, except, it seems, when *your family is around*."

Hers is the best plan we've got, so back in the corridor we go, down, down, down seven flights of dark stairs. The exit door in the first floor corridor doesn't appear to have been used in ages. It takes an appointment with Torvus's shoulder to finally give way. When it does, a corresponding crash of brooms, pails, and various other cleaning supplies confirms Dr. Novak's original guess. We have, in fact, emerged in a supply closet. *Thankfully*, I grimace, *no one had a pressing interest to keep the Gentles' health clinic clean today.*

We continue our path toward the back of the Center, ducking into offices and running through hallways to avoid being spotted.

They must still think we're on the eighth floor, holed up in the office like mice in a trap. When we reach the end of the long hallway, Dr. Novak holds up a hand. She peers carefully around the corner, then draws back quickly.

"They're guarding the door," she whispers, "just down there. It's not marked, but you can't miss it now."

Torvus, in turn, investigates.

"How many?" Jase asks.

"Thirty."

My stomach drops. But the numbers confirm we're exactly where we need to be.

We duck back into an adjacent room, the curve of a high wall obscuring us from chance passersby.

"I'm afraid I won't be any help getting through them," Dr. Novak says. "But if you can get to that door, you'll find a corridor on the other side." She removes a cord from her neck. "This key will also fit the lock at the far end. Inside that room is a metal case. That's what you're looking for."

I nod, silently running through the sequence one more time.

I grip the doctor's forearm. "Please keep my sister safe."

She nods and Ciela embraces me, whispering, "Mother would be proud."

I return her squeeze. Her surprising vote of confidence means the world. "I . . . love you, C."

Doctor Novak gives us a final tight smile, her eyes lingering on Torvus, then Jase, before escorting my sister down the hall with hurried steps. She's in good hands. I hope.

When they're out of sight, I turn to Bri.

"You don't have to do this either. It's not too late to turn back."

She looks at me like I'm a special kind of dense. "Nice of you, Rei, but really, offering an out would have made a lot more sense before you forced me to like these peccaries."

Her choice of insult forces several grins.

"Alright then," I concede, grateful to have her on my side.

We huddle closer, and Torvus outlines the plan, which can be summed up in four words: fight to the death. Phase two: if we miraculously reach the door, Rohan, Bri, Dáin, and I will destroy whatever lies inside while the six remaining Brutes stave off new visitors.

Fiddling with my horsehair bracelet, I glance at Jase. The thought of being separated from him feels all kinds of awful. But he's exchanging unspoken words with Rohan. They're like family to each other too, and their bonds have tied them together far longer than I've even known Jase existed.

Despite being outnumbered three to one, as we discovered upstairs, we'll have at least two advantages. One: Brute strength. Two: because the nondescript door is in the middle of a long, seemingly forgotten hallway no more than two meters wide, the Alexia are forced into a line two guards across, like an armed snake. If we enter from one end, the "head" will only be able to shoot two at a time, so as not to hit itself. It's not much, but it's something.

As he gives final instructions, I consider each of their faces. Weathered Torvus. Stoic Galion. Endearing Jase. Clever Jem. Carefree Dantès. Steady Théo. Even Dáin seems slightly less terrifying in this moment. They show no fear. Agitation, maybe, but their courage in the face of our probable annihilation inspires me to be braver than I am. Even Bri impresses me with her determined scowl.

As we ready our weapons, I look for one more face. Rohan meets my eyes, pulls me near, and grips the nape of my neck. "Please be careful."

"You too," I say, trying to draw just a little more strength from him. Anything else we want to say will have to wait until we make it through this. Otherwise, what's the point?

Before a single Alexia guard can reach for her weapon, before they will come to know about the Brutes waiting just around the corner, I step boldly into the hallway, my empty arms outstretched.

This might be my dumbest idea yet, but I couldn't let the Brutes charge the hallway without at least trying. I doubt Bri and I will be able to abstain from this fight, and I couldn't stomach harming my fellow Alexia before offering a way out.

"Our quarrel isn't with you," I say firmly, my voice filling the space between us, hoping the shock of seeing me unarmed will stay their hands until they hear me out. "Stand down—"

Every Alexia nocks a bow or draws a sword. Before I can add "or else," several arrows already whiz toward me. I jump behind the corner as the *tink-tink-tink* of arrows collides with the concrete wall previously shadowed by my optimistic butt.

"I told you they wouldn't back down," Dáin jeers.

I shrug. "Still, better odds than taking on the whole finca, right?"

We wait for the thump of echoing boots to near, ensuring they'll be too close to easily load bows. Except no footsteps come.

Galion curses. "They were supposed to pursue!"

I crouch low and carefully peer around the corner. Sure enough, all thirty Alexia stubbornly stand guard, weapons raised, bouncing with nervous energy, but holding. They must have orders to guard that door at all costs.

I turn to Torvus to ask what he wants to do now. But he's running toward the adjacent room.

"Where's he going?" I ask incredulously. He wouldn't run away from this fight . . . would he?

Scarcely a minute later, he's back with a table nearly as tall as him, and twice as wide. He rips one of the legs away, and Rohan— apparently catching whatever idea Torvus isn't sharing—kicks off another. They each shoulder one of the two remaining legs, heaving the table in front of them.

"Stay behind us until we're too close for them to shoot," Torvus commands.

Without objection, we file behind the pair, waiting our cue.

"Now!" Torvus shouts. He and Rohan lift the shield, we round the corner, and run toward our fate.

Immediately arrows strike wood like a crack of thunder, and I'm grateful Torvus thought like a Brute. We would have been skewered. Another round of arrows, another and another, before the table collides with guards. Torvus and Rohan give the shield a final push, then shove it aside onto a tangle of bodies, ready to face the remaining Alexia.

Shock blanches our opponents' faces as the Brutes climb over the debris with swords, spears, bows, club, and daggers drawn. The first strike of metal on metal reverberates deep into my chest, echoing like a tremor of nerves through my limbs. Successive blows create a cacophony of clanks, shouts, and lightning-fast movements, making it difficult to think, let alone assess tactics.

This is real. People are going to die.

I grip the hilt of my sword tighter, vowing it won't be Bri or these Brutes I've come to care so much for.

Torvus was right: the cramped hallway works to our advantage, creating a bottleneck that prevents more than a few Alexia from engaging us at a time.

Torvus and Rohan lead our charge, continuing to push the Alexia back with their mass as much as their skill with the blade. Those who slip past this defense find Jase's sword or Galion's spear, and on down the line, with Bri and me trailing last. Despite our disadvantaged numbers, the Brutes fight with incredible strength and remarkable precision, parrying each of the Alexia's textbook moves and countering with unexpected slashes and jabs.

"It's actually working," Bri says, behind me. But behind *her*, a swarm of seven Alexia sweeps around the corner. Having cleverly circled back, they'll soon trap us between two fronts.

"We have company!" I yell. As they charge toward us, Bri and I take down three with arrows before I'm forced to unsheathe my bone dagger and prepare to test its strength.

The force of the collision between my weapon and this Alexia's transports me to Arena training, where Trin taught us the proper mechanics of swordplay. It doesn't take long to realize my "combat partner" surpasses my skill, and her bold offense betrays that she knows it too. When I'm barely able to parry several moves, she lunges mightily. I stumble left, my shoulder barely avoiding her well-timed attack, but her thrust is met by another blade. A frightening fire fuels Rohan's movements, one hand wielding a sword, the other a spear. He blocks my body with his before finishing the Alexia. Bri's challenger glances at Rohan, and fear distracts her the split second it takes for Bri's sword to meet its mark. The Alexia crumples to the floor. Neither of us has time to process the implications of our actions.

Weapons clash everywhere. Brute and Alexia grunts, cries, and curses add to the chaos. Jem bleeds badly from his already-injured arm. To my right, Dáin cracks his club across a skull, then, seeing Dantès outnumbered, comes to his aid.

We're mere meters from the door now. The Alexia force is down by half, nearly evening our odds. Maybe we have a . . .

"Here come more!" Théo shouts. I watch in horror as another stream of Alexia sprint down the hall.

Torvus signals us to push toward the doors before we're over-run. "Go! We'll hold them!"

There's too many. I hesitate, guilt pricking my insides. *We can't leave them now.*

Rohan shoves two Alexia into each other and yanks open the

door. "Now, Reina!" he yells, providing cover while Bri and Dáin duck inside. I hesitate only a moment. Arguing will cost people their lives. I slip through the doorway, waiting on the other side for what feels like an eternity before Rohan backs in and slams the door shut.

We're momentarily engulfed in darkness, our eyes slow to adjust to the dim light of the long, steeply sloping corridor. The air's thick with must and time, the earthen walls damp to the touch—such a contrast to the clean tiles and advancements in Scientia and Medicinae a single door away. Anyone who chanced upon it would assume it's too ancient, too forgotten to be of importance. But we know what we're here for.

I don't need to tell them to hurry. If we don't get this thing destroyed and go back to the others soon, there might not be any others to go back to.

Don't think like that. This is going to work, and then we're all going to get out of here together.

We jog down the corridor, turning right at an elbow, and find the metal door, just as Dr. Novak described. The key slides easily into the lock, but there's no click when I turn it, as if it wasn't actually bolted. *Wait . . .* Did Rohan open the first door without needing a key? *Didn't Dr. Novak say—?* The thick door scrapes against the concrete floor as we swing it wide enough to rush through.

The bank is easy enough to find—a meter-high reflective metal case—perfectly centered between four Alexia guards, Adoni, and the toucan's party colors.

If bad luck were an art form, I'd be a blasted prodigy.

"I know you so well," Teera croons, "it's almost as if we're related."

She sets her slender shoulders like a woman half her age. Like a victor. Though her eyes flit, almost imperceptibly, to the Brutes around me, she doesn't give them the satisfaction of fear. I'd bet a two-minute head start I'm the only one who notices her silver brows lack some of their usual sharpness in the Brutes' presence. To anyone else, she appears to be the fearless Mother that Nedé needs.

Beside her, Adoni grips the hilt of her sword. She scowls at Dáin, both she and her dragon tattoo poised to pounce. The Alexia to their left and right, none of whom I recognize, couldn't have known whom to expect. They seem torn between drawing their weapons and running for the door.

Teera addresses me again. "I think it's time we have a little family chat." Her intonation could slice stone.

"We've said everything that needs to be said," I snap, taking in the rest of the room as I evaluate our options.

Metal shelves line the cinder block walls, holding dusty ledger books, glass jars filled with yellowing substances, crusty parchments. Strange relics pile haphazardly beneath the shelves and under a table that runs the length of one wall: odd machines rusting their guts out, tarnished metal tablets, and a few guns that look to have been chipped from cement. The space could pass for a decrepit museum, its centerpiece—the polished, guarded bank—its only valuable. Nothing else appears to have been touched in decades, if not centuries.

"Oh, I don't think we have," Teera counters. "Clearly, you have *not* heard enough or you wouldn't be here with *them*."

She turns on her heels, the movement causing both sides to twitch toward weapons. Reaching a shelf on the back wall, she retrieves a gray metal container the size and shape of a large brick.

"I told you: it only takes one Brute to bring evil back into the world, Reina. I tried to explain there were ample reasons the foremothers had to act." She sets the case atop the bank and opens the lid. "Reasons you and the rest of Nedé have been protected from knowing. The Gentles, if they knew what they once were . . . I'm afraid it would do more harm than good."

"Not to be rude," Bri gibes, "but can we get on with the fight? We're in a bit of a hurry."

Teera's nostrils flare, but her words come out smooth as her silken robe, its colorful panels strangely juxtaposed with the monochrome pale clay and old metal of the room.

"While your enthusiasm toward your pending demise interests me, Dom Pierce, I recommend you indulge me."

Bri scowls but stays quiet.

Teera lifts a stack of crinkly papers from the box. A few yellowing strips slip from the bundle, flittering toward the ground like flakes of ash. One skids along the cement floor before coming to rest so near my boots I could reach out and take it. Close enough to read the large black letters that form the words "Will Women Ever Be Safe Again?"

"When I recovered this box my first year as Matriarch, I immediately began fortifying the Alexia to defend against a Brute resurgence—from without or within. I may have been the first Matriarch to view these documents since Tristan Pierce herself brought them to Nedé, which is why I was the only other Matriarch to take similar, decisive actions. *I* understood the threats our foremothers faced. I knew what horrors those filthy Brutes had committed and why we must never allow them a foothold again. At the time, my measures were preventative; I had no reason to suspect we'd need them.

"In more recent years, however, strange stories originating along the borders—coupled with my own daughter's strange behavior—piqued my suspicion. When the attacks began—" she appraises Dáin coolly, and I'm reminded she thought he was the leader—"I was convinced that—against all odds—the plague had somehow returned. It appears I was correct."

"You're wrong about them," I counter. "You have no idea what they're actually like."

"Don't I?" she says hotly, then thrusts the stack of thick cards toward me. "Go on. Before we dispose of you, I'd like you to see them." She smiles wryly. "Call me vain, but I'm looking forward to hearing you acknowledge I was right."

My nerves are strung so taut you could play a song on them, but . . . curiosity claws at me. What could possibly be written there to make Teera so confident I will change my mind about these Brutes? Before we destroy Nedé's future, shouldn't I know the whole of our past?

I step forward. Rohan shadows me protectively.

"*Just her*," Teera warns.

I place a hand on his arm. "It's alright."

The tension's thick as mangrove-swamp mud, dragging against me as I take each of three steps across the room.

Adoni's eyes reveal nothing. The other Alexia fix their attention on Bri, Rohan, and Dáin. But Grandmother's gaze taunts me, dares me to be brave enough to see what she holds.

Forcing my hand to steady, I reach out. She shoves the cards into my palm.

They're made of a strangely thick paper—not full of writing, but . . . paintings? Like portraits, but so detailed, so realistic, they could live off the page. Their vividness terrifies me, because I hold unquestionable horrors.

In the first, Brutes in uniforms point guns at kneeling women, blindfolded and gagged. In the next, a cluster of unkempt little girls huddle on a bed, their eyes eerily hollow. Next, a woman with black-and-blue eyes and a bloody face.

My fingers tremble as I flip through nakedness, shackles,

death, and fear, until I can't bear to look at another relic. They slip through my fingers, spilling to the ground.

I barely hear myself ask, "That's what it was like, in the world before?"

"That is only the beginning, Reina. I found writings of other foremothers, who told of horrors they themselves experienced at the Brutes' hands." She flings a hand toward my companions, as if *they* were the perpetrators. "Our ancestors were willing to risk everything to stop the depravity. Why would we *ever* allow it to creep back into our world?"

"But depravity already *has* crept into Nedé, and it didn't begin with them," I say, rehearsing the reasons I'm standing here now. "The evil lives in us, too—certainly in you. What crimes might appall your great-great-granddaughters someday? That we crippled Gentles so we could feel safe? That we forced them into lives of miserable servitude? The inescapable pain and sorrow that pushed them toward the stinger? How about the Gentle you shot at the Hive, just to make a point?" My voice is trembling with anger now. "And what of me? What will *my* descendants say when they're told I sent an arrow through my best friend's heart?"

She starts to argue, but I have more to say and I'm tired of cowering to her.

"My choices have haunted me. But just as I can choose virtue, they can too. You don't know that because you don't know *them*."

"How can you be sure?" she suddenly yells, a frantic note betraying the only weakness I've ever seen in my grandmother.

I consider the question and deflate a little, knowing I can't actually be completely certain. I think Jase is trustworthy. I believe Torvus is honorable. I have to hope that Rohan will prove a man *can* be good to a woman. That our love will be enough to keep him from hurting me. *But* . . . I squeeze my eyes shut, trying to still the voices of doubt. The truth is . . .

"I *don't* know for sure," I say. If Mother's right, I'm not meant to. "But it's not my job to 'play God.' It's only my duty to protect the weak and do my part to ensure safety for all—including Gentles."

"Then you've disappointed me after all, Reina," she says.

I know what comes next, but before she can signal Adoni to take me out, my dagger is at my own grandmother's throat, the razor-sharp bone pressing dangerously against her skin.

Adoni knows she can't attack me without losing the Matriarch. Rohan, Bri, and Dáin stand off with the other guards.

No one moves a muscle.

Teera's breaths come in shallow wheezes. Fear drains her of the usual harsh veneer, revealing an old woman, made paranoid by hate.

I want to hate her too. I *need* to hate her to do what I must.

Sometimes people have to get hurt so the right thing can happen.

I've heard it from Dáin, from Jase—even from Rohan.

The right thing is for the gentling to stop. For Tre's death to mean something. The right thing is to let Brutes be the men they're supposed to be, come what may.

Mother knew this moment was coming. She tried to warn me. *Seeking revenge never offers the closure one hopes it will,* she said.

If I kill Grandmother, will I be any different from her? When I shot Tre for the greater good, it unraveled me. Will I be able to live with myself if I kill her, too?

Where forgiveness grows, new paths appear. Maybe sometimes the right thing can happen without selling your soul.

I meet Teera's gaze with unflinching fire. "I'm not like you. I won't take your life the way you made me take Treowe's. But I *will* stop you from hurting anyone else."

In one swift slide, I dive for the bank, barely avoiding Adoni's reach, swinging at the metal door with my dagger. It scarcely dents the metal, but the reverberating clang signals a riot. In the twitch of a cat's whiskers, the twin waves of Alexia and Brutes collide in the center of the room. Adoni makes a beeline for Dáin, Bri defends against two Alexia guards, and Rohan battles the rest.

I smack the case again and again, but rather than cracking the lock, the knife shatters. I hold the broken fragment of the basket-weave hilt in my hand, shock morphing instantly to anger. I scan the decaying debris under the tables for something heavy enough to break it open.

"Reina!" Rohan shouts, sweat dripping down his cheeks. "Behind you!"

Teera has taken a sword from the first fallen Alexia and rushes at me with surprising dexterity, robe billowing behind. Before I can unsheathe the dagger on my thigh, Teera closes the distance. She swings the sword overhead, bringing it down like an ax. In a flash, Dáin spins away from Adoni, positioning himself between me and my grandmother's fury. He meets her slice with a swift uppercut of his harpy-eagle club. Teera's sword flies across the room.

Time slows to a trickle . . . Grandmother's enraged eyes widen with fear as Dáin swings again. A wicked smile splits his mouth as his club collides with the side of her head. The crack is deafening, even in the chaos. My stomach lurches as her body crumples to the dusty floor, coiled in on itself like a limp snake. The Matriarch of Nedé is dead.

He raises the club to strike again out of spite, but Adoni grabs his wrist, twists him toward her, and thrusts her sword through his middle.

"*No!*" Bri shouts, hacking her opponent down and running at Adoni.

Dáin's freckled face drains of color while blood as red as his fiery hair seeps from the wound. Still, he musters the audacity to spit in Adoni's face.

She scowls, then twists her blade before jerking it free. As Dáin drops to his knees, Bri lunges wildly from behind, thrusting her sword at Adoni with the kind of rage that doesn't consider hopeless odds. For once, her brashness pays off.

Adoni tries to circle on Bri, but her body gives way and she stumbles forward, splaying across Teera. Even in this hell, the sight of the mighty defender's death rings strange and wrong. She's *Adoni*. She doesn't deserve to go like this.

Bri slips an arm under Dáin, trying to lift him.

"*I* wanted to kill her," he mumbles, blood staining his lips. Then he collapses into her.

Rohan yells in pain, and I remember that we're on borrowed time. He shifts his blade to the other hand, under the attack of the final three guards. Bri tears herself from Dáin to draw one away, leaving two for Rohan.

I snatch Dáin's club, swing it in a wide arc, and smash the lock on the bank's metal door. Again and again I swing. Finally, the door cracks. I jam the base of the club into the split and pry the bent hinges open.

Inside, thousands of tiny crystalline vials, lidded with shimmering gold seals, await my own fury. I sweep the shelves mercilessly, vials pelting the floor like glass raindrops.

"For Treowe!" I scream. "For justice!"

Once the last vial shatters, the room goes silent, the fighting suddenly stilled. Bri and Rohan stumble over. Together, we heave the whole case on its side, crashing atop the debris of would-be lives.

I don't look back as we race toward the door.

Outside the corridor, an eerie quiet gives me pause; the carnage stops me cold. Jase slumps beside the door, barely able to lift his head at our approach. Dozens of Alexia bodies line the hallway around him. *By Siyah—what have we done?* Across the hall, Torvus huddles over Dantès, ripping strips from his shirt to bind deep gashes on his arms and side. Torvus himself bleeds heavily, slices across his back and legs butterflying his skin like filleted cuts of steak.

Rohan falls to Jase's side, immediately evaluating his wounds. "Did you find it?" Jase asks weakly.

"More than we were looking for." Rohan adjusts Jase's hasty bandage work. "The dragon woman and the Matriarch, both dead."

Jase leans his head against the wall, smiling weakly. "We did it." Then he moans as Rohan cinches a final bandage around his leg.

Théo limps toward us, squeezes the back of Rohan's neck.

Rohan scans the hallway. "Jem? Galion?"

Théo shakes his head.

"Theirs were honorable deaths," Rohan mutters, standing. "As was Dáin's."

Jase shuts his eyes at the news. Théo nods blankly. For all the hate I've harbored against Dáin since our very first encounter, viewing his death through the grief of those who knew him when he was a reckless redheaded cub forces me to face what happened in there.

Dáin *saved* me.

We all have to choose. I consider Rohan's words from yet another vantage point. For all Dáin's selfishness, for all his vile scheming— no matter how many wicked decisions he made—each choice was still just that. And in the end, he *chose* sacrifice.

Bri takes Rohan's place next to Jase. He forces himself to sit higher so he can face her.

"So," she says indifferently, "you made it." But her eyes are moist, and she can't quite meet his gaze.

Jase's ragged laugh breaks some of the heaviness of the moment. "Sorry to disappoint you."

She loops an arm under his, helping him to his feet. "Come on, you big baby."

Théo supports Jase's other side, but I'm still worried.

"Should I get Dr. Novak?"

Rohan doesn't hesitate. "We're getting out of here before any more arrive."

"What about the injuries?"

I hate the resignation in his eyes. "If we can get back to the Jungle, I can find what we need. If we can't . . ." He brushes my cheek, but his words remain firm. "At least we did what we came to do."

So we gather our wounded, I salvage a sword, and the seven of us make for the front entrance. The secret corridors offer no advantage now. As we pick through the bodies, my own injuries finally break through my fading adrenaline. Nondescript aches begin surfacing, stings from lacerations, and one shooting pain where a piece of the bone knife must have ricocheted off my forearm. But, considering those who fought alongside me—fought *for* me—this pain doesn't deserve my attention.

The first floor is eerily quiet. Not a single guard intercepts us on our way to the entrance, and any other early workers must have cleared out in the commotion.

As we push the large glass doors open to a tunnel of flame vine and a brightening sky, I finally exhale.

Against all odds, Jase is right. *We did it.*

For better or worse, we destroyed the bank. With Teera gone, her Apprentice dead, and the Alexia leaderless, what's to stop us from finally changing Nedé?

Perhaps only one thing could. And as we step through the final arch, limping and weary, it waits for us like a cruel joke.

"This feels a bit like déjà vu, Candidate," Trinidad says, sword drawn, two hundred Alexia forming ranks behind her.

CHAPTER TWENTY-SIX

THIS IS DECIDEDLY BAD.

"You mean, you aren't here because you missed me?" I say, attempting to push down the panic resurfacing in my whole body. Jase and Dantès can barely stand. The rest of us might still be able to fight, but what is that against so many?

Trin meets my levity with a scowl. "*Let me guess*—you want me to *trust* you?"

I deflate under her scrutiny. She certainly has no reason to. Yes, I freed her at Tree Camp, but we're far from even. How many times can I plead for her trust before she has none left to give? I have a feeling the answer is one less than I need.

"I thought you were an Alexia," she glowers, hurt hardening her voice like the steel she wields, "but you made your choice when you aligned with them."

I eye their ranks—the women I was meant to stand beside—
rows and rows of mounted archers, even more on foot. If there's
a way out, I can't see it. We're helplessly exposed, too injured to
run far. It's over.

For the love of Siyah! I want to scream. We beat the odds, succeeded in eliminating the Matriarch *and* Nedé's source of Gentles,
only to meet our end here? At the hand of the one Alexia I want
to disappoint least?

Trin lifts a closed fist; bows are raised. Before she can signal
the onslaught of arrows, a strange sound fills the air, like voices
yelling, sprinkled with a metallic clanging reminiscent of wind
chimes. She stalls, noticing too. It seems to be coming from just
over a knoll behind the Alexia force. No—to the right? The left?
It grows louder by the second, now surrounding us from every
direction at once.

Trin turns slowly at the eerie sound; the Alexia look to each
other in confusion.

A mass of people crests the top of the rise, marching down
around the Alexia like a swarm of slow-moving termites—hundreds
and hundreds of them, a thousand or more—brandishing pitch-
forks and field machetes, shovels and kitchen knives and plow
hooks. Each and every one of them *a Gentle.*

At the front of the wave, a familiar face roars with a high-
pitched yell. *Neechi!* Domus marches on his left, Old Solomon on
his right. They hedge in the Alexia like a human dam, closing the
circle on either side of us. My arms beg to embrace Neechi, who
comes to stand beside me; my lungs ache to hoot and holler. But
I hold my ground, face placid. I need Trin to believe I knew this
was coming.

"We don't want to hurt you—any of you." I raise my voice so
every Alexia can hear. "It's over. We've already set in motion the

end of Nedé as we've known it, so a better Nedé can take its place."
I exhale slowly before dealing the next blow: "Teera's dead."

A murmur ripples through Alexia and Gentles alike. Trin grips
her sword, and the way her golden eyes narrow I know she's more
convinced than ever I'm a traitor. Will she ever be able to forgive
me for what I must say next?

"And . . . Trinidad is now the acting leader of the Alexia." I bite
my lip as I watch her digest the meaning of my announcement.

"How *could* you?" she seethes, dismounting Midas and racing
toward me until she's close enough to strike. I don't flinch, don't
back down. She positions her blade to run me through. Rohan
lunges, but I stop him with a hand to his chest, begging him to
trust me.

"You could kill me," I challenge. "You could kill these Brutes.
With some loss of Alexia life, you could probably decimate every
Gentle here—every Gentle in Nedé—with the full might of the
Alexia. But for *what*, Trin? I'm fighting to end tyranny and restore
virtue. I know you want that too. As of today, there will be no new
Gentles. Nedé stands at a crossroads. Why waste any more blood?"

The tip of her sword holds steady, poised to strike. "Adoni was
a *good* leader. Teera, flawed or not, was our *Matriarch*. You deserve
to pay for your crimes."

"Maybe we do. But what of Teera's crimes? Of Nedé's? Let me
defend our actions before the Senators. Then . . . I'll willingly
submit myself to our punishment."

She hesitates, taken aback by my request.

"High crimes demand a full trial," I press, pretending I haven't
just remembered this.

"Fine," she concedes. "But you'll stay in the cells until then.
And this time—" she almost, *almost* smiles—"no custard apple."

She takes in the sea of Gentles, their makeshift weapons glinting in the morning sun, and shakes her head.

"I don't know how you did it," she says, "but you had better call them off before I change my mind."

I'd love to know the same thing. As soon as she walks away, I sweep Neechi into my arms. He's sweating like a pig in July, and holding a sickle so tight his hand might be stuck. Jase slaps him on the back while the other Brutes grin. Rohan quips, "Not so gutless now."

"Neechi," I say, careful not to let any Alexia hear, "what in *bats*? How did you—?" I finally land on "You would have fought the Alexia head-on?"

Neechi laughs. "Fight? Dom Reina, you know Gentles better than that. I might have thrown some coconuts from a tree, but I barely convinced them to hold weapons and walk down the hill. If it came to fighting, we would have run as fast as our brittle legs would carry us."

We burst out laughing.

"We may not have the strength of a coyote—" he taps his head with a finger—"but Dom Leda helped us think like one."

"My mother?"

"She told the Gentles at Bella Terra the truth about us, like you told me, and they've been spreading the word that when her daughter got to Phoenix City, we should do whatever we could to help her, because she wants to help us. Old Solomon got the message going like wildfire. Eventually, word got to Domus—"

"Domus!" I interject, remembering now that I saw him in the crowd. He shuffles forward and I take his wrinkled face in my hands. "You're alive!"

"Yes, Dom Reina." He smiles meekly. "Happily, other matters kept the Matriarch preoccupied after your departure."

"But how did you end up with them, Neechi? We thought we lost you."

"You did." Neechi grins. "Or I lost you. Then Domus found

me near the stable—scared the scat out of me—and since I knew you were headed for the Center, we figured this was as good a place as any to help you."

"Well done, Neechi," I say. "Brave, brave Neechi. Now you can tell the others . . ." and I give him one last instruction before Trin returns with ropes and guards to escort seven prisoners to the Arena cells.

CHAPTER TWENTY-SEVEN

WHEN MY EYES FLINCH IN THE blinding sun of midafternoon three days later, I'm disappointed Trin doesn't accompany the guards. She stuck to her word about no custard apples, but she did provide food and medicine. It was an honorable gesture, and I had hoped to thank her.

In her stead, a full fifty guards escort us, our hands and feet bound with heavy shackles. Apparently, after the Brutes' last victory against impossible odds, they won't be taking any chances.

During the long, dark days underground, we grieved those we lost—told stories of Galion's mishaps and Jem's surprising naughty streak. And I came to terms with Dáin's sacrifice—whether he meant to or not, he gave his life saving mine. I told them, too, about the images Teera showed me, and though their expressions were impossible to read in the darkness, I could feel their quiet rage—perhaps even a little fear at what their kind could become if left unchecked.

The single star to these uncertain days and nights, the beacon of light, was that Rohan, once again, somehow managed a way to be near me. From the adjacent cell, he'd slip his fingers through the metal bars and find mine, and somehow that simple touch gave me the courage I needed.

That courage motivated me to rehearse what I'll tell the Senators today. If I don't succeed—if I can't convince them—Rohan will die. So will Jase and Bri, Torvus and the others. Our very survival depends on my ability to convince them within minutes what took me years to accept.

We're herded along the curving stone wall of the Arena. I expect to be pushed into a waiting surrey or marched through cobblestone streets to Finca del Mar, where Senate meetings are usually held. Instead, we turn abruptly into the west entrance.

Through the tunneled archway, a semicircle of tables materializes in the center of the Arena, chairs filled with unsmiling Senators. I recognize some of their faces, including Julissa Pierce. None of them—not even my own aunt—betray a single glimmer of hope. Dread turns my limbs to water. *You asked for this*, I remind myself. *Pull it together—this is your chance to save them.* It's just that my defense felt more substantial while mentally rehearsing in the secluded cells than it does before the scrutiny of the full Council.

A strangely familiar sound grows as we approach—like a river murmuring quickly downstream. When we emerge into the ring, the entire Arena seems to echo with a gasp, and now I realize what the sound is. The towering gray bleachers are packed with women, tense and muttering. When they see us—or perhaps more accurately, the *Brutes* among us—there are little inhales and heated whispers, even some hisses and boos, from the Senators' tables and bleachers of Nedéans alike.

It appears all of Nedé has come to hear the verdict: *What will be done to avenge their Matriarch?* I falter under their collective gaze. Preparing to face the full Council was intimidating enough; I never imagined *this*. How can I make *all of them* understand?

My heart pounds wildly, and my palms grow slick.

The guards halt the Brutes and Bri, but march me forward a few more paces so I'm standing in the middle of the unpretentious semicircle of leaders. No greenery or flowers decorate the tables for this occasion, so unlike our usual gatherings in this space. No flags fly overhead. There's not a drop of chicha in sight. It seems, with Teera gone, the Senators have already reverted to a greater simplicity. Austere, but not soft. On the opposite side of the Arena, a rectangular platform has been erected, where more Alexia guards stand armed and at attention, prepared for a pending execution. *Our* execution.

Seated in the center of the Council, Trinidad stares at me, unblinking. One half of her head has been shaved, the rest studded with short, gold-tinged braids. The tribute to her fallen commander makes her appear fiercer somehow, and I wince. Her metal arm cuffs gleam in the sun, and she wears her Alexia uniform like the leader she has become. Whatever she thinks of me, I am *proud* of her. Under different circumstances, it would be an honor to shoulder a bow in her service. But the sight of her also makes me ache. Even if no one else in this blasted Arena understands what I've done, I need *her* to.

Enough guards surround Torvus, Rohan, Jase, Théo, Dantès, and Bri to stamp out any notion of escape. I steal a glance at Rohan. His whole body is taut as a bowstring; his gaze follows my every move. Despite the worry he can't hide, his eyes tell me I have what it takes. That we'll make it through this somehow.

By Siyah, I hope he's right.

A Senator with gray hair and a taupe tunic rises, unfolding a piece of sand-colored parchment.

"Reina Pierce," she reads, "you stand accused of aiding and abetting these enemies of Nedé in the destruction of *vital* Nedéan property; the murder of Teera Pierce, eighth Matriarch of Nedé; the murder of Adoni Assad, leader of the Alexia; and fifty-two Nedéans, members of the Alexia destiny. Yet," she sighs, "in the tradition of Nedé's long-standing esteem of the Virtues, including justice, you may now make your defense."

I step forward and lift my chin.

Beneath a deepening blue sky, tens of thousands of faces stare down at the spectacle we've become, waiting to hear—not what I have to say, but what punishment we'll be given. I scan the encircling rows of my fellow Nedéans, wanting so badly for them to understand.

One set of hazel eyes, just behind and above the Senators, welcomes me with their love. My sisters, Marsa, and Dom Bakshi surround her. She risks much to be here. How like my mother. With the lives of Jase and Torvus also balanced precariously on my defense, her unconditional support fills me with a strange ache. A fresh resolve.

I address the Senators, Trinidad, and our sisterhood, projecting the words of our motto loud and clear.

"'Praesidete debiles. Salus omnibus. Vis sine virtute tyrannis est.' These are words Nedé has proclaimed since the foremothers risked their lives to allow us to live free from fear." Murmurs of assent ripple through the crowd. "Nedéans protect the weak. Nedéans ensure safety for all. Nedéans fight against tyranny with virtue."

I don't know how much they have been told, but the Brutes stand in plain sight now. Might as well address the obvious.

"It was in pursuit of those very virtues that one brave woman saved these Brutes from becoming Gentles. We've been told that Brutes committed atrocities against women because of inferior genetics. But now I know the truth: we Nedéans have made Gentles the weak-minded, brittle-bodied humans they are. To protect ourselves, we have been robbing Brutes of their minds and bodies. What right do we have to strip others of dignity because of their *potential* to hurt us?"

A tall, thin Senator with hollow cheeks interrupts. "The Brute atrocities in times past are irrefutable, and their current actions prove their danger remains."

"With few exceptions, the actions these Brutes have taken against Nedé—against the Matriarch—were in the name of justice and self-preservation. They only combated the tyranny against them to claim what was rightfully theirs: safety, health, happiness. Is that so different from what our own foremothers were willing to risk their lives to achieve?"

"You said 'with few exceptions,'" the Senator presses. "Do you admit they took excessive, *Brutish* measures?"

Even though he's dead, I can't escape the memory of Dáin pinning me against the damp earth in a Jungle clearing, or excuse the terror Jonalyn experienced at his hands. And Dáin wasn't the only one—those who followed him to the attacks hold blame too. I glance back at the Brutes, my eyes settling on Rohan. A flutter of familiar fear surfaces. *Will they go beyond reasonable measures again? Will they choose to do right more often than wrong?*

I beg doubt not to betray me as I respond. "The attacks against Nedéans were led by one rogue Brute and a few followers—they weren't sanctioned by the rest. That Brute is now dead."

"Yet he was capable of great harm against us."

A distressed murmur pulses through the crowd, and I have to raise my voice to be heard above their fear.

"What of our own evil?" I yell. "Was our Matriarch, Teera

Pierce, a model of virtue?" I scrutinize each Senator as I continue, settling on Aunt Julissa. She knows her mother better than any of them. "Would you be *very* surprised to know I watched her kill a Gentle with wicked indifference? That she forced me to do the same? The unscrupulous *indulgences* you overlooked were only one flea on the old dog's back. Surely you've heard? She tried to murder her own daughter! And she was intent on killing every Brute in existence simply for being born."

The Arena has grown so quiet I can hear the whoosh of a jay's wings as it swoops overhead.

"I stand with these Brutes because I've discovered they're no worse monsters than we are. Without virtue, *whoever* holds the power—Brutes *or* women—will eventually default to tyranny. The foremothers thought we could wield sole power without being corrupted. Look where that got us. But what if we *combined* our strengths to fight injustice—called each other to a higher virtue?"

I meet Trin's eyes. She betrays nothing. A few Senators scribble notes on their parchments.

I don't know if it's enough, but it's all I have.

Torvus, however, doesn't seem ready to leave his fate in the hands of my shaky defense. He pushes forward to address the Senators, dragging two Alexia guards with him. They coil to strike, but surprisingly, Trin orders, "Let him speak."

Torvus's deep voice reverberates through the Arena.

"I was raised as a *son of Nedé*," he booms, without suppressing his resentment toward the term. "You claim to have freed Gentles to use their best gifts for women, but I tell you, you've stripped them of more than you've given."

The Senator spokeswoman blusters, "But Brutes have *killed* women."

"Women have killed Brutes!" I yell back, enraged by the hypocrisy.

The Senator glares at me. "*You* have killed Nedéans!"

The Arena erupts in chaotic murmurs and shouts. I'm crushed under the weight of her words: I *have* killed Nedéans. The truth is—even though I joined these Brutes for a greater good—the Council sees only that two Nedéans conspired with Brutes and turned against their own. *Killed* their own. Regardless of what they plan to do with these Brutes, they believe Bri and I deserve to die today.

What can I say in defense of our betrayal?

Amidst the Arena's upheaval, women demanding justice, Rohan fights his way forward until he's standing beside me. He meets my gaze for only a second before shouting above the crowd's dissent to address the Council.

"Hear me," he shouts over the din. "If according to your law someone must die for justice to be served, take my life. This Nedéan has done nothing deserving of death. I'll give my life willingly in exchange for hers."

The frothing crowd stills at his words. *I* still. *What is he—? Why would he—?*

Jase's confident voice breaks the silence as he moves past Théo to stand beside Bri. "And take mine for hers."

Bri hisses under her breath, "You're an idiot." But her cheeks flush and her eyes glisten all the same.

Trinidad stands abruptly, leaning across the table to stare at Rohan. "Why would you do that?"

Rohan takes my hand. "Your Matriarch had power but no virtue. Reina has no Alexia at her command, but she has more virtue than anyone I've ever known." He takes another step forward and spreads his arms wide. "My life isn't enough for hers, but if you'll take it, I offer it freely."

The Arena erupts in a fresh wave of confused murmurs and shouts.

Panic grips me. "Rohan, *no*."

He retakes my hand firmly in his, meets my pleading glare, and whispers, "It would be the *most* honorable death." Then, with a lopsided grin, he leans down and adds, "Besides, you chose *Brute*. This is who we are."

I want to throw my arms around him and never let go. To discover every other unlikely virtue this Brute possesses. But even if I can't—if we never get the chance—a strange resolve steadies me. We were made to change the world together, weren't we, and whatever happens to us today, *we have already done just that*.

I tear my gaze from him as Jase gives his answer to Trin's question. "Dom Pierce has sacrificed much to protect the truly weak— to save children who couldn't speak for themselves. Children like us." He locks eyes with Mother in the crowd, and I understand which Dom Pierce he's really speaking of. She beams with purest love.

As the crowd works to understand his meaning, a strange hush hollows out the Arena. I glance back at the others, who stand stoically, when a voice pierces the quiet.

"Let them live!" it shouts.

I whip around and quickly scan the Arena bleachers for our unexpected ally. Dom Tourmaline stands in the bottom row, just below Mother—as eccentrically dressed as ever in sweeping yellow silks—and cries again, "Virtue before tyranny!"

Before I can make sense of it, the crowd erupts in a mayhem of hisses and whistles, some shouting "death for death," while others chant for mercy.

The Senators shift uncomfortably, some watching the Alexia— tense amidst the unease—others twisting in their seats to read the crowd.

As the temperature in the Arena mounts, Aunt Julissa meets my gaze, her brows drawn together in thought, before rushing to the spokeswoman's seat. The two exchange heated words for several minutes as chaos continues. When the Senator reluctantly waves a hand, Julissa speaks urgently with Trinidad. The Alexia leader nods. With some secret matter decided, Julissa stands and motions for the Arena's attention. After several attempts, the crowd hushes enough to hear her address.

"Our law is clear," she says, to those gathered as much as to us. "A life cannot be taken without penalty."

My heart sinks and my whole body clenches with dread. This is it. This is where we die.

"However," she continues, and that single word threatens to upend the peace. The Arena trembles with unease. She raises her voice. "*However*, in light of all that has transpired, there is much to discuss. We will need ample time to determine the just punishment." She addresses the guards surrounding us. "Return them to the cells. No one will die today."

CHAPTER TWENTY-EIGHT

NEECHI HELPS ME PRESS FRAGRANT EARTH around the little plant in the shade of the fig tree, being careful not to disturb the papery red petals of its first hibiscus flower—a fitting tribute to Treowe. The familiar swish of the Jabiru reminds me of him. So do our goats, and Old Solomon, and bananas, and just about everything good or kind. But especially the flower.

I untie Callisto's fraying two-toned braid from my wrist and lay it beside the plant. Returning to Bella Terra makes me miss them both something fierce. But I had to come back, one more time.

The Senators decided Mother could keep her beloved finca, now that she's an inaugural member of Nedé's Assembly of Justice.

It seems we underestimated the number of Senators already suspicious of Teera's actions and plans. They were kept informed, it turns out, by a certain Finca del Mar regular with orange-gold hair and a flair for curating fine clothing. My hunch about Dom Tourmaline's sharp eyes was correct. And when word got out that Teera had indeed ordered the death of her daughter, Leda Pierce—a woman well-known and well-loved by many Nedéans—any lingering loyalty to Teera's ways dissolved. Their outrage over her actions fueled a demand for change in the Matriarchy itself.

It also didn't hurt that—once Dr. Novak revealed the implications of the destroyed bank—they realized killing off the Brutes would sentence Nedé to extinction.

So, after nearly a week of deliberation, the Senators and Trinidad settled on a plan to move forward in the wake of our upheaval. The Senate will continue per usual—what Senator would vote otherwise?—to handle the affairs of the provinces. The Matriarch's role has been replaced by the Assembly of Justice, which comprises one representative from each of the destinies: Trinidad for the Alexia; Mother for the Maternos; Domus will now oversee Gentles Ministerium, which replaces Gentles Regimen; and Torvus was the natural choice to represent an entirely new destiny, Anthropos. Though Brutes and Gentles will be grouped within their own destinies for now, Mother assures me changes will continue as women adjust to having what they believed were their worst nightmares living among them. She trusts one day, Brutes and women will be able to do the same jobs, intermixed within the destinies.

Thankfully, the Senators' "plan to move forward" did not involve our deaths. *Though . . .* a hollow homesickness fills me as I recall our pending punishment. But now's not the time to dwell on that.

I take the trowel from Neechi. "Thank you for helping me."

He nods, smearing tears from his cheeks with the back of a muddy hand. We take our time strolling toward the villa.

"So," I pry, "Jonalyn tells me you've refused Ciela's antidote."

Though it's not a complete reversal, with actual Brute blood to utilize, my sister quickly closed the final gap in her research and created a "strength serum." She expects it to have the greatest effects on the young Gentles, but because it will require a lifetime of injections, she's unsure how many will actually utilize it. If Neechi's any indication, we won't have to worry about a population of Gentles-turned-Brutes overnight.

"How could you refuse the Center's new codirector like that?" I tease.

The moment I was reunited with Ciela, she made sure I knew about her new role—replacing a retiring Dr. Novak, who wishes to make up for lost time with her son. My sister plans to use the year's supply of life serum we didn't destroy to tide Nedé over while she figures out how to duplicate the process the foremothers used to create the bank. At least until Brutes and women begin having children like in the old world. Children like Jase.

Neechi shakes his head. "I'm happy as I am, Dom Reina. I like those Brutes enough, of course. But what do they have that I don't? I'm happy here, with Dom Pierce's horses to care for and a soft bed at night."

"Then you'll stay on at Bella?"

He shrugs, smiling. "It's what I know."

I smile back.

I suppose change sometimes provides the opportunity to continue doing what we've always done.

At least I've given him the choice.

Not that life at Bella will be *quite* the same moving forward. In the days since Ciela began testing Mother's little Gentles with the strength serum, Dom Bakshi and Marsa have had their hands full of squirming, playful monkeys. I've never heard Marsa threaten "Wap kon Jorge!" so many times in a day. And once Torvus, Jase, and Rohan return from the ruins with the rest of the cubs—along with any older Brutes who want to come—Bella Terra will transform into its own kind of Jungle.

Speaking of transformations, Little Boo—I swear, three centimeters taller already—has spotted me and sprints past the goat pen, high-jumping over low shrubs as he runs. He throws his little arms around my waist.

"You all done with your morning studies?" I ask, kneeling beside him.

He nods.

"Were you good for Dom Bakshi?"

He screws up his mouth, thinking harder than he should have to about the answer to this question. I ruffle his hair.

"She's the best tutor in Nedé, Little Boo. Go easy on her, for my sake. It's my fault she has her hands full."

"Yes, it is," Dom Bakshi protests, mopping her forehead with the edge of her sari as she overtakes us. But her face softens as Little Boo runs off to play.

"Have you seen Mother?"

"She went with Marsa to look into those supplies for—" Her words trail away as she averts her eyes.

"I'm going to be alright, *Domina Bakshi*," I say, in that nasally delivery I used to tease her with, trying to coax a smile. Though she and Mother, and especially Marsa, aren't so sure, *I'm* confident I—*we*—will be.

CHAPTER TWENTY-NINE

MAY 2267

ONE WEEK LATER

Sᴜɴ-ʙʟᴇᴀᴄʜᴇᴅ ᴘʟᴀɴᴋs ᴄʀᴇᴀᴋ ᴜɴᴅᴇʀ my weight as I scramble onto the platform of the two-hull. The midmorning sun blazes across a shimmering Halcyon Sea, a steady breeze promising fair sailing for our journey. Lazy clouds drift across the cobalt sky, and great gray pelicans sun themselves on the waves. The wind carries hints of salt spray and fresh beginnings. I have to say, the general charm takes some of the sting out of our exile from Nedé.

I hand Rohan the last rucksack, and he tosses it into the adjacent hull, where packs, flasks, and plenty of weapons take up half the space. The other half is chock-full of Bri's sour pout.

"If we die on this stupid 'mandatory hiatus,'" she whines at me, "my ghost still knows where your ghost lives."

I grin. "Hey, you were the one who just *had* to follow me into the Jungle. It's your own fault, really."

"Come on." Jase grins at her from the other hull. "It's going to be fun."

She sticks out her tongue at him.

"For the record—" I wince—"I'm still not convinced I understand a Brute's idea of *fun*."

Dantès raises the bone-white sail—a gracious gift from Trinidad—and a gust draws us slowly from shore.

I give a final farewell nod toward the small crowd gathered along the stretch of sand. Trinidad, who stands among a patrol of Alexia, winks at me, and I smile back. Our final conversation didn't contain many words, but I knew what she meant. When we return—whenever that might be—I can rejoin the Alexia. It was all I needed to hear.

On the other end of the shore, Mother wipes tears from her cheeks and Torvus pulls her a little closer. Jonalyn, who finally returned to La Fortuna, waves with one hand, holding little Finch with the other. Her reclaimed four-year-old son—who's receiving the serum—and daughter, Cassia, romp through the sand, pouncing playfully on Ori, who returned with Torvus to help with the cubs. Domus and Neechi are there too, waving and crying and making my heart ache with their care and worry for us.

Aunt Julissa and a few Senators observe from a distance, ensuring we keep our end of the bargain. When the Council conceded that our crimes were out of self-preservation and decided not to execute us, they still thought it best, given the current state of upheaval, for our newest Nedéans and their accomplices to remain out of the public eye. As much as I relished the prospect of spending those months or years sequestered in the musty Arena cells while things died down, I can't say I was disappointed when Rohan suggested an alternative. Explaining his suspicion of outsiders to the Council, he requested we spend our exile evaluating possible threats beyond Nedé. It sounded like thinly veiled code for *exploring* to me, but after exchanging apprehensive looks at the word "outsiders," the Senators eagerly agreed. We are required to vacate Nedé for a minimum of one year, and may be gone longer, depending on what dangers we encounter.

The Council granted Torvus an exception so he could oversee the cubs and establish the new Anthropos destiny: an occupation allowing Brutes to use their gifts for the good of all. And they allowed Théo, who took Jem and Galion's deaths particularly hard, to return to the ruins, where a handful of Brutes have decided to remain out of sight a while longer, giving the women—and armed Alexia—time to adjust to the idea of Brutes existing outside of their nightmares.

Finca del Mar shrinks to doll size in the distance, and eventually the mysterious Divisaderos—Jungle lands teeming with life and danger—fall away too. But before they disappear completely, I almost imagine the top of a very tall mahogany peeking from behind a misty rise, reaching its proud branches toward the sky.

Rohan comes to sit beside me on the front of the platform. The horizon stretches before us like so much possibility, like endless tomorrows.

"You know," I remind him, "when we return, you'll have to choose a destiny." I bump him with my shoulder. "I think you'd make an excellent Alexia."

He chuckles. "I wouldn't look nearly as good in those pants as you do . . . though I wouldn't mind getting my hands on one of those bows."

He slides an arm around my shoulder and kisses my hair. I like the way my head fits under his chin, how our fingers join just so. You'd think I was a perfect sunset for the way he looks at me, and I see the strength of El Fuego in him. When I'm in his arms,

I can feel our hearts fusing together, like we were *made* to love each other.

I imagine Tristan Pierce taking a boat across the sea into an unknown world, determined to create a society free from the tyranny of evil. She and the foremothers were brave enough to imagine a world different from what they had experienced. In that way, I suppose, our voyages aren't so different. Except I'm venturing out—have risked my life—for a different kind of freedom. Fear and hate motivated Tristan to alter Brutes in the name of justice. I've liberated them for the sake of a different virtue altogether: love. The one virtue, I'm now convinced, that is greater than them all.

Glossary

Ad Artium *(ad AHRT tee uhm)*—destiny of Nedé specializing in the arts

Adoni *(uh DO nee)*—leader of the Alexia

Agricolátio *(A gri ko LAH tee o)*—destiny of Nedé specializing in horticulture

Alexia *(uh LEX ee uh)*—destiny of Nedé specializing in peacekeeping

Amal *(uh MAHL)*—southwestern Province of Nedé, meaning "hope"

Apprentice—the Matriarch's choice of successor, selected from among four Candidates. The Apprentice trains under the Matriarch for one year, after which time she assumes the Matriarchal role and title

Arena—Alexia training facilities

Bella Terra *(BAY yuh TER uh)*—Materno finca managed by Leda Pierce, Reina's home

Bolas *(BO luhs)*—a hunting weapon made by attaching each end of a medium-length rope to a sphere made of a heavy material, used to capture animals by entangling their legs

Brishalynn *(BREE shuh lin)* **"Bri" Pierce**—Politikós turned Alexia from Amal; former Succession Candidate

Brute—an ungentled male, thought to be extinct

Callisto *(kuh LI sto)*—Reina's pinto horse, a Paint and Lexander mix

Camino del Oeste *(kuh MEE no del o ES tay)*—Nedéan thoroughfare, running north to south along the western border

Candidate—one of four women chosen to compete in the Succession, in which the Matriarch chooses a successor

Cassia *(CA see uh)*—Reina's niece, daughter of Jonalyn Pierce

Center for Health Services—aka, the Center; facility in Phoenix City responsible for medical and Materno services

Chicha *(CHEE chuh)*—an alcoholic beverage made from fermenting fruit and/or grains

Ciela *(see AY luh)* **Pierce**—Reina's older sister, lab technician at the Center for Health Services

Criollo *(cree OY oh)*—breed of horse native to Nedé

Dáin *(DAY in)*—Brute

Dantès *(dahn TEZ)*—Brute

Divisadero *(di vi suh DE ro)* **Mountains**—mountain range marking Nedé's western border

Dr. Karina Novak *(kuh REE nuh NO vak)*—doctor, coleader of the Center for Health Services with Leda Pierce

Dom *(DAHM)*—shortened form of *Domina*, a title of respect given to women of distinction (adult women who have chosen a destiny) in Nedé

Dom Bakshi *(buhk SHEE)*—Reina's tutor and educator of Bella Terra's Gentles

Dom Russo *(roo SO)*—advisor to Matriarch Teera

Dom Tourmaline (TUR muh leen)—Personal stylist to Matriarch Teera, assigned to Reina during the Succession

Domus *(DAHM uhs)*—Gentle 37628, major domus (finca manager) of Finca del Mar

Estrella *(uh STRAY yuh)*—Leda's horse

Fabricatio *(fa bri CAH tee o)*—destiny of Nedé dealing with manufacturing

Fallon *(FA luhn)*—Alexia

Fik'iri *(fik EE ree)*—northeastern Province of Nedé, meaning "love"

Finca del Mar *(FEEN kuh del MAHR)*—the Matriarch's estate

Finch—Jonalyn's son

Finglas *(FIN glahs)*—aka Fin; Brute

Galion *(GAL yon)*—Brute

Gentles Regimen—destiny of Nedé specializing in Hive oversight and Gentles' vocational training

Halcyon *(HAL see ahn)* **Sea**—body of water marking Nedé's eastern border

Highway Volcán *(vol CAHN)*—main Nedéan thoroughfare, running east from Phoenix City to Nedé's western border

Hive—live-in training facility for Gentles ages seven to fourteen

Initus *(IN i toos)* **Ceremony**—a Nedé-wide celebration at the Arena to commemorate the fourteen-year-old Gentles' departure from their respective Hives to begin vocations

Innovatus *(in o VAH toos)*—destiny of Nedé dealing with innovation, particularly repurposing materials, and maintaining technologies necessary "to increase convenience without compromising our core virtue of simplicity," as per Article V of the constitution

Jabiru *(JAH buh roo)* **River**—river running from the Divisadero Mountains to the Halcyon Sea, dividing Amal and Lapé provinces from Kekuatan and Fik'iri

Jamara Makeda *(juh MAHR uh muh KEE duh)*—Apprentice to the Matriarch

Jase *(JAYS)*—Brute

Jem—Brute

Jonalyn *(JON uh lin)* **Pierce**—aka Jo. Reina's eldest sister, Materno, finca manager in Kekuatan

Julissa *(jyoo LI suh)* **Pierce**—Matriarch Teera's younger daughter, Reina's aunt

Jungle—the land outside Nedé's borders, characterized by unexplored, dense vegetation

Kekuatan *(kuh KOO uh tahn)*—northwestern Province of Nedé, meaning "strength"

La Fortuna *(lah for TYOO nah)*—Materno finca belonging to Jonalyn Pierce

Lapé *(lah PAY)*—southeastern Province of Nedé, containing Phoenix City, meaning "peace"

Leda *(LEE duh)* **Pierce**—Reina's mother, daughter of Matriarch Teera, codirector of the Center for Health Services

Lexander *(LEX an dur)*—breed of horse developed by Lex Sterling; a Criollo-Thoroughbred mix prized by the Alexia

Little Boo—Gentle 85272, nurtured by Leda Pierce at Bella Terra

Marsa Museau *(MAHR suh myoo ZO)*—aka Dom Marsa, or just Marsa. Chef at Bella Terra, second mother to Reina and her sisters

Materno *(muh TER no)*—destiny of Nedé specializing in the birth and care of children

Midas—Trinidad's horse

Nedé *(ne DAY)*—the haven formed by the Safety Coalition in 2067 for the preservation and protection of women

Neechi *(NEE chee)*—Gentle 54901, former stablehand at Finca del Mar

Nyx *(NIX)*—Adoni's horse

Ori *(OR ee)*—Brute

Phase-out facility—a place for Gentles who are no longer useful to live out their remaining days

Pippin—aka Pip, Brute

Politikós *(po LI ti kos)*—destiny of Nedé specializing in politics

Reina *(RAY nuh)* **Pierce**—daughter of Leda Pierce, granddaughter of Matriarch Teera, former Succession Candidate

Rio del Sur *(REE o del SUR)*—river running from the Divisadero Mountains to the Halcyon Sea, marking Nedé's southern border

Rohan *(RO hahn)*—Brute

Safety Coalition—organization which fought for the safety and survival of women, founded in 2052 by Tristan Pierce

Salita *(suh LEE tuh)* **Pierce**—Teera's cousin, former Senator

Scientia and Medicinae *(see EN tee uh and med uh KEE nee)*—destiny of Nedé specializing in science and medicine

Siyah Assad *(see YAH uh SAHD)*—former operative for the Safety Coalition, first Alexia leader

Solomon—aka Old Solomon, Gentle 29811, major domus (i.e., lead Gentle) at Bella Terra; former preeminent horse trainer for the Alexia

Stinger—slang for a quietus injection, which ends a Gentle's life. An option for Gentles who are no longer useful and/or who suffer from debilitating pain

Succession—the competition by which the Matriarch chooses a successor from among four Candidates, one from each Province

Teera *(TEE ruh)* **Pierce**—Eighth Matriarch of Nedé

Théoden *(THAY oh den)*—aka Théo, Brute

Torvus *(TOR vuhs)*—Brute leader

Treowe *(TREE o)*—aka Tre (TRAY), Gentle 61749, finca worker at Bella Terra

Trinidad *(TRIN uh dad)*—Alexia second-in-command

Tristan Pierce—founder of the Safety Coalition, first Matriarch of Nedé

Valya *(VA lyuh)*—Alexia

The Constitution of Nedé

*We, the seventy-five founding women of Nedé, do hereby establish
the laws and code of conduct for our great society, to abolish the evils
of patriarchy and to rid the world of the Brutes who have harmed
women for millennia due to their biologically driven lust for pleasure
and power. The following five Articles shall serve these purposes:*

I. **MATRIARCHAL SYSTEM.** The peace and prosperity of Nedé
   shall be maintained by three cords of government: the
   Matriarch, the Council, and the Alexia.

   A. **MATRIARCH.** We hereby appoint Tristan Pierce,
      founding Council member, to serve as the first
      Matriarch of Nedé. The Matriarch shall hold executive
      power to act in the best interest of Nedé, in partnership
      with the Council.

      1. **SUCCESSION.** At such time as the Matriarch should
         choose to retire from service (but before she reaches
         eighty years of age), she shall possess the right and
         responsibility to choose a successor. Each of the four
         Provinces—Fik'iri, Lapé, Amal, and Kekuatan—shall
         supply one Candidate, selected by senatorial vote,
         for the Matriarch's consideration. Upon evaluating
         the merit of each Candidate, the Matriarch shall

choose one woman to become her Apprentice for a duration of one year, after which time executive powers will be transferred in full to her successor. Should the Matriarch perish or be rendered incapacitated before such a Succession can take place, the Council shall elect a successor by vote.

B. COUNCIL. The Council shall consist of four senatorial houses, each representing one of the four Provinces. Each provincial Senate shall comprise twelve members, elected by popular vote. A Senator's term shall last eight years, with one re-election possible. Senators shall advise the Matriarch in matters of state, serve as judges in civil matters within their Provinces, and serve as examples to all Nedéans of the Virtues we strive for.

C. ALEXIA. To guard Nedé against any threat—within its borders or without—we hereby appoint Siyah Assad to establish and organize a peacekeeping force, hereafter termed the *Alexia*, to uphold the Articles of this constitution, to maintain order within Nedé, and to protect our borders from any threat, present or future. The leader of the Alexia will report directly to the Matriarch, who will select and appoint future Alexia leaders.

II. GENTLES. Males born to the women of Nedé, hereafter termed *Gentles*, having been liberated from their aggression and lust, shall contribute to the good of Nedé—and maintain their enlightened state—through the important tasks of public and private service, as deemed beneficial by the Matriarch and Council. These duties shall not deny nor diminish the dignity of life but aim to make provision for the inherent frailty of Gentles and supply them with meaningful labor. For the good and safety of all, in perpetuity, the women of Nedé do make these sacrifices:

A. Between the ages of three months and one year, Gentles will be relinquished by their birth mothers to a Materno finca, where they will live until the age of seven.

B. Between the ages of seven and fourteen, Gentles will reside in special facilities called Hives, where they will be educated and trained to serve Nedé.

C. To prevent undue or inappropriate attachment, interaction with grown Gentles shall be limited to necessary instruction.

III. DESTINIES. To spread the abundant capabilities of Nedé's women across all necessary sectors, at eighteen years of age each woman shall choose, based on her own interests and abilities, a particular field of expertise, where she shall serve Nedé until she is physically unable to do so. These destinies shall include: Ad Artium, Agricolátio, Alexia, Fabricatio, Gentles Regimen, Innovatus, Materno, Politikós, and Scientia & Medicinae. A detailed description of these fields of employment can be found in the forthcoming document *Nedéan Customs and Practices*.

IV. MATERNO COMPENSATION. Without denying a woman's right to refrain from childbirth, to ensure the longevity of our population, special honor shall be bestowed on women who choose as their destiny the bearing and nurturing of children during the span of eighteen to thirty-eight years. These honors shall include: substantially comfortable lodging, a stipend for each delivery, and a stipend for each baby she breastfeeds for one complete year. Any woman who births ten or more children shall receive a pension for the remainder of her years. All others shall choose another destiny in which to serve the remainder of her years.

V. **VIRTUES.** Contrary to the rampant immorality of our respective origin societies, Nedé shall cultivate a haven of incorruptible ethics. All Nedéans, led by the Matriarch, shall endeavor to embody the core Virtues of diversity, harmony, ingenuity, simplicity, and self-restraint. The development of these Virtues shall remain the free responsibility of the people, whether through their religion of choice or without it.

A. **DIVERSITY.** Because Nedé combines the cultures and languages of dozens of countries of origin, to create a new, diverse yet unified society we shall:

1. Establish English as our common tongue, precious-metal coin as our common currency, and the metric system for measurement.

2. Preserve distinctive relics of our respective heritages, including food, dress, art, and religion.

3. Treat all women equally.

4. Rely heavily on the ancient roots from which many of our cultures of origin arose (i.e., the Greeks and Romans, with special attention given to Latin, mathematics, and music) while not ignoring the contribution and influence of ancient Eastern cultures.

B. **HARMONY.** Nedéans shall strive to live by this guiding principle: treat other women as you would treat yourself. Furthermore, because harmony shall prevail

380

as long as our citizens adhere to these Articles of the constitution, the Matriarchy shall guard them at all costs. Failure to adhere to these Articles shall result in fines, loss of privileges, or imprisonment. While capital punishment shall have no place in Nedéan justice, either for woman or Gentle, the Matriarch reserves the right to ensure—by any other means necessary—that all Nedéans benefit from our collective peace and prosperity.

C. **SIMPLICITY.** Nedéans shall endeavor to live in harmony with Mother Earth, respecting and cultivating nature in ways the old world—dictated by Brutes—failed to do. The location of Nedé, with its limited access to man-made resources and technology, shall foster the virtue of simplicity, as well as contribute to the previous Virtues. Gentles shall provide the manual labor necessary to work the land, care for animals, and enable a simple life for all Nedéans.

D. **INGENUITY.** In order to thrive in Nedé's locale, Nedéans will apply their minds to creative problem-solving, make do with what is available, and refuse to give up when setbacks arise. Without compromising simplicity, our limited technological resources shall be focused first and foremost on creating and maintaining life, public sanitation, and fostering harmony. Should additional resources be discovered in Nedé, they shall be repurposed at the discretion of Innovatus to increase convenience without compromising our core virtue of simplicity.

E. **SELF-RESTRAINT.** Recognizing the dangers and evil of primal lusts in every form, and to demonstrate our superiority over the Brutes who abused, suppressed, and mistreated us, the women of Nedé will adhere to the highest standards of self-restraint by denying any and all base urges; instead redirecting our passions into productive contributions for the good of Nedé. Unlike our brutish predecessors, women are capable of enjoying all the merits of platonic friendship and sisterly affection without digressing into crude gratification. Those not exercising self-control will be punished as deemed appropriate by the Matriarch and, if necessary, the Alexia.

Protect the weak. Safety for all. Power without virtue is tyranny.

Signed,
Representatives of the Safety Coalition,
founding members of Nedé

Tristan Pierce, Florida, USA	*Consuelo Medina, New York, USA*
Melisenda Juárez, Florida, USA	*Liz Carolina Rivera, Colombia*
Li Na Kuang, China	*Siyah Assad, Iran*
Stephanie Becker, New York, USA	*Chisimdi Okonkwo, Nigeria*
Meera Lopez, Belize	*Stella Williams, Australia*
Alicia Lavoie, Canada	*Annika Novak, Russia*
Farah Museau, Haiti	*Amadi Makeda, Ethiopia*
Amelia Chavez, California, USA	*Adaku Musa, Nigeria*
Charlotte Taylor, Australia	*Cora Cunningham, California, USA*
Camila Roberts, Texas, USA	*Ana Silva, Brazil*
Prisha Ananda, India	*Maria del Carmen Cruz, Mexico*
Fernanda Varela, Brazil	*Fatima Mohamed, Morocco*
Margherita Santoro, Italy	*Elena Chan, Canada*

Jaqueline Harris, United Kingdom

Dimitra Alexopoulos, Greece

Mila Ivanov, Russia

Islande Pierre, Haiti

Candela Moreno, Spain

Emily Carroll, Georgia, USA

Tamaya Khalil, North Sudan

Yael Dayan, Israel

Bjani Ngalula, Democratic Republic of Congo

Margot Du Plessis, South Africa

Zana Jafari, Iran

Mingmei Tan, China

Min Cho, South Korea

Ishaani Bakshi, India

Rebecca Allen, Texas, USA

Lee Nguyen, California, USA

Maria Alvez, Brazil

Grace Lynn Macdonald, Georgia, USA

Amira Suleiman, Syria

Lex Sterling, Kentucky, USA

Zala Tesfaye, Ethiopia

Anwen Hughs, United Kingdom

Susan Jones, Virginia, USA

Mae Lee, United Kingdom

Shandice Castillo, Belize

Andrea Tourmaline, Washington, USA

Blair Williams, United Kingdom

Adèle Leblanc, France

Sofia Dominguez, Spain

Genevieve Fox, Illinois, USA

Ji-woo Kwan, South Korea

Naomie Nadeau, Canada

Tahara Ahmed, United Kingdom

Caron Leblanc, France

Aliyah Morrison, California, USA

Soo-jung Pak, South Korea

Guilia Russo, Italy

Lauren Diaz, Louisiana, USA

Novah Ramos, Nevada, USA

Laurence Tremblay, Canada

Adriana Torres, Mexico

Claire Evans, Utah, USA

Ceylon de Silva, Sri Lanka

Alana Herrera, New York, USA

Zhi Ruo Xue, China

Olivia Fraser, United Kingdom

Thea Spanos, Greece

Tanner Bryant, Nevada, USA

Alipha Oliveira, Brazil

Acknowledgments

MADELEINE L'ENGLE, author of *A Wrinkle in Time*, wrote, "A woman who follows a vocation needs an unusually understanding husband." Mine is exceptional. Thank you, Paul Daniel, for taking on more than your fair share so I could finish this manuscript. Countless brainstorm sessions—not to mention those twelve pages of notes—made this a better book.

My daughters, Ryan and Logan, thank you for believing I could do it, and sharing me with this story so sacrificially.

Andrew Wolgemuth, your partnership, expertise, and availability are a gift. You are a class act and world-class agent.

Some books are refined by an excellent developmental editor. *A Brutal Justice* had the benefit of *three*. Nicci Jordan Hubert, Sarah Rubio, and Danika King, my heartfelt gratitude for your combined input that helped shape this story. I've learned much from your expertise, and am indebted to each of you for expecting and striving for excellence.

Linda Howard, Kristi Gravemann, and Mariah León, thank you for championing this series and humoring my outlandish ideas. Eva Winters—be my cover designer forever? Debbie King and Lisanne Kaufmann, your attention to detail and gift for language were a copyediting godsend. Andrea Martin, for your warmth and timely encouragement. And the rest of the incredible team at Wander who have believed in and worked on the Nedé Rising series, *muchisimas gracias.*

I have been blessed with the best team of alpha readers an author could ask for. Seriously. Abbie Dykstra, Ashley Paulus, Claire Zasso, Emily Weimer, Genevieve Nelson, Jen Johnson, Jen Schuler, Jenny Brannan, Jocey Pearsey, Noël Brower, Ryan Minassian, and Tamara Tilley, thank you for sharing in my excitement over the story, being brutally honest, and offering some killer suggestions. You make me look good.

So much gratitude to the Plouffes, Diehls, and Pearseys for offering quiet, secluded "shelter-and-write" spaces while my people sheltered-in-place. There's no way I could have finished without your generous hospitality.

Daniel Frost, the Nedé map is exceptional—the color version, exquisite. Thank you for lending your talents to bring my world alive.

Finally, thank *you*, dear reader. Sharing the world of Nedé with you—reading your reviews, talking about characters on social media, meeting you in person—has been one of the highlights of my life, let alone career. Thank you for joining me on this adventure.

Soli Deo gloria.

A Note from the Author

I CARE DEEPLY ABOUT WOMEN. Of course I'm biased. Not only am I female, I gave birth to two more. I care for my daughters' safety, honor, and futures even more than my own. But I also care equally for men, and believe that selfless masculinity, unleashed, has the power to change the world. My heart aches over the great divide between us—the blaming, shaming, and fear. I believe there's a better way—a partnership that brings out the best in us all, a world in which we choose the good of others above our own desires.

Most authors dream that their words will somehow make a difference in this world, and I'm no different. But words sail further when tethered to action. That's why I'm donating half of all my earnings from this series to the Corban Fund, which supports organizations seeking to end violence against women and promote change.

Men aren't better than women; women aren't better than men. We both have the capacity to choose good, so let's do more of that.

Safety for all,

Jess

About the Author

JESS CORBAN graduated from college with a degree in communications and, perhaps more instructive, thirteen stamps in her passport. After college, a chance interview at a small publisher for an even smaller position sparked a love for writing that turned into twelve nonfiction books (under various pseudonyms). Now Jess lives with her husband and two daughters in the Sierra Nevada Mountains of California, where she finds inspiration in a sky full of stars and hiking the Canyon of the Kings. *A Brutal Justice* is the second novel in her Nedé Rising series. Connect with Jess at JessCorban.com.

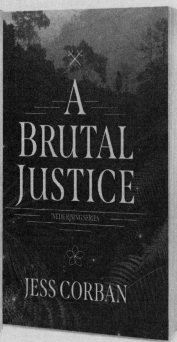

THE NEDÉ RISING SERIES

A GENTLE TYRANNY

NEDÉ RISING SERIES

JESS CORBAN

A BRUTAL JUSTICE

NEDÉ RISING SERIES

JESS CORBAN

WHAT PATH WILL REINA CHOOSE?
AND WHAT WILL HER CHOICE COST HER?

wander™
An imprint of
Tyndale House
Publishers

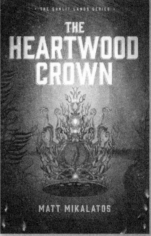

A MIXTAPE OF
BIG '80S STYLE,
HIGH SCHOOL ANGST,
AND A CLASSIC
JANE AUSTEN TALE